Unholy
Vengeance

K. L. DEMPSEY

PAGE PUBLISHING, INC.
New York, NY

First originally published by Page Publishing, Inc. 2019

ISBN 978-1-64544-606-4 (Paperback)
ISBN 978-1-64544-607-1 (Digital)

Printed in the United States of America

Dead…might not be quiet at all.

—Marsha Norman, Night Mother

Dearly beloved, avenge not yourselves, but rather give place unto wrath: for it is written, vengeance is mine; I will repay, saith the Lord.

—Romans 12:19

In memory of Raphael Zacher, kind friend, great human being to all, selected for early arrival into God's kingdom at age eighteen.

Friday, a Summer Night Shortly before Midnight

When death stares you in the face, it often travels at the speed equal to the downward propulsion of gravity. Most have the misconception that many faced with death die instantly after the impact of the bullet, the sudden unexpected crash of the semi into the family car, or when accidently falling through the ice while walking across some frozen lake. Only rarely is this true. Whilst the shock of the experience of stepping into the open air of an elevator shaft can cause a heart attack, most experiences of death provide you enough time to understand what is happening to you.

There are of course exceptions to every rule regarding sudden death, such as that end-of-life experience, which looks at you and chooses to allow you to enjoy what remaining time it has provided you. Such is the case when the most dangerous predator hunts you for the sole purpose of ending your life, but not before it allows you enough time to think about its intent.

As she sat in the chair bound by the leather straps, the woman couldn't believe what was now happening. By eleven thirty last night, she knew that she was in love. Well, maybe in lust anyway. And maybe her perception was slightly clouded by his ridiculously expensive liqueur and how he had sold her on the idea of her matching each drink of his with another one of hers. Only hours before, they had made love and had celebrated the occasion with his specialty drink of Frangelico, irish cream, and melon liqueur. After apologizing for its name, he had told her that professional bartenders referred to it as the fuck-me drink. She had restricted her laugh to politeness but was surprised somewhat by his choice of language in consideration of his occupation. The two drinks that she had downed had reacted faster to her system than that of the deadly kamikaze, a drink that she had once taken on a dare, only to find herself passed out in no time. In the middle of the night, as her head nestled into his shoulder, she had felt safe. She had raised her head and found him fast asleep with his hand gently resting against her thigh. Before she fell back to sleep, she briefly tried to read his expression, but it was dark, his face in the shadow. Despite the way she'd stared at him, she received no reaction, and thus she began to drift off to sleep like a baby, which told her exactly how much the past lovemaking had taken out of her.

Much later when she heard the chime of the kitchen clock, she had opened her eyes and for a moment had no idea where she was. Her arms hurt from the leather restraints, which tied her hands behind her back. The shock of the straps and the pain made her cry out for him, but there was no answer. Someone had moved her from her bed onto a chair, and she hadn't realized it. Dressed in the T-shirt that she had fallen asleep in, along with only her underpants that seemed to keep slipping off, she felt half-naked.

"Hey, what the hell is going on here!" she yelled. "This is not funny. Untie me."

No answer, but she knew he was in the room watching. She heard the noise immediately. It sounded much like the sound of someone unscrewing a jar of pickles, maybe jam or peanut butter. Then she suddenly saw it, fifteen feet in front of her, moving ever so slowly toward her chair. In her lifetime, she had seen many spiders, and all were frightening, but never had she seen one this large, which appeared to be about five inches, hairy, and fast moving. She kicked her legs out in an attempt to frighten the spider, but her movement appeared to only further anger the advancing spider.

"Help! I know you're there! Get this damn thing away from me!"

UNHOLY VENGEANCE

Suddenly three feet from her the arachnid stopped and displayed its prominent red jaws while lifting its front legs into an erect position. "Oh my god," she cried while watching the spider swaying from side to side with its several eyes focused on her. She moved her legs back and forth at it, only to find that her movement once again seemed to increase its aggressive state, not frighten it away. When it stopped swaying, she relaxed thinking that it was about to move away from her. Suddenly it leaped the remaining three feet onto her leg and bit deep into her right thigh. The pain was immediate as the spider released its venomous poison into her system. The sudden shock of being attacked caused her to faint.

When she awoke, the chair was gone along with the leather straps, and she found herself once again on the bed. Had she been dreaming? Looking down at her thigh, she noticed a large blister about the size of a half-dollar. Getting up from the bed, she walked to the medicine cabinet looking for any antibiotic ointment or itching cream. Finding a tube of clobetasol propionate, she spread the cream on the affected area. Something was beginning to make her feel uneasy, and she knew that it was only a matter of time before she would throw up. Her head now starting to pound from the onset of a headache, she quickly downed two aspirin. Alone and now panicky, she walked to the phone in the living room to call for the fire department's paramedics. The poison now swiftly moving through her body soon ended her attempt at holding whatever was moving through her under control. She fell and knocked the phone over. She had never been more afraid in her life, but she'd learned long ago that the only way to deal with fear was to take control of it, hold it at bay. Focus on other things, on the phone, rescue, and safety. Reaching for the phone, she dialed 911. The operator said that they would be on their way. Oh, but how long could she hold out? Inside her mental prison, it suddenly started to get dark, and her breathing became a struggle. Tears started down her cheeks, and it was then that she knew that she would die.

After he watched the event unfolding and she stopped breathing, he walked over to her, bent down, and kissed her cheek.

9

C H A P T E R   1

The Pastor

Reverend Paul Bergman enjoyed the silence of the morning. Like Jacob's angel, the morning often required that you wrestle with it before it bestowed upon you its personal blessing. As he glanced around the five acres of his property, he liked the fact that the location of the parsonage was devoid of human presence, unlike that of other congregations who often preferred that the parsonage was next door to the church. He sniffed the steam and took a first long sip, a little ritual he did every morning. "Nothing better than just made coffee early in the morning," he thought. Through the living room window, he could see the sun coming up, and he could tell that the warm air would soon burn off the ground mist.

Bergman was a loner, and this was one of the main reasons for him accepting a call to this small prairie town. Well, maybe one of the main reasons, he thought, because it offered the opportunity to hide his past life from the scrutiny of the typical member of a church who was determined to not only have a pastor but also own his life. He remembered with joy his first call to a Nebraska congregation, where they had treated him as a rare diamond among the 150 members of the church, unlike many of his future calls where church officers viewed him as a hired gun or a full-time paid Christian. Over the years, he had seen his fellow brother pastors trying to dodge the wrath of layman who given an opportunity would have fired St. Paul from his pulpit. Most congregations failed to understand or care that a Christian pastor held office under a divine call. That call was much more binding in a solid church than a written contract. Yet today, church after church simply gave pastors their walking papers for shoddy reasons that wouldn't hold up in a courtroom in a breach of an unemployment contract lawsuit. He had hopes that this call to Silver Valley would provide him the opportunity to forget recent bad experiences.

One of the simple pleasures of Silver Valley, Wisconsin, was not only being able to drive where there was no traffic but also there was something special about entering the country and immediately seeing 100 White Tail Deer or simply looking across one of the many rivers and just watch the cherry trees wake up each morning. He loved that feeling and would be happy if not for the continued and unrelenting pressure from Mrs. Betty Ogden, the wife of Head Elder Alan Ogden, or as he liked to be called Dr. Alan Ogden, owner of the only health clinic in town. Betty, who originally was concerned about the congregation accepting his call to the First Independent Church because of unanswered questions about his background, had always been the outspoken leader of a small group that continued to dig into the history of his ministry.

Walking down the steps from his attached porch, Bergman walked the 150 feet to his private shed, which contained the small yellow cub mower he used to cut the grass and clear the snow with its attached blade in the winter. Opening the door, Bergman hit the light switch, which brought into focus the neatness of his well-kept pride and joy secrets known only to its owner. Smiling to himself, Bergman reached into his wallet and retrieved the combination to the single black hanging lock that would open up the large gun cabinet next to his workbench. Next to the gun cabinet stood a Pendleton vault organizer containing the majority of his prized possessions, which would only open by knowledge of its S&G electronic keypad lock. That combination was never shared. Turning the combination, he opened the lock and admired his collection of handguns and long rifles. He wondered what the church officers would think once they realized that he owned an arsenal larger than the most avid hunter in the church. Satisfied everything was in place, he relocked the gun cabinet, turned off the lights, and relocked the shed door. Glazing one more time at the vast and green yard, he walked back to his porch and found a comfortable cushioned deck chair. Sitting down, he began to pondering the potential solution to Betty Ogden, the woman who now was attempting to interfere with his pastoral paradise. After all, her recent relentless interest in his wife and daughter could be a major problem if it was allowed to be continued, and that he could not permit.

It was just three years ago that he'd barely survived the past crisis that found him accused of his wife's attempted murder. Thinking back to that time, he recalled the rookie police officer Kate Heller arriving at his home on that fateful day when she had discovered that his wife had been choked with a cord and left convulsing on the floor of their garage. The attractive officer he remembered was flawless in her appearance. She was more than beautiful. She was spectacular. She had arrived with a revolver in a holster on her hip, and next to it was a shotgun that she held in her right hand. After listening to his explanation of how he had found his wife on the garage floor, it became clear to him that she didn't believe his story. His wife had never recovered from this savage assault on her life and remained in a vegetative state at a nursing home in Michigan. His daughter having read reports that her father had wanted to marry his lover, a member of the congregation, had left home fearful of her life and married an Air Force captain. He had not heard from her since.

At his trial in Funston, Michigan, prosecutors tried to show that Bergman plotted to kill his wife so he would be free to marry the church organist Gayle Browning, arguing that he knew that a divorce would jeopardize any chance of his receiving future calls to other congregations, let alone nullify any chance that he would have in becoming the rising star that most assumed that he would become. As he thought back to the day three years ago when the jury acquitted him based on his testimony that while he did cheat on his wife, at no time would he as a pastor resort to any attempt to murder the mother of his only child, a woman that he still loved. Bergman was still amazed that he had survived the accusations and was acquitted by the jury of attempted murder. His own daughter had rejected their findings and refused to talk to him.

Although he was later asked to step down as the pastor of his congregation due to the threatening letters from many congregation members, the local district president of the First Independent Church, fearful of legal action, decided to scrub any mention of Bergman's past involvement in this high-profile case to protect his right to participate in any future call opportunities. Like the history of the Catholic Church, their First Independent Church leaders were not opposed to transfer their problems to another congregation. Later when Silver Valley requested assistance on calling a new minister, he was placed on the call availability list by their local district president for consideration. Up to this point, Bergman knew that he had been lucky, and Lady Luck seemed to keep smiling in that his former mistress and only linkage to his involvement had later died mysteriously of a spider bite. Leaning back in his chair, he remembered what his college professor had said to him when he was depressed about his questionable grades that might keep him out of entering seminary school. "Paul, it's important to keep things in perspective and to remember that all things pass. The important thing for you to concentrate on is that you act, not react. Make it your goal to understand that those who continue to react to failure rather than act will never control their destiny."

Across the large lawn, he could see that the two shepherd-crook bird feeders had been tugged far out of plumb by the brown squirrels who consumed every attempt on his part to feed the many blue jays that searched for the food he put in the feeders daily. Bergman ignored the aggressive rodent hunger of the squirrels and even bought on occasion large bags of peanuts in hopes of curtailing their hunger away from the sunflower seeds that he left of the ground for the many deer that moved through his yard. Hearing the grandfather clock chime 7:00 a.m., Bergman knew it was time to make his twenty-minute drive to the First Independent Church. To be late was an invitation to a morning lecture by the church's self-appointed sentry, Paul Flowers, who at ninety-seven years old felt it important to remind every pastor that walked through the doors that the forty-two-thousand-dollar salary paid needed to be earned beyond just doing the Sunday sermon.

"Well," thought Bergman as he dressed, "at least the old man walked the walk not just talked since his weekly envelope never contained less than three hundred dollars each Sunday." Grabbing his black sport coat, Bergman locked the front door and entered his green Subaru Outback and headed to work.

The coffee he had picked up at the Speedway station had been a mistake. The old cherry-topped danish roll was a bigger mistake. The gas-station brew tasted as if it had been made two weeks ago and seemed to have an oil change taste to it. Bergman drank it anyway, a comfort ritual that came from his time served in the Army when caffeine-packed, tar-colored liquid could be downed without concern for lack of flavor or the fact that it was often cold and in the end didn't taste like coffee at all. Not so comforting today was the stale danish with the sudden discovery of its blue moldy surface. For the rest of the drive, Bergman kept thinking back to his jury trial in Funston, Michigan. The prosecutors didn't immediately bring criminal charges against him. It was in fact the state district judge that ruled that Bergman "intentionally, knowingly, maliciously, and brutally attempted to strangle his wife." That period of time was a tough stage of his life, but it had ended well because he understood the eureka fallacy and the judge did not. The eureka fallacy used often by police themselves is based upon the tendency of most people to put a lot more faith in things they discover about someone than the things that you want you to believe. The judge wanted the jury to focus on the cord around his wife's neck, while Bergman wanted the jury to remove its focus about the possibility of him putting that cord around her neck and concentrate on his role as a Christian pastor in love with his wife and daughter. By the time he was within two miles of the church, odd bits and pieces of the affair were still occupying his mind. He wondered whatever happened to Officer Kate Heller, the arresting policewoman who was the rising star of the Funston Police Department. She had been the first officer that had arrived at his house and had attempted to revive his wife. He had met her only briefly at his house and later while providing his deposition at police headquarters. During both meetings, her voice was quiet but clear, warm but not soft, and her accent sounded local. But what he remembered most was that she considered him guilty. Oh well, that part of his life was over, thought Bergman as he pulled into a parking space alongside the church rather than using his traditional reserved slot for him, which the head elder had some unusual issue with.

CHAPTER 2

Officers

Dr. Alan Ogden tossed his stethoscope in the back seat of the jeep and glanced with admiration at his new Complications watch, which had cost his wife, Betty, the price of a new Mustang. It had a simple brown leather band and a white chronograph face. You would have had to be an aficionado of watches to recognize this type of timepiece, which combined several functions within a single casing. Betty had read about the watch and its value when she had read an article on quality watches in the *New York Times*, which had done a feature story on Complications. At first she had struggled with the cost but then had told Alan that if a doctor's wife could give a car for a Christmas gift, like some wives did for some man who had not yet demonstrated a full six months of not hitting on his nurse, she could certainly make sure her husband of twenty-five years knew that she loved him for all he had done for the medical profession and especially her. Besides she had justified that it was perfect for her husband, a physician who was the director of medicine along with being the chief of the Infectious Diseases Department at Valley Medical Center. She had smiled at the time telling him that one shouldn't expect him to wear a cheap twelve-thousand-dollar Rolex watch like so many of the hospital colleague physicians wore. It was no accident, she had continued, that her husband's name consistently appeared in the *Castle Connolly* guide of the best doctors in the United States. No, it was because he was considered by his peers to be one of the most outstanding infectious disease specialists in the country. Alan was aware that references alone from physicians and hospitals that treated the ever-growing number of AIDS cases brought him patients and money that pushed his annual income over three million dollars per year. Betty had closed off any further conversations on the subject by saying she loved him dearly and wanted the best for her man, a man she was certain was already spending too much of his valuable time searching for a comparable woman's watch for her. Alan had burst out laughing at this remark, which had been typical Betty, his solid rock that always kept him grounded. The woman was truly amazing, thought Alan. Not wanting for money, Betty still felt the need to hold her job as the vice president of human resources at the largest bank in town because, as she had put it, she wanted him to always know that there was another hand on the pail.

Thinking of his growing medical practice, Alan Jeffery Ogden mumbled a curse as he pulled out of his private parking space next to the Ogden Medical Clinic, while at the same time activating his Bluetooth to dial Dr. Lynwood Silverman, a physician that under most circumstances he had little in common with. While Alan had developed a reputation with his patients as someone always approachable, Silverman on the other hand was a nasty, abrasive, watery cynic who took pleasure in talking down to his patients. Still, professional courtesy required that Alan offer his apology for being unable able to see Silverman's patient tonight because he had forgot his scheduled meeting at the church with the congregation's president. "You may be a doctor by day," thought Alan, "but when it came to the church you belonged to, well, being its president trumps that of a physician holding the position of head elder."

As he accelerated to fifty miles per hour, he reviewed in his mind the patient's diagnosis according to the advance information forwarded to him by Silverman. The poor guy had received some sort of insect bite that had continued to create open traveling sores that Silverman was unable to cure even though he had been treating the man now for four months. The report had suggested that Silverman had even ordered seven different biopsies, and all had come back negative, but the difficulties with the sores had continued. "What an ass," thought Ogden, "in allowing your ego to wait so long before contacting him." Any first-year infectious doctor understood that insects comprised the most diverse and numerous class of the animal kingdom. Their biting, their stinging, or even their feces could range in severity from benign or barely noticeable to outright life-threatening. It was clear to Ogden that Silverman had let his personal pride interfere with doing the right thing for his patient's health and now was trying to recover from his blunder. To make matters worse here, he was racing to a meeting when a patient really needed his specialty.

Ogden hoped the pompous Silverman would understand his missing this last-minute requested appointment since it was common knowledge in the medical field that most physicians were not sold on religion as important to their profession. At the same time, Ogden felt a sense of urgency to see the patient at the first opportunity and would encourage Silverman's office to tell his practice manager to give the patient his choice of appointments. The car speakers gave back a staticky silence indicating no one was going to pick up his call at Silverman's office. Frustrated, he hung up and dialed again. This time, he got a busy signal and suspected that the staff had left early and failed to set the answering machine correctly. Tapping his fingers on the steering wheel, Ogden decided to give up and concentrate on the forthcoming church meeting, which involved the developing concern over their controversial pastor, who had accepted the congregation's call for a new shepherd just a little over two years ago. Now there was a movement by his church elders and many strong-minded individuals to find a way to rid their church of what some considered the original bad decision to have hired him in the first place. Ogden realized that any solution would only be accomplished by some type of compromise, not by hysterical church leadership who failed to understand that pastors were called for the life of their call and were not at-will employees to be let go just because of differences. The divine call which it was referred to had long been the staple of the Independent Church, which insisted that it involved God's decision as well as the congregation, and thus God didn't make mistakes. While he himself had several issues regarding Bergman, he understood that the divine call was much more binding in a solid church than any written contract. Today it seemed church after church had officers that would give their pastors their walking papers for shoddy reasons that wouldn't hold up in a courtroom in a breach of an unemployment contract lawsuit. Because you didn't like his kids or his wife was not sociable were not enough. Rather than causing continued concerns in a church over unresolved matters, a Christian should use Matthew 18 in attempting to resolve these issues. Actually the concept was quite simple, since all it required one to do was for that person who found fault with another Christian, simply just go and tell him his fault. If he would choose not to hear your concerns, then you'd take one or two other people with you to meet with the offender. Ogden was going to recommend to Jack that they both do this.

Five minutes later Ogden circled the perimeter of First Independent Church and entered the church grounds through the back alley and toward the rear of the church. Though the temperature remained a little above freezing, the breeze was dead quiet, which allowed Alan's old Jeep Grand Cherokee to quietly pull into the church's reserved slot marked in bright-yellow letters Pastor Paul J. Bergman. Ogden scoffed at the newly erected wall plaque because as the head elder and chief contributor of Silver Valley's only Independent Church, he had encouraged Bergman to wear his pastoral power lightly, much like he did as the church head elder. Hell, if anyone should have a reserved slot, it should be the chairman of the congregation, who by definition was the chief executive officer of their church, not the pastor whom most expected to be the example of humility, not some dunderhead masquerading as a man of God but looking for perks. Shutting off his engine, Ogden sat for a few minutes thinking about what Betty had once said about Bergman. "He's a secretive man, Alan, the type who will always have you in the shadow of confusion." When he had asked her to explain this observation, she had simply pointed out that any conversations that she had with him all pointed toward him looking at life through bleak lens, meaning that he viewed any questions asked of him like someone wanting to get him. She also had felt that Bergman had a personal fear of the church council, which was a clear indication to Betty that he was not only mysterious but also hiding something about his ministry. Alan had at that time defended Bergman, pointing out to Betty that it was natural that he had some fear because if she would think back, she would remember that it was two other families plus them that originally objected to approving the acceptance of Bergman as their congregation pastor. Betty, as the appointed chairlady of the search and call committee, had felt that his provided documents that had come from the Western Michigan District President's Office had clearly contained too many ambiguous and cloudy characterizations of his past service with his former church. Since the rules of calling a pastor prohibited any direct contact with the former church he had served, the committee had to make their decision based only on the provided paperwork from that District Office. Betty, a highly trained and skilled human resource person, had always felt Bergman had outfoxed her call committee by volunteering himself to being available for a personal interview with the committee. This act in itself was unusual since the Independent Church clearly specifies this is not a requirement to the acceptance of a divine call. Betty had pointed out to the Church Voters' Assembly that when Bergman had presented himself and was asked by her and the call committee to talk about certain aspects of his past ministry, Bergman always found ways to change the subject and would instead bring up things he hoped to accomplish if offered the divine call to the Trinity. Betty, out of frustration, had told Ogden's Elder Board that her call committee was suggesting that they should take a pass on Bergman, if for no other reason than their inability to break through his reluctance to answer even the most basic questions about his past. "For God's sake," Betty had told Alan, "he wouldn't even talk about his wife or daughter like most pastors would." And then there was the matter of his call documents and that CRM code, which the church used as its incongruous claptrap to confuse both the pastor and the calling congregation. Betty had pointed out that the CRM code was used by all church district presidents as a double-edged sword. On one hand, it could mean only that the pastor was available for a call, while at the same time it was used as a red flag alerting each district president that the pastor had bumps in the road. Finding out the true meaning was private only to the local district president, and the chance of any district president sharing that with any call committee was equal to learning the code to the black box the president of the United States carried. In the end, the voters' assembly rejected the feelings of the three families and extended the call to Bergman. Now, that apparent error in judgment had consumed their congregation for the past two years trying to convince the local Independent Church's district president to help resolve these pointed concerns about Bergman by allowing them and their voters' assembly to reverse this divine call. It had become a matter of Bergman's total reluctance to share even the basic information of his personal life, especially that of his family.

Opening his car door, Alan got out and activated his Astra car alarm system while walking to the rear door entrance of his church. Pausing for a minute, he looked up into the approaching darkening sky and noted the glowing brightness of the new moon. Thinking back to his early medical classes on retinal sensitivity, Alan knew all about the phenomenon associated with looking directly at something rather than to the side. Now moving his eyes away from the moon, he started to pick up the stars that were originally lost when he focused only on the moon. As he entered the church, he began to feel that if solutions to their dilemma existed, it would only come by having an awareness of things as they really were. And what were those things pondered Alan? Shaking his head in obvious frustration, Ogden remembered that it took Bergman only two days of prayerful consideration to accept the church's letter that called him as their pastor. Right then and there, Betty had pointed out that was all the call committee really needed to know since most pastors took two to four weeks considering what this would mean to their family, while Bergman reached his decision quicker than a passenger on the sinking *Titanic* deciding if a lifeboat might not be a better option rather than going down with the ship. Still, the congregation voters insisted that they extend the call because many were concerned that few pastors were going to be interested in a church such as theirs with a declining membership and no grade school. If Berman's quick acceptance of their call offer was not enough of a concern, Alan himself always remained puzzled why not one member of the church council hadn't become suspicious about Bergman's reluctance to open up more about his family that still remained behind in Funston, Michigan, rather than joining him in his ministry here at First Independent. But in the end, Bergman still carried the day with the voting members of the congregation and brought to Silver Valley First Independent Church his empty vessel of spiritual guidance clouded in mystery and doubt. Walking down the church hallway, Alan noted the darkness of the secretary office and the apparent locked door of Bergman's office, which thus should have ended any idea conveyed by former pastors that their door was always open. Alan couldn't help wondering what in the hell could one be hiding in a minister's office. Seeing the glowing lights coming from the conference room down the hall, Alan assumed that the church president, Jack Koehler, had already arrived and was going over his notes for their meeting. Koehler, like all officers, to include himself, were voted into their respective positions by the voting members of the congregation, usually for a term of two to four years.

Alan and Betty both liked Jack, although he clearly frustrated them and the church council at times because, as is often the case with presidents of Independent Church congregations, they often bought into the Kool-Aid that came out of one of several district presidents' offices that formed the nucleus behind the election every four years of their national president of the churches. Alan almost broke into a laugh thinking about the politics of the church, which controlled its business so tight that while promoting the idea that each member of the congregation had a say in who would be the future leader of the church, he knew that it would be near to an impossibility to find more than five members in any congregation that could name who was the leader of their churches while more than 90 percent could name the pope. It was really the district presidents that controlled the destiny of their pastors and the local member congregations. Without their say, no pastor was ever granted a call regardless of the churches' insistence that it was largely the individual churches' decision. No, every pastor had to clear muster with the pleasure of his district president before being placed on a call list.

When Alan had been elected to his office as the head elder of the church, he learned one of the little secrets about being an officer of an Independent Church that even his money and position as a physician couldn't change. He learned after several visits to the district office that its president would use every quotation within the Bible to justify why your congregation could not overturn the divine call and why the complaining congregation needed to overlook any perceived weakness of their minister. In any other occupation, individuals were held accountable, but not when you were a called minister because God was involved in the process of sending you this Shepherd. That guilt trip was the continued message used to justify the retention of even the most hapless man ordained to lead a congregation. Now that this message was beginning to be broken down by many aggressive congregations, it shouldn't have come as any surprise that the pastors now removed by their church were placed in the hands of that same district presidents to find them a new church. This newly created pool of throwaway pastors resulted in each of the affected men having their lives now controlled by the same local district president. Like in all forms of politics, there became winners and losers in this game of finding new congregations, only now these divine-called pastors were seeking help from the same district office that usually turned a deaf ear to congregations.

Continuing his brisk pace down the hallway to the conference room, Alan pondered Koehler's last words encouraging his elder board to fix the problem, not disappoint the district president by taking the easy way out. Well, thought Alan, some might feel there is no chance to fix Bergman, a pastor who in the last three months had been acting strange, if one considered strange a pastor who allowed the Sunday service to continue while members of the congregation were attending to a dying member in a pew. Bergman, not able to cope with the obvious developing situation, compounded the tragedy by allowing the continuation of the passing of the collection plates down that same pew and over the stretched-out body of the now-dead member. And then there was his reluctance to accept phone calls to his parsonage home, which he considered an invasion of his privacy, or when working to reject inquiries from his secretary as to how she could reach him during an emergency. His reasoning was that his cell phone was his personal property and that members could call his home phone number, in which he maintained his answering machine. Alan knew that Bergman had many good qualities beyond his marvelous singing voice and his ability to deliver liturgical solos, which often brought tears to many members of the congregation. The man was a marvel with children and would bring the newly baptized children in his arms up to the altar, while at the same time performing the order of baptism installation.

As Alan entered the conference room, he was surprised to find Jack looking over what appeared to be a field and stream magazine along with the latest addition of handguns.

Looking up, Jack said, "Evening, Alan. I heard you pull up while I've been looking over this fantastic article on how to catch a pike as long as your leg. Hey, did you know that last year, Manitoba's Nueltin Lake produced two northern pike that were measured at 50 inches long, with 121 other pike over 41 inches? Most of those suckers were caught on a yellow Lazy Ike, just like old Elmer uses up near Spoon River and Harold Bean's old farm." He continued without missing a beat, "You know, Alan, you and I need to get the men's club guys together and run up their some Saturday, don't you think? We could catch some pike, walleyes, a few perch, and have a fish fry meal for the members and use the free-will offering to help pay for the new carpeting for the church. We could invite Bergman and the circuit representative at the same time and do a little bonding to help Bergman relax a little. Have you noticed how much he seems to sweat just delivering his Sunday sermon? The guy has some emotional problems, Alan, and people are beginning to talk. We need to do something to loosen the guy up, with his wife and family still in Michigan."

Unwilling to engage in the small talk, Alan snapped, "Damn, Jack, can't you put that stupid magazine down and concentrate on why we are meeting tonight. I didn't drive all the way out here after canceling an important appointment to talk about fish, plugs, spoons, or any other pieces of fishing crap. Unless you've forgotten your memo to me indicated that we're meeting tonight while Bergman is attending a steak fry with the men's club in Redwood."

"Lot of charm in that greeting, my friend," said Jack.

"Well, I'm tired, Jack," said Alan, "and to be frank, if it would have been anyone other than you, I wouldn't have tried so hard to be polite. So what's the reason for the meeting tonight, Jack? I had the impression that we were going to work on some exit plan for Bergman, or did you find some answers in that mountain of horse manure sent to you by the district president that I see hidden under that latest issue of *Handguns*? You know, Jack, the district is just continuing to play with us, don't you? They have absolutely no desire to get involved in our mess, and unless you've misunderstood all the signs, let me help you understand that it's not part of their DNA. Like all good deep thinkers of the white collar, they stick together against us common-pew occupiers. Hell, Jack, you know that I've personally written the national president of our synod for consideration of reassignment of Bergman to a more suitable congregation that would better fit his skills. That was over three months ago, and not even an acknowledgment of my letter."

"Now just for the record, Alan, I've been in your house several times and have had dinner with you and your lovely wife, Betty, on more than one occasion. You, sir, are not what one would refer to as common," said Jack. "All district presidents are busy, Alan, in particular the national president who has to deal with hundreds of congregations along with his other regional presidents who want his ear every day. One shouldn't expect that he has time to focus on our particular concerns, which in my opinion has not reached a crisis that can't be handled locally."

"Look," replied Alan, "please forgive my lack of manners, but we need to do something about Bergman, because frankly we have a lot of members that feel his train is not running on the track. Don't you remember our last elders' meeting when he told us that he didn't think it was safe to bring his family here because the country parsonage was overrun by wild wolves? Hell, he was so nervous that I had to ask two of our elders to pitch a tent over at his place just to relax him. And do you remember what I reported back to you that they found out, Jack? Yep, sitting there in the dark, lost in their thoughts about being eaten alive by Bergman's wolves, they discovered all the yipping and howling turned out to be a pack of maybe three or four coyotes chasing deer. Within the framework of traditional psychological testing, my guess is Pastor Paul J. Bergman might be approaching a condition that my psychiatry colleagues would diagnose as being just a little nuts."

"Maybe you're being a little hard on him, Alan. After all, he's out at the farm parsonage every evening by himself, so who wouldn't get a little spooked?" asked Jack.

"Well, the way he's been acting lately, it will be a miracle if he can find his way home in the dark," said Alan. "Let's admit it, Jack, we've made a mistake in calling him to our congregation. He appears uncomfortable around us and has a lot of anxiety disorders. Last week during communion, he forgot to give wine to Betty, and if that wasn't enough, he dropped a wafer down Lucy Dwyer's blouse. Heck I was holding my breath that he didn't try to recover it by sticking his fingers down her blouse. Two weeks ago he was conducting the Rodney James funeral, and Bergman referred to him as the wonderful, devoted Jesse James. He's becoming a joke, you know it, I know it, half the congregation knows it, and my guess is the district president's office has known about it when they cleared his call to our congregation said Alan. You know what they call the last graduating medical student when they award him his MD title, Jack?"

"No, I'm afraid that I don't."

"They call him doctor, my friend, so don't get hung up on the fact that the ministry doesn't have the same problems," said Alan. "I've tried to be fair, Jack, and look at his good side. He's good with kids and can sing better than Kenneth Copeland or Jimmy Swaggart."

"I know who Jimmy Swaggart is, Alan, but Kenneth Copeland, never heard of," said Jack.

"He's a televangelist that preaches prosperity gospel," answered Jack. "His believers are taught that you can become wealthy through tithing, giving offerings, and using faith as well as sound financial practices. Before he found, God he was a recording artist for Imperial Records, even had a record that made Billboard's Top 40. His only problem seems to be keeping one step ahead of the federal government, who questioned his twenty-million-dollar *Cessna Citation* airplane being used for personal vacations for himself and friends while claiming certain tax write-offs. Betty is a fan of his, or let's say a fan of his wife, Gloria Copeland, who is a best-selling author of religious books."

Jack sat back in his chair and looked up at Alan and thought back to the time when they first met a few years ago. He was impressed with him then as he was the day that Alan and Betty had applied for membership. Besides being bright, he had an imposing figure. Six feet, seven inches tall, and long, silver gray hair that he parted in the middle and combed back above the ears. His Vandyke beard gave him a decidedly European look, although from what he knew now, the closest thing to England Alan ever happened to be was when Betty and Alan took a London tour two years ago.

Alan had told him that he had graduated twenty years ago from Northwestern Medical School with two degrees, but it was his music background that was the most interesting to Jack. While certainly having a physician in the church with a PhD in pharmacology would be unique to any congregation, it was the music background that first caught the attention of Jack. Few things were more priceless to any congregation than having a member that could play the organ or, in Alan's example, also be able to also direct the church choir. Seated in a chair across from Jack, he couldn't help admire Betty's choice of the Armani three-piece suit for her husband. Alan had confided to him that it was his wife that dressed the man, not him. Yes, thought Jack, behind every great doctor was a wife that made certain that her husband looked the part of his medical profession that would give immediate confidence to his patients that everything was going to be all right. The only flaw in the image as viewed over time by Jack had already been covered over a couple of beers they once enjoyed together. His habit, as Jack pointed out, was not to smile but rather to scan the patient from top to bottom, being probably cognizant that his mere presence proclaimed that he was the doctor. As Jack had pointed out to that effect, while satisfying to him, only encouraged those that didn't know him to want to flee like Dracula running from sunlight. Overtime Ogden had corrected that image and now was considered by his patients to be the example of what bedside manner was all about.

Bringing his attention back to Alan's last comment, Jack said, "I understand the difficulty of the Peter, Principal Alan, where some people slip through the cracks and are either promoted beyond their capabilities or for that matter maybe awarded MD titles. Worse yet to you and I and some members of our church is having someone placed in charge of the spiritual needs of a congregation who often appears not competent to handling the concerns of this church. The responsibility I have, Alan, as president of this Congregation and you as the head elder is to ensure that we are embarked on the right course of action needed for the benefit of our members and that we not just assume because of perceived flaws that the captain of our spiritual needs is manning the boat minus a rudder. Before I give you my thoughts and recommendations, Alan, I would like to have you tell me what Betty thinks since she was, after all, the chairwoman of the original call committee that brought the pastor to us."

"Well, Jack, it's no secret that her committee rejected his original call and the district support of that divine call since she reported those findings of the committee to you and the voters' assembly. As you should remember, they wanted a better understanding of his CRM status that they had noted when reading his submitted documents, but that the district turned them down based on confidentiality."

"Yes, I remember that, Alan, and although I didn't agree with the answer given and pressured the president to rethink his position, he stood fast in his argument," said Jack.

"The problem with that, Jack," replied Alan, "is that he outright lied about confidentiality since when you check the requirements of disclosure on a pastor listed with a CRM, the guidelines specifically state that the contents can be released to the chairman or president of the congregation, just not to a member at large. The real problem on this subject is that the district prefers that every congregation not understand what a CRM actually is. It's a toy they are allowed to play with but prefer that we just accept the idea that it simply means that a pastor is not presently serving a congregation but is eligible for a call. Of course that's all baloney, but it's their meat market."

"I pointed that out to the district president," said Jack, "but he insisted that if in the judgment of the pastor's reporting district the contents were of a personal nature, that he had the responsibility to protect the confidentiality matters of the pastor. And thus Bergman's records were private."

"This reminds me of the South Dakota case," said Alan.

"What case was that?" asked Jack.

"It happened about fifteen years ago," said Alan. "There was a pastor that wanted a divine call to a congregation closer to the sick parents of his wife. Although he did place his name on the required call list of his local district president, despite his experience and spotless record, no church in the district he was located so much as offered him any consideration. After three years of frustration and not being allowed to review his personal file, he somehow discovered that his file had a CRM on it. Not satisfied with the explanation provided by his district president, the pastor hired an attorney to look into the matter."

"And what was the outcome?" asked Jack.

"Well, here's the interesting twist, Jack. The pastor was given a clean bill of health, but his wife was the roadblock to his getting a call," said Alan.

"The wife? How could that be?" asked Jack.

"Well, the district defended their decision on the basis that she was a divorced wife," said Alan.

"Divorced? For Christ's sake, half the married population gets divorced before seven years of marriage," said Jack. "As you are aware, I've been divorced myself for over ten years."

"It gets worse, Mr. President," said Alan, now laughing. "You see, their justification was not only stupid, but the truth of the subject was that she never ever was divorced in her entire life. Well, forgiveness is part of being a Christian, so the pastor withdrew his lawsuit and eventually got his new divine call near his wife's parents," said Alan.

"And if I might ask," said Jack, "what has this got to do with our problem and the future of Pastor Paul Bergman?"

"It's really simple, Jack," said Alan. "We don't know what we have here at this First Independent Church. Betty feels, along with my elder board, that the background of Bergman needs to be better understood since his insistence upon everything being of a private matter places the congregation in harm's way, especially since the pastor is the single person here that meets many of our members alone in their house, to include our children. In addition, he also has many meetings at the country parsonage that include our youth group and female members of our congregation."

"You're not suggesting that the pastor is doing anything immoral, are you, Alan?"

"No, of course not, but until we understand what his background really is, we owe it to every member to understand the person who is our shepherd."

"Anything else?" asked Jack.

"Betty also feels it's about time that the congregation's trustees review the condition of the parsonage to ensure everything is up to code," said Alan.

"She actually means doing a little snooping," said Jack.

"No, we're not snooping, Jack. It's something that has been an ongoing practice of this congregation for years in order that should the day come in which it becomes necessary to sell the parsonage, the church will know that everything is up to code."

"I'll go along with that, Alan, but Bergman must be invited to be present when the trustees make their inspection, and you must give him a heads-up that we intend to do this," said Jack.

"Fair enough," said Alan, "and Betty mentioned one other suggestion that she thinks will be helpful to both the pastor and the congregation."

"What's that?" asked Jack.

"As you know, she's the VP for the human resource department at the bank in town and attends a once-a-year retreat with other officers from around the country. This year in order to promote the relocation of their headquarters, it happens to be in Detroit, Michigan."

"What again am I missing, Alan?"

"Betty wants to visit the Bergman wife and daughter and hopefully his former congregation in Funston, Michigan," said Alan.

"Now, Alan," said Jack with a concern on his face, "we both know the rules about checking up on a pastor's prior church that he had once served at. Under the district guidelines it's not allowed because he's not our employee but a man of God."

"Betty said that no questions about his past ministry will be asked," said Alan. "She has a right to go to church, and it turns out his former congregation is only fifteen miles away from their meeting site."

"Where is the wife and daughter currently living?" asked Jack.

"It's my recollection from past conversations with Bergman that his wife and daughter are currently renting the vacant parsonage until they move here," said Alan. "The new pastor, a fellow named Christmas, and his family bought a home in the area, so they had no need for the parsonage. Betty had sent a 'We miss you' card to the Bergman parsonage and family last month."

"That was very thoughtful, commented Jack."

"And informative, Mr. President, as the post office returned the card indicating no such name at the address."

Looking somewhat perplexed, Jack thought about what Alan had just said. "Well, here's the deal. Your wife can visit the church while she is in Michigan, and if she's lucky maybe even have an opportunity to meet Bergman's wife and daughter, but under no cir-cumstances visit the church office and ask any questions about their former pastor. You may be the greatest doctor, Alan, this side of the Mayo Clinic, and Betty may be the smartest human resource vice president this side of General Motors, but I happen to understand how the First Independent District President's Office functions. They stick together and even instruct their own ministers not to revisit or communicate with their past congregations. In other words, no interference with the current administration at any church, or you can kiss goodbye any help from this district in the future for a divine call or, to be more specific, any assistance to get a new minister in the future," said Jack. "Now, my doctor friend, it's time that I go home to my dog and you to your family. You talk to Betty about what I recommended, and please impress upon her to be careful. We will do an inspection of the parsonage as she recommends, but if the deal in Michigan is not handled carefully, the district will come down on us like white on rice, or worse yet Bergman might file a lawsuit that this little church couldn't handle."

"Jack, you have my word that Betty and I will talk about this. We're all just doing the best that we can for our congregation."

"I know, Alan. Let's just go home."

CHAPTER 3

The Visitors

No one waits better than a farmer for rain or a Cubs fan for that World Series opportunity, unless you happen to be a First Independent pastor who has spent the last two years in endless meetings with the president of the congregation and head elder each attempting in their own way to find reasons to invalidate your divine call to the congregation that had called you. Nothing was worse, thought Bergman, than a layman provided the power to ruin your life. The Catholics had a much-better system in which the priests' fate rested usually with the local bishop, not some elected member of a congregation who would have the job for two years and then turn it over to another power-hungry layman after wrecking your life. Putting his hands to his head, he lamented over the changes since his graduation as a minister. The First Independent Church, once dominated by its heritage of male domination in key positions, which held dear to the male role of not being under the supervision of a woman, now found itself opening the door to women elders, who were often now being elected to the position of president of the congregation. He could remember his own mother not being allowed to be part of the voting assembly because she was a woman and telling him that she once only mixed with the women during church services.

As he sat in his office chair, Bergman decided that if they really wanted to open that door of his past history, it would be no easy task because of the safeguards placed on congregations invading any pastors' past life were almost equal to one attempting to have access to his health records due to the House Insurance Portability and Accountability Act. Still, the hunter seldom realized when he was the one being hunted. He remembered when he was nineteen years old hunting black bear in Wisconsin with his new seventy-pound pull compound bow. Walking in the woods, bow in hand, eyes alert for any sign of footprints on the newly fallen snow, it never had occurred to him that his prey was watching him behind a large hay ale, biding its time until he made a mistake. It would have worked for the bear if not for the sudden whistle of the Burlington Northern approaching. To this day he was not certain if the sudden sound of the whistle blaring was due to the freight train's approach to the unguarded railroad crossing or that the bear had been spotted by the engineer. Regardless the bear bolted from its hiding spot and ran across the open field to the cover of the nearby woods. In seconds, he had gathered himself and had retreated to the safety of his father's old truck, vowing never to hunt bear again unless carrying a handgun.

Checking his watch, Bergman noted that he had spent the majority of the day preparing his report for his upcoming elder board meeting, which required him to review the number of the members he had visited this calendar year, plus how he was going to handle the upcoming All Saints Day. As he got up from his chair, Bergman walked over to his small office refrigerator and removed a can of diet Coke. As he was returning to his desk, he walked over to the office's large window, which faced the rear parking lot and his reserved slot. In the space below was Dr. Alan Ogden's car with Jack Koehler's parked a few feet away. "That's odd," thought Bergman, "since I didn't even know they were here." He was about to check the basement conference room when both Koehler and Ogden appeared coming out the back door of the church and approached their cars. Each got in and drove away not realizing that he had been watching them. Whatever was going on obviously didn't include him since they didn't stop in his office, but then again they probably didn't expect him to be working late since his car was not in its usual place. Then he realized that they probably were unaware that he had to cancel his scheduled steak fry with the men's club because of a sudden request of a member to see him regarding a future wedding. Still looking out the window, the sudden ringing of his cell phone on his desk made him jump. Rushing over to the ringing phone, he picked it up.

"Pastor Bergman. Can I help you?"

"Oh, Pastor, I'm glad I got you," said Ogden. "I hope that I didn't disturb your dinner."

"So," thought Bergman, "they didn't see my car." He elected to ignore Ogden's comment about dinner.

"No problem, Dr. Ogden, I haven't started eating yet. Is there something wrong?"

"No, not at all, Pastor," said Alan. "I'm just giving you a heads-up about the board of trustees' requirement that we check out the condition of the parsonage. As you know, Pastor, our constitution requirements state that we have to do this at least once every two years just to ensure that everything is up to village codes. We are sorry to inconvenience you, but it shouldn't take more than two hours. You are, of course, welcome to be there during our visit."

Bergman, thinking about this, said, "That won't be necessary, Dr. Alan. Just have the men try to be careful about moving any of my church papers in the house. I usually leave all important church matters on my desk at home. Do you have any idea when they intend to stop buy since I would like to clean up a few things so it doesn't appear overly messy?"

"No, but don't worry, Pastor, the trustees are all men, and they are used to not vacuuming." Alan laughed Alan. "I'm truly sorry, Pastor, but I have another call coming in from what appears to be one of my patients. Betty and I will see you in church this Sunday," said Alan as he disconnected the phone.

Bergman didn't know what to make of the call since Ogden had appeared to be much too helpful. Pulling open his file cabinet, he found the copy of the church constitution and turned to the page covering the parsonage. It clearly covered the requirements of a parsonage inspection by the board of trustees. Putting the copy back, he wrote himself a note to ask his secretary if she could remember the last time trustees had performed this requirement. Well aware of the fact that most congregations had a hard time following the basic requirements of a yearly audit on their budget, or even concerned enough to keep up their church members' records, something bothered him about this request. Were they looking for something? Soon he would have to find a way to better explain the true reason why his wife and daughter were not yet here, because you could only count on the district's confidentiality so long. Although he was guarded with both the doctor and Jack, the real troublemakers were always the women who expected to know everything about your life. Well, the ball was clearly in his court because they had given him the opportunity to be present when they did their inspection, and he had refused. "Well, at least for now," thought Bergman.

In the fading twilight, Bergman got in his car and decided to drive past the Ogden's home on his way to his country parsonage, as he liked to refer to it. He had been in the Ogden home once at the invitation of Betty and Alan, who had hosted a steak fry for the men's club. Their house was hidden behind tall hedges set back from the street in what was referred to as the Garden of Eden Estates and as usual was protected by a wrought-iron gate at the entrance, which hung open. Although most homes were in the price range of $750 to $900 thousand, Betty has commented that the little community was safe and needed no guard security. Entering the gate, Bergman decided to drive around the perimeter of the Ogden home to obtain a better understanding of how First Independent's best contributor lived when not seeing patients at his downtown clinic. Although darkness was now setting in, Bergman could still see the ghostly white birches that filled one corner of the lawn where the massive colonial home rested. What he had not noticed before was that the house was set on a knoll, providing the Ogdens a circular view of the entire Eden Estates. It reminded Bergman of the usual high-end tombstones that usually was stationed at the front of a cemetery that welcomed all visitors. Pulling his car over, he noted that the majority of homes down in the valley of Eden Estates were within walking distance of an eighteen-hole golf course. After a few minutes of observation, Bergman put his car in gear and circled the block past the Ogden home heading back out through the gate onto the main highway. Reaching in his CD storage area, he located his basic lesson 1 Spanish tape and inserted it into the CD compartment.

"*Buenos dias*," said the Spanish-speaking woman. "Good morning" was the English response. "*Buenos tardes*" was the new response from a Spanish-speaking woman. "Good afternoon" was the English reply. Bergman smiled as he attempted to concentrate on the lesson while at the same time watching for the herds of deer that occupied the woods leading up to the entrance to the parsonage. The road ahead was perfectly straight with low forest on both sides and nothing but darkness in the distance. He figured that with any amount of luck the deer would not be interested in crossing the road tonight.

Turning on his bright lights, he continued the drive through the forest preserve. "*Buenos noches*" spoke the Spanish woman. "Good evening" was the English response. "Well, not too bad," thought Bergman. Turning off the CD, Berman decided it was best to focus on the remaining part of the drive since being hit by a deer was always a possibility in this country. Turning down the window, he noted that the night was windless, soundless, and had a dead stillness about it that made him uncomfortable. Seeing the curve about five hundred feet in front of him, he began to slow his vehicle when suddenly a large gray object bounded across the road in front of him. "Jesus Christ," said Bergman, "that was no fucking coyote." Slowing almost to a stop, he looked to the side of the road where the animal had disappeared. Fifteen seconds had passed. Gooseflesh spread up Bergman's back. He could feel the sweat dripping down his forehead. Rolling up his window, once more he turned his eyes in the direction of where the animal had vanished. Nothing, then some hint of motion in the dark. "That's enough," said Bergman, putting his car in gear as he raced to find the gravel road turnoff that put him to the driveway that would lead him up to his parsonage home. In a few seconds, he felt the welcome gravel on his tires and began to relax knowing that he had less than two hundred feet before he would be home. Pulling up to the front door, Bergman got out of the car and walked up the wooden steps. Pausing, he looked down toward the back of the vast yard seeing only the reflection of the water behind the parsonage shed. At that point, the yipping of the coyotes started but suddenly stopped. Perhaps, thought Bergman, they were now being hunted themselves. As he entered the building, he locked the door and retreated to his bedroom. Walking over to the king-size bed, he reached under his pillow for his P99 Walther hammerless pistol. Finding it, he carefully placed it on the side of the bed, removed his shoes, and closed his eyes.

Bergman woke suddenly in the dark of the early morning, his heart racing as the voices inside him became muted and dull, like when one closes a window near a busy street, and yet you still feel yourself being dragged down into sleep, descending into dark chambers that warn you of impending dangers unless you were able to escape the oncoming rabbit hole. Shaking his head to dislodge the demon's faint face, Bergman could see the digital clock glowing half past three. Somehow in the night, he had managed to crawl under the sheets, now twisted in a knot around his legs, his body dripping with perspiration. As he untangled himself, he sat up, putting both hands on his face hoping to rid himself of the nightmare. The other recurring dream was always better, thought Bergman, but it too was fading. Trying to remove his current fear, he envisioned instead Gayle Browning, his former church organist in Funston, Michigan. He remembered her waiting for him at her apartment, as was often the arrangement of their ongoing affair. Sometimes he would surprise her, arriving early before his church hours were actually completed, and she was not yet ready to go out. That was some of his best times as he liked to walk in her bedroom and lie on the bed and watch her get dressed and put on her makeup, with that look of impending promise, followed by a little smile in the mirror when all was complete. The sight of her stepping into a dress or tucking her blouse into her skirt and zipping up her jeans was almost better than watching her take off her clothes. His earlier fear was now vanished and replaced by the remembered sensuality of a woman now dead. He shook his head in despair thinking it should not have happened the way that it did, not to this beautiful woman he so had loved. He knew that denial was always a bad thing, carrying on one of his dialogues with himself. "At one time or another, we all have to engage in denial to some extent just to get by. It's a survival mechanism." Angry now, he realized that his hand was around the pistol grip pressing the trigger. With a conscious effort, he relaxed his fingers and turned his thoughts away from the original nightmare of what was once his and now had been taken away.

Thinking back Bergman remembered their last week together when he had accidently discovered that she had been seeing another man. His suspicions first had come to light when he had asked to borrow a writing pen and she had reached in her purse and hand him a Montblanc roller ball pen. He had not said anything to her at the time, nor had she considered that he might understand the significance of this little act. Bergman had become familiar with the expensive writing instrument when he had been asked to give the opening and closing prayers at a retirement party for state senator Marc Davidson. The politician, a devout Christian and former member of Bergman's first called church, had over the years kept in contact and requested his attendance for this part of the program. The Montblanc pen had been the gift of the senator's staff, coming at a price he was later to learn of $795. He knew at that moment that it was unlikely to be something that a church secretary could or would purchase for herself. It was the beginning of his suspicions, jealousy, and anger. That night represented the worse fight they ever had with each other. Bergman couldn't even remember what he had said, the specifics, the accusations, or even the threats. Getting up from his bed, he walked into the bathroom and splashed cold water on his face, but it didn't help. Reaching in the cabinet, he took two sleeping pills from the bottle, swallowed them, and walked back to the bed and lay back down waiting for the drug to take hold. Looking up at the ceiling, he had remembered the panic at the thought of being abandoned by Gayle for another man. As his eyes started to close, he thought back to the feeling that he was then out of control, the desperation of trying to stop and yet not able to. Now descending through a long corridor, past the dark chambers of memory into a world of regret, he fell into a deep sleep.

"Five thirty a.m., still an hour until first light," cursed Bergman as he rolled over on the bed, but he was through sleeping. He hadn't slept much anyway. Mostly just dozing, snapping awake whenever he heard the yapping of a coyote or something frightening in his mind.

Rolling out of bed, the first thing that he checked was his cell phone to make sure that it was charged, and a good thing because his battery was low. Walking across the carpet floor into his bathroom, he killed a few minutes with a hot-and-cold shower and a shave. Then he put on his traditional pastor collar with black shirt and tan pants. In the kitchen, he brewed coffee, poured himself a glass of orange juice, and made toast. Bergman found that he had no appetite, even though he hadn't eaten since the evening before. The coffee appeared to be too strong, and the juice was too sticky, too sweet tasting, and a couple of swallow of each was the best that he could manage. The parsonage's cold and silent emptiness was more than he could bear this morning. His world was coming apart fast. "Goddamn that nosey Betty!" he yelled. Picking up his car keys, he walked outside without bothering to lock the door and got into his car. Pulling away, he mumbled to himself, "I got plans now. Oh, baby, do I have plans now!"

Policewoman

Curtis Patterson wasn't thrilled over being selected to play church detective and the need to travel to Michigan. But like most things associated with his current church, he was doing it for his parents more than the church's current desire to learn about their genealogical history. Besides, Curtis had stated to the church council he considered their selected mission of locating the grave of the original founder of their church flawed and a waste of time because if they really wanted to do a good historical search, they would not just follow the single line where only the father's parentage is considered but rather examine the genealogy of all members of his family. His argument had suggested that from the standpoint of inheritance, his method was the only way to ensure biologically the rights of its current generation. In the end, the church council had accepted part of his suggestions but voted that their interest should be focused on locating the grave of Rev. Herman Karl Reusswig, the church founder, and everything else wasn't a priority. He had talked to his parents about why he considered the plan to be a flawed mission, but both his dad and in particular his mother were all caught up in the jubilation of the church's forthcoming 125th anniversary and the fact that the current pastor, Frederic Reusswig, was the descendant of the founder. Besides, they had reasoned, as a reserved pilot for Delta Air Lines, it wasn't like he had to report to work each day, and that he had plenty of spare time. Curtis loved his parents, but as an only child he certainly could understand how one could wish there had been siblings to share in these wonderful moments.

Curtis, after graduating from high school in Lift Bridge, had been accepted at the University of Illinois and later entered the aerospace engineering program, graduating with a degree in aeronautical engineering.

It wasn't long after leaving the university that he had read in the *Detroit Times* employment section about the airline's need for entry-level pilots and managed to secure an interview with Northwest Airlines. To his everlasting surprise, they hired him as a second officer. The following eight years were of flying second and first officer up and down the grain towns of North and South Dakota and living in more apartments than he could remember in Minneapolis.

Curtis was promoted to reserve captain and based out of Detroit Metropolitan Airport. His parents, now both retired, maintained a winter home in Key West, Florida, while spending their summers in Lift Bridge, Michigan. At the urging of his parents, Curtis decided to build a home in Lift Bridge and before long was convinced to join their new church, the Bethany Freedom Church. It had always been unclear to Curtis why they had so easily renounced their Catholic faith in order to join the Bethany Moravian Church, but at first it mattered very little since Curtis made it a point to avoid organized religion in favor of Sunday fishing. That changed soon after being convinced by his mother that he should use his talents to help out on a few committees that the church needed good men to serve on. The idea, he felt, wasn't going to affect much of his free time, so he made it known to the officers of the church that he would be available for some light committee work. It was not long after he had put his name in that he was elected to be on several committees, the most recent the anniversary committee that was assigned to locate the burial site of the original pastor, Herman Reusswig, founder of the Bethany Moravian Church.

Needless to say his parents were excited when they learned that their church selected him to visit Funston, Michigan, and to look for the burial site of the Reusswig family, now believed to be resting in a Lutheran cemetery. Although considered by most to be a Protestant faith, Curtis viewed his brown granite church and their peculiar ways to represent a more secretive religion than that of a traditional faith. What else, he thought, could one think when before he was accepted as a member, the church's pastor handed him a hundred-question personality test, which contained such questions as, "Do you feel that your size is against you?" Curtis had laughed to himself not knowing if they were referring to his height of six feet six inches or trying to learn something about other parts of his body. He remembered the second question being equally as weird when it asked, "Would you sing in an elevator just for fun?" In any event, he took the test when applying to become a member and agreed to help out by becoming the church's official archivist. So now, to the special delight of both his parents, he was volunteering to play detective for the next few days and visit some cemetery. But then again, as his parents had said at the time, he had no scheduled trips for at least the next ten days, and to the best of their knowledge, the only thing waiting for him at home was dirty dishes.

Curtis, now looking at his house and yard over for the final time, locked the front door to his split-level brick home and headed to the side of his house where he parked his black Chrysler 300. He had considered flying his new Cessna parked 500 feet away from the house but dismissed the idea knowing that it was more practical packing the car with the tools that he needed for this journey. Remembering that he expected to be gone for the next few days, he opened the trunk to make sure that he had packed his pump action 12-gauge Winchester and his newly purchased Smith & Wesson Governor that held six rounds of .410 2.5-inch shotshell or should he prefer could fire the same amount of .45 ACPs. Understanding the tough gun laws of Michigan, he opened up his wallet to ensure he had his proper firearms permit. Satisfied that he was prepared, he put his two suitcases in the trunk and slammed the lid. Moving up to the front door, he climbed in and pulled the 300 out onto the road, leaving his house, and headed for the main highway that signaled his departure from his hometown of Lift Bridge.

Although he had never visited the town of Funston, Michigan, his calculations indicated that the expected 225-mile drive should take no more than 4 hours. Heck, with any amount of luck, he should be in the area just in time for a late lunch. As he passed the town's only water tower, he smiled while looking up at the large brown acorn painted on the center of the tower. "Ah, yes," thought Curtis, remembering how often he had to fight his way out of a high school basketball or football game when the smartass local jock mocked his town and Curtis's team with the, "Look here, everyone, we have the team from the land of nuts." When the opposition visited Lift Bridge, it got even better because the shitheads from Watertown and Crest Hill arrived in their trucks, horns blasting as they threw nuts on the street leading up to the high school gym or football field. "Those were the good old days of black eyes and busted noses," thought Curtis as he passed the "You are leaving Lift Bridge" sign.

Curtis found the beginning part of the trip difficult in paying attention to the road when there was so much nothing to take in, with gas stations ten to fifteen miles apart and so little traffic for miles. The seemingly empty land was busy only with inhabitants that you couldn't see as you drove. Low to the ground would be mice, gophers, moles, grouse, pheasants, and prairie chickens, but nowhere in sight this morning could he hear the sounds of big John Deer tractors or even yellow school buses. "Where the hell are the jackrabbits, foxes, or the deer that I used to see growing up as a kid?" thought Curtis. Glancing down at the DVD slot in his console, he was reminded that he needed to call Terri Jensen, the Delta Air Lines simulator instructor, to set up time for his next class. "What happened to the days when everything was done in the air instead of behind some two-million-dollar simulator on the ground?" wondered Curtis.

The drive was becoming more miserable in a way that Curtis was finding more difficult to control. He was both distracted and seeking distraction at the same time as he watched the mile markers pass by and the endless telephone poles filled with red-wing blackbirds that moved from one side of the road to the other. Every radio station he tried was more boorish than the next with a multitude of unknown names recognizable only to that part of society that was probably now just getting up to head to their college class. Every commercial found him wanting to scream. "Tell us the truth, you jerks! Just tell us the truth!" he shouted to no one in particular. Good God, he was in a terrible mood, he thought, and it would take just one more reminder from some over-the-hill actor selling gold or silver or some reverse mortgage scheme to have him committed. He let his mind drift back to Terri Jensen and the simulator class, but of course not because of the flight training, but rather Terri, the single brunette with the brown eyes who made no secret that she was interested in him. The problem was Curtis knew where this was heading, and he was not the type of man who wanted relationships based on intriguing, lustful one-night-stands. What happened to the days when a man spent six months to a year courting some woman with the only expectation that she might just say maybe? No, he had experienced enough of that over the last two years, so he was holding out for the right woman. "Yeah," he thought, "the type that you took home to Mom and Dad, provided you could trust Dad." He laughed.

He had just passed the exit sign when he saw it across a yellow wheat field about a half mile off the road. Turning around, he approached the dirt road cut off and followed it down the wheat field until he came to the house built of straw. Butch Jacob Taylor, the Lift Bridge BP gas station owner, had told him about it several months ago. It was behind the home of a Tired-Out Ranch home near a town of Faith, Michigan—population, fourteen. Pulling off the dirt road, he shut the engine off and got out of the car for a better look at the house. The gas station owner had told him that the unique home was actually a thousand-square-foot straw bale home (outside measurement) and took five months to build. Curtis had heard that homes such as these had been built with straw over ten years ago, but he had never seen an actual one until now. According to the information that he had been provided, the home was built by the owner of the Tired-Out Ranch for his daughter and her husband. Looking at it for about five minutes, Curtis decided that he would stop by another time to actually understand the building process, although his initial feeling was that the big bad wolf could huff and puff all he wanted, but that this straw house wouldn't blow over. After Butch Taylor had first told him about the house, Curtis had looked the subject up on his computer and had learned that its fire rating was even higher than that of conventional homes, and if one believed everything that they read, the straw house could last forever. Turning around, Curtis returned to the highway and pushed the accelerator up to seventy miles per hour to make up lost time.

Soon he noted the approaching sign that said, "Funston, 80 miles, home of Wally Windfield." "Who the hell is Wally Windfield?" pondered Curtis. Pushing his Chrysler up to the maximum allowed speed of seventy-five miles per hour, Curtis looked across the road at the overgrown remains of what was once a sunflower field backing up to a dead or dying farmhouse, with the only suitable thing of value its thirty-foot windmill turning in the breeze. Seeing the rest stop sign, he decided to pull in and stretch his legs for a few minutes. As he exited the main highway to the rest stop, he was surprised that it turned out to be a small cement building that resembled more of a shed than the typical rest stops that promotes physical comfort and several other amenities. Getting out of the car, he walked into the building finding a single stall, shining urinal, and a simple but clean sink. Relieving himself, Curtis returned to his car and pulled it away from the entrance to the building and parked near the lone picnic bench. And then as though the uneasiness of the realization that you were alone wasn't enough, the realization that you were not was broken by the movement in the bushes, which produced a medium-size doe emerging followed by her fawn both walking up to his car. The mood of the moment was relaxing and kept him motionless. There was nothing he could do or wanted to do, so he just did the first thing that came to mind. He closed his eyes and drifted off to sleep.

Later after pulling back onto the highway, it was not long before he spotted a sign indicating, "25 miles to Funston and proudly proclaimed home of the second tallest man in the world, Wally Windfield, exit route 24A Windfield Drive."

"So that's who this guy Wally is," thought Curtis.

When he approached route 24A, Curtis noted a billboard advertising Cluck-Cluck Diner with the tagline, "Eggs fresh, waitress friendly, and free coffee." As he entered Winfield Drive, Curtis passed Wally Winfield High School, which displayed a life-size statue of the giant next to an American flag. Slowing down, he canceled the urge to stop and stand next to the likeness, fearing that this childish act would draw attention to his presence followed by too many local questions about a stranger visiting a town in search of the nonliving. After another half mile, a sign with a chicken head indicated, "Turn right for Cluck-Cluck Diner." Turning right, he pulled into the only open space at the diner between a police car and a Clark's propane truck. Exiting the Chrysler, Curtis walked a few paces toward the diner and while attempting to activate the car door lock accidently hit the trunk button on his car ring, popping his trunk open. As he started back, the state trooper, having got out of the police car almost at the same time, noticed the car trunk being opened and laughed at Curtis, saying, "It happens to me all the time, friend. I'll get it."

Curtis froze realizing that he had put the shotgun and the handgun in the trunk but couldn't remember if he had thrown the blanket over the weapons. He also realized that the officer was a policewoman under that Funston police trooper hat. Shit, he thought, the last thing he needed was to have to explain to a local cop why he had firearms, especially since hunting season was clearly over. Walking back toward the trunk, the trooper paused and slammed the trunk lid down while continuing her walk toward the restaurant. Breathing a sigh of relief, Curtis yelled thanks and followed the officer toward the door.

Kate Heller, now watching the stranger, had been a police officer now for over three years, during which time she had developed a well-earned reputation as one of the most capable, smart, and insightful street officers on the force. So it would be expected by anyone that knew her that she would not be fooled by the handsome stranger in the fifty-thousand dollar or so Chrysler 300 that was now seated in a booth several tables from her who was wondering if she actually did see the firearms he was carrying in the car. She had, and now it was only a matter of time before she would let him know that. But patience was the key to all success, she thought, as she laid her book on the table while looking at the specials listed on the menu board near her.

Laying his car keys on the table, Curtis walked to the men's room clearly marked Roosters. Entering, he noticed that unlike most men's rooms in small restaurants, which usually had a single urinal, this one had three side by side. It seemed like the owner had a sense of humor since he had installed each one to accommodate the individual patron, with the first designed to handle the little tikes, the second for men, and the third marked "Wally men." Curtis guessed that the Wally men urinal would remain clean as it appeared it had few, if any, takers since it started at chin level on most men. Finishing, he walked over to the sink, washed and dried his hands, and decided it was time to get back to his booth. Opening the door, he glanced over at his table and noticed that his car keys remained but now was accompanied by a menu. Walking over, he observed that the policewoman was now sharing a laugh with who appeared to be a high school-age waitress with an orange-and-white shirt who had sat down at her table. The only other waitress was occupied pouring coffee and taking the order of the propane driver, who seemed more interested in trying to read the name tag above her breast than the coffee she was pouring. Glancing at his menu, Curtis couldn't help overhearing the farmers in the room talking gossip, but in a small town, gossip provided the comic relief for people under tension. Even though they appeared to be arguing over who owned what car, inhabitants of a town as small as Funston would learn to recognize one another's footsteps along with the presence of strangers. They obviously had noticed him, so it came as no surprise when one got up and headed toward Curtis's table.

Extending his hand, the farmer said, "Name's Jacob. Haven't seen you around these parts, so guess you must be just passing through?"

Shaking Jacob's hand and getting up, Curtis said, "Name's Curtis. Just spending a few hours while handling a church project for my congregation."

"Really?" said Jacob. "What kind of a church project could exist in a little town like this?"

Curtis decided that a little information would do no harm, but that he would keep the real reason to himself.

Curtis answered, "Our church in Lift Bridge adopted a special theme this year called Christian history. It's some project where the ladies intend to gather information on all Independent churches so that they can share the faith with each other by putting together a reference guide that lists all churches that still exist within our district. One of the ladies seems to feel her kindred Joanne Schultz was buried in the Funston local Lutheran cemetery and asked me to take a picture of the grave. That's if I can even find the cemetery." Curtis laughed.

Just then the older waitress appeared, and Jacob said, "Molly, meet Curtis, who's just visiting and probably hungry as hell, so here's your chance to push the Wally special. Nice meeting you, Curtis. I'll let Molly fill you in on the rest of the town." Leaving, the farmer gave Molly a salute and wink and headed back to the table with the other farmers.

Curtis looked up at Molly, and the first thought that crossed his mind was how out of place she seemed to be in her orange-and-white Cluck-Cluck shirt. She reminded him of his best friend Mark's wife, Sue, a woman that seemed to give Mark the prairie fever so bad that when they were returning from fishing one Saturday a few years ago, he had Curtis pull over to the first phone booth they passed so he could call her. When Mark got back in the car, Curtis had asked him to explain the sudden emergency. Mark had replied, "No emergency. I just asked Sue to marry me." Thinking back to that day, Mark had explained his sudden decision as simply realizing that Sue was the woman he wanted to be with all his life, and he wasn't going to take a chance that this good story was going to be anything short of a happy ending.

Curtis thought that Molly was someone's good story also, but no ring on the finger yet, which was surprising to him. Molly, sensing that Curtis was in deep thought, gently asked if he would like some coffee while he finished looking over the menu. Curtis replied, "No, I'll just take the Wally special with the eggs scrambled and wheat toast and a large glass of orange juice."

Molly, offering a smile, said, "Be careful, Curtis, Jacob likes to pull that on all-out-of-town folks because the Wally special has eight eggs, six pieces of toast, and served with half a gallon of orange juice. I'll order it for you if you would like, but you would be the first here since Wally to actually eat it all."

Curtis smiled and told Molly, "I'd like the same order, just more for an ordinary mortal, not a giant."

Molly wrote down the order, turned, and headed for the kitchen. Curtis could hear the farmers laughing, so he figured that he was the center of their little joke, but as they say, no harm, no foul. Molly must be close to thirty, thought Curtis, with an empty ring finger and a maturity that seemed so out of place in this small-town diner. It was then Curtis noticed that Jacob had walked over to the booth where the propane driver was reading a newspaper and appeared to say a few words. Whatever was the message, the driver got up and walked over to the register, where Molly was assisting another customer. When the customer left, the truck driver then said something to Molly, which caused her to blush and then sprint back to the kitchen area. Clearly taken back from being apparently dismissed by Molly, the propane driver stormed out of the restaurant without another word to anyone. Curtis found the exchange interesting and wondered if it was a lovers' spat.

When Molly returned with his breakfast, she showed no signs of being upset. Smiling, she asked him if there was anything else he needed. Curtis thanked her and asked her if she could help him with directions to the Old Lutheran cemetery when she had a chance. Her smile suddenly changed to a sincere concern as she asked him if he was visiting a loved one.

"No," responded Curtis, "just on a church mission to verify the existence of another Lutheran church for the ladies who are putting this information together as part of their genealogy records." Curtis hoped that this would satisfy Molly since while he again didn't want to get into a discussion as to the real reason for his trip, something about Molly also didn't want him to outright lie to her either. Molly didn't press him any further and indicated when he was ready to leave, she would give him the directions, which she said only amounted to another four-mile drive on the other side of town.

Later when she returned with his bill, Molly poured him yet another cup of coffee and then to his surprise dropped off a handwritten map to the cemetery, while at the same time indicating that she thought that this would be easier than verbal directions. Glancing over in the direction of the policewoman, he couldn't help but feel that she was watching him. Why, he wasn't sure, but damn if he was going to show any concern. When he had finished his coffee, Curtis got up and headed toward the register, where Molly appeared to being doing double duty once again.

Passing the policewoman's table, he couldn't help notice that she was reading a book about spiders.

"Excuse me, Officer, but I rarely ever see someone interested in spiders," said Curtis, smiling.

Looking up, the attractive policewoman said, "Now I must admit, Curtis, that's a novel pickup line, but it happens to be that this spider book is about my work, and frankly I don't like spiders." She tried hard not to telegraph her real feelings about having been approached before she had been able to talk to him about those guns.

"Interesting that you should know my first name," said Curtis, "but word must get around in a small town like this."

"Well, it didn't happen that way in this case, Mr. Patterson. I just happen to have run your plate for priors. You know, police officers take an interest in folks who visit our town transporting a .45-cal. Governor pistol, but I'm sure you're licensed to carry, right, Mr. Patterson?" asked the policewoman.

"Wouldn't travel any other way, Officer, but I admit to you being right," said Curtis.

"Right about what?" asked the officer.

"That I need to improve my skill level when approaching an attractive police officer, even if I probably know more about spiders than the person reading the book," said Curtis.

Momentarily caught off guard once again, the stranger had struck an interesting cord with Kate. "Well then have a seat, Mr. Patterson, and share some of that knowledge that you have stored in your head. You may call me Kate if you wish. I have the book on spiders only because one of the little buggers is responsible for having killed someone a while back."

Curtis, sitting down, looked at Kate before responding, "While I don't doubt your information, Officer, but that's most unlikely."

Raising her eyebrows, she said, "What do you know about the brown recluse spider?" asked Kate.

"Well, to begin with, Officer Heller, out of the twenty thousand different spider species that inherit the Americans, only sixty are capable of biting humans. The brown recluse spider is one of those, along with having the dubious distinction of being one of the four most dangerous spiders in the world, actually ranks number four in its deadly bite," said Curtis.

"And how have you come about that information?" asked Kate.

"Besides actually being bitten by one, entomology was my minor in college, with spiders having my special interest," said Curtis.

"Really?" she asked. "What, pray tell, was your major? And please don't tell me it was the weaker sex," said Kate.

"Hardly my specialty since I haven't been on a serious date in two years. To be frank, it was aeronautical engineering," said Curtis.

"You have a very impressive background. That probably means you work for Boeing or some sister company," said Kate.

"No, just a plain old Captain for Delta Air Lines," commented Curtis.

Not telegraphing her interest, she said, "Tell me more about spiders, Mr. Patterson. Like, what are the chances that we would have any brown recluse ones here in Funston?"

"You could, but it would be unlikely since they are native to the Midwestern states and the southeastern states. Documented populations outside these areas are rare, but that doesn't mean that on occasion someone will spot one in Indiana, Michigan, or Wisconsin. My personal suspicions are that when most of these occur, the reporting individual has probably had been drinking several bottles of Miller High Life."

"So you wouldn't then put too much stock into a report that suggests that the brown recluse may have killed some adult?"

"Especially an adult," said Curtis.

"Why's that?"

"If one is to assume that your victim happened to be from here or that of a surrounding state, he or she would have had to beat the terrible odds that point out that brown recluse spider bites don't kill adults, just children. The only real damage of its bite is that some amputations do occur because the flesh is destroyed in the area of the bite. You might want to check with a local infectious specialist, Officer, since the bite would usually require his involvement to stop the spread of the venom. Few doctors have the ability to determine even that the patient has a spider bite, let alone if it was the deadly brown recluse."

"You're joking, of course," said Kate.

"No, it's the truth. Unless you have been lucky enough to have killed the spider or captured it so that it can be put under a microscope, everything else is just guesswork. I'd rather be bit by a black widow and be near a doctor than the recluse spider, which often takes a little longer to recognize that you're in trouble," said Curtis.

"What do you mean by being in trouble?"

"Well, if a black widow bites you, the venom is said to be fifteen times more toxic than the venom of the prairie rattlesnake," said Curtis. "You would need immediate help. On the other hand, a brown recluse spider bite could go undetected for a couple of days until that part of the body begins to show the infection. During that period of time, most people just begin to apply medication for the itching and rashes that they are experiencing, not realizing what may be actually taking place. The area of the bite has to be watched very close by a doctor because it can result in an amputation if you're not careful how you treat it. I would imagine that you couldn't tell me what your interest is in spiders, could you, Officer Heller?"

"No, I'm afraid not since it involves a cold case that remains unsolved. It's not my case, so at this point my interest is only curiosity, nothing more."

Getting up, Curtis said, "Well, good luck in your investigation, Officer, but should you have any other spider questions, here's my card and phone number. He handed her a card with the Delta Air Lines widget emblazon on the front.

Looking up, she smiled.

"No, really, Officer, this is not another bad attempt at a pickup line," said Curtis. "You may need help, and it's just part of my Delta inbreeding to be helpful, as the slogan says."

"Just what does that slogan say, Mr. Douglas?"

"You know, it's been around for a while. 'Delta is ready when you are,'" replied Curtis.

Kate didn't let Curtis see the amusement on her face at the implication of his words or her placing his card in her blouse pocket. Her instincts told her that the guy was nervous, but that didn't necessarily mean he was dangerous. After all, if it was true that he hadn't had a serious date in two years, his attempted ways to connect to females might just be a guy out of practice. He was good-looking and very tall, but that wasn't what had caught her eye. It was the shoes, she thought, the GJ Cleverley & Co brand that cost nearly a thousand dollars. Her deceased husband had bought a pair with his football pool winnings the year that he had died, after of course he had insisted that she spend the other half of the winnings on something for herself. She could feel the tears as she remembered the call from his commanding officer notifying her that he had been killed by a sniper in Iraq shortly after he had returned from his short leave at home. The shoes, goddamn those shoes that brought back the memories, but they also suggested that Curtis was more likely just someone who he advertised to be—a pilot, nothing more.

Walking up to the cashier's booth, Curtis was brought out of his momentary daydreaming by Molly's voice. "Can I help?" she asked.

Realizing that he had been caught looking back in the direction of the policewoman, Curtis said, "You already have, Molly, and I appreciate everything you have done. The directions you have provided to help this stranger find that Lutheran cemetery is most appreciated." He handed her his restaurant bill. "Maybe you could also recommend or tell me where the motels are located in your town, as I will probably be here two or three days," said Curtis.

"You'll pass by several on the way to the cemetery," said Molly. "We have the standard commercial types like the Holiday Inn, Howard Johnson, and the Westgate, and a few that cater to the truck drivers who are only looking only for a night's sleep. Nothing fancy, no pool or workout area, just a bed and sheets. But to tell you the truth, the Flicker Tail Inn across from the Holiday Inn is the popular place because the cost is reasonable and they serve a small free breakfast in the morning. Don't wait too long before making the reservations, especially at the Flickertail, because some of the local farmers like to just book it for its pool and game room when they come into town once a week. Sort of like taking the family to Disney World minus the high cost."

"Sounds good to me," said Curtis, "so I better get out to the cemetery before it gets dark." He started to walk away."

"Oh, one more thing, Curtis," said Molly.

"Yes, what's that?" asked Curtis.

"Police Officer Kate Heller, the lady you seem to have an interest in. The entire male population of Funston from eighteen to sixty-five have tried at one time or another," said Molly.

"I'm not following," said Curtis.

"The way you looked at her at the table as you walked away. She'll turn you down no matter how hard you try," said Molly. "Many have tried, and all have failed."

"It's that obvious?" asked Curtis.

"Well, remember, I've been a waitress for a few years, and I see those looks all the time, but yours seem to be sincere. She'll still turn you down, so be prepared to be hurt, although it probably won't be personal. We're friends, and I can tell you that she's not ready and might not be for some time," said Molly.

"Why?" asked Curtis.

"That I can't tell you for personal reasons as her friend," she said.

"Well, thanks again, and I'll remember what you said, but in life I've learned a long time ago that it's not the victories that make one's dreams come true but rather how well you handle the defeats. Something tells me that she would be worth a defeat or two. Anyway, it'll be dark soon, so I better be on my way if I expect to visit that cemetery," said Curtis.

Kate waited a few seconds before she followed Curtis out the door of the restaurant, giving him just enough time to pull out of his parking space before she got into her police car and followed him as he headed out of town toward the Lutheran cemetery. Staying just far enough back, she was able to observe him pulling into the cemetery, shut the car down, and proceed to walk down the slope toward the main burial area. Satisfied that his actions all appeared harmless and was just another visitor to Funston, Kate turned around and headed to the police station for the afternoon shift change. She was within five miles of the station when she noticed the backup of the traffic. It looked like pavement repair since the road workers were all following the blacktop repair crew. All six with the shovels were wearing hats on their head. Five mesh caps printed with the names of what she took to be agricultural equipment Manufacture's. The sixth waved at her as she passed him with his pheasant cap proudly proclaiming that this was "Big cock country."

"Boys will be boys," she thought.

CHAPTER 5

The Beehive

"Everybody has secrets," she thought as she reviewed her conversations with Curtis Patterson. People lie. Lawyers lie. Car salesmen lie. Cops lie. Life is a contest of who is telling the truth and who is lying. And we all know that. Still people engage in conversations knowing that they are going to be lied to and with regret to be lied back. The trick is to be a good listener, because the longer a person talks provides the listener a greater opportunity to uncover the lie. Being patient was her strong suit. What was that her dad used to say? "Patience is the element of success."

A few minutes later she pulled up to the station, and she noticed that her immediate supervisor, Jacob Henning, was parked a few slots over from her car. Looking his car over, she then opened up her car door and slid out of the vehicle and walked over and wrapped on his window. "What's up, Sergeant?"

Rolling down his window, Jacob said, "I've been waiting for you, Corporal. Come on and get in the car. I need to go over something with you before you go in today."

"I can't stay too long, Sarge. Captain Wagner wants to see me in about fifteen minutes," commented Kate.

"Yeah, I know, and that's why I wanted to get to you first and give you a heads-up," said Jacob.

Getting in the car and closing the door, she asked, "Is there anything bad coming down?"

"No, actually it's real good as I look at it, but it might cut into your social life," said Jacob. "Here's the deal, Kate. The big guy downtown has been taking heat over that murder two years ago involving that pastor and his church mistress. Do you remember the case?"

"Who can forget it? The press, politicians, and the brass from downtown all swarming around this little police station like it was a beehive that held the new queen bee," said Kate.

"Well, it did, Officer Heller, and the queen bee now turns out to be you. After all, it was you who answered the initial call that found the woman with the cord around her neck and still breathing and probably through your quick actions saved her life," said Jacob. "It was that effort that is making you the new rising star, and whether you like it or not, it has put you on the fast track to becoming the first female to wear the sergeant's gold shield."

"Little good it did, since I still ended up being a vegetable," said Kate, "and as you can see, I still remain a corporal."

"Well, you're wrong on both counts, lady. First, the pastor's wife has made news again as of yesterday. She never ever came out of her coma and unfortunately died. So after all that time with her parents at her side, she never said one word about who tried to kill her. Everyone thinks that her pastor husband attempted to murder her, except the jury which has set him free. The end result of this sad ending is that the case remains open, and the politicians remain angry as hell because the news outlets are busting their chops. Second, you should see the detective shield on your blouse before the weekend, although I've been told to keep quiet on that surprise in order that the captain can pretend that he had something to do with it."

"You mean over something like a pastor's wife dying gets me a shield?"

"Something along those lines, plus the fact her death has required dusting off the cold case and finding someone new to take the heat off a police captain. It's good for you as long as you remember that manure runs downhill in this case."

"You mean, someone takes the fall for the boss?"

"I just always knew you were my smartest cop," said Jacob.

"Yes, and this smart cop also knows that with her death also went our best witness," said Kate.

"Well, it gets worse. A reporter from the *Funston Star* wrote a big piece on it suggesting that the Funston police need to remove the grime from this cold case and find the killer," said Jacob.

"And this is where I come in?"

"It seems the brass is thinking about reopening the case, and you've drawn the short straw. I've been telling you for some time, Corporal, that the detective shield was moving in your direction, and nobody deserves it more than you. At the same time, with responsibility comes the curse of being put on the hot seat that often should be for someone else. The beauty, if there is a beauty to something like this, is that should you solve it in the time period that saves your boss's behind. It usually means another feather in one's cap. You've got the talent, Kate, and the perseverance to win at this game while others would melt like a snowflake. Last free advice before we go in, Howard Singer thinks that the detective shield belongs to him. Well, it could someday, but not now or maybe never until he corrects some of his ways. So expect some grief, but accept none. Now let's get inside."

She got out of the car without looking back and walked up the six flights of steps that brought her to the front entrance. She slowed and waited for Jacob, and when he passed her at the door, she said. "Wait!"

As Jacob turned to see what was on her mind, Kate pulled him close and whispered in his ear, "Thanks."

Smiling, he said, "For God's sake, woman, if someone had seen that, what are they going to think?"

"They'll probably think because you're twenty years older than me, that you're one lucky fellow," she said laughing while slapping him on the rear. She allowed him to continue down the hall into Wagner's office. She waited another two minutes before entering the room.

"Right on time, I see," said Captain Wagner.

"Yes, sir," responded Kate. Looking around the conference room, she noted that Jacob was seated next to some well-dressed, attractive middle-aged woman.

"Corporal Heller, I'd like to introduce you to Rachel Underwood, our new district attorney for the Funston area," said Wagner. "Ms. Underwood already knows a lot about your good work, Officer Heller, since she has met with Sergeant Henning earlier today." Underwood gave her one of those head nods that said hello, but not much more. Wagner continued by saying, "As you may have heard from Sergeant Henning, the *Funston Star* wrote a column about a past attempted murder case that involved the wife of a pastor from one of our churches in Funston. That column caught the attention of our mayor."

Kate, looking direct at Underwood, observed her favoring Jacob with a knee caress and the softness of her white cashmere sweater against his shoulder. Although it was only a guess, she somehow felt that it was still not her turn to talk, so she just listened.

Wagner continued talking, "Ms. Underwood has decided to revisit the circumstances of that case, along with the horrible death of Gayle Browning, the former organist of that same church that the Reverend Paul Bergman had served. Her death, as you might remember, happened within the year following the tragic attempted murder of Mrs. Alicia Bergman."

This brought Kate's attention back from watching the hand of Underwood, which now rested on Henning's leg. "Isn't she the one who allegedly was bitten by a brown recluse spider, Captain Wagner?"

"Yes, that's right, but how did you learn about that?" asked Wagner.

Irritated, Underwood said, "It's not really important at this stage of the new investigation, Captain Wagner, unless you want to continue to waste time. The fact that anyone knows anything about this case is a surprise in its own right regardless how they found out. Now I need to speak to Detective Heller alone, Captain Wagner. She is the one you told me is going to head up the reopening of this cold case, correct?"

"We haven't talked to her about that yet," said Wagner.

"Well, then maybe you should talk to her, Captain. Frankly I have a tight schedule, and I don't have all day," she said as she got up and walked out the open door of the conference room.

"Whew, what got her panties in a bunch?" said Wagner.

"I doubt, Captain, that she is wearing any," said Kate.

"What was that?" asked Wagner.

"Nothing, Captain. She's just under pressure from the mayor's office."

Wagner, now reaching into his uniform jacket, pulled out a piece a paper.

"Corporal Heller, I regret that you had to hear about being assigned to this case from our district attorney, but maybe this good news will out weight that oversight. The good news is that it's my pleasure to award you the gold detective shield, which now makes you our first female detective and newest member of our detective squad. Our custom at this police station is that you now have the responsibility to assist us on finding the next most qualified future squad leader to replace you. You've certainly earned this promotion not only because you were the best overall candidate but also because you have recently scored the highest grade ever achieved on the detectives' written examination. If that wasn't impressive enough to all your commanders, it's also has been brought to my attention that you also scored very high on the pistol range, coming in second."

"She actually tied for first," said Henning, "so we flipped a coin and she lost."

"Lost? Good God, why didn't you just put up another target?" asked Wagner.

"She declined to participate because it was the other officer's birthday and she felt he deserved it," said Henning.

"Oh, for Christ's sake, let's finish this meeting before Underwood knocks on the door looking for my ass," said Wagner.

"Now that I gave you the good news, the bad news, Heller, is that you're being assigned the Bergman case in the hope that we can find some new information on who actually might have murdered his wife. Any questions?" asked Captain Wagner.

"Yes, what if I find information that points back to Rev. Bergman having killed his wife?" asked Kate.

"That won't happen, and if it did, he can't be tried again since he was originally found innocent by a jury of his peers," said Wagner.

"What about Gayle Browning?" asked Kate.

"I don't follow you, Corporal. Sorry, I meant Sergeant," said Wagner.

"The brown recluse spider bite, Captain, it was listed as the cause of death," said Kate. "It would seem that the pastor, having now lost his wife to some unknown killer, has gotten real lucky to now have had his alleged mistress also out of the picture due to her death. One has to believe in the consistency of good fortune to not believe that something is very odd about both events. It could turn out that Bergman killed both women, so he may not be entirely free as a bird, if you know what I mean."

"I know what you mean, but how in the hell, Sergeant, did you find out about that spider bite anyway? asked Captain Wagner.

"I stopped a speeder outside Funston who happened to be an arachnologist. While I was writing him a warning ticket, he commented that he had heard some time back that a woman in our area had died of a brown recluse spider bite. It was his opinion that it was unlikely that she died that way regardless what the authorities or papers thought," said Kate.

"What in the hell is an arachnologist, and what led him to assume the authorities were wrong?" said Wagner.

"An arachnologist studies spiders, Captain, and according to the guy, brown recluse spiders are rarely, if ever, found this far north. I later talked to another guy in a local restaurant who had studied the subject and said that in the entire United States, there hasn't been one record death in the last five years. He suggested that the person who made that call was someone who had little training on the subject," said Kate.

'Well, the guy might have just trying to impress you and was just blowing smoke in order to get out of you writing him a ticket, so I'd be careful in drawing any conclusions," said Wagner. "Regardless, this is going to be your case to live and die with, Sergeant, so keep me posted all the way. In the meantime, I'll do my best to keep the DA away from you, but as you can well understand, she's going to be a pain unless we can give her something to calm her nerves. Therefore, don't count on getting any new cases for at least a month. This should give you an opportunity to get your teeth into the Bergman file and hopefully have something for me to take the pressure off. Any last thought before I end our meeting?"

"Just that I would like to have both case files to read, not just Bergman's," she said.

"You really are hung up on the spider deal, aren't you, Sergeant Heller?" asked Captain Wagner.

"Not really hung up on it, sir, but rather when facts contradict each other, then some of the facts may well turn out not to be the facts. Let's just say, Captain, that I'm uncomfortable with the way the pastor's mistress had died. You know, if she was actually bitten by this fiddleback spider, the report should show have shown some signs on the skin of a developing rash and, if not treated, would have kills the tissues," said Kate.

"Sergeant Henning, do you have any idea what the hell she's talking about?" said Wagner.

"Not a clue, Captain," he said smiling.

"Sorry, Captain," said Kate. "You see, the brown recluse is called the fiddleback because it has a violin-shaped appearance on its body. The truth is, unless the lab people actually had the dead spider turned into them when they examined the Browning woman, there is a very good chance that they were just guessing about the cause of death."

"How have you become such an expert on this subject in such a short time, Sergeant?" asked Wagner.

"The guy I stopped gave me one of his old books on the subject, and I like to read a lot," said Kate. She decided not to bring Curtis Douglas into the picture until she knew a little more about him."

Looking frustrated, Wagner said, "It's your call, Sergeant. Have my secretary assemble what you want, but cover your ass on any fast conclusions or you'll have a lot of people having panic attacks about my new detective. And by the way, Officer, just so you know, I understood your comments about Ms. Underwood's lack of attire.

You've been awarded points for artfulness of expression, but I suggest you be very careful when commenting or getting too close to the lady. She is dangerous to our careers. Until you understand that little fact, you don't know anything about what it feels like to have been bitten by a good set of fangs. Do I make myself clear, everyone?"

"I follow you, Captain," said Kate.

"Understand boss, said Jacob."

As she left the police station, Kate drove south over the hills of Funston and down toward the farms and ranches that represented but a part of the overall personality of a city that could mix wealth with the sweat of the working man that produced the milk and bread. Most residents didn't care that this particular section of their city was perpetually shrouded in mist, nor the odor of the farm animals that filled the air, any more than if one was passing by one of the many golf communities that were more prevalent near her home. As she passed an ancient Ford truck hauling what appeared to be corn with a trail of bluish smoke coming out its tailpipe, she noted the young teenager inside. The young boy was singing to the music coming into his headphones and was oblivious to the squad car as he faced straight ahead with his eyes barely open. The red tip of a joint flared brightly and then faded as the teenager moved back and forth to the music with not a care in the world. Pulling alongside the truck, she touched her horn several times and motioned for the boy to turn his window down. Seeing the uniformed policewoman, he became conscious that he had been caught and was about to be busted. Rolling his window down, the young driver then slowed the pace of his car down to match the speed of Kate's squad car. Now alongside the truck, she pointed to her mouth indicating with a motion to throw the joint out. The teenager, reacting quickly, tossed it out the window. Giving him the thumbs-up sign, she picked up her speed and quickly left the truck in her rearview mirror. Even a blind squirrel can have a lucky day, thought Kate, and today was his. She was just too exhausted to put the hammer down on youthful transgressions. Maybe, just maybe, he would have profited by a break in life.

It had been an interesting day for her to say the least as she thought back to her meeting of Curtis Patterson. "How many times in your life do you meet a real Spiderman?" She laughed to herself, and make no mistake, he had definitely hit on her, but why? The guy was certainly good-looking and tall, maybe six feet six inches, well-educated, with seemly a dream job as an airline pilot. The idea that he hadn't had a date in two years seemed to be a stretch for a guy with his obvious assets, which would attract most females. And then there was the surprise of the detective shield. Certainly she had made it clear from the day that she was hired that she was goal minded and had used every opportunity and training available to prepare herself for this promotion, but things were now moving fast. As she glanced ahead on the newly paved highway, she noticed the gleaming white beach of Lake Michigan off in the distance. The sight of cars pulling their recreational vehicles took her back to a few summers ago when she had met her future husband while enjoying a late-summer afternoon reading a book on one of these gleaming white beaches. Unlike the slow, boyish charm of Curtis Patterson trying hard to camouflage his interest in her, Mark never attempted to hide what he had in mind. He had shocked her when he had approached her with his rented Sunfish and the bright-pink tail. So many years ago, she thought, but clear nevertheless. He had tried the direct approach by trying to convince her that he was an accomplished sailor and spent a lot of his free time sailing the shores of Lake Michigan. Ruggedly handsome and beamingly confident, Mark had no intention of receiving any type of rejection, so in the end, she had bought his smooth description of his seamanship skills and had agreed to take a ride with him on Lake Michigan. What she later learned was that Mark knew very little about sailing or the shifting winds that were common on the Big Lake, as the locals liked to call it. His awkward efforts to tack had almost dumped them into the chilly waters and possibly cost them their lives. When it had become clear that he was in over his head, he had tried his best to right the boat, but the sail kept flapping uselessly. Finally in frustration, he simply admitted to her that he didn't know what the hell he was doing. As luck would have it, the shore patrol had spotted their difficulty and had moved in to offer them assistance and then towed them to shore. Undaunted by his misstep, Mark had overwhelmed Kate with perseverance in wanting to be with her. Love being what it was, she had decided to overlook Mark's minor flaws of arrogance and a demanding personality. Within a year, they were married, and Mark had taken his former background from officer candidate school in college and enlisted in the Army as a second lieutenant. Following basic training, she had joined him at Fort Hood, Texas, where she was hired as a radio dispatcher for the county police department.

She continued her drive, leaving the sight of Lake Michigan and its many boats but now only a picture in her mind as she turned at the next cross section and headed to what she always referred to as no-man's-land between the changing neighborhoods and ultimately where she lived. The area was lined with low-built commercial buildings, small shopping strips, several fast-food restaurants, plus several cemeteries. It wouldn't be long before she would be home and face the empty bed again that would remind her of the two different Marks that she had married, one that could be loving and gallant, while the other childish and fearful. But did it matter now since Mark had been dead for three years, killed by some faceless enemy miles away in Iraq? Pulling up to her townhouse, Kate turned off the ignition and entered her world of loneliness. Slowly she moved around the living room, touching familiar objects, remembering all the automatic tricks she had used for so long to make the sterile confines of her surroundings make it feel like home. She was alone, nobody trying to reach her. She was about to take off her shirt when she felt it the business card of Curtis Patterson, the Delta pilot. Studying it for a minute, she looked at her watch—6:15 p.m. Another hour and the Lutheran cemetery would be closed.

Picking up her car keys, she opened up her front door, locked it, and raced to her car.

CHAPTER 6

The Cemetery

The evening sunlight rolled in over the stubble, grass, and gravel that made up the entrance to the first Lutheran cemetery of Funston. The red-and-white water tower four miles off in the distance provided the only comfort suggesting that civilization really existed in the small town. Thinking back to his breakfast at Clucker's, it was impossible to dismiss the hidden story that seemed to surround the policewoman. She had been friendly, but guarded even when she had asked him about his knowledge regarding spiders. Clearly she had been struggling with the subject but had volunteered little about what that was or about herself. It was natural, he thought, to have stolen glances at her before she had invited him to sit down, if for no other reason than her outward attractiveness, which couldn't be hidden by her standard-issue uniform. Still, his experience of having lived in a small town himself for a good portion of his life had told him that outsiders with no family ties to a town were never fully accepted. Town folks had a tendency to avoid discussing important stories with strangers. They put these tales safely out of sight and out of mind when strangers would show up.

The policewoman was one of the town folks, and her life story was theirs, so he was on his own should he want to know anything about her. No ring on her finger was a good sign, but it was difficult to imagine that she had escaped the interest of the male population, as well as the women whose first look probably gauged the size of her breasts. She undoubtedly had some understanding that being young, smart, and sexy could turn men a sickly, pale green, and if she had detected his lingered gaze, she had handled it well and was not openly upset. While women in the past had always focused on his background as a pilot, the policewoman seemed more interested in his knowledge about spiders, not how well a Delta Air Line captain was paid. The only positive thing he could remember was that she didn't press the issue of his transporting the shotgun and the pistol, plus she had accepted his business card and had given him hers. Dismissing any further thoughts on the subject, Curtis reached for his light jacket for protection against any sudden cold winds that one would expect when walking through an open cemetery unprotected from the shelter of trees or buildings. Looking over his shoulder, Curtis saw what appeared to be a police car turning around and heading back to town, but he was not certain since from his distance cabs looked much the same as squad cars. Sighting the car, he returned his mind back to his meeting with Kate, with the secret hope that her interest had brought her out to the cemetery. Curtis sucked in a chest full of air as he contemplated the excuse he would use to contact her before he left. He had also remembered the words of the waitress, Molly, as she had provided him a warning about how Kate had in the past rejected all attempted outreaches to get to know her better. Curtis was by nature a careful man, and even though this was a chance meeting of a woman that had caught his interest, something told him that he must not pass up the opportunity to get to know this beautiful creature.

Being the appointed archivist for the Bethany Moravian Church in Lift Bridge, Michigan, Curtis had driven the last 250 miles in search of what his fellow members believed to be was the final resting place of the original eight families that came from Moravian, Austria, in 1837 and who had built in the United States their first original Bethany Moravian Church in Funston, Michigan. If the trip proved successful, thought Curtis, he would locate the final resting place of the church's first minister, the Reverend Herman Reusswig, who reportedly died in this area somewhere around 1859. According to the records provided, the church burned down around 1889, and a new Lutheran church was built in the same location of the Bethany church, and together past and present now shared the same land that held the history and bodies of both churches. The church records indicated that Reusswig and his followers remained in the area but were unable to build a replacement church, choosing instead to allow the continuation of their church to be in the hands of those who had relocated to other areas. Curtis understood that the big prize for the folks back home in Lift Bridge was in the location of the Reverent Herman Reusswig's resting place because the church council wanted to make his discovery the centerpiece for its 125th anniversary. They would then present this information to the members of their congregation and their current pastor, Adolph Reusswig, the great-grandson of Herman Reusswig, who now occupied the pulpit of this 77-member congregation and last remaining Bethany Moravian Church.

Curtis remembered the words of Pastor LaMar Schmidt, his last real connection to any faith: "God works for all good." When the old minister learned that Curtis had made a comment to an old classmate that "the bologna came fast and furious" regarding current organized religion, he had ended up meeting Schmidt's wrath. Taking him aside on one Sunday after church, he had lectured Curtis, "Christians are able to swallow and devour whatever evil confront them and confidently expect a thousand advantages for one disadvantage or loss. Someday, you will want something very bad, and you will see either the devils behind or the face of God. Have the courage to understand which of the two has the ability to make your dreams come true, Curtis, and the chances are, you will have a blessed life."

Patterson unhooked the six-foot chain that allowed entrance into the old Lutheran cemetery. With care, he drove his new Chrysler past the open gate, moving ever so carefully down the gravel drive until he reached the ten-foot iron cross that marked the center of the cemetery. A large aged copper metal sign pointed to the gray marble upright stone indicating the resting place of Wally Winfield, "the World's Second Tallest Man." It proudly proclaimed that Wally was the most famous former resident of Funston, along with being the former church organist. Reading on, the sign said that an overactive pituitary gland had produced a peppery growth spurt that lasted from age 10 until he was 24. When he was fully grown, Wally stood

8 feet 1 inches tall and weighed 438 pounds, with a shoe size of 24. He had died unmarried at the age of 49 from a heart attack while working in the local lumberyard. His marble stone, "Rest in peace, Wally," only made reference to his two homesteading parents and the date 1919–1968. Curtis couldn't help wonder where the tallest man in the world lived and if he was as loved as Wally had been. God, the shoe size 24 must have had every girl in Funston trying to guess many things about Wally, thought Curtis. Hearing a noise, Curtis turned to see a fast-moving propane truck kicking up the gravel as it moved past the cemetery heading to what he speculated was some farmer's yard in desperate need of heating fuel to prepare for the coming winter season. Although he couldn't make out the name on the truck, it reminded him of the incident at Clucker's that involved a propane driver and Molly. As he pondered the exchange between Molly and the driver, he noticed suddenly that the truck began to slow down and had turned off into what he guessed was a cross-country road used for local traffic. Again stopping, the truck turned around and headed back in the direction of the cemetery. Although Curtis never thought of himself as a loner, he knew that visitors would only ask questions that he was for some unknown reason still cautious about answering. Mentally reprimanding himself for his unnecessary suspiciousness of the driver, Curtis moved further into the cemetery while trying to ignore the sound of the truck driver, who clearly had entered the cemetery grounds. Curtis noticed that the driver had decided to park his truck and walk into the cemetery rather than pull through the gates. As he walked into the front part of the cemetery, he appeared to be trying to remember the location of some particular grave but was having trouble finding it.

Suddenly the man appeared to have located what he was looking for because he paused and put his hands together apparently in prayer for whomever was buried in that location. The headstone appeared to have brought back memories of another location because the propane driver moved toward the far end of the cemetery fence line. Curtis remembered from his early days in church that usually that section of the cemetery was reserved for those who had taken their own life or individuals not confirmed in the faith of those resting with the other members of that religion. Within a few minutes, the driver appeared to have found what he was looking for and kneeled down to place something on the grave. Although Curtis couldn't be certain from his distance, the burial place appeared to be well decorated with children's stuffed animals and some type of small rotating fan. Deciding it would be best not to be caught gawking, Curtis continued to move deeper into the cemetery grounds, following a small path that led to what appeared to be the most recent used area for new burials. After about five minutes, he could hear in the distance a truck starting up, suggesting that the propane driver was leaving after what Curtis concluded was his brief visit to a family member. This left Curtis to once again ponder the seemingly empty land that a cemetery offers to its visitors. A land quiet, yet busy with inhabitants like mice, gophers, moles, grouse, prairie chickens, pheasants, and the occasional snakes behind some broken-down marker. Along with the largeness of the visible iron fences, the distant trees, and the now-fading sunset, this land's essential indifference to the human could be unnerving. He wouldn't let himself be fooled by the meadowlarks, killdeers, seagulls, and hawks that he had noticed darting above as they hunted for prey. Instead he kept his eyes open for the lone badger and the skunks that lumbered busily through the grass. The badger was a major concern because although it would usually flee from strangers, its ferocity was legendary to those who had seen it pull a large dog into its badger hole. Curtis had remembered reading about how Indians on the plains would pass down through generations the stories about small ponies meeting the same fate as dogs. Ah, yes, Michigan, "the Badger State." It sounded less friendly than the Peace Garden State that North Dakota folks liked to refer to in reference to their state, thought Curtis. Finding and learning the truth about whether the Reverend Reusswig and his followers lay buried somewhere in this old Lutheran cemetery would not be easy. Unlike the cemeteries in the larger cities, those in the country, much like this one, could be depressing just by the dried grass that appeared everywhere. He remembered the image of Psalm 90, which spoke of grass being like flesh, where in the morning it would spring up and by nightfall would wither close to the ground. It was hard, he thought, to imagine that his parents' church was dying, almost impossible to picture it becoming yet another abandoned religion like the one he was investigating on this land.

Maybe, he thought, that it was a mistake that he had not being friendly to the driver and sought him out since he would have obviously known the grounds better than what he did. "It's absurd," thought Curtis, "that in the middle of nowhere that somehow I will stumble upon a tiny group of headstones that will mark the location of the family that started this church."

He could hear in the distance the bellowing of cows at what he thought would be their drinking from some water tank or feeding from some hay bale. Well, he thought, at least the sound was much more to his liking than meeting the hiss of some rattlesnake looking for a gopher. Kate would be a much-preferred companion than this goose chase, but then again, if he was right about what he perceived to be her many admirers, she was already spoken for, despite Molly's insistence to the contrary. Once again dismissing any further thoughts about the propane truck driver or the policewoman, he continued his search. Behind a large group of pine trees, he spotted a large cement outline of what appeared to be an open-face granite Bible. Walking further downhill until he was upon the display, he now could make out the German words of the Lord's Prayer on the face of the Bible, which was surrounded by rows and rows of old tombstones. Nearest to the granite Bible was a large gray cement stone bearing the name of Elizabeth Dehnhardt with the inscription 28 SEP 1732–12 APR 1791. Most of the additional stones reflected the same time period, with most dates impossible to read due to the weather eroding the names and dates of those now at rest. As he glanced to his left, Curtis noticed what appeared to be a small divided section of the main graveyard. Walking through and between the old markers, he came upon what appeared to be a family plot with twenty or more individual graves, all with German surnames of the family members—Schultz, Dill, Baumann, Wollin, Schwager, and Brehmer, but no Reusswig. None of the dates on the makers could be made out with any degree of clarity, and since the sun was beginning to set, Curtis decided to call it a day and return tomorrow morning after a good night's sleep at one of the local motels.

As he started to head back toward his car, he suddenly caught his foot on a piece of wood sticking out of the ground, and unable to regain his balance, he found himself falling heavily to the ground and just by luck missing a large flat headstone. The fall felt like a sledgehammer to his gut. "Oh Christ," he breathed, suddenly understanding that he was miles from home and might have broke his wrist. Sitting up, he carefully removed his jacket while at the same time moving his hurting left wrist up and down and checking his body for any signs of cuts or bruises. Finding everything seemly in place, Curtis breathed a sigh of relief and carefully eased his body off the ground. As he stood up, but still shaking from his close call, he walked over to where the wooden stake still remained. Grabbing the top of the shaft, he attempted to pull it out of the ground, but his effort produced no results. He then realized that someone probably had driven it into the ground with a hammer and was now several inches in the ground.

Bending down, he put both hands on the stick and attempted one last try to raise it out of the ground. It was then that he noticed the flat-shaped stone with a carved-out cross and date, "H, March 30, 1832; D, June 7, 1834; Baby Augusta R," with the remaining letters of the last name weather-worn beyond being recognition. Reaching in his jacket pocket, Curtis found the flathead screwdriver that he always carried in the jacket and gently put the blade under the small flat stone and attempted to raise it up enough to determine if he could remove it from the grips of the years of grass growth. After several attempts and picking his way around the stone, it suddenly came loose enough for him to pull it free. Still not certain what he would do with the stone, Curtis decided that he would take it back to the Chrysler and clean it up to determine if he would then be able to read the last name. Then he would return tomorrow and put it back in its proper location and continue his search. Picking it up, Curtis started to walk back to his car, which appeared now to be some distance away. Walking with care, Curtis found himself beginning to feel the effects from the long walk but remained grateful that the sky was clear and not howling from any sudden winds that often appear this time of year. Finally reaching the car, Curtis opened the door and carefully laid the flat stone on the rear seat, covering it with his jacket. Feeling the need to take a short nap, he walked around the front of the Chrysler and slid himself into the driver's side and locked the door. Reaching for his thermos, he took a long drink of the cold water and thought about his afternoon activity. It was ironic, he thought, that he was the one tramping through the grass and prairie of a cemetery looking for the past history of his church back home when he himself had never been eager to go to church in the first place, while his parents had attended church every Sunday morning as good, practicing Christians. Sunday was a day that he preferred to spend with his friends or just go river fishing. There was another reason, of course, and it had a lot to do with church services never starting or ending on time. The favorite saying of the parish minister use to be, "And not to be windy," which usually meant that was exactly what would be in store. Church was always supposed to be over by noon, but more often than not it would continue until one o'clock. All this could have been manageable, in Curtis's mind, if the doctrine of forgiveness and the parable of the Good Samaritan would not have been lost to the more aggressive attitudes of the self-appointed righteous members. Picking up the thermos again, Curtis splashed some water on his face and took a second drink while adjusting the seat so he could rest. Yes, these folks had gotten to him and had succeeded in removing any remaining hope for him to become the churchgoing son that his parents had hoped for. It had begun when one Sunday when a long-time member of their Church had announced that the current organist, who had been playing for the church for over thirty years, should no longer play the organ because she was not officially a member of the congregation. So in order to avert trouble, the church members acquiesced to having a less-talented woman play the organ because she was a member. The same woman member who didn't like the organist also had rejected another family who had a handicapped child who continued to cry throughout the service. She had insisted that the parents either leave the child at home to be watched by another family member or that she would withhold her contributions. Once again, both the minister and other church members, faced with the problem of losing their number one contributor, decided to ask the family to keep the child at home until she was taught to behave. Curtis, in short order, became familiar with the politics of being a member of a congregation and decided to do his praying at home and by himself, much to the disappointment of his family. Turning on his Sirius satellite radio, he leaned back in the seat and listened as Fibber Magee and Molly started to discuss when Fibber was going to clean up that closet. Curtis, now tired from the walk through the cemetery, found his body starting to doze.

CHAPTER 7

Ghostly Image

He was somewhere between night and day, shadows and daylight. All Curtis could see was a little boy walking alone at night with a bucket and lantern, down by the trees, by the tombstones, and the owl sitting in a large oak tree. He tried to fight it off because there was no room in his life for bogeyman or poltergeists and certainly not a ghostly yellow owl. Then the image suddenly changed as he listened to the voice of fear that seemed to be coming from the owl. There was silence, then the voice once again, communicating something urgent. Hearing the fear in its voice, the panic in the tone, he pushed his back firmly against the seat. He watched as his first officer was yelling something about not being able to control the descent of the aircraft. Numbers, she was calling out numbers, eight thousand feet, pulling to the left, seven thousand five hundred feet, losing control, descent increasing…

Rap, rap, rap. "Wake up!" came her panic call. It was like a play and he couldn't follow the plot. Suddenly the dream ended, and Curtis looked up seeing knuckles banging on the window. Sitting straight up, Curtis could see that it was the policewoman, Kate, rapping against the window. He shook his head trying to clear his confused state and at the same time turning the ignition key to the on position, which allowed him to lower the driver's window.

"Sorry, sir, I didn't mean to frighten you," said Kate, "but the cemetery is not the safest place to sleep. Funston is a quiet town, but it's been known to draw some questionable folks off the highway looking for a quick buck, especially from those that leave things in the car while they visit their relatives."

Still dazed from coming out of the dream, Curtis rubbed his eyes, saying, "That's all right, Officer, I was just dreaming about one of my flight trips, and things were going bad, so I'm glad you woke me up. Besides, it's nice seeing you since you've been on my mind all day. Sorry, excuse me, it seems like I'm always stepping in it."

"What are you stepping in, Mr. Patterson?" asked Kate, trying to hide her smile.

"Could we just start all over, Officer?" said Curtis.

"I don't think that will be any problem," replied Kate, "so here goes. Mr. Patterson, what are you stepping in?"

"Shut your eyes and think," thought Curtis. "Remember the old military approach that Grandpa told you years ago. Should you be faced with not knowing what the hell to do, always do something, right or wrong!"

"Have you lost your voice, Mr. Patterson?" asked Kate.

"No, not at all, Officer Heller, although I usually think better when I'm in command of a wide-body airplane rather than trying to navigate through these troubled waters that I seem to always be swimming in since I met you this morning. But here's the deal, Officer Kate, you've been on my mind because, well, frankly I was hoping for another opportunity to see you before I left Funston in the next two days."

No answer, just a stare from Kate.

"These things are complicated for a man like me, Kate, and almost impossible to explain," said Curtis

No answer, just a smile and that stare.

"You see, for years I've dated very little, always searching for the right moment in hopes of finding that special woman. I have a good eye for this type of individual, but having a good eye is not enough. One needs to look and act when the moment is right," said Curtis.

She was still silent, but the good news seemed to be that she hadn't put in a call for an officer needing backup.

"Well, Officer, you happen to be that moment in life that I've been waiting for. Think of it like someone searching for that plant that has three petals and suddenly it appears in your life. You are that, that orchid, Officer Kate, so ever since that moment at the restaurant, I've been stumbling through the flower garden making a fool of myself, if that makes any sense to you," said Curtis.

"Well, Mr. Patterson, I must compliment you on your improved pickup lines since this morning. Even my husband was not that good when we first met," said Kate.

"Oh god, I didn't realize you were married," said Curtis.

"I was married, Mr. Patterson, not now. He happened to be killed by a sniper in Iraq three years ago," said Kate.

"Jesus, my apologies for being such a dunderhead," said Curtis.

"Apology accepted, but not necessary since there would have been no way that you could have known," she said.

"Look, Officer," Curtis said as he started his engine, "I'll be on my way, but again, I do appreciate you looking out for this stranger."

"You stop looking for that orchid if someone has gotten it before you did, Mr. Patterson?"

"What did you say, Officer?" asked Curtis.

"I asked you if your search is over now that someone got your special flower first?" asked Kate.

"Of course not. Do you mean you?"

"Tomorrow happens to be my day off, Mr. Patterson. If you happen to be in town and want to talk more about flowers, you may call me later in the afternoon," she said, handing him her cell phone number. Kate turned and walked back to her squad car. Getting in, she drove off slowly toward town.

As he watched her pull away, Curtis was stunned but elated. It had been some time since he had asked any woman for a date. To say that he was thunderstruck with the idea that he had just met the woman that he had been searching for so long would be like saying that James Patterson liked to write books. He would call her tomorrow, that was as certain as the sun coming up in Funston.

The Inspection

Elmer pulled his car into the parsonage yard and glanced at his friend Ed Russell, who seemed preoccupied and concerned over their assignment to inspect the country parsonage of Pastor Paul Bergman. He decided to make light of the circumstances. "Isn't it nice this time of the morning, Ed, just before dawn and all is blue in the sky? You can barely see the lark bunting landing on that fence post down near the shed."

"Hell, Elmer, I don't even know what a bunting is," replied Ed.

"It's a brightly colored small bird, like that lark on the post. I'm sure you seen many in town as I have."

Ignoring Elmer, he asked, "Where's Pastor Bergman?"

"Doc Ogden said he wouldn't be here," replied Elmer. "He's attending to some personal matter and indicated that he had no objection with us doing it without him being here."

"Still, are you sure we can just go through his house and inspect his personal property without him being around? It does seem a little weird to me and could be asking for trouble," said Ed.

"Look, it's in our constitution that specifies that we have to do this once every two years, and besides, the Parsonage belongs to the church and is one of our major assets. None of us really know how long the Pastor will stay or, for that matter, when he may want to purchase his own home. You know, most Pastors today do own their own home rather than staying in the typical provided parsonage because unless they do have their own house when it comes to retirement, they have nothing. The whole purpose of doing this is to keep our costs down should it become necessary to sell the property. Remember, Ed, our job is not to open up his dresser drawers, but just to make sure that everything is in top shape and up to village code. Did you bring the camera so we can include the pictures for the board to review as part of our normal scheduled meeting with the church council?" asked Elmer.

"It's in the back seat of the car," said Ed. "Have you ever wondered why his wife and daughter are still in Michigan? He's the first pastor that I've ever run into who didn't bring his family with him. A lot of us have, but according to Doc Ogden and Jack, the Bergmans have had a difficult time selling their home, plus his daughter is still finishing college."

"What do you say, Ed, that we start with the shed down the hill?" asked Elmer. "Have you ever been inside it before?"

"No, and it's fine with me," he said as he reached for the camera and pulled it up to the front seat. "You know, Elmer, I forgot about that little lake behind the shed."

"Yeah, it was a good deal when we bought the property years ago. The water flows down here from the Rice River, and I heard that sometimes some of the men come down here to do some duck hunting, along with fishing. Sometimes the water level gets pretty high, but it has never reached the parsonage even though it gets close to the shed," said Elmer.

As they were walking down the hill, Ed commented to Elmer, "It's hard to understand why Bergman would want to come to this small town of Silver Valley rather than accepting a call to a larger city that would have a bigger congregation. He seems more suited for one that has a school and a church."

"Hey, we're not that small, Ed. The town is approaching ninety thousand residents, which makes it large enough to have its own McDonald's, and still what my wife calls a small-enough town to be filled with people who are full of good stories."

"Don't know what that means, Elmer."

"It means that if you like gossip, and most church people feed on that, you can still find someone who has a story about someone else."

Reaching the shed, Elmer used the provided key, and both men walked in the spacious storage building. "Good God, it's larger inside than I remember," said Elmer.

"Look, he's converted some of the space into sort of a makeshift guest house with a wide-screen TV and a couch that opens up into a bed and lounge chairs," said Ed. "Look over by the workbench in the corner, Elmer. It looks like a large gun cabinet to me. And isn't that a steel vault next to it? Big combination lock on that one, but it's none of our business, really, so we have no right to open it up even if we were able to."

"Remember when we were a kid?" asked Elmer.

"What do you mean?"

"Gym class, Ed. Remember the gym class before we had to go to speech down the hall?"

"Oh, you mean how we set the combination lock to grab extra time?" he asked.

"Yeah, the old trick thirty-eight right, back left to eighteen, and right to the click," he said as Elmer put his hand on the lock and turned the dial slowly until he heard the click.

"Bingo, my friend," he said as he removed the lock and opened the door to the gun cabinet.

"Holy shit," said Ed. "Do you see all those rifles and pistols?"

"Pretty expensive collection," said Elmer.

Picking up the Brown Special Forces carry weapon, Elmer remarked, "About $2,500 for this .45 ACP alone."

"How would you know that?" asked Ed.

"Have one myself. Bought it two years ago to remind me of my time in the Army overseas," said Elmer. "Looks like he has a favorite caliber," he said, now picking up a S-Para-Ordnance Warthog .45 ACP. "Guys like to carry this one when they're hunting wild pigs down in Arkansas."

"What's this?" asked Ed, pointing to what looked like a military rifle.

"That, my friend, is a Socom 11, with all the optional accessories, including a night vision scope," said Elmer.

"What would he want with that?" asked Ed.

"That, partner, is something that I have no idea about," said Elmer as he closed the gun cabinet and replaced the lock.

"Think we should say something?" asked Ed.

"No, remember that we're here to inspect the property, not snoop, so it's best that we just leave it alone," said Elmer. "The guns are his business, his secret, and as long as he's broken no law, what he's got them for is private, unless he wants to talk about it."

Continuing their inspection of the shed, the two men found everything in order, with the exception of two old wall sockets that needed replacement along with a broken doorknob lock on the rear security door to the shed. Taking a break while Ed replaced the second wall socket, Elmer sat down on the couch glancing up at a beautiful antique picture of a Victorian mother holding her five- to six-year-old daughter. The mother's eyes were blue and sensual and seemed to be staring right directly at him. Seeing that Ed was done, he picked up the tool bag while Ed grabbed the camera, and they both walked out of the shed then moved back up the hill to the parsonage.

"What's the matter, Elmer?" asked Ed as they walked up the parsonage steps and unlocked the door.

"Nothing, really, it's just the shed, Ed. Something just doesn't fit, but darn if I can tell you why," said Elmer.

"I know what you're talking about, friend. The shed gave me the creeps. Sort of like that back-door-to-hell situation that I read about last year."

"Must have missed that one," said Elmer.

"Some farmer around here unearthed an opening that he claimed led to a spiral staircase, which winded its way to hell."

"How long did they lock the guy up for spreading such a bizarre hoax? asked Elmer.

"They didn't, and as a matter of fact, its interest apparently caused curious outsiders to flock to the area. According to the report, the farmer, frightened to death at what he thought that he had found, had left. But those that stayed and looked around the farm area discovered an unusual cement structure located on an abandoned farmstead nearby. What they later discovered was an eight-by-twelve-foot cement vault that was three-quarters underground. The arched opening, with its wooden floor that had long since gone, led to stairs that went to a cement floor covered with mud. Most of the local residents who knew about the vault had always thought that it was a cyclone cellar. They even had called in many high-ranking Masons, who verified there were no such type buildings in Masonry. It had interesting markings on the wall, such as a winged human being with a cocked head, which some claimed to be ancient or medieval. Anyway, everyone left, but today the legend still remains as the back door to hell. So my point, Elmer, is that we may have our own type of back door to hell down in the shed, and it gives me the creeps.

Elmer studied his friend but didn't say anything more.

As they walked inside, both Ed and Elmer stopped and looked in amazement. Neither couldn't remember when was the last they had seen a house so clean. "No typical man lived here," thought Elmer. Everything was polished or waxed, with nothing laying around in the typical man fashion, just waiting to be put away. No dishes in the sink, coffee cups on the table, or magazines waiting to be read on one of the many tables. As they began to walk around, they found that shoes were all lined up side by side. Closets filled with shirts, suits, sport jackets, and dress pants with a few pairs of jeans and casual clothing. Amazing, all arranged on different-colored hangers representing the type of garment being hung. It seemed a little over the top.

"Have you noticed anything a little unusual, Elmer?" asked Ed.

"You mean the handgun under his bedroom pillow?" replied Elmer.

"No, although I couldn't help but notice the barrel sticking out," said Ed.

"What then?" asked Elmer.

"Pictures, Elmer, pictures! The parsonage and the shed have no pictures of his wife, daughter, or anything family. In fact, the only picture it the house or the shed was this one," he said, handing it to Elmer."

"Where did you find it?" asked Elmer.

"It was near his computer. Don't you find that a little strange, and who is it?" asked Ed.

Looking at the picture, it was that of a woman about twenty-five or thirty playing an organ at what could have been her home. She was clearly an attractive woman with an engaging smile and posing for whoever took the picture. Elmer had seen that woman before, but he couldn't place where. Instead of confusing and worrying Ed even more, he said, "Haven't ever seen her, and it does seem strange, to answer your question. Remember, Ed, that Pastor Bergman operates somewhat different at times compared to the other ministers that we've had. Anyway, it's about time that we wrap this up and go home. The place looks good, well-kept, and the only thing needing repair seems to be replacing the toilet wax bowl ring, and we'll need to send the trustees back for that job. Everything else is good to go, as they say."

"Well, look at that," said Ed.

"What?" asked Elmer.

"The guy's got a Macintosh computer," said Ed. "These babies are considered the best at handling viruses, but his choice in a screen saver seems a little unusual for a guy who seems to be a little edgy living in a Parsonage located in the woods. Didn't he indicate that he's a little concerned about animals, asked Ed?"

Walking over to the computer Elmer could see what Ed was talking about since Bergman had programmed the screen saver page to advertise the world's five most deadly spiders. Elmer recognized the black widow spider and the brown recluse spider, but the others were not familiar.

"Well, who knows," said Elmer. The guy likes guns and spiders, but again, it's his business, and we're supposed to just check out the buildings, not snoop into his personal life."

"You're right, Elmer. Besides I have no desire to open Pandora's box."

Looking at the expression of concern on Ed's face, Elmer said, "It's time to get on the road before we hit one of those deer feeding times of the day. It's getting about that time, and I personally don't need to have one of them bust of my fender," offered Elmer as they both walked out the door and got into Elmer's car.

Ed watched Elmer, who had been sitting still for three minutes while staring down at the shed but hadn't started the car. "What's the matter?" he asked.

Elmer, thinking about the question, answered, "Tell me about the landscape in which you live, and I will tell you who you are."

"What?"

"It's something that my father always mentioned when I would ask a question about an individual that I just met for the first time. The quote comes from some Spanish liberal philosopher born in the middle 1800s."

"So what does this have to do with anything,?" asked Ed.

Elmer stared straight ahead through the windshield, his hands clamped around the steering wheel. His eyes burned, but he refused to show any of the emotion that was running through his body. He wasn't the type of man who let others see that anything was worrying him. "Ed, something is very wrong in that house, something very evil, but I don't know what. The house is too sterile and staged to represent that everything is correct, but it is not. At the same time, Pastor Bergman has done nothing but keep a clean house with some unusual hobbies. It's just the landscape that puzzles me," he said as he started the car and pulled away.

"Well, I think that we should include everything in our report and let the officers decide what's right and what is wrong. That spider crap is not what a pastor should be interested in, for God's sake, and what the hell does he need an arsenal of weapons for? Sleeping with a gun under his pillow is a little eccentric, wouldn't you say, Elmer?"

"What I think is that every time I drive out this way, we either run into layers of fog or flocks of geese," said Elmer. "I'm so spooked with fear of some deer hitting this car that it's hard for me to even worry about Bergman until we get out of these woods. But you're right, Ed. We may have to at least give the council a heads-up about the guy's strange interests, if nothing else."

"We live in a small town, Ed, and how the heck does a person tell the truth in a small town where everybody knows each other's business most of the time? If we say anything to anybody about his guns, his computer interest, or what type of toilet paper he has hanging in his bathroom, it's open for public consumption," said Elmer. "You know how some members can be like. This gets out, and most of them would shrug their shoulders and say, 'What's the big deal?' while folks like Margret and Lester would demand that Doc Ogden and Jack lock the doors and nail the pastor in his office until the white jackets arrive. Christians are not what you call patient folks, Ed. You can negotiate with a Presbyterian, have a drink with a priest, maybe even with a Baptist on a good day, but always remember Lutherans feel that they actually wrote the King James Bible."

"Hey, watch out, you almost hit that buck that just crossed the road," cried Ed. "He was one big bastard and could have cost you a few thousand in car repairs, if not killed us."

"The fog is so darn thick I didn't even see it," said Elmer. "You better help me keep an eye on the road. That bend up ahead is notorious for packs of those buggers. There's a farmer's field down to the left of the crest that's full of sunflowers, which they feed on."

The drive continued with neither man aware of the individual that patiently waited in the tall, uncut sunflower stalks as he admired his Ed Brown tactical rifle. The heart of any rifle, he pondered, was in the action, and his Ed Brown model 702 was one of the best bolt action rifles ever made. He watched the Chevy began its climb to the top of the hill and could tell by the speed that the driver was being cautious and attentive to the road. As he looked through the Nightforce 3.5-15×50 scope, he could see that the car's passenger was moving his hands back and forth and providing verbal instructions to the driver. He was probably telling him to watch out for animals, thought the man. As he placed the lightened tactical stock against his cheek, he slid the rifle forward across the sandbag rest and sighted in on the passenger riding in the car. He knew that the 300 Winchester 167 grain Scenar HPBT match bullet would do the job that he had in mind. If anybody built a better rifle with a softer recoil and light pull on the trigger, he had yet to find one as he moved the crosshair slightly to the right of the passenger and fired the weapon. He smiled as he watched the car window explode and the vehicle suddenly jerk and lose control then disappear below the hill. Gathering his rifle and the rifle rest, the man walked the 100-feet distance where he had parked his car. As he looked around to be certain that he was still alone, he opened the rear car door and laid the rifle rest on the floor while carefully placing the gun on the rear seat. Shutting the rear door, he moved to the front of the car and got in. Double-checking that he had everything, he started the engine and proceeded to drive the vehicle down the dirt path as he found his way back to the paved highway and turned his car in the opposite direction of the vehicle that had disappeared over the hill. He knew from the sighting and scope that his was not a kill shot. He had intended it to be that way, not a funeral.

When the window exploded, Ed felt glass pieces and a rush of wind hitting him. His reflective action, plus the shock of the exploding window had pushed him in the direction of Elmer, who now had jerked the wheel of the car sharply to the left, pushing the vehicle across the road and down an embankment. Holding on to the wheel with both hands, Elmer avoided the first large tree, but hit the picket fence full force and continued on for another fifty feet. When the car finally came to rest, Elmer turned and said, "Ed, you're bleeding. Where have you been hit?"

Reaching up to his face and feeling the blood, he said, "It doesn't hurt any place, Elmer. Maybe the blood is from a glass cut. What the shit happened to the window? It sounded like an exploding rocket hit us."

Opening up the car door, Ed pushed himself out and stood on the dirt field, while Elmer had opened his door and came around to see how he was doing.

"Say, that's a nasty cut above your eye, Ed, but everything else on you looks good and seems to be all right. How do you really feel?"

"I'm good, but what the goddamn hell was that all about," continued a shocked and pale Ed.

"Probably a stray bullet from some hunter," said Elmer.

"Well, the son of a bitch almost killed us," said Ed. "I thought that hunting season was all over by now."

"Well, we got lucky, friend, so let me get that old towel I have in the trunk, and then you can hold it against that cut until I get you into town." Opening up the trunk, Elmer got the towel and gave it to Ed while he looked over the farm area to determine which way provided the best opportunity to reach the highway from the field. Seeing the tractor's path, Elmer told Ed to get into the car. Within a few minutes following the created path by the farmer's tractor, Elmer had found an open gate that led to a gravel road. Within two miles of driving on the gravel, they had reached the main road to Silver Valley and its medical outpatient clinic.

"Well, do you feel better now after seeing the doctor?" asked Elmer.

"Yeah, but those twelve stitches are going to leave a zipper scar," said Ed.

"At our age, the glass is always half full, my friend. The good news is that you're too old to go to a prom, so what difference does it make? And second the bullet didn't hit a vital spot, so all in all it's still a good day," said Elmer.

"While you were getting sewed up, I gave the county sheriff the report as to what we think happened," said Elmer.

"Think happened? That city slicker trying to play Daniel Boone almost killed us both, Elmer," said Ed.

"Maybe, maybe not," said Elmer.

"What are you saying?" asked Ed. "He could have killed one of us with that bullet, or if not that, the car could have turned over going down the hill. Except for your good driving, both of us today could have ended up with more than a few stitches."

"That's very kind of you, Ed. What I'm saying is, I'm not sure that it was a hunter," said Elmer.

"What do you mean?" asked Ed, looking puzzled.

"Well, for one thing, I think gun season should be just about over, and if it's not, that's an awful lot of damage for a shotgun to make," said Elmer.

"Shotgun? Who uses shotgun to hunt deer?" asked Ed.

"I see you haven't hunted in years, Ed. Our township changed the law years ago and now only allows deer hunting within twenty-five miles of a major city to only be done by shotgun," said Elmer.

"What did the sheriff think?" asked Ed.

"He's not sure about anything, Ed. He wasn't buying the theory about it being a rifle because he said that many hunters using shotguns use loads that are the size of ball bearings and could easily explode the window," said Elmer.

"Well, maybe he's right," said Ed, while touching the four-inch bandage above his eye.

"No, Ed, in this case, he's wrong, but I didn't tell him why. That will come after I see my friend that operates Bill's gun shop in town." He held out the palm of his hand for Ed to see.

"What's that, Elmer?" he asked, seeing him holding some type of bullet.

"That, Ed, is the frontal portion of a flat-nose shell, which was on the floor below my seat. While I can't tell you what grain bullet it is, it definitely is not a shotgun slug. Anyway, let's get the hell out of here and worry all about this tomorrow. I need to get the window fixed, see Bill tomorrow at the gun shop, and turn in our report to the church on the inspection of the parsonage. When I drop you off at your house, I want you to get a good night's rest, and I'll take care of everything else and call you later tomorrow," said Elmer.

"I'll take you up on that. All in all, it hasn't been a bad day considering our families could have been singing at a couple funerals."

"You're right, and until we figure this out, I for one will start carrying a weapon in the car, and I would recommend that you do likewise," said Elmer.

"Geez, you think that's a good idea? Michigan has some tough gun laws, and we don't want to go to jail," said Ed.

"You won't be going to jail, Ed, but let's just assume that today we could have had to shoot someone in defending ourselves instead of just having a window blown up. Speaking only for myself, I would not like to be carried by six, but rather be judged by twelve," said Elmer. "We live in a different world today, where even in Michigan, the antigun, Flat Earth Society folks would have you and I believe that by simply carrying a gun in a car for self-defense makes us Wild West gunfighters ready to participate in bloody road-rage wars. They're full of crap, my friend, so don't be intimidated by wacky left-wingers."

"Point well made, friend."

Just as he was thinking about telling Ed his theory about actually who might have been behind the ambush rather than a stray bullet, the sky opened up, and sheets of rain started to come down. "Never underestimate the fact that things can always get worse," thought Elmer. A big question that had been running through his mind was whether or not Bergman had changed his mind about his house being inspected and had decided to send a message. In the end, though, he was gratified that no one was actually hurt very bad. Seeing Ed's house in the distance, Elmer said, "Well, here we are, so get some sleep, buddy, and I'll keep you posted on what I find out about that bullet from my gun shop friend."

Getting out of the car, Ed ducked his head. The rain was hitting him in the face as he made it up to the front door of his house. If he'd ever been more physically miserable in his life, he couldn't remember when. Turning, he waved quickly to Elmer as he turned the doorknob and entered his house.

CHAPTER 9

What to Do

"Do you have any idea what type of bullet this is, Bill?"

"Well, it looks very much like a 167-grain Scenar HPBT matched round, Elmer. You don't see much of that stuff around these parts, though. It's something used most often in high-end tactical rifles and generally designed to be used by the police or military personnel," said Bill. "But don't get me wrong, Elmer, because this type of ammo could have found its way into the civilian market for anyone who might be looking for custom-grade quality in a medium-bore competition rifle. The point is, it's unlikely to be from a gun used by weekend gun hunters trying to bag that 7-point buck. That's provided, of course, they would even try to fire a rifle near town since shotguns are the only thing allowed, as you know."

"So if you were to guess, Bill, how does this thing end up blasting our window out if rifles are not allowed for hunting?" asked Elmer.

"Remember that rifles are not illegal, just hunting with them. It's still legal to test shoot with a rifle because many hunters prepare for the hunt and test the bullets before they actually go hunting. My guess is that what hit your window was just a bullet that went off the reservation and just found its way to your window," said Bill. "By the way, Elmer, what were you and Ed doing out in the country anyway?"

"Just doing work for the church, and we were heading home when it happened," said Elmer.

"Well, sorry I couldn't be more helpful, but I wouldn't worry too much," said Bill.

"Why's that?" asked Elmer.

"Because if I'm guessing correct, the rifle he was using wouldn't have missed the intended target if he really was trying to do you any harm. In my opinion, it was just being in the wrong place at the right time, nothing more."

"One last question before I leave," said Elmer.

"What's that?"

"Do you have much call for that brand of bullet, since it seems to me that it's specialized for only certain uses?" asked Elmer.

"No, we don't stock it, but if a customer requested it, we would secure it through one of our suppliers. If you want, I could check our past records to see if we ever had such a request, but I doubt it ever happened."

"No, don't go through that trouble. Just let me know if anyone requests that bullet in the future," said Elmer.

"You got it," said Bill as he watched his friend walk out the door and cross the street.

As he walked down the street, Elmer thought about one of the nice things about living in a small town, if one called just under ninety thousand small. "Many of us are interrelated in a community like this, whether or not we're related by blood. We know without thinking about it who owns the main hardware store, who owns the lumberyard, who owns what car, and who's sleeping with whose wife that one is trying unsuccessfully to hide. You have your local restaurant with the same regulars every day that allows you to know who is sick or in the hospital before you go to church on Sunday and when the pastor officially tells you. Privacy takes another meaning in such an environment, where you are asked to share your life, humbling yourself to your every weakness that a large city would never reveal to its neighbors." Crossing the street, Elmer walked toward Alan Ogden's clinic while wondering if he would be lucky enough to catch him between patients. Like himself and his wife, many in the congregation used Doc Ogden as their regular physician not only because he was a member but because he held a dual specialty being the only internal medicine doctor in town and who also was considered one of the top infectious disease specialists in a three-state area. When they had first met years ago for a simple case of having an upper respiratory problem, Doc Ogden had insisted on doing a full examination for his records. He had at the time noticed a small scar on his leg and had commented, "Oh, you've been bitten at one time by a nasty spider, haven't you? Who did you see for it?"

It had happened out of state, so he had told him that the doctor had said it was nothing to worry about and just gave him some type of ointment as he remembered. It was then that Ogden had told him about his second specialty and cautioned him not to take such answers in the future so lightly, since the wrong type of spider bite could be sometimes fatal, if not just damaging to the skin. He remembered asking him why a doctor became an infectious disease specialist as opposed to picking another field such as psychiatry or neurology. Walking up to the entrance of the clinic, he could still see Ogden's smile when he had answered.

"Because, Elmer, it's so interesting, and what other type of doctor has the opportunity to look the monster straight in the face and stare him down knowing I've found out who you are and can do something about it? Take that little bite on your leg. If another doctor looks at it, he sees confusion and a multitude of different possibilities as to what it might have been, and most of them will be dead wrong. In my case, the little bastard has walked into a bear trap because I'll find out who he is and kill him Elmer, simply kill him." Thinking back to that time period, Elmer remembers being happy to have finally found a medical professional that had such confidence in his work. It wasn't about money for Ogden. It was about restoring the patient to good health.

Remembering that he was in the clinic, he looked up at the receptionist. "Hello, Holly, is the doctor in the house?"

"He is, Mr. Stein, but he's with a patient right now. Why don't you have a seat and I'll let him know that you're here. It shouldn't be more than five minutes," said Holly. "Should I tell him what's wrong, or is this just a social call?"

"Just social, Holly, nothing more," he said as he took a seat. Picking up the latest issue of *Good Health* magazine, Elmer started to review the front pages screaming a warning about prostate cancer and how every man over the age of fifty needed to be tested. "Jesus," thought Elmer, "you can't even enjoy the world of denial without someone tracking you down." Thumbing through the magazine, he started to focus on the recent government position that the PSA test gave to men regarding an enlarged prostrate was often flawed, and then he noticed that Alan had come out of his examining room with two cups of coffee. Alan's expression looked like it was going to take more than a cup of coffee to get him going again, but suspected that the second cup was probably for him. Alan gestured for him to follow him down the hallway to his office, where he closed the door when both men were inside.

"Well, Elmer, it's nice to see you," said Alan. "This is one break that I needed with all the emergency appointments, plus my regular schedule, and the hospital not sending me the intern that they had promised to do today. On top of that, Betty called and reminded me that tonight's our standard date night, so be sure and not schedule any late patients. Sometimes I envy you being retired and look forward to the day when that comes for me."

"Say, Doc, this may be a bad time for me to have stopped in, so maybe we can pick this up later. It can wait. You look like you're overloaded today, and I want to keep my doctor healthy in case I need him," said Elmer, with a wide smile. "You know that this town needs you, Alan, and remember, even doctors can get burned out."

"Wait nothing, Elmer. We don't see enough of each other, and Betty keeps reminding me that we've got to get together and start planning for the annual steak fry that will be at our house this year. You did get stuck with being chairman of that committee, didn't you, Elmer?"

"Yes, I did, thanks to you, my good doctor, who if I remember correctly was the one who nominated me at the council meeting," he said laughing.

"Well, let's not worry about the small things, Elmer. Besides, as your doctor, worry isn't recommended for a healthy heart," said

Ogden. "What are you downtown today for anyway? Wasn't it yesterday that you and Ed were to be at the parsonage by the river? I actually love that location with all the possibilities that it offers. Fishing, hunting, and a lot of open land to have a good church picnic at."

"We did the inspection yesterday, Alan. As we were coming back, I had encountered some damage to the passenger window, so I was having it replaced on the car today while I was downtown visiting my old friend Bill at the gun shop," said Elmer.

"Why do I believe there's more to this story than what I'm hearing?" said Ogden.

"There is. The inspection went fine, except for a couple of things that we need to talk about some other time, but it was when we were coming home and had just reached the top of Buffers Hill that we ran into a little trouble. Out of nowhere a bullet shattered the side of the Ed's window. The impact of the window exploding scared us, and I lost control of the car, and we ended going down the side of the hill into a farmer's field. There was no other damage to the car, although the breaking of the glass put a cut on Ed's face that required a few stitches. You know how he is, Alan. He won't call your office and let you look at it even though to me it appears to be all right. Maybe you could have Holly give him a call and encourage him to stop in for a checkup."

"I'll do one better, Elmer, and call him myself. Cuts are nothing to fool with in a day and age when infections are growing unchecked, even in some of our top hospitals. For God's sake, Elmer, did they find out who fired the gun?"

"No, and we probably won't since the sheriff feels that it was probably someone hunting and we just caught a runaway bullet from some hunter."

"What the deal with Bill's gun shop, since I believe you told me last year that you had given up hunting because of your eyesight?" asked Alan.

"I have, but I found the bullet under my seat, and I wanted to find out what type of gun it came from," said Elmer.

"Did you?" asked Alan.

"Yes, and it's an uncommon type of bullet used generally by the military, some police forces, but not by the average hunter," said Elmer.

"So you have doubts Elmer as to the cause of that bullet?" asked Alan.

"I'm just that way, Alan, until I have the answers that I'm looking for," said Elmer.

"Maybe the problem is not that you're coming up with the wrong answers, but rather you're coming up with the wrong questions, Elmer," said Alan.

Elmer was about to answer when a rap on the door brought both men back to attention.

"Yes," said Alan.

"Doctor, your patients are building up," said a female voice.

"I'll be right out, Holly. Give me a minute please," said Alan.

After Holly left, Elmer said, "You get going Alan. Give me a call later tomorrow, and we'll continue this conversation. Maybe at your house or mine," said Elmer.

"Yes, it would be better tomorrow if we can hold off, since I'm taking Betty out for our date night, remember? She's a very understanding wife, but pretty solid on not breaking this schedule. Plus my guess is she will give me an earful about Bergman, so I'm anxious to hear about your inspection of the parsonage."

"That's fine, Alan. Enjoy the evening," he said as he got up and held the door open for Alan as both men walked out.

As he was driving home, Elmer kept thinking about Alan's last comment regarding wrong answers being wrong questions. Maybe he thought he was paying far more attention to the bullet fragment that he had found rather than to the gun it was fired from. While he had asked the gun store owner if he stocked the special bullet, he had neglected to ask him if he had ever sold the type of rifle the bullet was fired from. Sometimes he thought the dots that one's mind tried to connect and couldn't was staring you right in the face. After all, he was Elmer Stein, the former insurance investigator for World Wide Insurance, and should be able to focus much better than what he's been doing the last twenty-four hours. And then it hit him suddenly as he pulled the car over on the shoulder and pulled out his hand-kerchief to wipe the developing sweat from his forehead. "It's right in front of us," he thought as he pulled out his cell phone and dialed Alan Ogden.

"This is Dr. Ogden I'm sorry that I'm not available. Please leave a detailed message, and I'll get back to you."

"Alan, this is Elmer, and I'm truly sorry to disturb your night out with Betty. Something just came up from our visit today, and it's important that you arrange a joint meeting that includes Jack, your-self, and me sometime real soon, maybe tomorrow at the latest. It has to do with our inspection of the Bergner parsonage. Thanks again and call tomorrow please. Elmer."

CHAPTER 10

The Wolf Stone

The alarm went off at 6:00 a.m., a high-pitched siren loud enough to wake the dead if not the next-room lovers, now fast asleep after attempting to wear each other out until three in the morning. Curtis felt thirsty and reached for the leftover bottle of Diet Coke that he hadn't finished the night before. It didn't seem to make sense him being in the Flickertail motel miles away from his house on a mission that he didn't want to have for a church that he had no interest in. He had brought the small headstone to his room in his Delta Air Lines overnight bag and laid it on the small provided nightstand. Getting up from the bed, Curtis walked over to the stand and now for the third time studied the date and the inscription. Last night he had taken three pictures of it from his cell phone camera and texted it back to the church secretary for their records with the only comment that the stone had promise and that his search might be paying off.

He had received no response from anyone, but since it was a church, one shouldn't expect anything to be acted on right away, thought Curtis. The date on the stone was well within the expected time period that the family should have lived in the area, and the child's last name beginning with the letter R could represent the family he was looking for. Turning away from the table, Curtis reached for his cell phone guessing that Kate would be getting up about now, or at least if she didn't have her cell phone turned on, he could leave her a message regarding their planned get together this afternoon.

Curtis gave up calling Kate's cell phone number after hearing the voice mail that said, "Neither Channing or Kate are available now. But please leave your message and one of us will call back as soon as possible."

"Channing! Who the heck was Channing?" wondered Curtis. "Maybe it was her live-in boyfriend? Well, what can one expect after he had made such fool out of himself in his attempt to get to know her? After all, he had been acting like a teenage boy in his attempts to impress the woman, so it's no wonder that she probably decided to teach him a lesson by giving him her phone number, which would send him packing once he got the message. Anyway, the weather was expected to be warm and sunny and overall a good day to continue walking through the Lutheran cemetery in search of history, while giving him time to imagine Channing with his arms around the policewoman.

"Shit. Doesn't anything ever work out?" he said to himself as he walked into the bathroom then took off his clothes and stepped into the shower. It was a little late by the time Curtis left the Flickertail, but he was in no mood to really care. His mind was filled with disjointed thoughts tumbling in circles, coming round and round again before he could catch hold. "I suppose she had a right to do it this way because she's used to being hit on all the time, but for God's sake, she was the one who chastised me for giving up on her, so I didn't, and then she seeks to teach me this hard lesson," thought Curtis. Nothing ever seemed to go right for him when it came to finding the right woman. He had no damn luck at all. Sometimes it seemed like the gods or whoever had it in for him even before he had even got to first base.

Turning into the cemetery, Curtis drove through the gate, bringing his car as close to the young child's burial area as he could. Getting out of the car, he opened up the rear door and grabbed the Delta bag with the headstone in it. He then closed the door and proceeded to walk the few hundred feet to the grave site. Replacing the stone on the exact same spot, Curtis stood up and once again stared at the marking, "H March 30, 1832; D June 7 1834' Baby Augusta R."

"Nothing like mysteries and oddities to make one's day," pondered Curtis. "If the baby below this burial location is actually a member of the Reusswig family, the remainder of the once-existing family must be close by." Part of the problem in locating the correct site was the lack of information provided by his church. When pressed for any type of information, the best that the current council could provide was that it was believed that the Bethany Church was originally part of the Moravian Church, a Protestant church that originated in Moravia, Austria, until it came over to America. That much he already knew. He also knew that history had suggested that the Catholic Church had apparently provided ruthless persecution of the Moravians with fire and sword, although their aggressive action failed to stop the religion from spreading in Central Europe. So if the story was true, they were constantly on the run, even in America.

What was he missing? Hell, he didn't even know what the name of the family actually meant, and if anyone within his church knew, they apparently were not even into sharing that information, thought Curtis. The origin of family names was important since many names were changed as they were passed down through the generations. While he was in college, Curtis had taken a course regarding the origin of names and knew that a name such as Schultz meant "magistrate" or "mayor of a village." He had remembered that the professor had explained that the oldest form of some names, like Schultzheis, were then shortened to Schultz, and of course there were several other spellings of the name, such as Schultze, Schulz, and Shulz. His own mother's former name was Dill but originally came from the name Dillenius. They had laughed together about that his dad always called her his little pickle. What was he missing? he asked himself again thinking about his favorite uncle's words of wisdom that he would always bring up while they fished together. He would always say, "Curtis, when you can't figure something out, back up ten steps and think it over again."

Once again Curtis glanced at the small headstone and reviewed the inscription. Shaking his head, he started to move away when suddenly it came to him. They had left the clue in the letter *H* where the family graves were located. The letter *H* contained the imaginary outline of the grave, with the crossbar pointing in the direction he would need to follow. Getting on his knees, he could see the period at the end of the crossbar on the right hand side of bar. Standing up once again, he focused on the imaginary *H* and smiled at the simple logic of the clue. Most people never remembered that the term *headstone* was actually in reverse order of how a person was buried. In the placement of a stone, the headstone would usually be at the foot of the grave, not the head of the deceased. Walking forward to the top of the grave site, Curtis looked to his right and began to move slowly down the grave site area toward the fence about fifty feet away. He had walked about ten feet when he spotted the pathway lined with small trees and a few shrubs. As he continued his walk, Curtis passed a few pieces of wood and field stone, which he thought were probably used to mark some early graves that were now worn down to just rotting wood and weather-beaten symbols of early attempts to identify departed family members. As he stared at them, Curtis was unable to determine any dates let alone family names. As he eyes circled the surrounding grassy area, he noticed what appeared to be a toy granite animal resting on the ground a few feet away. It was at that moment that Curtis felt the sudden surge of anxiety that one usually found in the hunter that unexpectedly flushed a trophy buck. As he got closer, his suspicions confirmed that it was not a toy but rather an iron-cast wolf head attached to a flat, worn-out field stone. He knew from visiting old cemeteries over the years that during the early 1800s that wolf stones were commonly placed on graves in hopes of deterring scavenging animals. Reaching in his back pocket, Curtis removed a large rag he had brought from the car and began to wipe the dirt from the face of the flat stone. "Bertha R. Born Jan. 12, 1829. Died Aug 4, 1876. Mother-wife of Shepherd." Trying to digest what he had found, Curtis felt the vibration of his cell phone in his pants pocket. Before he could stand up, he heard the phone registering the voice message as received. Standing up, Curtis pulled the phone from his pocket and hit the menu button to display his drop-down feature to multimedia in order to use the cell phone camera. Satisfied that the three pictures he took would be enough, he transferred them to the church secretary's email address asking her to review them with the pastor. Noting the two messages waiting for him, he began to clear both.

"Hi, Curtis, this is Kate. Sorry I missed your call, but I turned off the phone accidently. Please call." When he cleared the second message, it was Kate again. "This is Kate. Going out to get some groceries and do a few off jobs. Call soon."

Curtis, confused knowing that she was living with someone, put the phone back in his pocket and continued walking around the general area where he had found the Bertha stone. After thirty minutes of finding nothing more, he decided to return to the car and put together a small report for the church council on what he found.

CHAPTER 11

Regards to You

Leaning back, Curtis reviewed his report and decided that he would visit the site one more time tomorrow morning and then head back home. If his church wanted to continue the project, he felt that it was time that the officers of the church got involved because he had accomplished more than he had expected, plus the fact was that he was still trying to get over the obvious disappointment of making a fool out of himself over that policewoman. Well, he thought, he was no more a fool than her leaving such an obvious tagline on her voice mail, so maybe she needed a lesson also. Picking up his cell phone, he dialed her phone number with the intent of leaving a message, but Kate picked up.

"Hello, Curtis, I'm glad you called. I was hoping you wouldn't think I'm brain-dead in having turned off my phone. Do you still want to meet for dinner today?" asked Kate.

"Well, that depends," said Curtis, sounding somewhat irritated, "on how Channing might feel."

"Channing? What about Channing, and how in the heck did you find out about Channing?" she asked.

"It's pretty easy since you specified that either of you would call back on your answering voice mail," said Curtis.

Suddenly Curtis heard Kate laughing and laughing. "Now you definitely won't want to have dinner with me," she said, "after this major boneheaded thing I've done after telling you to call me. Channing, Curtis, is my dog. I put that message on my phone line to discourage unwanted male calls. I just forgot to change the message back to my own name. Please forgive me."

"God, you've made my day. "Here I've been thinking all day that you were seeing someone and just trying to just teach this guy a lesson for his teenage attempt to date a beautiful woman," said Curtis. "It sounds like I may still be in the running."

"Can we start all over?" said Kate. "And thank you for the compliment."

"Gladly," said Curtis. "I'm still at the cemetery and heading over to the hotel to clean up. You know the town better than I do, so pick the restaurant of your choice, and I'll meet you there."

"Do you like seafood?" she asked.

"Tonight I like what you like, Officer Kate, but to answer your question, I've often enjoyed Joe's Crab House on my many overnights in Atlanta and Chicago," said Curtis.

"Well, we're not big enough to have Joe's Crab House, but I'll meet you at Barneys Lobster and Swordfish at 5:30 p.m. It's on the outskirts of the airport, so it should be easy to find."

"I'll find it," said Curtis as he hung up, while telling her he was looking forward to their dinner.

Starting the Chrysler, Curtis pulled out of the cemetery and headed back to the motel to take a shower and a quick shave. Hope springs eternal that Kate would even consider allowing his face to get that close. Curtis smiled thinking about the coming evening.

As he circled the airport looking for Barneys, he imagined himself flying into the airport. It appeared to have the capability to handle commuter aircraft with the major runway appearing to be over five thousand feet. By the looks of the high volume of personal aircraft parked, it was popular for small-business travel that even included a small amount of helicopters with the company name Fox Valley Commuter Service. As he continued the drive, he spotted the two blue swordfish in the front of a large driveway. Turning onto the main road, he followed the signs that took him to the back of a wooded forest area and the entrance to what appeared to be an upscale restaurant. Parking his car alongside a black Lincoln, he walked up to the front entrance and found Kate was seated near the door entrance waiting for him.

"Good evening, Capt. Curtis," said Kate as she got up to greet him.

For a moment, Curtis was stunned and speechless for the woman in the police uniform had transformed herself into a remarkable stunning woman that reminded him of the front page of *Cosmopolitan* magazine.

"Wow, you look wonderful," said Curtis. "If I really said what was on my mind, you would certainly excuse yourself from this dinner, so just wow, and maybe you'll just overlook my admiring gaze."

"Overlooked, and thank you. I've made reservations for us, so let's go in," said Kate. As the hostess acknowledged their reservations, she walked them over to a secluded table near a window that overlooked a large pond filled with white geese and a few ducks. As they both studied their menu and later placed their order, Curtis kept staring at Kate's ring finger and the beauty of the unusual ring that she was wearing tonight.

After dinner, she asked him, "Well, what do you think?" asked Kate.

"About the restaurant, the food, or the company?" asked Curtis smiling.

"Why don't you try all three," she answered, "and please be honest."

"Well, the restaurant and food couldn't be better, and my guess is from the parking lot that it's a favorite spot for the locals. The food was excellent, and the ambience, especially being seated near the pond with the geese and ducks, was perfect, but of course my guess is that you requested this seating," said Curtis as he noted Kate's smile.

She reached over and touched Curtis's hand gently while whispering, "Thank you."

"The company tonight, and especially for this lucky man, is best explained by William Wordsworth's poem 'I Wandered Lonely as a Cloud.' The poem contains some sadness as does the search for an elusive flower, which the Greeks refer to as the daffodil, the flower and symbol of unrequited love," said Curtis.

"So my company makes you sad?" asked Kate.

"No, not at all, because as you probably know on the subject of unrequited love, sadness only sets in when the recipient of your love turns you down. So far you haven't turned me down yet, and that makes my evening perfect. Changing the subject, that's a beautiful ring you have on tonight," commented Curtis.

"It was given to me as a Christmas present three years ago by my deceased husband while he served in Iraq. He was killed before he actually got to see me wear it," she said. "That's how things can happen when one is so far away, especially in a war zone."

"Well, you meant a lot to him, Kate, and in truth, he told you that by giving you that special ring, but you already understand that," said Curtis.

"Yes, he was not shy about his feelings, but this dinner is not about him, Curtis. It's just a ring, after all," she said.

"A regard ring, Kate, is not just a ring. It's a promise of everlasting love," said Curtis.

"I don't know what you mean, Curtis, or for that matter what the term *regard* means," she said.

Looking at her, Curtis could tell from her expression she was telling the truth. "The regard ring was popular in the Victorian period when it was customary to give the woman or man you loved a ring pledging your love or your heart. Look at the different stones on your ring, Kate. It tells the story," said Curtis.

"What story?" asked Kate, now more confused.

Reaching for her hand, he pointed to the gems on the ring finger, saying, "You have a ruby, emerald, garnet, amethyst, ruby, and diamond. You were his regard woman, and he was showing you his love. The custom started around the Victorian time period of 1840 and was given as a token of love and friendship."

"Now I'm really the fool, Curtis, for wearing this ring and spoiling your dinner," Kate said with moisture filling her eyes.

"Don't be foolish, Kate. I can handle a ghost if you can help me through this unrequited love stage," said Curtis.

"Let's change the subject. Tell me more about you and your cemetery visit today and when you have to leave."

"I'm leaving tomorrow because I've done everything possible I could have done for my church. Although I located the burial site of the family, to include, I believe, one child and the wife of the Reverend Reusswig. However, his grave still is missing, and my free time is not unlimited because I have an Orlando and New York trip to fly this weekend. Until an opening occurs on the bid schedule, being a reserved captain means I take the fill in routes as they are offered. But now I'm going to gamble a little, being a pilot, and you having such a nice small airport, and I being the proud owner of my own Cessna. Hope you will see me soon in the future when I can get back," said Curtis.

Kate, looking at Curtis, said, "So the flower hunt continues?"

"No, the hunt is over. It's just a matter of being careful not to lose sight of where I first found it," said Curtis.

"It shall remain waiting, Curtis" she said, handing him her home phone number and address. "Remember, though, when you come next time, bring some good doggie cookies for Channing," she said, giving him a hug and a kiss on the cheek as they walked to his car.

CHAPTER 12

The Shepherd's Cave

Hearing the sound of the local firehouse siren and the constant howling of her dog ended whatever was left of her sleep. Kate sat up and rubbed her eyes, checking the time on the nightstand, which flashed 3:00 a.m. Patting the bed, she called Channing over and began to rub his head, telling him it would be all right soon. Within in a few minutes, the fire siren ended, followed by the sounds of fire trucks and police cars and the blaring of the paramedics as they all traveled down her street to reach the destination of the latest crisis. Getting up, Kate walked into the bathroom and turned on the shower while glancing at her five-foot-eight-inch frame. Tall as she was, she had felt small standing next to Curtis, a man much taller than her former husband and somewhat admittedly more complex. Taking off her nightgown, she stepped into the warm water, allowing the spray to caress her breasts while cascading down her body with the gentle sensations of a lover's touch reaching for the hidden pleasures, long forgotten and now hiding in her pubic hair. It's been a long time she thought as she bent her head to allow the water to prepare for the shampoo that she now applied to her long auburn hair. Her husband was the last man she had been with, now over three years ago when she had visited him in Fort Hood, Texas, before he had left, never to return. A little guilt began to form as she started to feel the sensations beginning to overtake her body. Stepping out of the shower, she walked into the bedroom and began to lay out her police uniform that still contained the corporal rank instead of the gold detective shield that now designated her true rank. The fact was she would probably be using her uniform very infrequently since detectives were more incline to dress in casual clothes. It should be interesting to learn what her captain had in mind for his first female detective. Reaching up on the dresser, she found the gold shield along with the belt clip, and while laying it on the bed, she accidently knocked her ring to the floor that she had worn to dinner with Curtis. Reaching down, she picked up the regard ring and studied it for a moment. Regard, that's what Curtis had called it anyway. It was certainly beautiful, but she wondered now why her husband, Jason, had never mentioned that word. In fact, as she remembered, when she got the box containing the ring, there was not even a note other than "Merry Christmas to my wife." Curtis seemed to be—what was the word—deep, while Jason rarely showed that side. Still, Kate had always felt protected by her husband, and why not? He had been, after all, a former college star football player and starting tight end for Notre Dame. At six foot one, men would think twice about crossing the line in his presence, except maybe someone as tall as Curtis Patterson. He, on the other hand, at about six feet six, gave the appearance of being willing to downplay his obvious advantages in a man's world, thought Kate. Those that underestimated him, however, would probably pay a heavy price, much like those who had underestimated the willingness of her father to engage, if pushed. What did he used to say when the barroom bully used to annoy him when he had one of those infrequent relaxing beers on a Friday night with his trucker friends? "Go away before I give you two hundred and six other reasons to stop bothering me."

Not understanding, they would of course say, "What?"

"That's how many bones you have in your body. I could break them all before you realized what happened."

She never remembered anyone challenging his words. Somehow Curtis gave her the feeling that he was from the same school.

She laid the ring back on the dresser and put on a matching light-blue blouse and skirt. Today she decided to use her nighthawk custom ostrich companion holster to hold her Ruger 9mm pistol. What was the saying? A good gun in a bad holster is like having a race car with lousy tires. Picking up her cell phone and knowing that Curtis was obviously still fast asleep, she dialed his number and waited for the answering system to kick in. In a second, it did, "This is Curtis. I'm away from my plane today hunting for the most alluring flower known to mankind. When I locate it, I will return your call right away." Bursting out laughing, Kate wondered what kind of man would open himself up for kidding with such a message. "A confident man, obviously, that's who," she said to herself. She left him her message telling him that she loved his creativity and hoped that his flower hunt had allowed him to sleep well last night.

Kate spent most of the drive to the church thinking about Paul Bergman and his world of failure and grief. She wondered, was it possible that he had escaped any detection of his affair by members of his congregation or those close to him? Then again, maybe he hadn't, and that's why his now-deceased wife ended up with a cord around her neck, either by Bergman or someone else. She thought that it was unlikely that you could carry on an affair without someone knowing, but that person was in no hurry to discuss it, and why? Unless of course that person was somewhat involved in the mystery. And then there's the matter of his district president, who gave him that get-out-of-dodge card by sending him to another congregation. Well, doctors bury their own mistakes, and police have the blue code of honor to never rat out their bad apples, so one has to imagine that the Lutherans, Catholics, and Baptists protect one another as well. Kate knew that most homicides to a typical town was nothing more than just a little murder, and after a few days, its effect on the city would be short-lived. Maybe in a city, but not in any church that she had ever been familiar with. Any murder involving a pastor or a priest stays with a congregation for a very long time until it's resolved. Gossip remained one of the books of the Bible, to many.

The Lutheran Church was nestled behind a long drive and ended adjacent to an open field that seemed to go on forever. Kate noted that the lot had only two cars in it today, which probably was not unusual since, unless it was Sunday, her guess was this was a typical day in which the secretary and maybe the pastor were the only two people in the building.

Looking up the brick building, she found it strange that the church had no traditional bell or steeple reaching into the sky. Churches made Kate uneasy since as a Catholic in name only, she found that most often they were doors to sadness. Most she found stressed good versus evil and specialized in guilt and punishment. She thought about the last priest that she had given her confession and remembered that he had the strained expression of a person who found daylight unpleasant. Getting out of her car, she walked up to the door and found it locked. To her right, she noticed the buzzer and pushed it. Soon an attractive, middle-aged woman appeared and opened the door for her. Kate decided to not acknowledge that she knew that Pastor Bergman had transferred out.

"Good morning, can I help you?"

"Yes, I hope so. I'm looking for Pastor Paul Bergman. I'm Detective Kate Heller of the Funston Police Department," she said, now showing the woman her shield. "Would you mind if I stepped into the building please?"

"Certainly, come right in. My name's Laura Staple. I'm the church secretary." Kate followed her down a hallway, which then turned into a large room adjacent to a much larger area, which she guessed was the pastor's office.

"Can I get you something to drink, Officer?" asked Laura.

"No, I'm good, but thank you for asking," said Kate.

"I'm sorry, Detective Heller, but the Reverend Paul Bergman is no longer part of our ministry here at Trinity. He has accepted another call to a different congregation over in Silver Valley and hasn't been our pastor for well over a year, maybe longer. It's difficult to keep up with time, you know."

"You mean he was transferred?" asked Kate.

"Not really. In our church, another congregation can call for a pastor should there be a vacancy in their church. Congregations throughout the United States that are looking for another pastor are provided with a list of those pastors seeking what we call a divine call to a new congregation," said Laura. "If a pastor, even one at your own church, has an interest, he can notify the local district of his availability to be considered." Seeing that the policewoman appeared confused, Laura continued, "A divine call under our description is when a congregation has lost a pastor and wants a replacement. That church receives a list of candidates from their local district, and with God's help and the members voting on the name of their preferred candidate in time brings a new pastor to a congregation. I know that it sounds confusing, but that's the best explanation I can give."

"I think I understand," said Laura. "Where is your new pastor, and do you think I could see him for a few minutes?"

"He's in the church library now preparing for the Sunday service. If you just give me a minute, I'll speak to him," she said as she got up and walked around the corner.

Within the next few minutes, a tall, balding man in general street clothes came into the office following Laura. "Pastor, this is Detective Heller from the Funston Police Department."

"It's very nice to meet you, Detective Heller. I'm Pastor Gabriel Christmas, although Laura had indicated you had hoped to see Pastor Bergman? Yes, I know it's a strange name, Detective," Christmas said smiling, "but it does have its moments, especially around that time of the year, as I'm sure you can understand. Pastor Bergman, as Laura has explained, is no longer the shepherd of this church, but I hope that I can help you with any questions that your might have. Please follow me into my office, where we can chat." She followed him across the secretary's room to his office. As they were about to sit down, Christmas offered to take Kate's light jacket, which she handed to him. Noticing the empty holster, he said, "Thank you, Detective, for leaving your weapon in the car. It's not that I object to weapons, but in the house of the Lord, what do we really have to fear?"

"You're welcome, Pastor. There's a place for everything, and I felt that the church was not the place."

"Now if I could only convince my two Funston police members of that, then I might feel that I'm making headway. And should you be thinking about their names, well, you know the rule, Detective."

"Yes, it has something to do with what happens in Vegas stays in Vegas. And besides, those officers are not why I'm here today, Pastor, but it is nice to know that they spend time in church."

"Have we broken some law, Detective, or is one of our members in trouble?" asked Christmas.

"No, nothing such as that, Pastor, but before I explain the real reason for my visit, am I to assume that you are the current full-time pastor here for the immediate future?"

"Yes, I've been the pastor for almost two years," he said.

"Has Pastor Bergman ever contacted you or visited this congregation since he left?"

"Neither, and to be honest, it's unlikely that he would since he no longer has any connection to Trinity Lutheran."

"Isn't that unusual to just forget about old friendships that existed, especially for a pastor who has been so close to so many members?" asked Kate.

"Not if you understand how the system is designed to work, Detective. You see, most district presidents give an outgoing pastor a letter suggesting that they totally remove themselves from these relationships in order to give the new pastor the best opportunity to bond with his new members. Many laypeople get very close to their former pastor, and he as well to those members. It's hard enough to establish a new trust with those you serve without having to deal with how the former pastor operated as well, if you know what I mean, Detective."

"Yes, I can understand that would be a problem," said Kate. "What about Christmas cards, or telephone calls and emails, etc.?"

"Sorry, Detective, I don't follow?"

"Has he or do you communicate with former members in that way?"

"In my case, I follow the guidelines of my former district, which discourages any communication. To the best of my knowledge, Paul Bergman has done the same. Now could you explain to me what your role is in this matter is, Detective, since I'm somewhat concerned about providing any other answers."

"Fair enough, but please remember that the death of Mrs. Paul Bergman, wife of the former pastor of this congregation, still remains open, along with the unusual death of the former organist of this church. Because this is an ongoing investigation, there are certain limitations regarding matters of my investigation that I can't share with you. You are not a focus of this investigation, Pastor, or is your secretary. What I can tell you is that I've been assigned the responsibility to reopen this current cold case involving your former pastor, his now-deceased wife, and regretfully the late Ms. Gaye Browning, the former organist of this congregation."

"Yes, those were difficult times for our church, Detective Heller, and being the new minister didn't necessarily mean that the members of the congregation have let it go," said Christmas. "In the beginning, my new ministry was faced with a decline in our attendance by over twenty-five percent. People, as I'm certain you can understand, were confused and upset over what had happened and were looking for answers to this unfortunate set of circumstance. Answers that were and still are impossible to provide. Laymen expect perfection from the clergy and often fail to understand that we are human and have divorces like them, disobedient children like they have, and commit sins like them."

"How is it now?" asked Kate.

"Better, of course, but when something like this happens, it paints with a broad brush over all of us wearing a collar. The attendance now is still about five percent below what it should be, but God has been good in helping us recover. What can I do to help with your investigation, Detective?"

"Have you ever met Pastor Bergman in person at any meeting or convention Pastor?"

"No, our system usually self-governs on a local level. What that means, Detective, is that each district has its own president, and he has his own scheduled series of meetings several times a year, which at our level brings us together maybe two, three times. There is what is called a president's council, which is made up of all the district presidents across the United States, and they meet about four times a year, but of course we're not included. Pastor Bergman would attend only those meetings as authorized by his district president in Wisconsin and would not attend anything that I do here in Michigan," replied Christmas.

"How did you get assigned to this congregation, Pastor?"

"The term, as Laura may have explained, is referred to as being called, Detective. With all due respect to our Catholic friends, it is the priest that is generally assigned a new parish, while we Lutheran pastors are called by individual congregations. The idea is that each individual congregation is able to make their own independent decision as to the shepherd that will sit in this chair."

"How did they know that you would be interested in this opportunity," asked Kate.

"Like most pastors, our life is built around changes. Your family grows up, your parents grow older, or it's just time to move on for the betterment of your family and sometimes the congregation. Most pastors my age have worked with at least three, if not four, different congregations. In my case, I was the associated pastor of a congregation in Montana and had a desire to be a solo pastor of my own church. About four years ago, I put my name on a list with that of other pastors that would accept a call to another congregation. My name was shared with other districts since my desire was to be located in Michigan because my wife's parents live here."

"So your call to this congregation was a slam dunk."

"Nothing is a slam dunk, Detective, since each calling church receives at least five names of pastors that wish consideration. And of course, each of those names must be recommended by the local district office before the church receives the list."

"Sounds a little political to me, Pastor."

"It can be, but the intent is to make sure that each congregation gets a pastor best suited to their situation. As example, some churches have what is called a dual ministry. Therefore, you would want a pastor who has the experience of working with a principal, teachers, and school parents. The political part enters the picture when preferred pastors of the district president are included on the list. Although the congregation makes the final choice, the district can and does remove those candidates that they deem not a good fit."

"What's not a good fit, Pastor?"

"That's a question I'd prefer not to answer, Detective. It's better addressed by the district president of this region."

"Can you tell me anything about Ms. Gayle Browning, your former organist who died not so long ago?" asked Kate.

"You mean about the affair with Bergman or about the type of person she was?" he asked.

"The subject of the affair is public record, along with how she died. Pastor. No, my interest is in what type of person she was according to your observations," said Kate.

"Gayle was an excellent organist and the only one of the three that played regularly for us that enjoyed doing a contemporary service, which required working with the younger set. Not everyone likes doing that type of service. The music is not always acceptable to senior organists since they prefer the more traditional-type service. Lutherans have a well-deserved reputation of being stuffy at times, you know. We don't like changes, but Gayle was younger and enjoyed it."

"Was she married, divorced, or seeing anyone that you might know about besides the former pastor?" asked Kate.

He paused for a moment, probably trying to determine how much he could say without crossing the line between being helpful and personal information that was considered private between members of a congregation and their pastor. "Much of any information that I would have on that subject has come from the members, since the affair had been going on when I wasn't the pastor. She was young, or relatively young compared to Bergman," said Christmas. "To the best of our records, she had never been married."

"Did any of your current members ever comment on her ever seeing someone else besides Pastor Bergman?"

"I understand that she did, but have no direct knowledge. Gossip in a church is not healthy for a pastor to participate in, Detective Heller, so this line of questioning makes me uncomfortable," he remarked. "She was young, as I mentioned, and since she was single, one shouldn't be surprised if men did seek her out. The real surprise was in the fact that Bergman did."

"Understood, Pastor, so I'll move away from those questions, in your case. Are you aware that the organist allegedly died of a spider bite?" asked Kate.

"The papers reported that at the time, Detective Heller, and I didn't get the feeling that it was allegedly but rather the cause of her death," said Christmas.

"Last question, Pastor. As you certainly are aware, Mrs. Bergman also died recently, having never recovered from her original attack. My records indicate that you weren't the pastor who officiated at the service of either woman even though this was their home church. Is that correct?"

"Yes, that's true, but I'm sure that you understand that this would have been difficult for everyone, including Pastor Bergman. Regardless, he elected to have his wife cremated. Although it's somewhat unusual for a pastor, it is done now more regularly with clergy since it doesn't violate any creed, and to be honest, Detective Heller, most of us are not paid the kind of money that makes it possible to afford a ten-thousand-dollar funeral. Gayle Browning was also cremated and, like the pastor's wife, was not handled by this church."

"Something you would consider, Pastor?" asked Kate.

"No, but that's my personal choice," he said, getting up from his desk indicating that meeting was over. "I'm truly sorry, Detective, but I have a scheduled appointment with our circuit councilor and have to run. It's about an hour from here, and he's one of these guys that takes offense if we're late. You're always welcome to come back or give me a call if you have any other questions."

Getting up from the chair, she shook his hand and thanked him for taking the time to see her on such short notice. Walking past Laura's office, she stopped and thanked her for her helpfulness and made her way out of the church and back to her car. As she drove away, she couldn't help feeling that Christmas knew a lot more about Ms. Browning and Pastor Bergman than he wanted to admit or share.

CHAPTER 13

Along Came a spider

Sitting at her dining table, Kate opened the police report on Gayle Browning and began to review the notes. Reading from the report, she noted that according to the initial investigation from the responding police officer, Ben Smith, the deceased had failed to report to work at her place of employment at Red Carpet Cruises, where she was the assistant manager. The police report indicated that when the other associates were unable to get into the office, they called the owner. When he was unable to reach Browning, he drove directly over to her townhouse. When he had arrived, he noticed that the employee's red Honda Civic was still parked by the house but was unable to get any response on her cell phone or by ringing the doorbell. It was at that point that the owner had called the Funston Police Department. Shortly after they arrived, the police officer began rapping on her bedroom window, with no response. After a conversation with the duty officer in charge, the officer gained entrance by breaking the back door lock. Reading on, Kate noted that the report indicated that Ms. Browning was found on the floor in her bedroom dead with no noticeable signs of injury or foul play. The original feeling by Officer Ben Smith was that due to the condition of the body, it was his opinion that Ms. Browning probably had died of natural causes. The officer had then called for the Funston paramedics, who transferred Ms. Browning to Funston General Hospital, where she was officially pronounced dead, and due to the unusual circumstances as required by law, an autopsy was performed by Dr. J. L. Patel.

Kate then picked up the autopsy report filled out by Patel and noted that his resulting examination had concluded that the deceased had been bitten by a member of the arachnid's family of insects or, in the opinion of the doctor, a brown recluse spider, one of the five most deadly spiders in the world. She picked up the enclosed pictures in the file, one showing a leg of Gayle Browning just above the knee. She could clearly see on the leg a mark about the size of a quarter, which represented the bite from the spider. The photo was clear enough that Kate cold tell that the bite had caused small red blister marks to forming at the edges of the bite. The doctor concluded in his report that the victim had realized she had been bitten based on his finding traces of a 1% hydrocortisone cream on the affected area, which he concluded that she put on the area to reduce itching caused by the bite. Since the venom was slow acting, the deceased had probably fallen asleep thinking everything would be all right. She had probably woken up later and realized the effects of the poison in her system. The report contained the signature of Dr. J. L. Patel and his business card.

Kate got up, poured herself a cup of coffee, and located the book on spiders, which was given to her by the speeding motorist that she had stopped a few days earlier. Sitting back down at the table, she opened the book to the table of contents and noticed on the page that the motorist had written his name and address just above the index of categories. "Professor of Entomology: Joseph William Davis, 1515 Thornberry Drive, Bunker Hill, Michigan." Copying down the address, she placed it on her notepad and put it in her purse.

Laying aside the book on spiders, she picked up the business card of the doctor and noticed that his card said "American Board of Pathology" and that he was board certified in internal medicine. Credentials seemed in order, but one never knew how long before any doctor had to recertify his specialty, if at all, she thought. Reaching for the spider book, she turned to the page on brown recluse spiders. Halfway through the section on the brown recluse, she found that the speeding professor had underlined a section on the recluse with a yellow marker. "Please note," the sentence began, "that it's impossible to be conclusive with any spider bite being the actual cause of the skin irritation without the actual spider submitted for study." It went on to suggest that many spider bites were incorrectly blamed on actual tick or mite bites, and unless the actual spider was brought in for examination, the determination was often just an opinion by most doctors. Reading on, the section explained that in order to fully determine the exact species of the Loxosceles, the spiders genitalia needed to be examined under a high-powered microscope.

"Jesus," said Kate as she closed the book. The guy could have been only guessing what caused the death. "Both the speeder and Curtis had indicated their doubts about the brown recluse, and here we have the medical examiner coming to a rapid conclusion based on really what?" Rubbing her eyes, Kate jumped when her phone started to ring. Getting up, she walked over to the hall phone and picked it up without looking at the call identifier.

"Hello," she said.

"My god, you actually do have a home," said Curtis. "How are you doing, Kate? I hope you won't shoot me the next time we see each other for calling you so early."

"Hardly, and it's wonderful to hear your voice, Curtis, and you only need to worry if you've lost your interest in that special flower," said Kate.

"No, she's been found, and now I'm working on a way to stake a claim. I'm currently on the last leg of my flight trip and hope to be home in a couple of days. Please look at your schedule as I've missed you from the moment that I left," said Curtis.

"I have some time off this coming Saturday and Sunday. It's been busy around here since you left, so give me a call when you get back. I hope we can work something out, and should you not be able to tell, I've missed you also," she said.

"Well, I hear the gate agent making the final departure announcement, so regretfully I have to run, or should I say fly. Passengers are funny when they are all on board. They expect their captain to get them home. Bye for now, my dear."

"The man sure is careful with his words, or is it that he's still uncertain about being rejected and is saving the *love* word until he hears it from me?" she wondered. Walking back into the kitchen, she picked up her files and arranged them neatly on the counter for her to examine later when she had finished her visit to the station.

As Kate pulled into the Funston Police Station, she parked in one of the five slots marked for detectives. She couldn't help but feel a little uneasy using this little perk, especially since she still considered herself Corporal Heller. "Damn," she thought, "I have to start adjusting to the new promotion or I'll catch hell from Wagner, if not Henning, who enjoys busting my chops." Locking the car, Kate moved up the steps of the station and entered the puzzle palace, as Jacob liked to refer to it. She started to pass Captain Wagner's office when she heard a female voice yelling, "You're trying to bury me in bullshit, Captain, and that's something that won't work with this district attorney."

Clearly it was Rachael Underwood, thought Kate, as she moved passed the half-open door, still hearing the conversation growing louder.

"I'm the master of understanding the eureka fallacy, Wagner, so back off before I find a way to have the mayor place you on school guard patrol," said Underwood.

Kate found Jacob Henning at his desk and came in without knocking.

"She's a real bitch, isn't she, Detective Heller? After Wagner gets done getting his ass chewed out, he'll be looking for something to yell about, and I wouldn't want to be the new detective who still hasn't had her new shield clipped to her waist or that new outfit, would you?" asked Henning.

"No, of course not, and I've got the damn thing in my car but just having a hard time getting used to it Jacob. I'll get my act together before long, but the Bergman and Browning files, as you might expect, has taken up all my time," said Kate. "Besides, now that I'm a detective, don't sergeants have to show a little respect to a superior officer?"

Ignoring her little smug smile, Henning changed the subject and asked Kate, "Anything new yet on the cold cases?"

"Nothing yet, but I wish someone would have told me that he's moved out of state and that his former wife who died a short time ago was cremated. Plus, it's highly unlikely that his special squeeze just happened to have died by a brown recluse spider, as the report indicated. Other than that nothing is new but I'm working on it, Sarge," said Kate.

"Sorry, Kate, don't go sensitive on me. We're all under pressure to give the black widow down the hall something to feed to the mayor," said Henning.

"Yeah, I know. Say, what the heck is the eureka fallacy anyway?" asked Kate.

"It's the tendency of people to put a lot more faith in things they've discovered about someone than in things that person has told them. It's sort of like me having discovered long ago that you will do things at your pace, not what I've told you to do. Now if you will get the hell out of my office, get what you need, and leave this building, you might happen to live another day before either Underwood finds you or Wagner mows your cute little ass for leaving that detective shield in your car like it's nothing more than a prize out of a Cracker Jack box," said Henning. "And by the way, Detective, never forget my mother's favorite saying, 'I brought you into this world, and I can still take you out of this world,'" said Jacob while smiling at Kate.

Taking Henning's advice, she walked out of his office, exiting the back door, and circled the building until she came to her car parked in front. The trip to the office had seemed to be a total waste, but she knew that her comments to Henning would find its way to Wagner regarding her suspicions about the cause of death of Browning and Bergman no longer living in Funston. Getting in the car, she closed the door, punched the gas pedal, and left behind the morning aggravation that she didn't need. Being on special assignment had its advantages since she didn't have to report in each day for inspection and could work the case as she saw fit or until she couldn't feed the brass some new information. Then they would be all over her like white on rice, and that day would be coming unless she could move this case forward. Pulling over into the local Kroger food store parking lot, she reached back for her small briefcase and brought it up onto the front seat. Pulling the medical examiner's card, she looked at it once again and decided to see if Dr. Patel was in his office. She figured that it was worth the chance that he might be in, so she dialed the number on the card and got his answering service, which indicated that he was seeing patients at his Lakeview office today. She copied down the provided phone number and called.

"Dr. Patel's office, can I help you?"

"Yes, this is Det. Kate Heller of the Funston Police Department. Would Dr. Patel be in?"

"Yes, but he's with patients now. May I take a message?"

"Yes, I need a few minutes with him. Please check and see if there would be a convenient time that would be possible for me to visit him. Hopefully it would be as soon as possible. It has to do with a past autopsy that he performed." Kate suddenly found herself being put on hold as she heard elevator music in the background. "Weird," she thought, "the girl didn't even tell her what she was doing before placing her on hold. Obviously the doctor's gatekeeper wasn't impressed by a call from the police."

Suddenly a foreign voice came on the line, sounding irritated. "Dr. Patel, what can I do for you?"

Kate repeated her request for an appointment, this time explaining her need to see him regarding his autopsy on Gayle Browning and her assignment regarding the reopening of her case.

"Well, I'm busy now, as is the case with most doctors, Detective. The medical field is not what it was years ago when you see ten to twelve patients a day. Today most of us routinely see twenty to twenty-five patients each day, if we're that lucky to have a slow day. Tell you what, though. If you don't mind talking business over lunch, I can meet you at the Gaylord India Restaurant, which is located within five minutes of my office. They serve Bihar Indian food, along with a few meat-based dishes. If you can be there in the next hour, I can give you a little time today, Officer. Otherwise, we may have to wait until sometime next week."

"That will be fine, Dr. Patel. Thank you for your cooperation," Kate started to say, only to find that Patel had already hung up the phone. "Jesus," she thought, "where the hell have all men's manners disappeared to?" Pulling out of the parking lot, she decided to head directly to Gaylord's Restaurant, which she estimated to be about a thirty-minute drive considering traffic. She knew that it would be important not to allow one to read too much into Patel's apparent self-worth of his profession since experience had taught her that the medical profession often considered themselves heir apparent to sitting on the right hand of God, or was it the fact that he was an Indian doctor? She never thought of herself as being prejudiced, but then neither did her father, who never allowed ethnic slang into their house, yet despised the French, or the frogs as he liked to refer to them. It was her mother, ever the diplomat, who put an end to the subject by reminding her dad at dinner one night about 1876. Puzzled, he had asked her what that had to do with the subject, and she forcefully mentioned that it was the French responsible for the 150 pieces of copper that rested in New York's harbor called the Statue of Liberty. Kate couldn't help but remember her mother waiting for her dad's comeback, but it never happened, and the frog comments somehow left the house. Glancing at her watch, she noticed that she was well ahead of her scheduled meeting.

CHAPTER 14

Culture Shock

Kate pulled up to the Gaylord India Restaurant several minutes ahead of her scheduled meeting time and began looking for anything that resembled a doctor's car. "There I go again," she thought, "prejudging a guy based on the fact he's a doctor. The guy could well be driving a KIA for all that I know." Seeing nothing that caught her eye, she pulled into an open slot about fifty feet from the main entrance and shut off the engine. Flipping the tuner on the radio of her car, she checked in on one of the local news stations. The story was front and center on most of them, and a bulletin on most of the rest. Her beloved Red Wings had one of their key players hurt in last night's game by one of the notorious goons from Philadelphia. His medical condition had been reported on for the last several hours. The news report was indicating that the league would be deciding how many games' suspension that the Philadelphia player could expect to receive. "Maybe Patel is inside already," she thought as she exited the car and walked up to the building and entered.

"Are you looking for Dr. Patel?" asked the short, dark-skinned lady.

"Yes," said Kate.

The hostess, starting to walk, indicated that Kate should follow her as she led her to the far corner of the restaurant where Patel was seated reading what appeared to be a medical journal. As Kate approached the large table, she offered her hand and said, "Dr. Patel,

I'm Detective Kate Heller. Thank you for making the time to see me."

Nodding as if he were bored, he pointed for her to sit down, and without acknowledging her presence or attempting to return her handshake, he said, "You must work for Commander John Whiteside?"

Kate understood the implication right away: scare the new kid on the block by impressing her with the fact that you're a buddy with the top dog. It was an old trick that she had heard before. "Actually, Dr. Patel, I work for Captain Wagner, although we both do report to the division commander, John Whiteside. You must be a friend of Commander Whiteside, so I'll make certain to pass our meeting on to Captain Wagner that we've met today."

Seeing that Patel had waved her over to the table, the waitress appeared, and without giving her a chance to ask, the doctor placed an order for both himself and Kate.

"Detective Heller, I eat here every day and meet guests often who like you have probably never eaten Indian food, so I've ordered for both of us with a little American food mixed in," said Patel, never looking her in the eye.

"Oh, I've eaten a little boiled rice and cooked vegetables for lunch before, Dr. Patel, so not to worry," said Kate with a smile.

Looking at his watch, Patel asked, "What may I help you with, Officer? I thought the report that I submitted to your office would have answered all questions regarding Ms. Browning."

"It was an excellent report, Dr. Patel, and it was very helpful at the time, but we've been asked to re-examine the case because the new district attorney for our county has received pressure from the news media to find the killer of Pastor Paul Bergman's wife. As you may be aware, Ms. Gayle Browning had a connection to the pastor, and with the unfortunate recent death of the pastor's wife and the circumstances of her death being still unsolved, plus the mysterious death of his mistress Gayle Browning. Well, as you might appreciate, the local media feels we haven't done our job," said Kate.

"I still don't see what this has to do with me," said Patel, still not looking Kate in the eye. "Doctors are notoriously busy professionals and have little time to spend worrying about the latest gossip of who did what to whom, if you understand what I'm saying. Ah, the food has arrived. This is probably the last time I can relax before the next appointment arrives. Ever feel like you are overwhelmed, Detective?"

"All the time, Doctor. As we say in our business, 'Death seldom takes a holiday.' What you have to do with this is the reopening of the investigation and more to do with Gayle Browning than Pastor Bergman. He was acquitted, if you remember the newspaper accounts, and no longer lives in Funston."

"Yes, I remember reading that his church released him."

"That is true, but he's now the pastor of another church in Silver Valley, Wisconsin."

For the first time, Patel appeared genuinely puzzled. "Really? How unusual and forgiving, based on what I remember of the circumstances. So I repeat my question, Detective, what does this investigation have to do with me?" Glancing at his wrist watch, Patel said, "Go ahead, Detective Heller, ask your questions as we have limited time."

"Did you know, Dr. Patel, that there have been no recorded deaths from a brown recluse spider in the United States in over five years?"

"So what's your point, Detective?" asked Patel as he continued eating. "To the best of my knowledge, we haven't had any reported sightings of a whopping crane in our town, but it can happen tomorrow, can't it?

"My point, Doctor, is that the brown recluse spider is not native to this area. They are very rare to the medical profession, and their bite is most often fatal to children, not adults. In fact, the problem seems to be that most doctors can't even identify the difference between a spider bite and that of a tick or mite, and thus often misdiagnose the patient's problem."

"Are you questioning my report, Detective? First of all, I'm not your average doctor. I happen to be the head infectious disease doctor at Funston General Hospital, along with being a board-certified internal medicine doctor, who also just happens to handle the majority of autopsies in this area. I have a splendid reputation, Detective

Heller, and would not be bashful about defending it in court if it came to that."

"Your credentials are not being questioned, Dr. Patel, nor should you underestimate my desire to extrapolate existing clues to solve a murder case. My research on the subject indicates that the majority of doctors confuse the brown recluse spider bite with thirteen other species found in the same family. I'm not saying that you made any mistake, but rather that I just need your help because a killer is loose and he or she may strike again unless everything is looked at regardless of personal sensitivity. In addition, our new district attorney requires that the Funston Police Department reopen the investigation and hopefully bring needed closure two these open cases."

"I've not overlooked anything, Detective, so you can move beyond my autopsy report and concentrate your efforts in other directions. As I have said, my time is short today, and my patients look forward to my return. Please tell Commander Whiteside that I hope to play a few rounds of golf with him in the near future at the Flying Eagle Country Club."

As Kate started to get up, she paused, looked at Patel, and said, "I did not see any laboratory test results in your report to confirm that you reviewed the deceased blood count or possible blood clotting nor any developing damage to the area affected by the bite. These usually help validate the type of spider bite, especially in the case of the brown recluse, whose venom is notorious for causing a breakdown in body cells."

"Well, I can see that you have done your homework, Detective," answered Patel as he wiped his face with the provided napkin, "but I must move on."

"Yes, I understand what it feels like to get behind on one's work. At the same time, Doctor, we have a lot more that needs discussion, and I would like to arrange another meeting when you are less stressed with your patient schedule. Ms. Browning represents a clear path to my solving more than one possible murder and possibly the prevention of more such tragic events. As we both know, an immunologic test for the brown recluse spider bite has been developed that would have allowed you to positively confirm that the bite was that of a brown recluse, but no such test is offered by Funston Hospital. My guess is that this was probably due in part because of the unlikely hood of the spider reaching this part of the Midwest, plus of course that old budgetary concern. But I do thank you for taking the time from your busy schedule, Doctor. Unless you have a time on your calendar later today, I will call your office sometime later this week," said Kate.

"See how confusing the world is, Detective. Some opinions, including yours, suggest that it's hard to determine what a brown recluse spider bite looks like, and me, while I being an infectious disease doctor, have no doubt that what I examined was that little fiddleback's bite, so in my world a future discussion is of little value. I do have time for one last question, Detective Heller."

"No, I don't want to delay you any more, Dr. Patel. You've already indicated that you're behind schedule," said Kate.

"Dead patients never put pressure on me, but those hoping that I can prevent the inevitable present the most challenge of my time. Regardless of my time, I'm still interested in your last question Detective."

"The police report stated that you found traces of a hydrocortisone cream on her leg. Is that true?"

"If the report says that, then it's true. Again, what's your point, Officer?" asked Patel.

"Well, the police report indicated that they found on her nightstand a packet of Azithromycin tablets, which could also indicate treatment with other antibiotics," said Kate, "possible even some form of steroids."

"So what?" asked Patel.

"Well, it could mean that she had seen another doctor for some bite, and that doctor considered it a mite or tick bite and not a spider bite," said Kate. "Unlike you, Doctor, these medical professionals may not have realized what they had actually encountered or asked the right questions of the patient."

"Sorry, Detective, I didn't realize that you had a medical degree and knew what questions to ask."

"No, Dr. Patel, I have hardly any medical knowledge and to be honest hated chemistry in high school and college, but I still understand the value of preparation, if you know what I mean. For instance, when dealing with a brown recluse spider bite, I do know that one should not apply any hydrocortisone cream to the affected area, yet my report says that's what you found on her leg. It's my guess that she either did it on her own or received some encouragement from some practitioner. That part has to be looked into, not as a means to suggest incompetence on the part of any doctor, but just to be helpful in the overall investigation."

"What do you mean by that," asked Patel.

"Well, you know, Doctor, not everything is as we have been told. Some doctors, I'm told, actually still believe that the black widow spider kills its male after mating, which of course is not true. Then there are some well-meaning doctors who would never consider the possibility that what might be going on in their patient's body could be Hansen's disease, not a spider bite, tick bite, or mite bite. You have a tough job, Dr. Patel, and I respect the amount of time and effort that you must put in to resolve the many different possibilities of each of our individual illness."

As she again thanked the doctor for her lunch and was moving away from the table toward the exit, Kate noticed that Patel remained behind and was placing a call from his cell phone. In her mind, that was almost a certainty that he was calling the doctor whose name appeared on the prescription. It didn't matter what the profession was, cover one's ass existed at all levels. It really didn't matter as she would be seeing him soon anyway. Getting in her car, Kate let her emotion flow and pounded the steering wheel as she pulled out of the lot fuming at Patel's comments and manner. She had met him before, although if he remembered her, he didn't let on. Patel was one of the first doctors that she had to see as part of the police department's wellness program designed to meet the city requirements of the former mayor. She had learned that he was a father of three, with a trophy wife twenty years his junior, and prided himself on being a history buff. Like many physicians that she had met over time, Patel could play bluegrass, jazz, or country music on several instruments, depending upon what group he was attempting to please at the time. Word had it that Patel was also an accomplished pianist and enjoyed performing for his colleagues at various medical conventions. The only two drawbacks in his life seemed to be his temper and feeling that a stethoscope around one's neck was a guaranteed invitation for his female patients to undress for the many physical examinations that seemed to be part of the wellness program he was running. Kate had been sent to his office two years ago to review her potential for sleep apnea since much of her time would be driving the squad car at night. Patel had made it clear on the visit that he considered her to be a candidate for a full sleep test that would require her to spend an overnight at his sleep clinic, where he informed her that he would personally supervise the results. Uncomfortable with the developing arrangements, she had declined the sleep test and cancelled the scheduled weekend testing. His office had never called to reschedule, nor did she hear from him again. This has not been a good day, thought Kate, still unable to shake from her memory how easy it appeared to be for Patel to dismiss her concerns while protecting his apparent rush to judgment on his autopsy report, despite all signs pointing toward a different conclusion. And then there was his damn habit of not looking her in the eye almost to the point of ignoring her existence.

The sun was still high in the sky, although the cloud cover darkened its brilliance, making Kate think of its appearance now much like that of a ripe pumpkin. She could imagine how much fun it would be to share the experience of the sun going down with Curtis while sitting parked by Lake Michigan in downtown Funston. As a girl growing up in Michigan, she softly giggled to herself remembering the secret that she and her girlfriends used to share with one another about their experiences with their dates as they would drive over to Detroit in the summer and watch the submarine races with their dates. She had been shocked when her own mother had questioned her about this subject years ago trying to compare her experiences with her dad to that of her daughter and her boyfriends. Nothing much really happened watching those pretend submarine races and dates, but what it conjured up in the minds of those talking about it was, well, just growing up in Michigan, and their little secrets made for wonderful memories. She was within fifteen minutes of her house when she spotted the billboard sign with the Maytag man sitting in a house waiting for the appliance to break down, which of course everyone knew that it wouldn't. Do they still have a Maytag man? she wondered. And what happened to the Muntz TVs that she remembered her dad talking about? Before she had left home for college, Kate had found a black-and-white sixteen-inch Muntz TV stored in the family garage and had asked her dad about it. He had sat her down in the living room and talked endlessly about Earl William Muntz, the American businessman and engineer. Like the modern Bill Gates, he also hadn't finished high school, but as her dad proudly said, he was better than Gates. The guy had a madman persona and made his fortune selling seventy-two million dollars' worth of cars, and later fifty-five million dollars' worth of television sets, having produced and marketed the first black-and-white TV receiver, which he sold for less than one hundred dollars. Later her dad had said that Muntz created one of the earliest functional widescreen projection TVs and only went out of the TV business because of the introduction of color. But her father, smiling, had told her he still had plenty of things to occupy his mind, having married seven times. He went on to tell her that Muntz had Hollywood friends that wouldn't stop, being friends with Dick Clark, Gene Autry, Dean Martin and Bob Hope. Although Detroit had been a major market for his products, he sold cars and TVs all over the country. She drove a few more minutes before pulling up to her townhouse.

CHAPTER 15

Return Visit

Entering her house, Kate laid her small briefcase on the kitchen table and picked up her cell phone and dialed Laura Staple, hoping that the church secretary would still be in her office.

"Trinity Lutheran Church Office, this is Laura."

"Good afternoon, Laura, this is Detective Heller from the Funston Police Department. We met not too long ago when I visited Pastor Christmas. Is he in?"

"No, today he usually visits our shut-ins, and based on past history, he probably won't be in at all. Is there something that I can help you with?" asked Laura.

"Yes, when I visited Pastor Christmas, I forgot to ask him some additional questions regarding your former organist, Ms. Browning. Could you check your records and tell me if she had any close relatives since I understand that she was not married? Also could you tell me what funeral home handled her arrangements? Pastor Christmas had indicated that he didn't handle either the Bergman funeral or Gayle Browning," said Kate.

"Ms. Browning was an only child, with her parents having passed away years ago," answered Laura. After her death, we did get a phone call from someone who identified himself as her half brother, but to the best of my knowledge, that was the first and last time someone indicated having any family connection to her. She was, as you probably have learned, only one of our three organists. She appeared to maintain a very private life and seemed to keep too herself. Her relationship with Pastor Bergman surprised us all, Detective. It was so awful when you think about him often giving communion to both women at the same time. Well, Mrs. Bergman and Gayle, that's what I mean, Detective. Communion is such a sensitive subject to us Lutheran Church members, as I'm certain that it is to most religions. In our faith, most of our members even shy away from taking communion with someone that they are in conflict with. That can even include our pastor."

"Who handled her arrangements?" asked Kate.

"The Johnson Brothers Funeral Home," answered Laura. "They do almost eighty percent of all our needs in that area, and sometimes they even have waved the cost of their services when a fireman's or police officer's family is involved."

"Were the church services conducted at the Johnson Brothers Funeral home as well?" asked Kate.

"Yes, actually Pastor Christmas wanted to do both services here at church, but because of the unusual circumstance involving Pastor Bergman and her, the elder board refused to approve either situation. Gayle was cremated, so regretfully I can't tell you where her remains are," said Laura, "but if it was important to your investigation, the funeral home would have all that information."

"Was there any memorial that came from the outside that would have suggested any ties to any family members?" asked Kate. "Anything that you might have felt was unusual?"

"No, just that from her Trinity family members who attended her wake and funeral. There was, however, one gift from an anonymous source for $1,500, which specified that the money be used for new hymnal books as needed. I guess that would be called unusual."

"Just out of curiosity, did the anonymous donor request any name be used in the hymnal book such as 'In memory of'?"

"Let me put the phone down for a minute and check our records." Within a few minutes, Laura had returned to the line and stated that the records indicated a Mr. And Mrs. B. Phoneutria. Nonmembers with no return address."

"Thank you for this information. As always, Laura, you folks have been very helpful, and I appreciate your cooperation. Please have Pastor Christmas call me if he has any questions regarding my call or if anything else comes to mind."

"I will. This Bergman situation sure has drawn a lot of interest, Detective."

"Really?" answered Kate.

"Yeah, I just got a call from a woman by the name of Betty Ogden who wanted to visit our church and meet the pastor's former wife and daughter. Said she was attending some special meeting in the area and hoped to say hello. I didn't have the heart to tell her anything about Mrs. Bergman passing away nor that her daughter was no longer a member any longer, but I did leave a note for Pastor Christmas to give her a call."

"Did this Ogden woman specify any particular reason why she wanted to see the Bergman family?"

"Not a thing I can recall."

"Well then, maybe soon I'll give the pastor a call in the future and touch base with him on our conversation," said Kate.

After hanging up, she sat back in her chair and tried to digest her conversation with the church secretary, that of Christmas, and her lunch with Patel. Something just didn't balance, she thought. What was the name of that person who donated $1,500 for the Gayle Browning memorial? Looking at her notes, she wrote on a piece of paper, "Mr. & Mrs. B. Phoneutria." Why does that name seem familiar? she wondered. Her ability to interrogate was considered one of the reasons she was on the fast track to a command position at the police department. When asked by her superiors what was her secret, she had said, "The eyes." It was always in the eyes. It was part of the lore, which her friends since high school had commented, that Kate could kill you with a look that would induce such a deep sense of guilt at your having failed to tell her the truth that you would just curl up and confess. It hadn't happened with Dr. Patel, but only because the coward wouldn't look at her, thought Kate. There would be another chance, that was for certain, and maybe soon. Christmas was a different situation, because she doubted that he would outright lie about anything, but he didn't have to. While she was not close to any one individual church, she understood the rules of engagement when talking to clergy. Regardless if you were a policeman or not, in the eyes of those that wear a collar, you were but a layman who didn't understand who sits to the right of God first. If there were any secrets within the walls of Trinity Lutheran Church, Kate was certain they would not be volunteered by Christmas. The history of this particular religious group was built on a foundation that kept all their pastors on a short lease. So tight that breaking the established rules put in place by one of the local leaders across the United States was an absolute guarantee that you would either finish your career at the last church you served or be allowed to be released by your congregation and struggle until others helped you. There was a reason for the nickname Misery Lutheran Church, thought Kate. Suddenly the barking of Channing and his racing to the door brought Kate out of her chair. The doorbell ringing clearly announced that someone was paying her a visit and wouldn't stop ringing until she opened the door. Looking through the peephole, she could tell that the young man held at least two dozen roses. Smiling, she opened the door and accepted the delivery, asking the kid to wait while she found her purse. Giving the young man a tip was something that she had learned growing up in a house where them motto was, "Never stiff the little guy." It had stayed with her all her life.

Taking the flowers, Kate walked them to the kitchen and found the vase that hadn't been used in over three years. Placing them in the vase, she removed the card. "Miss you, my Kate. Hope that this Saturday will work for you. Love you. Curtis." Well, he crossed the line and took a gamble on the *love* word, she thought to herself. Picking up her cell phone, she called his number and heard her call go into his voice mail. "Hello, Curtis, this is Kate. Thank you for the lovely flowers. They were beautiful, and your words also. See you this Saturday. Bye for now." After she hung up, she thought back to these last few days since meeting Curtis, something she was not quite prepared for. Her career had been the salvation to the loss of her husband, and letting another man into her life had been something that she had guarded against. But here he was, the flower hunter, and she liked it.

Rubbing her forehead, she thought back to her meeting with Patel and wondered if she was letting her prejudices begin to control her. She never viewed herself that way, but the fact was that the man had gotten under her skin when she had first visited him as a patient and now recently as part of her investigation. From the minute she had walked into the restaurant and greeted him at his table, it was a relationship much like that of a mongoose meeting a Cobra—actually when she thought about it, more like a cobra meeting a baby goose. He didn't approve of her, and she certainly felt that he had much to improve upon as a doctor. Tapping her fingers on the kitchen table, Kate also thought back to her recent phone conversation with the church secretary, Laura. The woman was pleasant and helpful but was holding something back. It didn't matter what job or company a secretary worked for. She was usually the first person that always knew where the bodies were buried and who kept the shovel. It was clear that the secretary knew more about the relationship between Bergman and the Browning woman than she had let on, but seemed to prefer that Kate only think of her as a woman who minded her own business. And that $1,500 anonymous gift to the church from a family by the name of Phoneutria needed to be further checked out. As she finished writing brief notes to herself, Kate got up and walked over to the water cooler and poured herself a glass of spring water from the dispenser. Returning to her chair, she examined her notes covering her conversation with Christmas. The man walked like, talked like, and acted like what most laypeople would expect the prototype of a pastor to be. She doubted that he was holding much back on Bergman and was probably, as he had suggested, still trying to heal the wounds left by the former pastor. In her opinion, the key that would open the box and solve these two open files always came back to Bergman, and that Browning, while a participant in this massive play going on, was but a supporting actor, nothing more. Still, one couldn't ignore the beginning of the movie or all the credits, she thought, as she glanced at the business card of Prof. Joseph Davis. She detached the card from her notebook and laid it down on the table in front of her. She would visit him.

CHAPTER 16

The Entomologist

Most mornings Kate started early, well before six. Today was no different as she finished her shower and began to dress. It now seemed strange putting on civilian clothes, especially since it had been only a few days ago that she was wearing the traditional blue uniform of a Funston police officer. Now she was a detective and trying her best to find a concealed location for her service pistol. With men, it was easy since all you needed was a shoulder harness and a suit jacket, and you were in business. Women were a little more complicated, and most often unless you were trying to just look like the boys, you placed a weapon in your purse. Well, she was not one of the boys, nor did she need to look like Dixie Tracy to be a woman detective. Since she had decided to wear slacks today, her recently purchased ankle holster was one possible option, but she liked her Kahr CW 5 for its stopping power, not the pea shooter designed for the ankle. Putting on her slacks, she belted her brown compact holster to her waist and inserted the Kahr. Satisfied, she walked over to her bedroom window glancing at the rotating small windmill that she had in the backyard. She could tell it was going to be what her mother used to refer as a good laundry day. The windmill and the tree in the yard were both displaying a steady wind, but not too strong. She could still see her mother pulling clothes in from the sky on a line that ran from a pole to their porch window. "Hanging up wet clothes while it was still cool outside gave the clothes a unique freshness to them that no modern equipment could compare with" was what her mother almost always repeated during this process. Her mother was a farmwoman at heart, her "backyard clothesline the most typical give-away" would comment her husband over and over. Reaching for her jacket and detective shield, she walked into the kitchen and secured her cell phone to her belt.

Putting her notebook in front of her, Kate called Captain Wagner, giving him what she had uncovered, and told him that she was meeting with Prof. Joseph Davis, the entomologist she had stopped a few days ago over in Bunker Hill, Michigan. Wagner, still burning over his meeting with District Attorney Underwood, had advised her that he would need some solid results by the middle of next week because Underwood had scheduled a sit-down with the mayor, and he was tired of being used as a pincushion to advance the DA's career. Kate acknowledged his concern and said the investigation was moving at a fast pace and that she would be in on Monday and hopefully would have something for him. The phone call had lasted less than twenty-five minutes, ten minutes of which had been devoted to Wagner making a promise to her that unless she cracked the egg, a return to street duty could be arranged, despite the fact that he considered her his rising star. In this business, he warned it was all about keeping your bosses happy and off your back.

Giving Channing one last affectionate hug, she locked the house and slid into the front seat of her Honda Civic and headed to the outer drive, which would take her to US 12 and the short drive to the home of Professor Davis's house.

As she drove along the Michigan coastline, she was in awe of the beauty of the clear blue water, the white sand near the shoreline, the beach spots with the young couples holding hands and laying on the blankets, the parking lots with the boat trailers, the rest areas, and the other hangouts used by those lucky enough to be off today. It made Kate wish for the coming weekend to hurry, when she would see Curtis. She thought about Professor Davis and his willingness to see her on such short notice this morning, indicating that he could give her a couple hours if she could meet him at his home in Bunker Hill, which he had described as just a twenty-minute drive from Funston. It was almost like he was anxious to show her his world of knowledge about spiders. Kate had elected to downplay the detective police look in hopes that a more casual appearance would allow the entomologist to speak more open. At the last moment, she had removed the belted holster, along with the pistol, and put it in her briefcase and left it behind her seat in the car. She did, however, drop her subcompact P2000 .40 S&W in her purse before she had left the house. As she entered the exclusive, gate-controlled subdivision, the uniformed guard asked her for her identification, and she produced her driver's license, avoiding showing him her new gold shield. Pulling his head back in the guard shack, he placed a call to alert Davis that she had arrived. Waving her through with specific directions, Kate found the white brick home at the end of the block. Parking the car on the street front, she walked up to the front door, finding it open.

"Come on in, Officer!" yelled Davis. "I'm finishing a call and will be with you in a few minutes."

Walking into the home, she took a seat on the large camel-brown couch. The place looked like it must have at least six thousand square feet, she thought. The house smelled of wealth, from the rich oak flooring to the original and reproduction paintings that hung from each wall. The seventy-inch flat screen TV with an adjacent small bookcase containing a library of movies seemed to represent the lowest-price furniture in the room.

"Good morning, Officer Heller. Sorry to keep you waiting," said Davis as he entered the room.

Getting up, Kate extended her hand. "Thank you for seeing me, Professor Davis. You have a very beautiful home."

"Thank you, it's a little big for one person, but being the senior entomologist for our school, I have to entertain a lot, plus I needed extra rooms for my experiments and pets."

"What kind of pets, professor? I didn't hear any dogs bark when I pulled up," remarked Kate.

Smiling, he said, "I'll show you before you leave, but first, what do I owe the pleasure of your visit, Officer Heller? Certainly you haven't changed your mind about the speeding ticket since you would have just sent me the summons, correct?"

Laughing a little, she said, "There is no ticket, Professor, although I'm certain that paying a little fine wouldn't be any problem considering that beautiful Claude Monet that you have hanging in this room. I take it his painting the 'Lady with the Parasol' is a reproduction, not an original?

"Just a simple reproduction, along with the Van Gogh located above the fireplace. I'm afraid the university doesn't pay quite that well to allow me to afford the original."

"I requested a little of your time today, Professor Davis, because of your knowledge about the brown recluse spider, which continues to puzzle me as part of my investigation into the cause of death of a young, healthy woman. As you may remember from what the papers had reported, her autopsy listed it as the cause of death. I just interviewed the physician who did the autopsy yesterday, and he maintains that his findings were correct, even though my initial review of the subject suggests otherwise."

"Impossible to highly unlikely," said Davis. "You see, as I may have mentioned when we first met under those unfortunate circumstances of my speeding, most doctors misdiagnose the bite. With regret, the physician family mistreats the bitten area because they simply can't tell what actually caused the bite. That is unless the arachnid or spider has been captured and brought in for someone like me to look at under a microscope. So in the end, they end up prescribing creams until finally, after a few weeks if they're lucky, the bite usually goes away. With regret, many doctors and their patients are not so lucky and pay a price for their ignorance or pride in not handling the situation more carefully. In the United States in the last ten years, there hasn't been a single death recorded by the brown recluse, although left untreated, the little fellow has admittedly caused several unnecessary amputations," said Davis.

"Why is there the necessity of an amputation, Professor?"

"Because, while not causing death in the traditional fashion, the venom is so powerful that the bite of a typical true brown recluse will result in necrosis, that is the death or decay of the skin, not the person. If not treated in time, a person could lose a limb or develop a wound that will take months to heal, but death is hardly possible. Did this event happen in this area, Officer Heller?" asked Davis.

"Yes, and just so you are aware for your records should you ever need to call me, it's Detective Heller now since we last met. The Funston police captain has decided to take a chance on promoting a woman to that position."

"And at the same time gave you the challenge of solving an open murder case?"

"Yes, but more than just a single murder case, Professor. Although I must limit the information that I can discuss with you, the case involves a high-profile pastor and this woman who were having an affair."

"Ah, yes, the pastor whose wife was murdered," commented Davis.

"That's correct, so as you can see, this is a very high-profile case, and both are mine to investigate and hopefully resolve. It's my belief that the death of the pastor's mistress by what was originally thought to be a brown recluse spider bite is the linkage to the death of the pastor's wife."

"You mean the connection to the pastor who I remember reading had convinced the jury of his innocence and, as the saying goes, beat the charges?"

"Would love to comment on that, but I better leave it alone," said Kate.

"Most spiders, Officer, are not dangerous, just scary for some people to look at. Take the well-known black widow spider. You'd have a better chance of finding one of those in the Michigan area than the brown recluse. I've heard of that lady appearing at your favorite food store arriving with a shipment of muskmelons. And if you happen to make that lady upset, the venom is 1.5 times stronger than your timber rattlesnake, and yet if bitten, most people will only get sick for a couple of days, not necessarily kill you. Still from 1965 to 1990 across the United States, they have killed about 35 people. What I'm trying to tell you, Officer, is that we must not get caught up in the stories that are spread around and deal only with the facts. Those tales spread by those that don't really know make for a good story, but they represent nothing more and do a disservice to the many hundreds of harmless spiders. To be a real killer, Detective, you have to be a Brazilian wandering spider or, as layman refer to it, as the banana spider. Although it's indigenous to the tropical and subtropical regions of most areas in South America, this bad boy is a real nomad and likes to travel the world, arriving in shipments of bananas, thus the more common name being banana spider. It's extremely dangerous, Detective Heller, with one bite sometimes proving fatal."

Kate, now thinking about what Davis was saying, asked, "So from your professional background, you feel that a person would have been unlikely to have ever died of a brown recluse bite, but on the other hand, it wouldn't necessarily rule out the possibility that the victim ran into another type of spider that you described?"

"Yes, but let's remember that in this country, while although most of us are unfamiliar with this pest, food stores handling bananas are always on the lookout for the banana spider, so the chances are slim that it would reach the home of your victim, if that's what you were thinking," said Davis.

"It's my nature, Professor, to find what others wouldn't know about or care about. In my business, somewhat like yours, we avoid allowing our resolve to erode by time, because it's the facts of the situation that make one a good policewoman, or as in your case at the top of your field. Is it possible to handle a dangerous spider and bring it into a person's home without it just finding its way there?"

"Yes, but you must be an expert or place your own life in harm's way. Those that are careful can accomplish the task of simple trans-portation. The greatest danger is in the release of the spider, especially the banana spider, because it's basically mean-spirited and will hunt you down just for fun. I must admit I've never encountered a case where any spider was used to kill another human being. It is an ingenious concept, though, I must say."

"Well, Professor Davis, my visit has produced some interesting things for me to think about. Much of our work turns out to be just a shot in the dark. But when you're trying to unravel a very compli-cated murder case, you need to rule out all possibilities. In this example, the medical autopsy suggested that the woman died of a brown recluse spider, while your professional experience supports my own feeling that lean away from this conclusion. Nevertheless, the criminal still is a few steps ahead of me, and his secret remains as quiet as the inside of a casket buried in the ground. You have been extremely helpful, Professor, and by my watch, I've overstayed your invitation, so I'll be on my way, and thank you once again for granting me this time."

As Kate got up to leave, Davis said, "Wait, Detective. Remember, I wanted to show you something earlier."

"Yes, something about your pets," said Kate.

"Follow me please," requested Davis as he walked down the hallway to the door that led down into the basement.

Following, Kate walked the eight steps that took her to the basement below, at which point Davis pointed to the two large ten-gallon tanks, which were placed against one of the far walls. Seeing no water in either tank, she was puzzled thinking that the professor had not filled what she at first had thought were fish tanks. Walking over to the tanks, she noted the peat moss on the bottom of the large floor tank with a small lizard moving slowly across the moss, apparently chasing a cricket.

"What am I looking for professor?" she asked.

"Watch behind the lizard, Detective," said Davis.

"Suddenly, she now saw it and jumped back, shocked at its ugliness. The spider was about five inches in length, maybe having a two-inch body, with scarlet red hairs covering its fangs. Before she could even form a question, it stood on its back legs while putting its front legs up in the air and began to sway its body from side to side. Looking up at the professor, she heard him whisper, "It's an act of intimidation designed to frighten its victim before its attacks. You see, the Brazilian wandering spider doesn't care about creating a spiderweb. It chooses, as I mentioned upstairs, to hunt its prey, and that's what they do all day as they wander the tropical areas they so love. Don't be frightened, Detective, because as you will note, I have a solid top cover for this pet, because they are dangerous beyond your imagination and should only be kept as a pet by someone who understands their habits. I keep one in each tank for my private study since the insurance rates to cover the liability exceeds the school's budget and they won't allow them. I just wanted to show you how they live outside of their natural environment, but we're ready now to go upstairs since there's no point in you having to watch the kill. Remember, though, that nature has its own way to balance life and death, and even the most deadly of God's creation must eat to live."

As they were walking upstairs, Kate paused and asked Davis if he had enough time to answer two more questions before she left.

"Certainly. One of the nice things about my work is that the schedule is my own, unless of course I have a lecture to give," said Davis. "A lot of people would love my gig. No daily requirements or reports to submit. I'm pretty much free to roam the entire campus each day unless I have a lecture to give. So what's your first question, Detective?"

"Professor, let's say that you were going to move that spider that you have downstairs and yet as trained as you are you still suffered a bite. What would you do under those circumstances?"

"I never take a chance, Detective. I have great respect for what can be the result of an error in judgment. You see, as a man, even escaping death does not mean that you have escaped the pain of the banana spider bite. The pain for a man is excruciating because it causes unfortunately a long-lasting painful erection. It is because of that scientists are now studying the composition of the venom as a potential use for helping men with sexual disorders. That's why I never take a chance," he said while reaching for the chain around his neck and pulling it out of his shirt.

"What's that?" asked Kate.

"This little container, Detective Heller, has the antidote for the banana spider. It was discovered by a Brazilian sanitary physician by the name of Carlos Chagas, a great scientist and bacteriologist, around 1934. If I were so bold as to offer you an opportunity that might help you find the individual who might have introduced the killer spider to your victim, I would suggest checking hospitals or infectious disease doctors for any recent request of this antidote. What's the other question, Detective Heller?" asked Davis.

"Where is it that I need to go to purchase this dangerous spider if that was going to be my pet of choice?" she asked.

"Why, to any exotic pet store that handles snakes, lizards, scorpions, and other arachnids. We live in a world, Officer, where extreme is the norm and norm is, well, boring. Good luck on finding what you're looking for, Officer. If you need my help on this subject in the future, don't hesitate to call me."

Shaking Davis's hand, Kate walked down the steps into her Honda and headed back to US 12 and the foot-high pile of papers and notes that awaited her on her kitchen table. She had scoured over the last two weeks' countless stories from the many newspapers on the deaths of Bergman's wife, along with that of the church organist. She has even managed to secure the six editions of the *Northern Beacon* of the Lutheran Church that covered the period of Bergman's difficulties. As she continued her drive home, she diverted off the main road and passed the outskirts of Loveland, an upscale residential area, which the locals referred to as their contribution to the president's 1 percent. Homes in Loveland rarely sold below three million. Kate had been there years ago with several girlfriends, all imagining what it would be like living among the rich and snobbish as they giggled their way around the town.

C H A P T E R   1 7

Pandora's Box

He was a lean five feet eleven inches tall and wore wire-rimmed glasses. His graying hair was clipped short on the side, but the full head of hair was impressive for his age, which was about sixty-two, guessed Bergman. Over the years, the requirement to attend these district president's meetings were not Paul Bergman's favorite way to spend a weekend, but Pastor Lance Schultz was the newly elected president of the Wisconsin region, so it was his first opportunity to kiss the ring of the new sheriff. And according to all reports, Schultz enjoyed his local power and was a hands-on president who liked to show up unexpectedly at local congregations. As Bergman watched him work the crowd of assembled pastors from all over the state, he could tell that Schultz basked in all the attention. Bergman studied the man with the walrus mustache as he tried to find the right moment to introduce himself to the president so that he could then slip out the door of the large banquet room and head back home. What was the mustache all about with men of authority? Well, it was highly unlikely that they could appear with the latest tattoos appearing above their collar, so Bergman imagined that this was their way to establish their self-importance. Bergman could hear in the distance Schultz telling some pastor that "God works for all good." He watched as the First's vice president of the region seemed to guide Schultz to particular pastors that headed up the largest congregations. Bergman smiled knowing how the game works since these congregations could be counted on to exceed the area's request for annual financial support that would move the Wisconsin district to the top of the money chart. His guess was these pastors were little different than the politicians in Washington, DC, with the same anticipated outcomes on their minds. "We promise to provide you with the local juice to make you look good, and you in turn help us get that divine call to Fort Lauderdale or Key West when the time comes." Bergman loved being a pastor, but he didn't enjoy the little governments within the Lutheran Church at this level. It was hard enough being an outcast pastor without being silently threatened by presidents who considered themselves part of the imperial council. Moving closer to the crowd of well-wishers, Bergman could hear some of the pastors cracking sly jokes that had something to do with how the vice president was dressed for this occasion.

"Can you believe the guy is actually wearing that neckwear, and what the heck is with the Italian-made trousers?" said one voice.

"Well, if you want to get ahead, you have to be noticed," said another.

As Bergman was about ten feet away from any unwanted visits, he felt a hand on his shoulder.

"Paul, it's good to see you. When was the last time? It must have been at the graduation in St. Louis?"

Bergman, glancing at the name tag, observed that it was AJ Winters, his old roommate. "AJ, it's good to see you," said Bergman.

"Good to see you also, friend. You're the pastor for Trinity Lutheran in Silver Valley, aren't you? I read about the transfer in the *Beacon* newsletter."

"Yeah, that's true, but what about you?" asked Bergman as he tried to change the subject, hoping that no other details had been mentioned.

Winters was about to answer when suddenly the tanned hand of the Reverend Lance Schultz reached out and said, "Good to meet you in person, Pastor Winter. I've heard nothing but good things about you. Are you still studying for your doctorate, or did our First vice president provide me with the wrong information?"

"I'm about to finish it, Pastor Schultz, and thank you for asking. My doctorate is based on apologetics and how ignoring it can lead to a defenseless Christianity."

"Well, when you complete it, please send me an update as there are a lot of churches that are waiting for a man like you."

As Schultz started to walk away, he suddenly turned and faced Bergman. "You're the pastor from Silver Valley, aren't you?"

Wondering how the area president knew that, Bergman answered, "Yes, I'm Pastor Paul Bergman, and it's a pleasure to meet you, Pastor Schultz."

"That's a solid congregation, Pastor Bergman. I've met your chairman, Jack Koehler, and his head elder, Alan Ogden, several times. Dr. Ogden is a special friend of mine from way back when I had to travel to Funston on a matter related to Hanson's disease, something that I never heard of. Ogden knew right away that my family doctor had misdiagnosed the problem. You are a fortunate man to have been given a divine call to that Congregation, so do your best," said Schultz while moving further into the crowd.

"Wow, what was that all about? He didn't even give you a chance to talk. The guy was not what one considers warm and friendly to you, or was it just my imagination?" said AJ.

"Don't read too much into it, AJ. After all, I wouldn't have gotten the transfer to Silver Valley without his approval. Local presidents always have the last word on who gets what call opportunity to a congregation, despite the feeling that the local church has the total say in the call process. We both know the drill, partner. My former congregation was a gold card contributor to the local district, and they willingly moved me along, so it's wink, wink to the new church. If they wouldn't have been happy with me, I would have been treated like someone who committed suicide and buried alongside the fence in Funston's cemetery."

"You mean your call would have been denied?"

"They wouldn't have said it that way. They just kill you with silence while making certain that you never are put on a call list. Eventually you get the picture and realize that it's all over. Meanwhile, they take care of their buddies, place the new graduating kids in churches that would prefer to have your experience, and you're left with the last church you'll ever have or start considering changing your occupation. Anyway, AJ, it was nice seeing you again, but I've got to get home early tonight. Besides, what's left other than the area bigwigs patting themselves on their back? It's the same old thing," said Bergman. "I've seen this movie before. Keep in touch, and if you got the time, stop in and we'll talk about the good old days."

As he walked to the door, Bergman glanced over his shoulder and observed the vice president approaching the lectern and adjusting the mic.

"Everybody having a good time?" came tonight came the voice of the vice president as Bergman cleared the room and passed the front desk.

"It's my great pleasure to introduce your president of the Wisconsin region," the VP continued as Bergman walked out into the parking lot. Entering his car, he stared the engine and followed the winding driveway out to the main road that connected to the main highway.

CHAPTER 18

The Chairman Investigates

Jack Koehler sat in his chair somewhat troubled about the parsonage report that had been submitted by Elmer and Ed. He wasn't sure exactly what the reasons for his concerns were, but it was obvious the men were holding something back. Both had stated that the parsonage was in excellent shape, along with the attached building that served both as a storage area and living quarters. The report had not covered the accidental shooting of the car's window that Elmer reported verbally to him and Alan, but the rest of the report seemed complete. The rogue hunter shooting made no sense to Jack since everyone in the area had a clear understanding that long guns were not to be used to hunt deer that close to town. No, something just didn't add up, especially the part about Ed asking for his peaceful release from the church soon after the incident. That was more than strange. Jack knew that Ed had been a member for over forty-five years and had received his baptism at the church and later had married his high school sweetheart here. Jack knew from experience that people like Ed just didn't just disappear from the church in which they had developed long friendships with, but from all accounts, that's just what has happened. Ed had dropped off his letter resigning his membership with the church secretary and just said that he and his wife were planning on going to Florida. Later when the church secretary had attempted to call Ed's house for the additional information to update his request for the transfer, she had found that his phone number had a message on it indicating they were not available. When Jack had learned about the resignation, he immediately had called Elmer to see if he could shed any light on what might be troubling Ed. During the phone conversation, Jack could tell that Elmer was uncomfortable discussing the subject, so he had asked him if it was possible to meet him and Alan Ogden at the church so that they could talk about the visit a little more. Elmer had thought that it was a good idea and mentioned that he and Alan were already planning on meeting over the same thing. Later when Jack pulled up to the church, he noted that both Elmer's and Alan's cars were already there, obviously well in advance of his arrival. Walking up the steps of the church, Jack opened the door and headed to the main conference room, where he could hear the voices of Alan and Elmer already talking about Ed.

"I think that Jack needs to be told everything," he heard Alan say to Elmer as he entered the room.

Looking up, Alan said, "Evening, boss. Would you like some coffee? Elmer brought in a container of Dunkin Donuts best coffee?

"Thanks," he said, picking up a stray cup from the table and pouring himself a cup.

"Thanks for coming in on such short notice, fellows. I know that Dr. Ogden had nothing to do but go over his portfolio of investments tonight, but you, Elmer, have to be really disappointed having missed the latest rerun of *Law and Order*."

"No problem. My son tapes all the past shows for me anyway," Elmer said laughing. "Besides, while we were waiting for you, Dr. Alan gave me a good tip on the Facebook stock. Problem is, I have no friends that I want to invite into my circle, so I'm not even on Facebook. Most of them are dead now anyway," he said laughing. "You, on the other hand, being the president of this growing mega congregation probably brought us together today to discuss the latest idea of how we can reach those lost souls who fail to come to church on Sunday through introducing the wonders of Facebook."

"You are a laugh a minute," said Jack, "but the truth of the matter is, I asked you to come in because we have a problem, or at least I think that we do." Sitting down at the conference table, Jack explained the concern that he had about Ed suddenly leaving the church without any real explanation. "Do you have any idea what this is all about, Elmer? You were the last person that he spent any time with him while doing the parsonage inspection, and then of course there was that bad experience with your car window being shot out."

"Ed is an unusual guy, Jack," said Elmer. "He always seemed to be somewhat edgy to me long before the car incident. No one can ever question his devotion to his church, but even while serving in church, when we would ask him to just pass the collection plate, he was always a basket case. We were lucky to get him on the trustee board, which was the first responsibility he accepted in over fifteen years. Still I found him very helpful on the parsonage inspection, but I will admit he was not the same after the car window blew out from that rifle shot. He was cut by the glass, you know, and required some stitches. I took him home right after they were through with him at the clinic, but he started to change right after that experience."

"Maybe it had something to do with things that you left out of the report," said Jack. "Sorry, Elmer, but I did overhear Alan suggesting to you that I needed to know everything about that trip to the parsonage. It could be important, guys, so let it all out, please."

"Ed was fine during the inspection, Jack, until we accidently came upon Pastor Bergman's computer, and he noted the unusual screen saver that was full of spider images. Ed was concerned that I would include what we found on the pastor's computer on the trustee report. This seemed to make him feel real uncomfortable, and he had commented that he didn't want to open up Pandora's box regarding certain aspects of pastor's personal life.

"I'm a firm believer in that pastors need to be allowed to enjoy their own particular interests just like you and I. Too often members of a congregation want to control their pastors' movements and lives twenty-four hours a day. Admittedly, there were other personal things that we also left out in the report, because while inspecting the property and the house was one thing, but his lifestyle was something else altogether," said Elmer.

"Pardon my lack of history, but would one of you tell me what is meant by opening up Pandora's box?"

"It's taken from Greek mythology," answered Alan. "Pandora was the female version of our Adam, and she was instructed never to open the box given to her. In any event, in Greek mythology, it said that she couldn't resist the urge to find out what was inside and opened the box and released into the world everything that was evil. The one remaining item that didn't escape was hope. In today's meaning, to open Pandora's box means to create evil that cannot be undone. It's sort of like trying to get the toothpaste back into the tube."

"So you think that what really got to Ed was the inspection done on the parsonage more than having a bullet almost kill him?" asked Jack.

"Just my guess," said Elmer, "but it could be something more, and by us doing what we were asked to do, Ed might have felt that the box was opened."

"If your guess is correct, Elmer, that would mean to me that Ed was more concerned about what the pastor might do to him in the future than about the bullet that just missed him," said Jack.

"Well, the man does have enough weapons to arm a small platoon of soldiers," said Elmer.

"What do you mean by that?" asked Jack.

"See what I mean," said Elmer. "If I answer that question and had put it in the report, we could be accused of crossing the line and invading his personal rights to own firearms. Knowledge of his interest in that area could even affect his relationship with our members."

"Elmer is right on that account, Jack," said Alan. "We have to be very careful on this subject or open up the door for the area president to come down hard on our little church."

"There is absolutely nothing in his call documents that says anything about his owning firearms. If he were the pastor of a far Western state such as North Dakota or Montana, he would almost be expected to own at least a shotgun and a rifle."

"What about twenty-two firearms, maybe fifty or more," asked Elmer.

"What did you say?" asked Jack.

"What if he owned five shotguns, eight rifles, and nine hand-guns, plus an unknown amount of others?"

"You must be kidding, Elmer."

"The man owns, in addition to a gun cabinet, a fortified personal gun organizer. It's the ultimate vault organizer that can rotate 360 degrees for easy access to any gun. Unlike the gun cabinet, which has a simple padlock, the vault organizer couldn't be opened except by Navy SEALs since it has machine fail-safe, turning handles like a small safe. This I think scared Ed. The truth is, he could have anything in there, and probably has, but in the end, it's his little secret."

"Still makes no difference," said Alan, "but it does cause one to wonder why all the firepower."

"Is there anything else that was left off the report that we should discuss, Elmer? Anything that might help us understand what caused Ed problems? You said he might fear Bergman. Why?"

"That I don't know, but I believe that he'd seen something on the pastor's computer that spooked him. He was sitting at the pastor's desk when I walked into the room and saw him looking at the computer. I asked him what he was looking at, and he said nothing important. I knew that he was lying, but I let it go. He definitely had learned something, but he kept it to himself. I originally thought that it might have had something to do with the picture we found on his desk. It was another strange thing we discovered in that Bergman only had one picture of anybody in the parsonage, and we weren't certain who it was. It was a picture of a woman around maybe twenty-five to thirty-two years old playing an organ. The interesting thing about it to me was that the woman looked to be the same woman that appears in a painting that he has hanging in the shed of a Victorian lady with a child. Darn spooky, but again, I didn't say anything about the connection to Ed."

"Well, a lot is going on with our pastor as he must have caught the interest of Pastor Lance Schultz also," said Jack.

"Lance Schultz, the regional president of the Wisconsin region?" asked Alan.

"That's the one. The new district president who replaced Pastor Conrad Wilson, the one who approved the transfer of our current

Paul Bergman. He called the church office and indicated that he knew you from the past. It appears that he's going to be the featured speaker at what is called the Council of Presidents meeting here in Michigan next month. Wants to stop by and visit us after he clears it, of course, with our local guy."

"I had him as a patient some time back, but it turned out only to be a one-time visit because the original diagnosis was wrong. He went home happy," offered Alan. "Did he say what was on his mind?"

"No, but I'm willing to bet it has something to do with Pastor Bergman since he did volunteer that he met him recently at a Wisconsin convention for pastors. Well, Elmer, it would seem that your report contained the information that our voters needed, so it doesn't make any sense to speculate on what is not our business," said Jack. "Let's leave everything alone at this point. At the same time, Alan, see what you or your elders can do to help us track down where Ed may have gone. We certainly do need to talk to him no matter where he wishes to go. I can't believe that he hasn't shared any information with someone in this church. I would feel much better knowing that he is all right."

"If this meeting is over, I think that I can still get in nine holes of golf," said Elmer.

"Meeting is adjourned, fellows," said Jack. "Elmer, I just happen to have clubs in my car, so if you want a partner, I'll join you," said Jack. "Alan, how about you?"

"I'll pass, guys, and spend some time with my bride. Betty says my patients see more of me than she does. She's been talking about cancelling her Victoria Secret account if I continue avoiding her."

CHAPTER 19

The Date

Curtis woke up at 6:00 a.m. and walked to the guest room and looked out the window facing the backyard. The grackles were attacking his birdfeeder, along with a few cardinals and English sparrows, all attempting to compete with one another for the seed that he had put out the night before. Curtis enjoyed the yard pets that often included a visit by an assortment of squirrels and on rare occasions even a few mallards looking for corn. He missed having a dog, but with his Delta schedule, he had no one to care for the animal when he was gone. Glancing at his watch, he noted that he had plenty of time before he was to meet Kate at the Funston Airport terminal. He was too nervous to get back to sleep, so he went into the bathroom to get ready for what he considered the most important meeting of his life. This was a woman that he clearly felt attracted to and had built up high expectations that she would feel the same way about him. Under normal circumstances, Curtis wouldn't have been so anxious about dating a woman, because the truth was the airline business was full of attractive women that he had met over the years. When you wear an airline uniform with four gold stripes on the shoulder and a hat with the scrambled eggs on the bill, it's a ready-made advertisement for women seeking companionship. It didn't hurt that the news media often romanticized the job by pointing out the $250,000 annual salary paid to those that fly the wide-body aircraft. But aside from the benefits, Curtis, to the dismay of his parents and self-made matchmakers, had not found that special woman. He had always felt that his patience would find him the one woman that he would spend his life with, but until Kate had showed up unexpectedly, none had captured his heart as this woman had. And why was that? he pondered. It was obvious that she was drop-dead gorgeous with a figure that challenged the heart of any man over the age of eighteen, but there was something else since he had met flight attendants that could make the cover of the monthly *Playboy* magazine. No, Officer Heller carried that special confidence that was as rare as the Hope diamond, and with her beauty, it was the glue to the whole package.

Curtis started in the mirror at his half-shaved face, observing the first signs of gray hair now appearing on his sideburns. Well, it happened to men in their middle thirties. It wasn't like his cabinet was full of blue Viagra pills. Still, nothing about his above-average looks or personal history was today enough to convince him that Kate would find him a better prospect then possibly the many doctors, lawyers, and the business executives that undoubtedly have hit on her over the years. He was tall, sure, with a full head of brown hair, a straight nose, and clear blue eyes. He had been an above-average athlete who was good enough to be the best hockey player on his championship team, but his athletic skills had never found an interested scout. Certainly he had done well enough in college to be given the opportunity to fly for the second largest airline in the world, but then again Kate had probably had her choice of many professionals that would be home more often than a guy flying around the world for his living. Until today, he had been a fairly calm and confident individual, but she had changed all that. And then there was again Molly, the sweetheart waitress who had cautioned him about Kate's reluctance to date, but with no real reason why.

Well, at least that part Molly got wrong since the woman had agreed to see him today. Curtis finished shaving and reached for the hanger that held his best casual clothes. Before going downstairs, he pulled the shade aside and gazed at his new Cessna parked at the end of his five-acre property. The adjacent farmer, Gifford Matthews, a private pilot himself, had created over the years a paved N/S double-paved runway that he used and made available to Curtis for a small fee, which he refused to accept. Gifford and Curtis had become more than friends since meeting, so in order to satisfy the relationship of free access to the use of the runway, Curtis had convinced Gifford to accept the free buddy passes on Delta Air Lines that were part of the employment package at Delta. The sky appeared clear, and the colors looked even more intense from the window in the strong morning sunlight. Curtis turned away from the window and headed down to the kitchen. He had no appetite but knew he had to eat. He would need all his energy when he met Kate this morning. Fixing himself a bowl of Cheerios and toast, he managed to eat half his bowl of cereal before he got up from the table and grabbed his overnight bag, locked the door, and walked out the kitchen door to his plane. Walking around the aircraft in his typical preflight checking routine, he found everything to his satisfaction. "Well, big guy, showtime for better or worse," he said to himself as he climbed aboard his aircraft, started the engine, and taxied over to the runway.

It had been an uneventful trip. All good pilots that live to retire someday all have a single thing in common with one another, he thought. It was the little things that they notice first. Birds in the airspace that shouldn't be there. A small plane overlooked, and probably one who didn't file a flight plan. A burned-out bulb on the console that hadn't been replaced. None of that mattered today as Curtis was able to fly under visual flight rules the entire trip without a cloud in sight.

The short flight was coming to an end as Curtis could visually see the long wide strip of asphalt before him. Even at fifteen miles out, he could see the hangar to his right, with the words Wally Funston Airport painted in billboard-size letters along the side. He recognized it from his map as the locator for Funston's runway 14, facing to the Northwest. Looking down, he noticed a muddy parking lot full of cars adjacent to a large hall. Smiling, he watched as a bride leaning on the window of a car was talking to another couple inside. She looked up and waved at his aircraft.

Turning away, he now concentrated on his final approach to Funston's airport as he listened to the ATC say, "Clear to land, Skyhawk 414, winds SE at 12-14, use R14."

"Roger that," said Curtis as he lined up the aircraft and dipped the nose to begin his descent. The 180-horsepower engine with the Garmin-glass cockpit was Curtis's pride and joy and was reported to be the safest Cessna ever built. Maybe he could convince Kate and Channing to take a ride in his $265,000 investment, he thought as he lowered the wheels in preparation for the landing. Seconds later he heard the familiar slap of the wheels on the asphalt runway, using up about 1,600 feet before he turned and exited onto the pathway that would lead him to the parking area, set aside for business travel. Having reached the designated area, he shut the engine down and was met by one of the hangar's mechanics.

"Hey, buddy, we haven't seen this model Cessna Skyhawks before."

"It's a 2014. Just got it a little over three months ago," said Curtis.

"Name's Mason," said the mechanic. "We'll look it over for you and top it off so it's ready to go for you when you come back to leave. We'll have the bill ready, so all you have to do is swipe your card and you'll be ready to go."

"That's fine, Mason. I'll probably leave tomorrow afternoon, so there's no rush," said Curtis. Walking over to the storage compartment, Curtis grabbed his small overnight suitcase and headed to the waiting area. Inside the small terminal, waiting for him was Kate with a big smile.

"That's quite a piece of transportation that you used to come calling in. Do you do this that often to impress your lady friends?" she teased.

"You're the first, and with any amount of luck on my side, you will be the, well, hopefully, you know what I mean."

"I do, Curtis, but we have to do something about that redness in your face every time you talk to me."

"It only happens when I'm trying to avoid having you shoot me for saying another stupid thing."

"Well, don't worry so much, Curtis. I never shoot on the first date," she said, laughing. "Let's get in my car. I want you to meet my bodyguard before we begin the day," she said, giving Curtis a soft kiss on the lips. "That's for the beautiful flowers," she said as they walked to her car and got in. As she entered the drive that connected to the main highway, Kate said, "That looks like a mighty expensive form of transportation we left back there."

"It is, but you have to remember it's like buying a car. You trade in the old model for a new one so that in the end the price is not as brutal as one might think. It's the third plane that I've owned since working for Delta," said Curtis.

"What's the flight range on your Cessna?" she asked.

"This model's range is about 650 miles. In layman's terms, it costs about 97 cents a minute to operate, but what the heck, flying is my life. Speaking of life, how are you doing on your investigation into the brown recluse spider mystery and the two cold cases?"

"It could be going better, but these things take time since there are so many pieces to the puzzle. Everyone has a story to tell, and you have to listen to those first before anything really happens. Anyway, I rather talk about you and I today and let work wait until another time since today is special to us, right?"

"You are right, and I do want to talk about us," said Curtis.

"Well, we're about home," said Kate as she turned onto Monarch Drive and pointed to the white-and-black townhouse.

"You live close to your police station?" asked Curtis.

"About five miles away, but remember, Funston is a small town," she said. Pulling up onto the driveway of the townhouse, Kate remarked, "Here's my castle, Curtis. Let's go in and meet the man of the house." Walking up to the house, she unlocked the door and told Curtis to walk in first and not be afraid.

Looking somewhat hesitant, Curtis said, "Are you certain that the man of the house is ready to meet another guy?"

"Don't worry, he's in my bedroom, waiting for my command. I've trained him well, and he listens, so just relax. He wouldn't hurt anyone unless he hears the right word from me," said Kate. "Why don't we just walk in and sit on the couch, and I'll call him." Curtis sat down with Kate seated about five feet away from him. "Channing, come now," said Kate.

Curtis heard what appeared to be Channing jumping off the bed onto the floor. Shortly he came into the room walking ever so carefully and gazing at Curtis like a hunter evaluating the worth of the deer he was stalking. The dog looked momentarily at Kate, as if waiting for her command, then turned back to Curtis. Kate patted the open space between her and Curtis, at which point Channing jumped unto the couch and put his head on her lap. Reaching over the dog, Kate touched Curtis's leg while looking at Channing and said, "Good man, Channing, good man." The dog, hearing the command, got up and ran back to the bedroom, leaving Kate and Curtis once again alone in the living room.

"That is one beautiful Doberman. He must be close to one hundred pounds," said Curtis.

"He's actually ninety-seven pounds, and he will be full grown at one year, which he'll turn in about a month."

"Why did you name him Channing?" asked Curtis.

"The name comes from old English and French origin. It means 'young wolf,'" she explained. "The name just felt charming to me and gave him his own personal moniker rather than the standard dog names like Buster, Jack, or Pepper."

"I noticed that Channing hasn't been docked and still has his tail and natural ears," commented Curtis.

"Yes, I didn't have the heart to put him through the process. In my opinion, doing that is silly anyway since the only real reason they did it in the beginning was so that the tail couldn't get in the way of a working dog. By the way, I'm impressed that you knew the term *docked* since most people aren't familiar with it."

"I've owned a lot of animals Kate, especially when I was younger. Now that I'm flying, I don't have any pets because I can be gone for a week at a time. I never was a fan of the docked look, so none of my animals had to lose their tail or for that matter needed to worry about their ears being cropped."

"Say, you know a lot about dogs, Curtis," said Kate.

"As I said, they were a big part of my life when I was younger and actually would be today if I were home more. You've got a good one, Kate, since the pinscher is considered by most to be highly intelligent, alert, and loyal to their owner, plus a natural protector of its master or mistress. Long ago when I was dog shopping, I actually considered getting myself a Doberman but backed away because they couldn't find the fawn color like you have. The kennel had a number of black ones, one or two red ones, but no fawns. Let's change the subject for a moment before we look the town over and have lunch. How's the work going at the station? I don't mean your casework, but rather being accepted as that first female detective?

"As you have already guessed, police work is the easiest part of the problem. Being the new girl on the block who was just been promoted to detective is the real challenge and requires special handling of hurt male egos. As you know, being a police officer has for years been dominated by men, so it requires patience in bringing them around to acceptance of a female. But it is getting better than what it started out to be."

"It has been the same, Kate, in the airline business. To this day, we still have men and woman who will demand to change their ticket if they see that the captain happens to be a woman."

"Will the airlines do that?" asked Kate.

"In most cases the problem is solved by the simple fact that most airline tickets cannot just be changed at will because of the fact the customers have gotten a low fare based on the conditions of that ticket. You'd be surprised at how many people forget their prejudices when you want another $125 to change the ticket in order that they can fly on another flight."

"What is your personal feeling," she asked.

"Everything comes down to experience with me. Remember that a typical airliner captain is transporting around 155 passengers. Remember also that the majority of airline pilots with the most experience is a result of their time in the military, which most women don't have. That's probably the reason why Northwest originally hired me. A woman applicant wouldn't have the luxury of that type of background, so if she's hired, she's had to past extensive qualification requirements exceeding that of her male counterpart. In my case, I've found women pilots most competent and welcome them in the cockpit. The guys that you work with will eventually recognize that she didn't get the job just because of a pretty face. Those that don't will find themselves on the outside looking in. Of course I may be a little prejudiced being that my heart is pounding in anticipation of you sitting across the table from me shortly, but that's my answer and I'm sticking to it."

"You're doing very well, Curtis, so keep that playbook on the same page." Kate smiled.

"You mentioned when we were driving over here that the cold cases involving the pastor and the organist have been moving slowly. Without spending too much time on the subject, is that only because of the time it takes to break down each of the stories from the participants, or is internal politics slowing the process? You know, not wanting another police officer in particular one who is a female playing in their sandbox and solving the case?"

"Both, actually, because as I'm certain that you can imagine, not everyone wants to tell a police officer the truth for different reasons, inside and outside of the investigation. Everyone has secrets that they want to hide to protect the original investigator, or in many cases, people just don't trust the police. You know right or wrong the public doesn't view us in the same way as that fireman holding up his boot at the intersection asking for a donation. Police are pictured as the one who gives you the boot and spends his day at Dunkin Donuts waiting for their free double chocolate. I've interviewed several people in the last two weeks and have made some headway, but the key to the safe hasn't been found, Curtis. It will come with time."

"Maybe you've found the correct key, just not the right lock," offered Curtis. "My guess is that you'll soon find what you're looking for, Kate. Just remember that patience is the element of success. It also doesn't hurt to remember the words of the most extraordinary president of the United States, James A. Garfield. He once said, 'If a man murders you without provocation, your soul bears no burden of the wrong, but all the angels of the universe will weep for the misguided man who committed the murder.'"

"That means what, Curtis?

"It means that life is not always fair and that you should not be overly hard on yourself, because in the end some angel is helping you look for the lock. You don't walk alone, Kate."

"Maybe that angel could help me with Dr. AJ Patel, the physician that did the autopsy and is steadfast in his belief that a brown recluse spider was the cause of the organist's death. He refuses to consider otherwise. Not only does he object to the findings of my investigation and research, but dismisses the opinion of a noted entomologist that believes that the doctor's opinion and results most likely were misdiagnosed."

"Maybe he can't change his opinion because you're a woman, not because you're wrong, Kate."

"What does my being a woman have to do with him not considering the obvious?"

"You must remember that the India culture, particular the republic in certain parts of India, has strong male domination, where women are expected to be subservient to their men. You may have run into a situation where the doctor just couldn't deal with a woman challenging his authority. Should you have to deal with him in the future, sometimes by bringing a male partner with you might break the ice. One thing is certain, you can't change the culture."

The frustrations clearly beginning to set in, Kate moved away from the subject. "Let's talk about us, Curtis. How long does your schedule allow you to stay?"

"Well, I was hoping that we could go sightseeing first, then have dinner, spend some time talking for a while, and then I'll bring you back home and, depending how late it turns out to be, either get myself a motel or fly back tonight," said Curtis.

"You can't fly at night, Curtis."

Laughing, Curtis said, "That's what I do, dear. I fly for a living day and night, remember?"

With a faint look of hurt on her face, she said, "Are you making fun of me, Curtis? I know that you fly for a living, it's just natural to worry. Is the airport open all night to accommodate you guys who go calling on a lady friend?"

Sheepishly Curtis answered, "The Funston Airport is open all night, while the runway in Lift Bridge is privately owned and adjacent to a cornfield near my house. It's owned by a farmer friend of mine who lets me use it. We've installed very good lighting all around the field, and unless prior arrangements have been made, we generally are the only two people who ever use it."

"I'm not sure I want to learn any more about this, Curtis. Let's make the best use of our time. Give me fifteen minutes, and we can be on our way. There's water and pop in the refrigerator in the kitchen. Don't be alarmed if Channing visits you because he knows that the refrigerator door usually means some food for him. There's usually some extra lunch meat in the front for him if he comes calling. Make yourself at home. I'll be done shortly."

The Decision

When she walked into the office and saw the blinking red light on her phone, Laura somehow knew this was going to be a difficult day. Pressing the button, she heard the sound of the person hanging up. Well, she thought, maybe it won't be as bad as she had imagined. Reaching for a coffee filter, she started to prepare the morning coffee when the phone rang again.

"Hello, this is Laura."

"Laura, my name is Betty Ogden. You don't know me, but I belong to a sister Lutheran church in Silver Valley, Wisconsin. I happen to be attending a business convention in your area and hoped to stop by and say hello. It just so happens that your former pastor is now our shepherd here in Silver Valley, and I just wanted to leave a little something for his wife and daughter, who I understand are still members of your congregation until they wrap things up and join the pastor here. I was wondering if I could leave the items with you since we don't have their current home address."

Laura, confused about why Betty would not be aware that Mrs. Bergman had passed away, paused for a moment trying to think how best to answer Betty's question.

"Are you still there?" asked Betty.

"Yes, sorry about that. It's still early in the morning. When do you expect to be in the area?" asked Laura.

"Sometime after 3:00 p.m. if that's all right with you, Laura? Is the church office still open at that time? If not, I'll be able to drop the items off tomorrow."

"Yes, that will be fine, Betty. We don't close the doors here until five. I'm looking forward to meeting you," said Laura. "When you get here, just buzz me at the front door, and I will come down for you."

"That will be fine. Have a great day, Betty, and I'll see you a little later today," she said as she hung up.

"Good god," thought Laura. "The poor woman doesn't even have a clue that the Bergman woman is dead or that the daughter has left the area and is married. What in the hell has Bergman told those poor folks, or better yet, what hasn't he told them? And of course to make makers even worse, Christmas is out for the entire week. This is definitely is about to turn out to be a shitty day." Sitting back in her chair, she thought back to the time that this all started. It had been a time when she should have made better decisions and told Christmas everything rather than to try and handle it by herself.

Laura had been so certain that she could handle it. Although the pieces had fit together so perfectly, she still chose to close her eyes about Bergman's affair with the church organist. Had it been because of fearing Bergman or just poor judgment? She knew at the time it was wrong to allow it to continue and that something needed to be done and that she needed to talk to someone.

But instead she had elected to deal with the problem as if Berman was just going through a mid-life crisis. Thinking back, it was just a matter of fate, she later reasoned. If only she wouldn't have been so damn dedicated and had not returned to her church office that night to finish the Sunday bulletin, she wouldn't be part of this mess today. Even her husband had complained that she was working too hard and had encouraged her to stay home that night. But she had ignored his advice. Returning to that dreaded night, she remembered walking into her church office and seeing that the pastor's office light was on, but that he was nowhere in sight. Concerned and deciding to make sure everything was all right, she had walked down the hallway and entered the darkness of the unoccupied sanctuary looking for him. At the time, she had been puzzled by seeing that the church candles were lit. It didn't make any sense to her, but not seeing him, she was turning to walk back out of the church sanctuary when the noises from the balcony made her turn and glance up toward the organ area.

Seeing no one but hearing the continued noises that sounded much like two people laughing, Laura had walked over to the balcony steps that would take her up to the organ loft area. As she was deciding if she should walk up the stairs, she had heard a female voice, "Ohhhh, ohhhh," as if almost pleading. As Laura began her first steps that would take her to the upper level of the church's balcony, the sounds continued, and now somewhat afraid, Laura stopped. As she listened for a while, there were no more noise, so Laura continued her climb up to the last two steps of the stairs. Now able to look over the top of the landing toward the organ area, she was still unable to see what was causing all the noise. As she reached the last step, her eyes had adjusted to the darkness, and once again she looked toward the area where the organ would be located and felt her cheeks grow hot as she suddenly seen the naked back of Bergman bending over kissing the woman's breasts as the woman was moving beneath him. Laura knew that she would never forget his passionate words that he was uttering loudly to the woman.

"We're going to make love tonight, Gayle, until all the candles burn down. Until I have you completely. Don't hold back, give yourself to me," was the passionate command coming from the strange sounding voice of Paul Bergman.

"This can't be," reasoned Laura. She must be mistaken and seeing something or someone else, not the pastor of her church with the sanctuary but a few feet below. This was a place of refuge and protection, not to be used in this way. What was going on?

Then the woman was saying, "Oh, Paul, I want what you want now. Let me feel all of you." The heated encouragement continued from the woman crying loudly and almost demanding, "You must be mine tonight. I want us to have a child together, here in God's house." He seemed to be kissing her frantically now with the woman giving off the first sign of pleasure, pleading, "Don't stop now, don't stop now. Oh god, oh god."

Laura, in seeing and hearing these words of passion, took a deep breath and started backing down the stairs one at a time until she reached the last step, where she turned and walked back toward the door exiting the church body. Stopping, still trying to come to grips with what was going on that night, Laura remembered glancing one more time toward the balcony as she heard the woman screaming, "Now, yes, now, Paul, pull me closer, please, for God's sake, don't stop." Gathering herself, Laura had turned and started to walk away when she knocked over a metal wastebasket that the cleaning crew had forgotten to put away. She remembered the fear that ran through her body hoping that in their passion they had not heard. It was not to be.

"Who is there?" Bergman yelled as Laura continued her retreat, now running to her secretarial office. She then had grabbed her purse, shut off her lights, and ran down the steps of the church to her car. At the time, she was hoping that her escape was not seen by anyone, but had been unaware that Bergman had watched her from the balcony window as she had pull away from the church grounds. She had arrived home crying and discussed the incident with her husband, who suggested that she bring the matter to the attention of the church president. He had told her that he would join her in any discussion if she needed him but had also cautioned her that it could become one person's work against another. Weighing the situation as carefully as she could, Laura had decided to first have a discussion with the pastor in hopes that he would repent and appreciate her actions to help him avoid this embarrassment to the congregation and possibly his family. But Laura continued to wonder about who was the woman that she had seen in the balcony.

Unable to sleep, Laura had gotten up early the next morning and had arrived at her church two hours before the normal arrival of the pastor. Opening the back door of the building, she then walked through the basement directly to the steps that would bring her into the rear of the church and the stairs leading up to the balcony where she had witnessed Bergman and the woman together. Walking the six steps, she reached the top and walked directly to the organ area where she had seen the couple engaged in lovemaking. Now noticing to the right of the organ was a closet for the choir with its door half open and the light on, Laura then pulled the sliding door open, all the way discovering a purse and cell phone that had been left on the top shelf. Her guess was that the woman had probably left the items there before their lovemaking began and during the period that they had feared being discovered had rushed away, forgetting both the purse and cell phone.

Reaching for the purse, she opened it and discovered to her horror that it belonged to Gayle Browning, the church organist. Laura had only met Browning on one or two occasions but remembered that she played beautifully and looked even better. Still she doubted that Browning could be the woman that Bergman was involved with since she was much younger than the pastor by at least fifteen years and that she had never seen them together. Reaching to put the purse back up, she heard the unmistakable sound of the cell phone on the shelf alerting its owner that it was receiving a message. Laura, now unable to contain her curiosity, removed the cell phone from the shelf and lifted the flip-top cover noting that the caller identifier indicated that it was Bergman's cell phone number. Pressing the menu button on the phone, it took her to the section called My Images. As she pressed the button, Laura almost dropped the phone when a serious of pictures came up with Bergman clearly making love to the organist Browning in various positions. How in the hell had she done that without him knowing it wondered Laura, or did he know it and that these were just their private keepsakes?

Replacing the phone, she then walked back down the steps to the basement and quietly left the church and back to her car. Shaking from what she had learned, she then drove to a local McDonald's restaurant, sat down, and waited until it was her normal time to arrive at work. When she had finally returned to the church, there had been a phone message indicating that Bergman would not be in that day as he was at a circuit meeting. Relieved, she decided that upon his return that she would discuss this matter with him. She knew that this would not be easy since it was obvious that Bergman would be nervous and worried about his future with the church and his ministry. Again she had been wrong, seriously wrong about the man whom she had now become to fear. It would be much later today that she would be meeting with a stranger who would be asking questions about things that she would prefer forgetting. Those things that she now knew were best left alone. What could she tell her about the pastor's former wife that would not usher her into the dark world of a man that she had hoped was out of her life forever? Laura walked around the office staring at the clock and practicing in her mind the meeting that would soon come. How would she begin? "'I'm going to tell you something I haven't told anyone else. Can you keep a secret?' No, maybe I'll begin like this. 'I don't know what happened. I guess it's my fault that I didn't communicate with your church about how sorry we were to learn about etc., etc."

Betty had found the church without any difficulty and parked her car directly across the street from the front entrance of the old brick structure. Getting out her car, she looked across the street and admired the two large stained glass windows, which pictured Jesus wearing the crown of thorns. The remainder of the front of the church was covered with ivy vines that seemed to reach almost the top of the bell tower. As she crossed the street, she noticed that at the top of the front of the church, it had a stone plaque that indicated the year of its construction, 1889. Holding in her two hands was the large fruit basket for the secretary and two different types of Fanny Mae boxes of candy for Bergman's wife and daughter. Betty had been reminded several times to low-key her visit to the church by Jack and Alan since they had insisted that the local district presidents of the Lutheran Church frowned upon asking any questions related to any pastor's previous service at congregations other than their own. Although Betty considered this foolish, she had given her word to both the men that her visit would be nothing more than an attempt to let the Bergman family know that the congregation was looking forward to their arrival in Silver Valley. As she looked up at the church's service board, she noted that the new pastor's name was Gabriel Christmas. "What a neat name and meaning for a pastor," thought Betty. Smiling, she thought, "Hollywood couldn't have come up with a better casting name for a leading actor." Finding the call button, she pushed and waited.

"Yes, can I help you?" came the voice.

"It's Betty Ogden from Silver Valley, Wisconsin. I called for an appointment earlier today."

"Hello, Betty, this is Laura. I'll be right down to let you in." It took but a couple minutes before she arrived to open the door.

"Hi, I'm Laura. Come right in," she said, holding open the door. "Can I help you carry something?" she asked, seeing the fruit basket and candy.

"No, I'm fine, but I have some things in the car for Mrs. Bergman that I still need to get," said Betty.

"Why not leave them in the car until we have a chance to talk?" said Laura.

Puzzled, Betty followed her down a hallway that led into her office, where Laura asked her to have a seat while she got them both something to drink. Returning with two bottles of spring water, she handed one to Betty and sat down. "Well," asked Laura, "how long are you going to be in town before you have to return to Silver Valley?"

Noting the nervousness of Laura, she said, "Just today, thank heavens. I've only been gone three days, but as the saying goes, there's no place like your own bed, or is it home?"

"Yes, I know," said Laura. "My husband and I feel the same way each year when we visit the kids, who both live in South Dakota. They went to college out there and met their future husbands, so with regret, we can only see them on occasion. You said that you were in town as part of a business trip?"

"Yes, I work for a large banking firm who is relocating their headquarters to Michigan, so they have brought in their officers for a general overview meeting."

"You're an officer of this bank?"

"You know how titles are passed out in the banking business, Laura. Big titles, smaller salaries. I happen to be the chief operating officer for the human resource department. What it simply means is I supervise the hiring and dismissal of our employees with the cooperation of the department heads. I noticed that your pastor has a wonderful name for a shepherd of your congregation."

"Yes, it sure is. When he first came here, the members of the congregation couldn't get over it, especially around Christmas, when his wife and him surprised everyone by making dozen of Christmas ornaments for the church Christmas tree. They said it was their personal business cards that they loved to pass out once a year."

"Cute," said Betty. "I would love to have met him if it was not for the conference."

"He's going to be sorry to learn he missed the opportunity to meet you," said Laura. "How's Pastor Bergman? We know that this opportunity was special to him."

"Well, she opened the door," thought Betty. "Oh, he's doing fine. He lives in our parsonage, which is located out in the country about five miles from the church. His wife and daughter are going to love it because of its seclusion, so one never has to worry about some member checking on you to make sure you're at work," she said smiling. "We purchased the property many years ago, which allows us to hold our annual picnic out there on the extra five acres. It's a great location if you love hunting and fishing and general wildlife. When we sold the original parsonage in town, one of our members donated the location, which originally was part of his farm. We just fixed things up, and today it is what it is, as the saying goes. Which, speaking of the parsonage, now reminds me that I need to go downstairs and get those two boxes of select Wisconsin cheese for Mrs. Bergman." Betty started to get up.

"Wait," said Laura. "Please sit down for a moment. It's obvious that you don't know what has happened, and I'm somewhat at a loss for words as to how to discuss this. Pastor Bergman's grief must have prevented him from sharing his loss with your congregation. Why, I have no idea about the reasons, but—"

Betty could tell from the woman's expression that something was very wrong since she looked frightened. "I'm sorry, Laura, but I don't know what loss you're talking about. I make every church service along with my husband, who is the head elder of the church. Pastor Bergman has never mentioned that anyone was sick. In fact, he was rather upbeat last week when he was talking to the members about our church starting the forty days of the Word Bible study sometime next month. In fact, he was almost bubbling in joy that the author of the program was sending a representative to kick off the event."

"God, I'm sorry to have to tell you this, Betty. Actually I don't know what to say or how to explain it without Pastor Christmas being here. Please don't ask me any questions since I'll be unable to answer what you want to know, but by now you should have learned that Mrs. Bergman has passed away some time ago and that her daughter no longer is living in the area."

"Oh no," said a shocked Betty. "We had no idea. Was it sudden? Honestly he hasn't said a word about this to anyone."

"Remember, I said no questions without the pastor being here, but no, it wasn't sudden. The poor lady has been gone now for at least three months, and her daughter hasn't been a member for over eighteen months. Even if she wouldn't have died, it would have been most unlikely that she could have ever joined him, but it's my guess you aren't aware of that either."

"I'm just stunned, Laura, as I'm sure that you can understand. We never knew what you just told me. My husband, as I mentioned, is the head elder of our church and conducts monthly, sometimes weekly, meetings and would be the first person that the pastor would have talked to regarding this terrible thing and anything else regarding family situation. My husband would have certainly shared this with me, and he didn't," said Betty."

"I'm so sorry, so sorry, Betty, but please try and understand that we had no idea that you folks never knew," said Laura. "God, if Pastor Christmas was here, he could tell you more. I wish that I could, but it would make him very uncomfortable having me talk about matters relating to another pastor, especially about something so private. What I will do is give you a name to contact should you have any need for further questions about Mrs. Bergman's death. Pastor Christmas is a very wonderful pastor, but because of the way the local district feels about these matters, he most likely will follow the same careful approach regarding releasing any information on a previous pastor of this church." Laura then handed Betty the name of Officer Kate Heller of the Funston Police Department.

Betty looked at the note with the officer's name and then at Laura. "You seem somewhat scared, Laura. Don't be," said Betty, "or am I reading something incorrect into this?"

"Please, no more questions, Betty. I want to help, but it's not in my best interest. Thank you for the fruit basket, but I'm afraid I've said too much already." She got up and walked Betty to the door. Betty turned and gave Laura a hug and then walked down the stairs, puzzled about what she had learned and not learned. Getting in her car, she pulled away and dialed Alan's cell phone number. Getting only his voice mail, she asked him to return a call to her at the first opportunity.

Laura watched Betty's car pull away and saw her taking on her cell phone. Somehow she must reach Christmas and tell him what has happened because it won't be long before Bergman's story finds its way into the congregation in Silver Valley. Everything was about to come apart, and her attempt to remove Christmas from what she really knew was a continuation of a lack of judgment on her part and would probably cost her dearly in the end, maybe even her job as the church secretary. Her husband had tried to tell her this was after all not her fault but rather those who sat in the district office's, who played the politics that few pew sitters really understood. His guess had always been that Bergman's lifestyle and problems were well documented and not a surprise to anyone. Angry now, Laura thought back to how smooth the district had handled the Bergman court case and the affair. Like the Catholic Church, the difficult problems usually find their way either out of town or are ignored and left up to the individual congregations to resolve rather than to remove the disease that is affecting the church itself. Her original mistake was attempting to biblically try and resolve the affair herself by private conversations between her and Bergman. She had underestimated the power of the brotherhood that protects itself at the expense of layman. When she'd get home tonight, she would tell her husband that she intended to call Officer Kate Heller. She was just tired of swimming upstream all by herself.

It's All in the Mind

"She said that Bergman's wife was dead?" asked a shocked Alan.

"Yes, but she wouldn't give me any more information. That why I had to call you before I got home. I wanted to give you a little time to think about it before I arrived. That poor secretary is scared of something, Alan, but I don't know exactly what. Their new pastor was out of town, which made things more difficult because she didn't want to say too much in his absence."

Alan took a moment to think before answering. "You know what, Betty, I recall sometime back that Bergman did request a few personal days off. He said that he had some family matters to attend to. I didn't ask any questions because family matters are his own business regardless how we feel about his lack of candor, and he didn't share any information at the time. Certainly as an officer of the church, I would have hoped that he would mention things with us especially since he had advised us that his family would be joining him eventually. In view of the fact from what you learned about her being ill and unable to care for herself, it does seem that he has been dishonest about the entire thing. But we always must remember that his call was extended to him, not his family, and as long as he's performing to the extent that his call documents required, we would be well advised to move carefully on the subject of his personal life. We expect the same consideration when it comes to our matters of confidentiality, so we have to treat him the same way."

"So we do nothing at this point, Alan? Is that what you're recommending?" asked Betty.

"No, what I'm saying is that we give him an opportunity to validate his current married status on his own, nothing more. We extend the love of the congregation to his family and see how he handles it. What makes you feel that the church secretary is scared of something? Did she hint at all what might be the cause of that?" asked Alan.

"No, she did not, but she did provide me with the name of the police officer that investigated Pastor Bergman's wife's death."

"What did you say, Betty?"

"That Laura, the church secretary, gave me the name of the police officer that knew the circumstance of his wife's death."

"Honey, I don't know if you realize what you just told me. Generally police officers don't handle a natural death situation. You never mentioned how she died, Betty. Are you saying that the pastor's wife didn't die of natural causes?" asked Alan.

"You know, Alan, she was so nervous in attempting to get me out of the office that I never asked that question. Now I feel real stupid, to say the least," said Betty.

Alan wrote down the name of the police officer in Funston, Michigan, and put the note in his wallet.

"Are you going to call her?" asked Betty.

"No, and I will be recommending to Jack that he not do it either when I bring him up to speed on what you learned. I'm a doctor, Betty, not a lawyer, but my instincts tell me that unless we have good cause to ask these questions or make any accusations that we are just one step away from a lawsuit by suggesting or hinting that he has done anything wrong. There was a case not too long ago in which a district president prevented a pastor from receiving call consideration to another state because that pastor's records indicated his wife had been divorced," said Alan.

"How silly," commented Betty.

"More than silly, Betty, since the pastor's wife actually never had been divorced. That pastor sued the district and his home church for slander and won. We will not make that mistake, Betty, by dealing in gossip about what we might think about the pastor's wife's death. Instead we will demonstrate the patience of a farmer waiting for it to rain and give Bergman a little more time to answer these questions on his own. I think that I mentioned to you that the new district president, Lance Schultz, will be visiting us in the near future. He met Bergman at a recent pastor meeting and even brought up his name when he called Jack a short time ago to tell us he would be coming. I think that I had mentioned to you at the time that I even had treated Schultz on a minor concern sometime back. Now, Betty, I think that I need to hang up and call Jack to see what he wishes to do. After all, he is the president of this congregation, and he might have a total different opinion on how we need to handle this. Meantime, you drive carefully, and I'll see you when you get here, darling." Reaching for his phone, Alan dialed Jack's cell number and left him a message.

It was afternoon, the sun was shining, and Jack was enjoying his day off at Deer Lake. He had just finished putting a large eight-pound northern pike on his stringer and was attaching it to the eye screw on his boat when he could feel the vibration of his cell phone alerting him to an inbound call. Ignoring the interruption to his good day of fishing, he allowed the call to go into his cell mailbox. "God, how does one get away from everyone wanting a piece of his time," mumbled Jack as he continued casting his lure into the lake in hopes of finding that elusive twenty-pound pike that the lake was noted for producing. As he was reeling the line in, the cell phone gave that irritable electronic signal reminding him that he had a message in his voice mail. "Damn it, go away," he urged but knew that he would have to check on the message since he was the executive vice president of his company, Alternative Solutions, which specialized in aiding sleep apnea patients. Putting down his fishing rod, he pulled the cell phone from its holster on his belt and listened to Alan's message. After playing Alan's message twice to assure that he had heard everything correct explaining Betty's findings, Jack laid his rod down in his boat and placed a call to Alan's cell phone.

Surprisingly Alan picked his call up on the first ring. "Thanks for calling back, Jack. I know this is your day off and that you are probably fishing somewhere," offered Alan.

"I was, but it doesn't matter, Alan. I think we're in the middle of a cyclone. When our former pastor moved away a few years ago, if you remember, we were left with the task of filling the pulpit for an indeterminate period. It was not an easy time, Alan, as both you and I had to do double duty running the service on different Sundays while maintaining our current jobs. You being a doctor with a full schedule did it, of course, and I on the other hand had to contend with my own ghosts, among them some personal sins, but yet managed to do it, and then magically the district president provided us with a list of several candidates to fill the open vacancy. Remember he provided us with a list of five men wanting to be considered to replace our pastor."

"Yes, I remember," said Alan.

"Do you also recall that of the five candidates, four declined for various reasons, to include two pastors who had admitted to us that they had long ago asked to be removed from the call list?"

"Yes," said Alan.

"One other said that he preferred to remain with his congregation, and the fourth who lived in Florida never returned our calls," said Jack.

"Yes, but where are you going with this?" asked Alan.

"Think back, Alan. You had requested another five candidates from the district president's office, but the only names provided were that of new men newly out of seminary school, or commonly referred to as God's men who still hadn't shaved."

"Yes, but I still must be missing your point, Jack."

"The point, Alan, is that the only real candidate offered to us from the beginning was Paul Bergman. It almost now appears to me that he was sent to us with existing baggage and we had no idea what it was or what the district was trying to cover up. It shouldn't be a surprise to anyone that Bergman was not what he was advertised to be, but Bergman not telling us that his wife had died signals a new low, especially since he has always maintained that she would be arriving soon. How did we miss the signals?"

"It's not our fault. We both looked at the call documents, Jack. There was nothing on them other than a simple CRM that meant nothing."

"Did it mean nothing, Alan, or was there something that under the laws of privacy and HIPPA, the district office conveniently prohibited itself from mentioning, which in the end served its own purpose of moving damaged goods?" remarked Jack.

"What is your opinion, Alan? Is this officer of this small church looking for something under a woodpile that's not there?"

"Well, as you already know, I've had my reservations about Bergman for a long time. On the other hand, he can deliver a sermon without any notes, and the congregation membership has increased by fifteen people during the last year. Don't forget that it was through his efforts that our constitution was changed, allowing more women to participate on male-only boards within the church."

"Regardless how well he sings, Alan, we have to consider that we may have a future problem upon us soon based on what Betty brought back," said Jack. "Your elder board is not going to like what she's found out, and a lot of old-time members are going to call for his resignation."

"The difficulty is that the handcuffs are on tight until he wishes to tell us anything," lamented Alan.

"We're not going to wait long, Alan. Either Bergman's going to sing like a canary and tell us what the hell is going on back there in Funston or both you and I will simply give him his walking papers and say to hell with the divine call concept. Remember, there is a morality clause in his call documents, so he is on thin ice. The constitution of this church says I happen to be the chief executive officer of this congregation and in charge of all departments with the responsibility to govern its operations," said Jack. "We got something going on here that appears to involve our pastor, yet we don't know what. We've have a report from Elmer and Ed that leaves a lot of holes to fill in. And as of this date, we still have no idea where Ed had vanished to. On top of that, we have a pastor who has decided to remain mute on what has happened to his wife and daughter, lives in our parsonage out in the woods, with some interesting things going on out there. Therefore, I consider the trustee's report on the parson-age incomplete and reserve the right to do a walk through to satisfy myself since I have to approve the future sale of that asset. It's time, Alan, that we step up to the plate on this one."

"I didn't know we were selling it," said Alan.

"We're not at this time, but nothing prevents us from bringing the matter to our voters. A lot of congregations are selling their par-sonage and just providing living expenses to their pastors. It takes money to run a church, as you know, Alan, and churches that are smart are now investing the money from the sale of their parsonage to protect themselves when times are tough. We of course will assure the pastor should this happen, that we will provide him suitable reimbursement money for any necessary housing," said Jack.

"When are you considering the need to do another inspection?" asked Alan.

"I would like to give it a few days and let things settle down. It's my guess that before long, the district will begin to communicate with their counterpart here knowing that the truth is leaking out."

"And what is the truth, Jack?" asked Alan.

"That unfortunately I don't know, but my guess is we are about to learn a little more."

The Pagoda

"You certainly have a lot of nice places to eat," commented Curtis as they drove away from the Lion's Steak House.

"It's just because of the company I keep and often arrest." Kate laughed. "You'd be surprised at how many lawyers, judges, and just general citizens want to have me be their guests at one of these four-star restaurants just to overlook a ticket."

"I can well imagine," said Curtis. "How often did it actually work?"

"You certainly don't really expect an answer?" Kate smiled.

"Well, not really." Curtis laughed.

"The answer, dear Curtis, is never. I will admit that on occasion the thought did enter my mind that enough time had passed since my husband's death, but until now my work was the only thing that mattered."

"And now?" asked Curtis.

"And now I'm going to show you something special," she replied as she turned her car down what appeared to be a deserted road and drove for what was almost half a mile.

"Hey, this looks like fun, Kate. In about another two minutes, you're going to park and explain to me that you've unfortunately run out of gas. I like this," said Curtis.

"No such luck, flyboy, but patience can always bring hope," she said. "There it is. Can you see?"

"What the heck is it?" asked Curtis.

184

"It's called the Funston pagoda, and it's one of a kind, Curtis. It was completed in 1976 by a retired engineer who was just plain bored. He did most of the work himself."

"It must be seven stories high," said Curtis.

"No, it has actually eight," she said. "He was a great engineer but short on marketing sense since his idea was that each floor would have its own decorating theme and could be used for specialty offices, and he would rent out all the floors."

"How did the customers reach each floor?" he asked.

"That was the problem. Ladders were the only access to the floors," said Kate.

Curtis burst out laughing. "So if grandma wanted to visit the knitting and yarn department, she had to climb a ladder?" he said, unable to stop his laughing.

"That's it, no other way."

"But it's still here?" questioned Curtis.

"Yes, the city didn't know what to do with it. Another town down the road had offered to buy it and have it moved, but the guy just wouldn't sell. He died a few years later, so the town council had to decide if they wanted to make something of it or burn it down. It was then that someone came up with the idea to advertise it on the highway as a town landmark hoping that enough people would come into town just to look at it and spend a little money at the same time."

"So let me get this straight, Kate. You have signs on the highway encouraging those passing by to visit the site of this pagoda? A building that has nothing, so to speak, other than a dream that went bad?"

"Well, yes, Curtis. Everyone has to go through downtown to reach it, and they buy gas, eat lunch, and shop for groceries," she said snickering.

Curtis opened the car door, got out, and started to walk up to the pagoda before she realized that he was going to climb up one of the remaining ladders.

"Hey, what you doing?" asked Kate.

"I'm going to the first floor and see what the guy had going on. Have you ever climbed the pagoda?"

"No, never had a reason to. Besides it would have been my luck to pick the time when Funston had some of its high winds and the darn thing would topple to the ground."

"You need to come up here, Officer Heller, and look at each of these individual rooms!" Curtis yelled down. "After all, you represent the law in these parts, don't you?" he said as he disappeared around the corner of the pagoda's first floor.

Climbing the ladder, Kate reached the first floor and moved around the circular building until she bumped into Curtis on the other side.

"What do you want me to see?" asked Kate.

"This," he said as he put his arms around her waist, while pulling her close. "I've been thinking about you all week," he said as he moved his lips to cover hers. He felt her heart beating as she returned his kiss, drawing him into her. After a few seconds, he pulled back, just looking at her smiling face, her blue eyes soft and inviting, like nothing he had ever witnessed before. And he kissed her again as if he didn't want it to end.

Kate raised her hands to his head, returning the kiss once again while moving close to him and whispering in his ear, "I can feel, Curtis, you wanting to make love to me."

Realizing what she was telling him, he started to pull back embarrassed, but she held on.

"It's a good thing, Curtis. I'm just telling you that I can feel your love, nothing more, but maybe we should get back in the car before someone catches us," she said.

Climbing down, they held hands as they walked to her car and got in.

"What made you do it, Curtis?" she asked gently.

"Kiss you? I already told you that I missed you," he said.

"No, telling me to climb the pagoda so you could do it up there?" she asked.

Looking at her, Curtis said, "You told me you had never been on the pagoda, so I wanted to pick a spot that was only for you and I, no one else. That was our moment, that belonged to just us. It seemed to be the right thing to do and the right moment to share how I felt about you. As they say, timing is everything."

The only thing preventing her from crying was the sudden ringing of her cell phone. "This is Detective Heller. Yes, Monday morning at your office will be fine. I can be there at 10:00 a.m., Laura. You have a good weekend. Call me if you need me sooner," she said as she hung up." Looking at Curtis, she knew that she had to tell him. "Just a little police business, sorry about that. Now please tell me more about that pagoda kiss," she said while pulling back on the road and touching his cheek with her hand. Kate's heart was pounding as she had a feeling that her life was going to change this night, but somehow the man with her made it seem all right.

As he watched her drive, he inhaled the scent of her perfume and admired the gorgeous woman seated next to him. She had caught a glimpse of him staring at her and returned a smile that suggested that she had caught him but accepted his admiring eyes.

"Penny for your thoughts?" asked Kate while keeping her eyes on the road.

"A penny would not be enough in your case, but since you asked, it's only fair that I answer," said Curtis. I was thinking about the last few minutes on the pagoda when I had pulled you close. In life, there are but a few special moments that one always remembers. One such moment happened for me tonight when a stunning beautiful woman was in my arms and unbelievably was returning my kisses. I was thinking about how was it possible that I could be so lucky to have all this happening to me. That was what I was thinking about, knowing that you could have chosen countless men over me."

"It was a special moment for me also," she said as she flicked a look in the rearview mirror before crossing the lane that would lead to her townhouse. "Yes, there have been opportunities, that I will admit, but until now nothing that I cared about."

Watching her hand on the steering wheel, Curtis became aware of what he had not noticed at the restaurant. The ring finger tonight was missing the Regard ring, and he wondered why, but he decided not to comment on it, instead choosing to just admire this woman. As she made the final turn to her townhouse, Curtis noticed that

Kate's caramel-colored skirt was now ridding up her legs and that her matching shirt had the top button open to reveal a flash of cleavage, probable a result of climbing up and down the pagoda, he thought.

"Hmm," said Kate, "those thoughts I'm picking up might be worth an awful lot of money. Do you wish to share or keep them to yourself?"

"It might just sound too immature to the woman I'm trying to impress," said Curtis.

"I doubt it, Curtis, but like they say, nothing ventured, nothing gained," she said with a warm smile as she pulled up in front of her townhouse.

As Kate shut off the engine, Curtis looked at her before he said, "The venturous side of me suggests the time has come for me to say what I feel, Kate, since life doesn't always provide one with these opportunities. Remember that I've already held you close, tasted your lips, and looked into your soft blue eyes."

"Yes, you have, but you seem to be having a hard time with this, Curtis, so be a gambler and tell me the truth about what you're thinking," she said.

"It's something that you've heard many times before, and I want it to come out right tonight, which is hard to do. You have a personal attractiveness beyond a terrific figure, Kate, and those amazing legs," he gushed. He could feel the perspiration running down his face as he waited for her response.

She offered a smile but nothing else.

"You have a sensuality that makes my heart thump just at the sound of your voice, and never in my life have I seen such beautiful seductive eyes. But most of all, Kate, most of all, nothing come close to just the magic of being near you."

"Those were wonderful words, Curtis. Three years ago another man, my former husband, had talked about my figure, but never with the hunger that you've displayed tonight. He was a good, kind man, but his look was more about the sex entitlement of marriage and not containing the raw hunger that yours contained since we left the pagoda."

"I'm sorry, Kate," said Curtis.

"What are you sorry about, Curtis? A woman wants to feel wanted, not just used. I like your honesty," she said as she kissed him on the lips. "Let's go inside and I'll make us a pizza and something to drink," she said as she opened the car door and walked toward the front of the house. Walking up the steps with Curtis behind her, she opened the colonial door and yelled for Channing. The dog came running directly toward Curtis, who stood his ground as Channing stopped in front of him waiting for his first move. Reaching for the dog, Curtis gently lowered his head while hugging the animal and rubbing its back. The dog started to lick Curtis on the face while wagging its tail in a furious fashion of affection.

"Wow, I'm impressed. You showed no fear, and Channing seems to be rewarding you by offering to help you move in," she said laughing. "You two enjoy each other. The bathroom is in the bedroom down the hall, so please look around if you wish while I get the pizza going and a little food for Channing," she said.

As Curtis began to look around, he had always felt that you could tell a lot about someone by the type of reading material they had laying around but was surprised by the absence of any books or magazines. He heard the sound of the microwave oven humming, and Kate saying from the kitchen. "What would you like to drink, Curtis?"

"Do you have any cream soda?"

"Did you say cream soda?" asked Kate looking around the corner.

"Just funning with you. Nobody drinks cream soda anymore. Any type of Coke will do," said Curtis.

The microwave buzzed, and soon Kate had rounded the corner with the pizza, sitting it on the large oak dining table. Returning to the kitchen, she then picked up the two glasses of Coke and returned. Curtis had already found his way to the table, sitting opposite of her. "I notice that you're not wearing that beautiful ring you had on the last time we went to dinner," said Curtis.

"You mean the regard ring?" she asked.

"Yes, it must mean a lot to you," said Curtis.

"Well, it did, but to be honest until you mentioned its name, I never knew the significance of what it meant because my husband never explained its background. He was not like you, Curtis, looking for special flowers and telling a woman she has seductive eyes. No, Rod's idea of a compliment was telling her she had a good ass, if you'll excuse my expression. But don't get me wrong, Curtis. He fought for his country, was kind to animals, and I'd never seen him drunk. He was not just as the saying goes, 'Thoughtful about love.'" She was about to continue when the house phone started to ring. Making no attempt to pick up the phone, the answering machine kicked in after a fourth irritating ring from the insistent caller. Curtis listened to Kate's recorded voice announcing that she was not available to come to the phone right now.

"Hi, this is Laura again. I just wanted you to know that Pastor Christmas will join us on Monday. Have a good weekend," she said, hanging up.

"Must be an important meeting," said Curtis.

"It is," said Kate. "Remember when we first met and you told me about the fact that you had knowledge about spiders because of your entomology class?"

"Sure," he said while finishing another piece of pizza.

"Well, it just so happens that my visit on Monday with the church secretary, her pastor now will result in probably having to deal with my concerns," said Kate. "It's a messy situation, Curtis. The former pastor was having an affair with his organist while his wife was dying as a result of being attacked in their garage. Someday we'll talk more about it, but not tonight."

Curtis started to say something, but Kate came over to him, saying, "Let's forget about work for a while, Curtis, and just go sit on the couch."

As Curtis sat down, Kate joined him and moved close to him, putting her forehead on his shoulder, one hand trailing lightly, tenderly, possessively over his chest.

"What are you thinking now, Curtis?" she asked. "Are you on the pagoda or looking at my legs in the car again?"

Curtis realizing that the attractive woman on the couch apparently didn't miss any of his staring, started to withdraw.

"There you go again," admonished Kate. "It's all right to be honest with each other, Curtis, so don't be embarrassed about love. We're both are grown adults and only have to answer to each other. As I remember, you haven't had a serious date in two years, and my husband was the last man in my life over three years ago, and he's gone now."

Curtis paused for a moment and then began. "I was thinking about the pagoda again," he said as he moved back closer to her. "To that moment when I couldn't hide the fact that I wanted more than anything to feel you," he said, now moving his lips down to her throat and kissing it softly. Raising his head and looking into her eyes, he continued, "I'm back in your car watching you drive and seeing your skirt move above your legs and dreaming about how you smelled so sweet, soapy, and just damn sexy like I imagined you would in the morning after a shower."

"Go on, Curtis, I love how you're not afraid to show your feelings. Here, hear my heart beating," she said as she placed his hand against her breast while she used her other hand to caress his leg. Her eyes shut, holding on tight as if holding on to a dream, she whispered, "It's time, Curtis, if not for you, for me." Getting up from the couch, she walked down the hallway, motioning for him to come as she simultaneously started to shed her clothes while entering her bedroom. Naked, she climbed on the bed and watched as Curtis removed his clothing and walked toward the bed, his eyes blazing as he was taking in her beauty.

"Please talk to me, Curtis. I love your dreams," she said.

As he climbed onto the bed, he looked at the woman now waiting for him. His newfound confidence vaporized, leaving pure terror in its wake with the realization that all that he had dreamed about was but a few feet away, naked and inviting. He watched as she moved to opened her legs while placing her hands above her head in an act of total surrender.

Moving to her ear, his warm breath whispered his love as his fingers moved gently down to touch her breasts, then he cautiously placed his hand on the inside of her legs, now opened to receive him. "Is this really something you're ready for, Kate, want as much as I do? There is time, I can wait," he offered.

"Yes," she said as he paused to accept her answer and then leaned down to kiss both her aroused breasts. Feeling her excitement growing, Curtis slowly began to kiss the skin between her breasts as he was now sliding so lightly up to meet her body. She felt his weight as he continued to slide upward while looking in her eyes, which were looking at him with heated anticipation. Curtis paused one more time as he heard her softly cry, "Oh god, it's going to happen." She raised her knees, wrapping her hands around Curtis's warm back, and shut her eyes as Curtis slid firmly into her.

"Ohh, oh, oh god," she cried as he was kissing her frantically, his tongue circling her nipples, then kissing her eyes and her neck. His breath, now burning hot against her skin, made her tingle with passionate anticipation of what was yet to come. "Oh, oh," Kate cried as she held on and moved with him, feeling his steady rhythm. She had to open her eyes and see for herself the as he continued to bury himself in her. Up, then down, to meet her. She could feel the soft tremble in her body developing into the sudden scream that now escaped her lips as Curtis exploded without warning. Moments passed as they looked at each other with realization of their happiness.

Kate sighed, looking up at him, the afterglow of love's passion still present and warm throughout her entire body. The passion had lasted only a few minutes, but she couldn't ever remember a moment like this with her former husband. At that time, it had been for him, while today it had been for her and Curtis.

After a few seconds, he raised his head, smiling. "What a beautiful moment. I've just made love to the most sensuous woman in the world. Thank you for being my special flower that I looked so long to find," he said.

"I'm so happy that you did find me, Curtis," she said, while still feeling him growing deep in her. She didn't want it to end as she reached up and pulled him down into a long kiss, wet and hard, their tongues probing. For a brief moment they held each other. They didn't speak. But she knew that had aroused him further. They made love a second time, ending with his kiss, his face buried beside hers, his hand holding hers as he claimed her as his. An hour later, Curtis was dressed and again kissing her good night.

Sitting up in bed, Kate pouted. "Why don't you stay?"

"If I do, dear, I may not have enough energy to fly my scheduled trip tomorrow, nor will I want to. I wish you a pleasant sleep to think about us, because I will be thinking about you every minute I'm away."

"Dreamily?" Kate asked. "What will you be thinking, Curtis? I so love to hear you talk to me."

"I'll be thinking about this night and nights to come. How real love can make a man crazy. How just a few moments ago after making love to you for a second time, I just want to grab the lamppost outside and swing myself around it, tap dance, and sing like Gene Kelly in the rain. I was thinking about how you opened to me like a blossoming petal and received my love unconditionally, unprotected, and through your trust and warmth made me burst apart as a man into what I've been searching for so long, my forever woman."

Sitting up and kissing Curtis, she told him how much she loved him but warned him to call a cab before she locked the doors and pulled him back in her bed and had Channing stand guard should he try to leave.

Superstitious

Christmas leaned on the window frame and pushed the drapes aside. He peered down to the street and saw the policewoman step out of her car and move to her trunk, where she seemed to be storing her sidearm, before coming inside. "Maybe she's superstitious about bringing it into the Lord's house, thought Christmas. Turning, he walked past the secretary's office, watching as Laura finished the coffee and was assembling a tray of sweet rolls.

"Cup of tea or coffee, Pastor?" she asked from between the separated rooms of his office and hers.

Christmas shook his head at her. "I think that I'll pass this morning, Laura, but thank you anyway. I noticed the policewoman has just arrived. Maybe you can find me something stronger, like maybe a whiskey and soda perhaps?"

"I doubt that would impress either your members or the policewoman," said Laura.

"I hope this is not a surprise that she's bringing. I hate surprises, Laura, God in heaven, I don't handle surprises very well. The Bergman affair was enough for a lifetime of working for Christ. I can still remember the district president telling me that the congregation was going through a healing process, but other than that, it was a typical divine call that I was accepting. They of course failed to tell be that this typical divine call was as typical as Peyton Place. There's the buzzer. Maybe you better go down and let her in," said Christmas.

"I'm coming!" yelled Laura into the intercom. Walking down the two flights of stairs, she found the policewoman waiting with a wide smile. Opening the door, Laura asked, "You look extremely happy for a Monday morning, Detective Heller. Did you win the lottery," as they were walking up the steps.

"Maybe better," she replied.

"Oh, as a woman, I must tell you that your comment sounds an awful like love." Laura smiled. Without answering, Kate allowed her eyes a little telltale sparkle. Walking up the stairs and behind her, she followed Laura into her office. The secretary told Lisa to take a seat while she would see if the pastor was ready for them. Walking across the hall, she entered the pastor's office. "Are you ready?"

"Send her in, Laura. We might as well find out what is on the detective's mind."

As Laura entered the room, she noticed the rather robust, curly-haired man was in sports clothes today. If not for the large crucifix around his neck, he could have passed for a middle linebacker, if not for the fact of his age. She also noticed the apparent mission of the church displayed on a wall, "Love the word. Learn the word. Live the word."

Getting up, Christmas extended his hand saying, "We meet again, Detective Heller, although if my memory is correct, the last time you were carrying a different title."

"Your memory is good, Pastor, but since that visit, my captain has seen fit to include a woman into the detectives' men club. The world is changing so fast that one day they may even invite a woman to be a member of the Masters Golf Club."

"Well-earned promotion I'm certain, Detective, but I wouldn't hold my breath to be invited to wear the green jacket. I hope you haven't found any outstanding parking tickets on me since your last visit."

"No," laughed Kate. "We try to avoid ticketing speeding pastors for fear of getting on the wrong side of those who are trying to help some of us get to heaven."

"You are not excluding present company from that help, are you, Detective?"

"It's a very long story, Pastor. It may be best for another time. My visit today has been at the request of your secretary, Laura," she said as she gazed in her direction.

"Oh, you didn't say anything to me about any concerns, Laura. Have I missed something?" asked Christmas, looking more than just a little perplexed.

"You haven't missed anything, Pastor," said Laura. "This just happens to be something that you were unaware of regarding our former pastor, Bergman. It needs to be discussed with Officer Heller since she is handling a cold case that involves the former pastor and our former organist, Gayle Browning, and there are things she needs to know. I've asked that you be invited into this conversation because you are the pastor of this congregation."

"Well, well, this is a surprise, but I'm glad you did want me to be part of this meeting, Laura. Being a pastor of a congregation is difficult enough, without failing to understand what might be in the closet. Before we start, though, may I ask you, Detective Heller, what is your practicing religion?"

"I'm Catholic, Pastor, but I don't practice the faith," said Kate.

"Why is that?" asked Christmas.

"As my father used to put it, 'Sometimes religion is for those who are afraid to go to hell but spiritually is for those who have been there.' In my case, the jury is still out on where I fall."

"Well, in the book of Genesis, it says, 'In the beginning, there was only darkness until God created the light,'" commented Christmas. "Maybe you will find the light during your search."

"That is true, Pastor, but I'm reminded what a comedian once said on the same subject," said Kate.

"That is what?" asked Christmas.

"He said, 'In the beginning there was nothing, and then God created light. There was still nothing, but you could see better.'" Kate smiled.

Christmas couldn't help but laugh out loud before saying, "You may have hit on something, Detective Heller, or at least provide me with new material for a future sermon. In any event, it's clear behind that new rank of yours is a very well-informed woman."

Kate was about to ask Laura a question when her cell phone started ringing. "This is Officer Heller, can I help you?"

"Hello, Detective, this is Polly, the front-desk officer at the police department. We just got a delivery of three dozen roses for you."

Turning to Pastor Christmas, Kate said, "Please accept my apology, but I need to take this call, so please excuse me for a minute." Walking out in the hallway, she continued with the conversation. "Is there a card or anything?" asked Kate.

Polly replied and said smiling, "It would appear to be from someone named Mr. Curtis Daffodil. What the hell did you do, or should I say, how many times did you happen to do it? You better share the good news with me, or I won't put these flowers aside for you."

"I will, but can you hide them until I get there? Otherwise I'll have to be dealing with the whole office besides you," said Kate.

"You've got it, Detective Heller," she said as she hung up.

Walking back in the room, Kate said, "Sorry about that, there will be no more interruptions,", not mentioning that she had shut her cell phone off. "Now, Laura, you had mentioned on your recent call to me that you needed to talk further about Pastor Paul Bergman and his past ministry of this congregation. Before you start, am I to assume that Pastor Christmas is familiar with the relationship between the former pastor and the now-deceased organist of this church? My guess is also, Pastor Christmas, that your district president had a sit-down conversation with you about their sexual relationship before you agreed to accept this position?"

Christmas decided to answer Kate's questions before Laura responded. "With regret, Detective, I unfortunately probably know too much," said Christmas, "but none of that information was originally communicated by my superiors."

"Then how did you first learn about the situation?" asked Kate.

"You mean aside from the 125 members of this congregation, who made this a standard topic from the first day I arrived?" asked Christmas.

"Yes, who first brought this matter to your attention, if not your members?"

"The district office only indicated that the congregation needed a healing pastor, and I assumed that like many congregations, what that meant was that this church was dealing with the typical conflicts involving the lay leadership and disagreements with its ministry. This is very common in most Lutheran congregations, as with other religions, since pastors have been asked to leave their pulpit over the selection of hymns and their day off per week that they have requested," said Christmas. "So please understand that I initially wasn't worried."

"You've got to be kidding," responded Kate.

"No. Members are forever complaining about Lutheran hymns being too funeral like, and as far as the day off is concerned, officers of a church have a tendency to like to meet the evenings of a pastor's day off. When I accepted the call here, the subject of the pastor's former relationship with our organist just started to come up little by little, as most things do in a church. To answer your question as direct as I can, no official from the district gave me a heads-up about the affair. You must remember, Detective Heller, just because I'm a member of the clergy doesn't mean that I'm not still on a need-to-know basis with my bosses, just as I suspect you are."

"Why do you feel the former pastor was given an opportunity to transfer or rather accept another call to a new congregation?" questioned Kate.

"Forgiveness is the cornerstone of our Christian teachings, and with that, it would be pretty hard to justify denying a new start for any pastor."

"Even one who is alleged to have murdered his own wife and possibly his organist?" asked Kate.

"My understanding is that he was not convicted of his wife's unfortunate death, and as far as the situation with his organist at the time, that case has not been proved either," said Christmas. "In any event, Officer, you will need to check with the district president on matters related to Pastor Bergman, because I have no further comment."

"How about offering a guess?" asked Kate.

"I don't guess, Detective, just read the newspaper, and those papers have clearly indicated that the jury had acquitted him. Secondly, for what's it worth, the district probably didn't want to face a lawsuit by removing his collar," said Christmas. "It's pretty common knowledge, Detective, that with society being so focused on legal action as the recourse for every solution, the district didn't want to gamble on having a minister that was cleared of a crime turning around and filing legal action against a district because they elected to punish him."

"But wouldn't they have that right just based upon his affair that he had admitted to?"

"Yes, and that's why you might need to talk to the district, to determine what caused them to overlook that part of his divine call to this congregation. I have heard of pastors whose broken marriages or divorces have been managed by the district through counseling methods. Besides, one must remember that Pastor Bergman was a rising star within the Lutheran Church, and just maybe the saving of his career was more important to his superiors."

Kate thought about his comments as she pondered her next line of questioning. "One more question for now. Has Pastor Bergman ever called you or visited you since the time he was transferred?" asked Kate.

"I think, Officer, that I answered that question the last time that you visited. No, there has been no contact by him or any outreach by this office. Smart pastors, especially one like Bergman, understand how important that it is to remain distant from their past and focus on their current assignment only."

"Thank you, Pastor Christmas," replied Kate. "Now, Laura, we can do the next part private or Pastor can stay."

"I'd like him to stay," replied Laura.

She noted that Christmas showed no outward concern about the decision. "That's fine. So what concerns you about Pastor Bergman that you felt that I needed to know about?" asked Kate.

Laura explained how she had first discovered the affair in the church balcony and her original intent to keep the matter between

DEMPSEY

herself and the pastor, so as to not cause damage to his marriage nor inflame the church. After all, they had a good professional relationship, and she had felt that he would welcome her help, she said.

"And did you, or what changed your mind about keeping silent on this matter and not seeking advice from Pastor Christmas?" asked Kate.

"I didn't change my mind. Pastor Bergman changed his," she said.

"How did that happen?" asked Kate.

"I tried to arrange some time for us to talk about the affair, but he kept avoiding the subject. After a full week of excuses that he was too busy or had appointments, I just walked into his office one morning and shut the door and told him that we needed to talk about Gayle and the evening that I found them together up in the balcony," said Laura.

"How did he handle it?" asked Kate.

"He initially denied it and tried to use the weight of his collar to make me feel guilty about even bringing the matter up that involved a pastor. When that didn't work, he said that even if it was true, it would be his word against mine unless I had a witness. He went on to say if I continued with these lies, it would not be in my best interest," said Laura.

"Did you consider his tone a threat?"

"Yes, he seemed very confident that few people would believe me over a pastor. He had pointed out that he had experience with jury matters and that I would end up looking like a fool."

"What did you say after that?" asked Kate.

"I told him that I'd seen the pictures of him making love to Gayle, and that unless he would stop threatening me, I would take the matter up with the board of elders," answered Laura.

"What pictures are you talking about?" asked Kate.

Laura then explained about her return visit to the balcony the next day and finding them on Gayle's cell phone.

"What did he say then?" asked Kate.

"He still remained adamant that it was his word against mine since, in his opinion, no proof existed."

00

"He was wrong, wasn't he?" said Christmas, speaking up for the first time.

"Yes, because as most cell phone users are aware, you can transfer pictures form one cell phone to another in a heartbeat. He had forgot about that little feature when he threatened me, so once that dawned on him, he became most willing to accept my offer to end the affair and concentrate on being a husband and an honorable shepherd to this congregation."

"Do you still have the pictures, Laura?" asked Kate.

"No, because the truth is, I never really transferred them. He just thought that I did. In many ways, he was right about the collar effect, and the thought of destroying a pastor's career wasn't my deal. We are taught that a pastor is sent to us from God, and many of us take that very seriously."

"How was your relationship with Bergman after that meeting?"

"He avoided me, but I doubted that he ever ended the affair with Gayle. My guess is he felt that we had our conversation, and that I would accept his pledge as the truth since he was, after all, my pastor."

For a time, no one spoke, and then Christmas said, "What you went through, Laura, breaks my heart as a pastor. The church to most of us is a rock, but I'm also aware that the rock isn't malleable. At times, like in any walk of life, you encounter situations like what happened here at Trinity, and usually in our faith, those ministers are weeded out of the system."

"But he wasn't, and two people are now dead," said Kate.

"Is there anything that I should do or can do, Detective Heller, to help heal these wounds within the congregation?" asked Christmas.

"Yes, but it's against human behavior. You can begin by making sure that your church officers understand that sometimes the past is best left buried. For with the bones of the dead can lay some dark and very dangerous secrets."

"For someone who gives the impression that she's not connected to a particular faith, you certainly have some good insights into our field," said Christmas.

"Thank you, but any insight is nothing more than pure luck, Pastor."

"Laura, did the pastor have any other secrets that you became aware of?" asked Kate.

"No, but I don't understand what you actually might be looking for? Do you mean other secret women in the congregation?"

"Not women, actually, but rather interests in things that one would find unusual for a pastor to have an interest in. Maybe he was a collector of rare art, gold coins, or foreign stamps. Possibly something that involved exotic pets?"

"He did like jewelry," answered Laura. "One day I noticed that he had a women's Bahia ring on his credenza," replied Laura.

"What is a Bahia ring?" questioned Christmas.

"It's a ring that you often find on celebrities' fingers," said Kate. "With all due respect, Pastor, it's an unlikely ring that you would find that the majority of clergy would be involved with unless you are willing to spend upwards of two thousand to six thousand dollars, maybe even more. Do you remember what color it was, Laura?" asked Kate.

"As I remember, it was a beautiful blue color. I recall thinking that the intense-blue color was like a sea you've never seen before. I knew it was a Bahia ring because my husband's sister has one, which was given to her by her husband for their twenty-fifth anniversary. He's a lawyer with a major law firm in Chicago. Frankly I was suspicious that he might have intended it for Gayle and was keeping it hidden in his church office. If he ever did give it to her, she never wore it to church that I was aware of. Maybe he thought better of it considering the fact someone might have started to ask Gayle about where she had gotten it."

"All this was of course before the pastor's wife was attacked in their garage?"

"Yes, about six months prior would be my best guess."

"I take it, Detective Heller, that you are still investigating the circumstances of his wife's unfortunate death?" asked Christmas.

"Yes, and that of Gayle Browning, which still remains an open mystery as well," answered Kate.

"But the papers said she died of a spider bite. They reported that autopsy results confirmed that as the cause of death," continued Christmas.

"Yes, that's true, but I've been asked to take a second look." Recognizing that the conversation was moving in a direction that she didn't feel suited her visit, Kate got up from the table.

"Laura, I appreciate the information you have provided me today. I want you or Pastor Christmas to contact me at any time should you have any other concerns. My guess is that you will continue to have little or no contact from the former pastor since he has his hands full at his current assignment. If that changes, Pastor Christmas, please contact my office. Do either of you have any other questions that I need to address before I leave?"

Both Christmas and Laura responded that they didn't and together joined Kate as they walked to the front of the church building. It took her less than two minutes to reach her car and a total of fifteen more minutes more to reach her office to pick up the flowers.

C H A P T E R   2 4

Missing You

It was very peaceful in the sunlit garden. The pond was covered with huge water lilies, a stone bear spewing water from its mouth. Bergman sat on his favorite chair on the parsonage deck as he enjoyed the afternoon heat drinking a glass of cold tea and wondering about his future. It was just a few weeks since his wife, Peggy, had passed away in an undisclosed nursing home. His daughter had not allowed him any contact due to the simple fact she still considered him guilty of her condition. Thinking back to that late April 21 day when the police arrived at his home and found her choked with a cord and left convulsing and near death on their garage floor, it still made him angry. He had called the Funston Police himself upon arriving home from his fictitious late board meeting at a local junior college when they had found her on the cement floor. But still that rookie police-woman Kate Heller had put him through the third degree, making him her number one suspect. If not for her, there probably would never have been a grand jury or indictment of him. If not for her, he probably would never had stood trial. Taking another sip of tea, he remembered taking the witness stand, swearing to the jury that he wasn't covering up trying to kill his wife as Officer Heller had sug-gested in her report but just trying to hide his affair with the church organist, Browning. He had told the jury that he was ashamed as a father that his daughter, who needed him, had to read about the things now being written about him. Throwing his tea glass on the ground, Bergman remembered how that rookie cop had pictured him to the jury by her testimony in saying that he was nothing more than a clever cheating husband chasing after a younger woman. However, he had carried the day as the jury acquitted him, and later the Funston Police Department had pulled Heller from any more involvement on the case, instead assigning a more seasoned officer. Sad as it was, his church had not been so kind. The chairman of the congregation had demanded his resignation, feeling that his divine call to their church had been violated. He had considered threatening legal action against the church until his secretary at the time had also threatened exposure of pictures, which Gayle had taken when they were together. Although he couldn't prove it, his suspicions were that the secretary had participated in the pressure from the chairman of the congregation. Laypeople were the easiest to figure out, since most made your business their business. It was the nature of what church life was all about. They always had issues, if not with you, then something was wrong with your wife or children. Never happy, many looked for problems that were not there.

Faced with the ever-growing pressures of the church and a fifteen-million-dollar civil judgment in his wife's attack from her family, he had to plead with the district president to find him a new call. As luck would have it, not only did a new divine call develop, but the civil judgment was set aside when he had agreed to leave the state of Michigan.

Later moving to his church office, he sat down on his leather chair and opened up the locked file cabinet nearest his desk. Reaching inside, he removed the ring box that he had found one night while visiting Gayle at her apartment. Memories of that discovery brought back his days with his former congregation and his former life. Carelessly she had left it on her bedroom dresser, with the ring box nearby. Suspicious that the ring was from another man, Bergman had opened the box and found the receipt with the name Perry Sinclair. Never letting on to Gayle his anger, he later had visited the jewelry store whose name was on the bottom of the box. When he had told the clerk that the ring was purchased by him and he wanted to see if they had a matching ring for himself, the clerk simply asked for his last name, which he gave as Sinclair. The clerk quickly had brought up the file and verified the address and phone number provided by Perry Sinclair. Telling the clerk that he needed a little time to think about the cost of the matching ring, he had left the jewelry store. "It had been so easy," thought Bergman smiling as he checked his rolodex to make sure the information was still there. Opening the box, he pulled the ring out and studied its beauty. The ring was confirmed to be a ruby, formed by two stirrup-shaped loops that cradled the red stone. Its value was enhanced by diamonds on each side of the ruby. After Gayle's death, he had it appraised and was shocked to learn that Sinclair had spent twenty-two thousand dollars on his love gift. Putting the ring back in the box, he returned it to the file cabinet. Walking over to the living room picture window, Bergman began to think back to the time that he first became interested in Gayle. Oh, certainly she had been a most competent organist, and her willingness to play his contemporary music did set her aside from the other two women who were more traditionalist in their style and preference. Gayle seemed to enjoy the challenge of the new music, which brought the youth to the service, and besides she would comment, "Any organist can follow the Lutheran hymnal and play Luther's 'A Mighty Fortress Is Our God.'"

Looking out the parsonage window, his eyes settled on the greenhead mallard watching over his hen while she ate from below his bird feeder, confident that her partner was watching for any danger while she enjoyed her morning breakfast. His thoughts quickly returned to the moment, as he liked to refer to it, when he knew that Gayle would become more to him than the church organist. He remembered when she had walked into his office one Wednesday afternoon with the music that she had intended to play at the contemporary service on Sunday asking if he would like to sing the first verse. He had leaned across his desk, an amused smile on his face when his hand brushed across hers while reaching for the music sheets. The touch had startled him more than her at the time. "Oh, sorry," he had said, remembering a strange, guilty smile crossing his face as it turned red. "Sometimes I'm a little clumsy," he had stammered. Trying to recover from his awkwardness, he had encouraged her to sit down so that they could discuss her selection of the dismissal hymn. He smiled to himself as he closed his eyes remembering how when it was time for her to leave, she had stood up and pulled down the hem of the short skirt with her free hand. He had stared at her legs. Had he deliberately been so obvious? Or did he think back then that Gayle hadn't noticed? She had, of course, and it wasn't long after that they started meeting in a park near her townhouse to jog and talk about church business and their common interests. "There's something about changing sexual appetites," he thought, watching the two ducks through his office window lift off the ground and fly away. "It starts quiet but evolves with the little things. You ask yourself, was she flirting or was it you? If she did, did she single you out, or was it you that made you decide to tarnish your clergy reputation?" When days later she had mentioned the problem with her kitchen door lock one afternoon after jogging, he had volunteered to look at it, correcting the problem within a few minutes. She then had made them sandwiches and tea while he had worked at the lock, and everything had ended innocently, both resuming their lives, one as pastor and the other a senior bank teller.

That innocence had ended three weeks later when he heard the raucous laughter upon leaving Funston's most celebrated pie shop, having been disappointed that his favorite banana crème was sold out. He had turn to see Gayle with two rather young women raising their beer glasses in a toast. One of them had said something, and all three tossed back their heads and laughed again. As he had watched the group, he noted that the two other women had put on their coats and were leaving Gayle alone at the table to finish her coffee. Her smile was radiant when he had approached her table, telling her that he had heard her voice and wanted to say hello. "Oh, it was just girl talk," she had told him. They had been toasting one of the women's recent engagement and her pending Bermuda honeymoon. He remembered asking her if he could join her and that the pie shop had cheesecake that was astounding and as heavy as cement. Then to his surprise, she suggested that he pick up the cheesecake and go back to her apartment around the corner for coffee.

Gazing out the window again, Bergman thought back to how easy the words had tumbled casually from her mouth and how willing he had been to follow her lead. He knew that when she had suggested that they go back to her apartment, she was going to sleep with him. When they had stepped into her apartment, she had reached for the light switch, but he had grabbed her hand. They quickly undressed each other in the semi darkness, laughing somewhat at the struggle and the awkwardness of his attempt to remove her panties. But the bungling and his falling over his own pants soon ended as she pulled him to her bedroom and onto her bed as he kissed her and finally entered her.

Tears flowed down his cheeks as he thought back once again to the ring box that he had found on Gayle's dresser. He had not met Perry Sinclair, nor did he really care that much about him. What he cared about was inflicting the same kind of pain that one experiences when they lose the one that they love. He was about to return the ring to the file cabinet that he had kept it in when he noticed that the picture of Gayle had been moved. It was his favorite picture of her playing the organ that he had taken a week after they had first made love. Those bastards had snooped, not just inspected the parsonage. He had originally been suspicious of what Ogden had told him about the required inspection and was only sorry that the rifle shot had had just been a warning, not a kill shot. "The little weasels were going to pay a price that they hadn't counted on," thought Bergman as he tossed the pencil and pen holder at the wall. Getting up from his chair and not paying any attention to the floor covered with the writing instruments, Bergman walked over to the standing bookshelf and pulled a copy of the church directory and turned to the page listing Edward Simon. Smiling, he wrote down the address and returned the directory back to the bookshelf. Maybe it was time to pay a visit on old Ed, he thought.

CHAPTER 25

The Gift

The school bus driver waited patiently as Mary Sinclair stepped down from the bus and walked directly up the sidewalk to her home. When Mary had reached the front door, she turned and waved to the driver, who was slowly pulling away. Finding her key, Mary opened the door and walked inside leaving her school bag in the dining room. Getting a Coke from the refrigerator, she was about to sit down at the kitchen table when she heard the ringing of the doorbell. Walking back into the dining room, she looked outside and watched as a car pull away. She was about to go back to the kitchen when she noticed the large package sitting on the front steps. Seeing that no one was around outside, Mary opened the door and brought the large box inside and carried it into the kitchen. Curious about the contents, Mary decided to call her dad at his office.

"This is Perry, what can I help you with?"

"Hi, Dad, it's just me, Mary. Sorry to bother you at the bank, but someone sent you a box, and it says open immediately."

"A box? What do you mean, Mary? Maybe your mother has ordered something. Are you sure it's meant for us and not a mistake? Check and read the name carefully and the address. The darn postman always seems to be delivering the wrong mail to the wrong house."

"It's wasn't the mailman who delivered it, Dad, and it's got only your name on it. It says in big letters Mr. Perry Sinclair."

"Is there any return address, Mary? It would be located on the top left-hand side of the box."

"None that I can see, Dad. It does have a sticker on it that says Baskets for all Occasions."

"Baskets for all Occasions really sounds weird, Mary."

"Want me to open it, Dad?"

"No, let me get back to you, Mary, after I speak to your mother."

"All right, but don't take too long cause one of the stickers says 'Open right away.'"

"I won't, Mary, but hold on opening that box until one of us calls you back. It will probably be Mom since she should be home in about half an hour anyway."

When her dad hung up, Mary walked into the living room and turned on the television. Within ten minutes, the phone rang.

"Hi, this is Mary."

"Is this Mrs. Barbara Sinclair?"

"No, this is her daughter, Mary."

"Mary, we're calling to ensure that you received a box from Baskets for all Occasions."

"Yes, it came just a few minutes ago," she answered.

"This is just a courtesy call. Please be sure that the box is opened right away since it contains some special fruit that will spoil if it's left in the box too long. The instructions on the box should suggest that also," said the caller.

"All right, I'll do it right away," said Mary as the caller hung up.

She placed the phone back in the cradle and walked over to the box and thought about what the caller had said. Having made her decision, she started to reach for the box when the phone rang again.

"Hello, can I help you?"

"Hello, sweetheart, this is mom. I understand from Dad that someone sent us a box."

"Yeah, and it's pretty big, Mom," said Mary. "They just called before you did to see that we got it."

"You said someone called regarding the box?"

"Yeah, some man from Baskets for all Occasions. He said to open it right away or else the fruit might spoil."

"You're sure it's for us, not some mistake?" she asked.

"Dad asked me the same thing. I'm eleven years old, Mom, and it says Mr. Perry Sinclair and our street address."

"Isn't there any return address, dear?"

"All it says is Baskets for all Occasions, 4700 S Lincoln Way Drive, Funston, Michigan. I gave Dad all this information already, Mother. It's just some dumb box, so what's the big deal?"

"We're not trying to make a big deal out of it, Mary, just trying to be careful because it has come from someone that we don't recognize. No matter what it is, don't open it until I get home, Mary. It won't spoil in that short time regardless what it says. Dad is working a little late at the bank, but I should be home in another hour or less, and we'll look at it together, okay, dear?"

"Okay, Mom. See you soon," said Mary.

Turning to her office secretary, Barbara said, "Angela, would you hold all my calls until tomorrow. I got something going on at home, so I have to run. I have no more homes to show today, so if anyone calls, tell them I'll be in tomorrow at nine sharp. If they press, you can give them my cell phone number to call."

"Hot date tonight, Barbara?" asked Angela.

"Those ended years ago, Angela, after we had Mary. I've just have to make a stop on the way home," she said, now walking out of her office past Angela. Reaching the underground parking lot, Barbara got in her Lexus and drove past the unmanned security gate onto Butterfield Road. The address Mary gave her was as she remembered, close to the Huntington Shopping Center and only about five miles from their house. It was a shopping complex that neither of them shopped at very often since it was considered by most as just having high-scale, pricy clothing. She found it hard to imagine anyone leasing space to sell just fruit baskets or gift items in that location. Reaching Lincoln Way Drive, Barbara followed the address numbers to 4700 S. Lincoln Way Drive. The address turned out to be Rogers & Son Jewelers, a name she recognized as dealing in top-of-the-line jewelry. Puzzled, Barbara parked the car in the lot and walked up to the white brick building store entrance and was greeted by a female sales clerk.

"Are you looking for anything special that I can help you with?"

"Yes," said Barbara. "I certainly must be lost since your address was used by a company that specializes in gift baskets, and it appeared on a box delivered to my house this afternoon. Have you any knowledge of any business in this area like that?"

"No, nothing such as that which deals in gift baskets or anything near to that subject, and I've been working here for five years, and the store has been at this location for nearly eighteen years. If you would like, I'll be happy to locate the manager for you?"

"No," said Barbara, "it's clearly a mistake. You've been very helpful. It appears that some individual just mixed up the wrong address. Thank you for your time, though." She walked out of the store, returning to her car. "What in the heck is going on?" she wondered out loud. "No return name on the box and a wrong return address on top of everything. Maybe someone is playing a joke," she thought as she started up the car to finish her drive home.

Mary was looking out the window when she saw her mother pulling into the garage, and hearing the garage door close, she waited by the back door.

"Hi, Mom, was it a busy day at the office?"

"Every day is busy, Mary, so try your best not to grow up too fast. Enjoy life all you can because work comes to all of us eventually and much too fast. Now where is that surprise package you were talking about?"

"It's over on the table, Mom. Can I open it please?"

"Let me look at the box first," said Barbara. As she checked the address on the box and the company's name, everything was just as Mary had said. But who the heck was sending this surprise? Maybe some client was trying to win more business.

"Who delivered it, Mary, or didn't you see?"

"That's the funny part, Mom. It wasn't the mailman or the UPS truck, just some car stopped and dropped it off and then pulled away before I could get to the door. Now can I open the box, Mom?"

"All right, but be careful not to rip of the address so your dad can read it when he gets home," she said.

Being careful, Mary ripped the package paper off to expose the box. Opening up the cardboard top, Mary saw the red cellophane-covered fruit basket. Reaching in, she lifted the basket out and placed in on the center of the table. "Wow, Mom!" she yelled. "You have to see this. Someone sent us a big basket of all kinds of fruit."

"All right, dear, I'll be there in a few minutes," said Barbara.

"Waiting anxiously for her mother to return, Mary looked through the red cellophane paper at the selection of fruit trying to decide if she would grab an apple, pear, orange, banana, or some grapes first. As she put her hand on the bottom of the cellophane to lift it up, she jumped back and screamed, "Help! Mom, come help!"

"What is it, Mary?" asked Barbara, running from the bedroom.

"I don't know," said Mary, pointing at the basket. "It looked like a hairy bug or something. It went under the fruit."

"Are you sure?" asked Barbara.

"I think so because it had a lot of legs and it was ugly. It had a red mouth and looked mean."

Lifting up the fruit basket, Barbara began to turn it around to examine all sides of the fruit for any sign of the bug, but nothing seemed to bring it from its hiding place. Sitting down at the table, she reached inside one of the kitchen drawers and pulled out the spare flashlight she kept handy just in case the lights went out. Turning it on, Barbara moved the light from side to side over the various fruits hoping that the light would bring to the surface whatever was hiding. Nothing moved. Mary looked at her mother and was about to plea for her to believe her when suddenly they heard the car door slam outside.

"Dad's home," said Mary.

Coming in the front door, Perry yelled, "Anybody home? Where is everybody?"

"We're both in the kitchen, honey," said Barbara.

Waking into the kitchen, Perry looked at the fruit basket for a moment. "So that's the big surprise, huh? Why haven't you opened it, you guys, or were you waiting for Dad to have the first shot at it? Here, let me open it for you," he said.

"Wait, Daddy, there's some type of bug in it."

"What's she talking about, Barbara?"

"She seems to feel that the fruit basket has some type of bug in it, Perry."

"Well, it is a fruit basket, and that shouldn't be so surprising. Bugs like fruit, so let's open the package and see if the fruit is all right," said Perry.

"It's ugly, Daddy, and very hairy with a red mouth," said Mary.

"You said it was a bug, Barbara? What the hell is she talking about?"

"None of us are really sure, Perry, what it is, so do what you think is best," she said, somewhat irritated. "And by the way, the address on the box is not where it came from. There is no such fruit basket company at that address. It happens to be a jewelry company, and they have been at that location for many years."

"How do you know that?" asked Perry.

"I decided to stop on the way home and check it out thinking that the company would have a record of who sent it," she answered.

"Do you remember the name of the jewelry company, Barbara?"

"Why is that important, Perry? Do you happen to know some-one there?" she asked.

"No, just curious, so just forget it," he said, now looking more intently at the fruit basket. "I think we better open it up and get the little bugger out of its hiding," he said, now starting to lift the cel-lophane wrapping. "It's time to let the little bastard know who is in charge of this castle, don't you think?"

CHAPTER 26

The Funeral Arrangements

Kate was bored out of her skull. After almost a week interviewing most of the principals associated with the two deaths connected to Pastor Paul Bergman's wife and his mistress, Gayle Browning, she was no closer to having a solid lead than the first day she was assigned these cold case files. Clearly Bergman, regardless of the fact that a jury had acquitted him in the death and savage assault of his wife, was the connection to both these deaths. He had admitted at during his court hearing that he wanted to marry Browning, and it was obvious to anyone that Bergman's wife stood in the way. What was not clear was how and why the organist later herself ended up dead due to what was reported as a brown recluse spider bite. Even her visit to entomologist Prof. Joseph Davis, who had disputed the cause of death by a brown recluse spider bite, didn't change the opinion of the medical examiner and his findings. Nothing in her visit to Bergman's past church and conversations with the church secretary and new pastor told her much beyond the fact that Bergman was a just like millions of other men trying to have something new to twiddle with. "Face it, Kate," she thought, "you're missing something, and if you don't start connecting the dots, your future might go as cold as this case."

Reaching in her briefcase, she put her notes on the kitchen table and poured herself another cup of coffee while looking at the roses that Curtis had sent to her office. She would have to have a talk with him about that regardless of the fact that she had felt excited about his expression of love and she missed him terribly. He was a caring person and wonderful lover, knowing just what made her happy during those moments. Taking another drink of coffee, Kate started to reread her notes on her interview with Pastor Christmas and Laura. Both seemed to be sincere and truthful about what they knew about Bergman. Without a doubt, the experience witnessing Bergman and Browning in the balcony making love justified the woman's right to be nervous and afraid of Bergman then and in the future should he return to the area. Something was missing, but what was it? Picking up her notes for the third time, it was then she saw the possible missing link. "How could I have overlooked it?" she said, slapping the notes on the table. Jesus, it was right in front of her, and she had let it go. Laura had told her that the organist was seeing another man, but somehow Kate had not pressed that point with her during her last visit. What if Bergman knew about his competition? For that matter, what if the competition himself had found out that Gayle was doing more than playing the church organ for Bergman? It certainly wouldn't be the first time that men were beat at their own game of infidelity. Damn, she had been stupid. If Laura knew about the relationship, it was possible that Gayle might have mentioned his name to her or someone else in the choir or congregation. Picking up her cell phone, Kate dialed Trinity Lutheran Church and heard the recorded voice, "Hello, this is Trinity Lutheran Church. We are not available now but will call back as soon as possible. Please leave your name and phone number and a brief message. Thank you, and God Bless you."

"Damn," thought Kate, "why is everybody always away from their phone when you need them?" She was bending down toward her purse on the floor to see if she by chance she had picked up a copy of Trinity Church bulletin that might list Pastor Christmas's phone number when her cell phone rang.

"Hello, this is Detective Heller."

"Detective Heller, this is Laura calling you back. I just happened to stop in the church and noticed that your phone number appeared on the answering machine. You didn't leave a message, but I'm calling back to see if you needed pastor or me?"

"Actually, Laura, you were the one that I needed to speak to, if you have a few minutes," said Kate.

"Should Pastor Christmas be part of the conversation, or will you be stopping by the church?"

"No, his presence isn't necessary, and I think we can do this over the phone, since it's unlikely that he knows anything about the subject that I need to ask you about."

"Well, what is it that you need to know?" asked Laura, sounding somewhat concerned.

"You had told me when we first talked about the affair Pastor Bergman was having with Ms. Browning that she might have been seeing someone else besides the Pastor Bergman. Did I understand you correctly?" asked Kate.

"Yes, but remember, Detective Heller, this was just church gossip since I never actually met the man personally," said Laura.

"I understand that, but this could be important to my investigation regarding the circumstances of her death."

"The papers reported that she died of a spider bite," said Laura. "I don't understand why her seeing another man makes any difference regarding her death."

"It does, Laura, since it could mean that more than one person had an interest in her future. This is police business, so I can't comment on the reasons why that may be the case, but I can assure you the answer to my question could speed up my investigations."

"This whole thing makes me nervous, Detective Heller, and I'm trying to move on with my life."

"I'm sure you are, Laura, and that's the reason why I prefer to talk to you over the phone instead of revisiting you at the church," said Kate. "Look, Laura, I will share this much with you. My job is to make sure that both Pastor Bergman's wife's death and that of your organist's death are not connected in any way that still leaves a killer loose. So one more time, Laura, and off the record at this point. Do you or anyone at Trinity know the name of the man she was seeing?"

"All that I can tell you, Detective, is that she called him Perry. Gossip has it he is some big bank executive, and that's all that I honestly know," said Laura.

"How did you learn about all of this?" asked Kate.

"One of the ladies in the church choir during an evening prac-tice noticed her wearing a beautiful, expensive ring and had asked her about it, and she said it was a gift from a male friend. She also said his name was Perry, but as I told you, I have no last name, Officer."

"This was not the Bahia ring that you've seen on Pastor's desk?"

"Oh, no, this was much more expensive. Those familiar with jewelry thought that it was around twenty thousand dollars, maybe more," she said.

"That couldn't have made Bergman very happy," said Kate.

"I'm sure she didn't wear it when she visited him," offered Laura.

"Probably not, but I have one final question, Laura."

"Yes."

"I believe that you had told me that she had no relatives listed on your church records, is that correct?"

"Yes, she had no relatives that we were aware of, and from what I understand from Pastor Christmas, the only people that he heard that showed up at the funeral parlor were church members. You know that she was cremated, don't you, Detective Heller?"

"Yes, that I'm aware of, but someone must have had to pay for that service, and if she had no relatives, well, that does seem to leave me with other questions, but that's my worry, not yours. Thank you, Laura. As usual, you've been very helpful. If you can think of any-thing else, please call my cell phone number any time of the day or night," said Kate as she said goodbye.

The next morning walking from the kitchen to her bedroom, Kate sat down next to her computer and asked for a listing of all the banks in Funston. Printing a copy of the banks, she then checked her files that had been provided to her on the death of Gayle Browning.

The report listed that the arrangements were handled by the Gilbert Funeral Home. Checking for the address, she noted that it was not far from the Lutheran Church. Checking her watch, the time was 8:00 a.m. Picking up her phone from her small computer desk, she placed a call to Curtis, leaving him a voice mail telling him that she missed him and asking him to call her sometime this evening. As she thought back to their evening together, she smiled as she remembered taking off her clothes and how modest he had acted being naked. He even had gotten up after the second time making love to her and put on a pair of pajama bottoms. Any additional modesty was quickly overcome when he had felt her now familiar fingers snake through the fly of his pajamas and caressed him. He then had moved back far enough in bed so he could pull down his pajama bottoms as he whispered in her ear that she had such a wonderful woman's sex drive that should be bottled so he could take it home with him tonight. "Oh, Curtis Patterson," she thought. "You have awakened this woman, and you fail to give yourself the proper credit, instead thinking I'm so special in bed while it's how you talk to me that releases that passion." Suddenly she felt a presence behind her and realized Channing was watching her. "Hey, big guy, I've been neglecting you, haven't I?" she asked. Channing, realizing he was being called, trotted over to her and put his paw on her lap. "Oh, I get it," said Kate, "you're hungry, aren't you?" She got up and walked into the kitchen to open one of his favorite cans of dog food. While Channing started to eat, Kate walked back into her bedroom and retrieved her sidearm, strapping it around her waist, and grabbed her leather police jacket. She figured that once she had let Channing out for his morning doggy break, she would be visiting the Gilbert Funeral Home in hopes of finding more answers about the private life of Ms. Gaylord Browning.

It was sixty-five degrees outside as Kate got in her Honda Civic and pulled away from the curb of her house, heading toward Butterfield Road. The drive should be less than thirty minutes, she figured. The sun had been high overhead as she started out, but now she could see a great swash of gray clouds begin to darken the sky, rolling in from the Northwest and stretching over most of Funston. "Darn, it's going to rain," she thought, "and I bet I forgot to close the windows. Smart policewoman you are." Kate continued her drive to the funeral home. In the distance, she saw the flash of lighting and could only hope that the storm would pass Funston and spare her the further concern about water coming in her bedroom. The only good thing was that Channing wouldn't be bothered by the thunder and lightning since for some strange reason unlike most canines he could sleep through the worst thunderstorms without fright. Seeing the large Gilbert Funeral building ahead, she slowed down and pulled into the parking lot. Kate had been here one other time when she had attended the chapel service for one of the relatives of her boss Captain Wagner. As she remembered, it was a sad case where the young man had shot himself in a hunting accident. Getting out of the car, Kate walked up to the front door and entered the chapel. Remembering from her past visit the location of the administrative office, she walked into the room and approached the receptionist.

Looking up, the middle-aged woman asked, "Can I be of assistance, Officer?"

"Yes, I wonder if I might speak to someone regarding a Ms. Gaylord Browning. I understand that your funeral home handled her final arrangements. This is official police business, and I'm the investigating officer regarding her death. I need a little information regarding who made the request for her arrangements."

The woman looked at Kate for a moment and then asked her to have a seat as she needed to locate the director of the establishment. Sitting down, Kate looked at the magazines near her, which were all typical of most offices where most issues were several months old. Laughing to herself, she noted that several were golf magazines and vacation-orientated places in which to enjoy family fun. Funny, she thought, you come to bury the dead, and they're promoting fun in the sun at the same time. As she was about to read about the Princess Hotel in Bermuda, she heard a voice speaking her name, which brought her back from the clean waters of the island that she had once visited to the business at hand. His sudden presence caused her to look up from the magazine she was reading,

"Detective, Heller I'm Winston Gilbert, the director of our funeral home. I understand that you are seeking some information regarding a Ms. Gaylord Browning."

"Yes, the needed information is part of my ongoing investigation of her death."

"We were told she died simply because of an insect bite, a spider as I recall," said Gilbert.

"That appears to be true, but our office has decided to take a second look. Spider deaths are most uncommon," said Kate. "Were you the individual that processed her remains?"

"You mean did the embalming?"

"Yes, the person who handled the preserving of the body until burial," asked Kate.

"This is a family funeral home, Detective Heller, so many of us participate in the preserving of the loved ones' remains. Since this was actually a cremation, my brother Walter was in charge of the arrangements," said Gilbert.

"Do you do the cremation here?" asked Kate.

"No, that is handled by the Forest Lawn Cremation Home. We just prepare the person for the family viewing," said Gilbert.

"There's an actual viewing for a cremation service?" asked Kate.

"There can be if the family wishes that to be the case. Sometimes the family requests it for the deceased family and friends, and other times the immediate family requests that the remains just be cremated without any viewing. Ms. Browning was prepared for full viewing for all."

"I understand, Mr. Gilbert, but in a case like hers having few family members, what happened to her the personal items such as rings, watches, clothes, etc.?" asked Kate.

"Those items are returned to her family if there is a family, and those items left unclaimed are kept here as required by state law for six months. After that, the establishment can either donate such items to worthy causes or, in rare cases, sell them," said Gilbert.

"Do you have a list of what those items were?" asked Kate.

Pausing for a moment, Gilbert asked Kate to join him in his office, where he kept all the personal files on such matters. Following Gilbert into his office, he offered her a seat while he opened up a massive file cabinet to search for the Browning file. Kate, sitting down, noticed the office was neatly decorated with family portraits of the owners and certificates of his professional background. Holding her smile, she observed that Gilbert had a signed picture of himself and Arnold Palmer, which was obviously taken at the Masters.

"Here it is, Detective Heller, the complete file on Browning. There were only her clothes and her watch," said Gilbert.

"You said she was cremated, Mr. Gilbert?"

"Yes, it's the new trend officer, with about 38 percent of families now choosing that method. The cost is substantially less, and most religious orders have no objection," said Gilbert. "With modern society so caught up in green and saving land, it's the way people are going these days. We of course would prefer traditional burial, but it's the family that makes that decision of course, so we leave that matter up to them."

"Just a few more questions, Mr. Gilbert. Our records indicated that she had no immediate family, so can you tell us who paid for her services and cremation?"

Looking at the file, Gilbert said, "The payment came from an anonymous donor."

"Isn't that somewhat unusual, Mr. Gilbert?" asked Kate.

"Unusual, yes. Illegal, no," said Gilbert.

"Was there a name on the check?"

"There was no check, Officer. The male individual just came in and paid for it with cash. As a matter of fact, he paid $300 more than the bill of $4,200 just in case there happened to be extra expenses. His instructions were to give the remainder of the money to her church if there happened to be any left over," said Gilbert. "There is a strange footnote here, though."

"What is that?" asked Kate.

"Like you, he asked if there were any rings on the body. We told him, of course, no."

"That does seem like an unusual question, Mr. Gilbert, considering that the benefactor should have no interest in any item from the deceased, let alone a ring. Wouldn't you agree?"

"Yes, that's true."

"Those are my only questions, Mr. Gilbert, but I would like you to talk to your brother and ask him if he could describe the benefactor in some detail such as age, height, and weight. Here's my card. I'll stop by and pick up any information he might recall. You've been most cooperative, Mr. Gilbert. The Funston Police Department is appreciative of your help."

Shaking his hand, Kate returned to her Civic, still wondering what this all meant.

The Prey

"Are you sure that's a good idea?" asked Barbara.

"What, opening a simple fruit basket just because Mary saw some little insect or bug?" asked Perry. "For Christ's sake, Barbara, the way you two are acting, one would think that we have a goddamn tarantula inside the basket rather than some simple bug."

"Watch your language, Perry. We're not your golfing buddies."

"You're right. Sorry for the poor choice of words, gang."

"It wasn't little, Daddy," said Mary. "It had a lot of hairy legs."

"Maybe you should leave the basket for a while, Perry, and see if it comes to the top," offered Barbara.

"Nope, this mystery has continued too long," he said as he lifted the cellophane off the fruit basket. "See, there's nothing there but fresh fruit, but I'll let it sit for a while just to satisfy everyone, all right? Now I'm going to wash up and change clothes, everyone, so no more talking about little critters in that fruit basket until after dinner," said Perry as he walked into the bedroom.

Barbara, following him into the bedroom, said, "Maybe you're being a little unfair about this subject, Perry."

"Really? What makes you think that?" he asked, somewhat irritated.

"Well, for one thing, we don't know who sent us this little gift, and second, it seems to me that I remember within the last year that some women in Funston had died from a spider bite. It was all over the news, or have you forgotten? And another thing that still bothers me is why would anyone use that jeweler's address?" asked Barbara.

"Yes, I remember," said Perry without turning around, although now concerned about where Barbara's conversation might lead. He couldn't help but wonder if she suspected anything.

"If I remember correctly, the woman that died was involved with some church pastor, wasn't she?" asked Barbara.

"Your memory is much better than mine, dear, but let's change the subject. Your point about Mary is understood, so give me a moment and I'll have a nice talk with her and tell her I'm sorry for being a jerk."

"I don't think that you're a jerk, Perry, just tired like me," said Barbara. Walking back out into the kitchen, she saw Mary pointing to the corner of the table.

"Don't move, Mommy, he's at the end of the table."

"What's at the end of the table—she started to say before suddenly screaming.

"What's going on now?" asked Perry as he rushed into the kitchen.

"There, don't you see it, Daddy?"

He had seen many spiders in his life, and most of them would scatter when they saw humans. This one was acting different and appeared to be inching down the table toward him, not running away as most spiders always did.

"Everyone, be calm and don't move an inch," cautioned Perry. It looked to be a full four or five inches in length, but what was unnerving was the sudden appearance of the spider's distinctive red jaws. The bastard appeared to have several sets of eyes, all now focused on him.

"Be careful, Perry," said Barbara. "I never have seen a spider like that in my entire life."

Now moving at a faster pace, the spider had inched its way to about three feet from Perry. "He's actually stalking me," thought Perry. The goddamn thing is acting like a hunter, not a spider. Perry could feel the perspiration forming on his forehead. Suddenly the spider's front legs stood straight up into the air and began to sway horizontally from side to side. "What the hell is that all about?" he wondered, now clearly frightened. And then it hit him. "Barbara, the bastard looks like he's going to attack me. If he does, I'll try to kill it somehow, but you get Mary and yourself out of the house fast," he said. The spider continued its swaying back and forth before abruptly stopping for a split second. As Perry was considering his next move, the spider leaped the remaining three feet onto Perry's shoulder. As Perry grabbed a kitchen towel, he crushed the spider, but not before he felt the bite and stinging feeling that ran up and down his arm. Barbara had taken Mary and retreated to the front door as she heard Perry yell, "I killed the little shit, Barbara! It's all right now, you can come back."

Crying, both Barbara and Mary came back into the kitchen and watched Perry dump the dead spider into the garbage can.

"Daddy, does it hurt very bad?" she asked.

"Yeah, it really stings, honey. Mommy needs to look for some antibiotic if we have any," he said. As she started to go to the bathroom to look for some medicine, Perry suddenly said, "Stop. Wait a minute, Barbara, something is wrong. I don't feel well."

"What's wrong, honey? Tell me," asked Barbara, now looking frightened.

"I feel like I'm breaking into a cold sweat, Barbara. I can tell that my heart is beating funny," he said, salivating at the same time. "Better call for the paramedics quick. I think the spider's venom may have been poisonous."

"Is Daddy going to be all right, Mommy?" asked Mary, now crying.

"Yes, now you stay with Dad while I call for help," said Barbara picking up the phone and placing a call to the Funston Fire Department Paramedics. After explaining the nature of the emergency, it was less than three minutes before she could hear the sound of the siren in the distance.

"Mary, you stand by the door and let the men in while I watch your dad!" yelled Barbara. Now going back into the kitchen, she observed Perry doubled over in pain. "They are on their way, honey. Where does it hurt now?" she asked.

"God, it hurts all over and doesn't let up. The venom seems to have caused me to have an unbelievable painful erection, Barbara. It's just so crazy and hard to explain," said Perry.

"There are here, Mommy, they are here!" yelled an excited Mary. In the next minute, the paramedics came through the front door into the kitchen, where they found Perry sitting on the floor in obvious pain, sweating profusely. Placing him on a stretcher, the three men carried him to the ambulance while telling Barbara she could ride with them or follow in her car.

"Wait!" yelled the third attendant at Barbara. "Find where you threw the dead spider. Bring it along if you still have it so the medical team might be able to tell what type of spider that they're dealing with."

Telling the paramedics that she would follow them, she grabbed the wastepaper basket and ushered Mary into her car as they sped off to Funston General Hospital. Five minutes later as she raced her car trying to keep up with the paramedic vehicle, she wondered why this was happening to her family. Now parking her car in the patient emergency section, Barbara and Mary were greeted by a Funston paramedic who told them to sit in the waiting room until a doctor came down.

"Why can't we go up and stay with him?" asked Barbara.

"The doctors are taking your husband to the critical care unit right now. There's nothing you can do but be patient, Mrs. Sinclair. I have to leave for another call, but I've asked a nurse to check in on you. Everything will be all right. These folks know their business," he said as he left to join the other paramedics outside.

As she paced the floor and watched Mary, she tried to decide what to do and whom to call. Trying to gather herself and make some sense out of what was happening, she heard the elevator door sounding its arrival. When the door opened, service people and nurses walked outside followed by an older man in a long white coat looking very much like a doctor. He walked directly over to her. "Are you Mrs. Sinclair?"

"Yes. Is he all right?" asked Barbara, talking nervously and looking very frightened.

Putting his hand on her shoulder, he said, "My name is Dr. Ogden. Your husband is fine at the moment, but in a lot of pain. I'm with the infectious disease department, and it's obvious to me that your husband has been bitten by some type of extremely venomous and dangerous type of spider. We haven't been able at this point to actually identify the type of spider, but from my preliminary examination, and early opinion, it would appear to be a Phoneutria-type spider from Central or South America. I have sent the dead spider's remains to our lab, where they can examine it more closely under a microscope, but from the symptoms, it would appear to be a Brazilian wandering spider, not common to this country."

"How could that be possible having spider of that type coming into our country, Doctor?"

"Sometimes they slip into our country by attaching themselves to fruit coming from these hot weather climates," said Ogden. "Regretfully those working in the produce departments at grocery stores often miss them hiding under the fruit, and we unwittingly become their victims like your husband. However, having said that, this is the first case that has ever appeared in this hospital, and admittedly we're all scrambling to find ways to treat it."

"This one came from a fruit basket delivered as a gift," said Barbara, now crying.

"The spider arrived in a fruit basket? That seems odd since someone would have had to pack the fruit," said Ogden, now looking puzzled.

"Is there something you can give him to kill the poison and reduce the pain?" asked Barbara.

"That's part of the main problem, Mrs. Sinclair. There is an antidote, but because this hospital hasn't ever had a need for it, the hospital doesn't store the antidote. The spider is not a native to the Funston area, or for that matter to the state, so as you can well imagine, there's a lot we don't know. However, we have located the antidote at another hospital, and they are sending it by air ambulance, so we hope to have it soon. Meanwhile, Mrs. Sinclair, we're doing our best to keep the situation under control. Now I have to get back upstairs, but we'll call you when you can come up, so just try and be calm. The good news is you were lucky to have a smart-thinking paramedic to have advised you to bring in that spider. He could have saved your husband's life," said Ogden.

"Thank you, Doctor," she said as she watched him reenter the elevator to head back upstairs.

Seeing her daughter still crying, she walked over to where she was seated. "It's going to be all right, dear, Dad is in good hands. We just need to wait and say a little prayer." She sat down and pulled Mary next to her.

"I hope so, Mom. Do you think that the spider that bit Dad was the only one in the basket?"

Stunned at her comment, Barbara didn't know what to say. The thought that more than one existed had never crossed her mind as she pictured the fruit basket still sitting on her kitchen table.

Black Friday Afternoon

The flight had taken only thirty-eight minutes to cross the coast of Lake Michigan and then a large swath of farmland, which brought him to the back end of the Jake Lindbergh runway. The runway's name had no connection to the original aviator but rather was simply a five-thousand-foot asphalt landing strip that had been created over the years by the Lindbergh lumber Company founder, Jake Lindbergh. It's location just happened to be adjacent to Curtis's home and Jake's son, Randy, a friend and owner of the farmland that butted up to his property that he allowed Curtis to use free of charge. While others had to provide a modest landing fee for its use, most didn't complain since it was the only landing strip in his hometown of Lift Bridge. Curtis was only obligated to take Randy to his choice locations for fishing largemouth bass.

Last night and tired from the evening with Kate, he had carried his small overnight bag up the five-minute uphill walk to the house and tossed it inside before he had taken a quick shower and went to bed. He heard it squeak under his weight and felt that it sank at least three inches. Tomorrow would be another day. But first, of course, there had to be another tomorrow.

Curtis had slept soundly during his six hours of rest. He had awoken at 5:00 a.m. from the sound of Randy's John Deere in the distance. He stretched his tight limbs, then felt a creak and then a pop in his left shoulder. "Thirty-eight years old and on the downhill slide," he murmured to himself. Pulling his body out of the bed, he walked over to mirror in the bedroom bathroom and looked at his face and the day-old stubble, now showing a few gray hairs. His height was always impressive at six foot six inches, with a rock-solid two hundred and thirteen pounds, but the nose? His nose had been broken once, and although he had it reset, he chose to not forget the mistake of years ago when he didn't keep his head up while trying to score a goal for his university hockey team. His hair was naturally brown, and he had a lot of it, but preferred to keep it short rather than the current style of over the collar. His facial features were highlighted by a cleft in his sharply defined chin. Tilting his head back, he examined the small quarter-size scar directly under his chin, which had been with him since birth. For whatever reason, few if any people that he could remember have ever commented about it, and certainly not Kate, who had every opportunity to see it last night. His mother always felt that it was God's special branding of a special son. Turning from the mirror, he walked to his bedroom window and pressed his face to the cool glass. The morning sky was brilliant. It was often that way this time of the day, and he wished that Kate were here right now to share this moment with him. He checked his watch. It had been less than twelve hours since he had held her, but the emptiness was building. Reaching for his cell phone on the dresser, he placed a call to her house, only to find that it went on her answering system. "Probably taking a shower," he thought. Wishing her a safe day and telling her that he loved her, Curtis ended the call by telling her how wonderful their time was together. Removing his clothes, he turned on the shower and stepped in. As he finished and was drying himself, he heard the unmistakable sound of his phone vibrating. Moving swiftly from the bath rug to the bed, where he had laid his phone, he quickly picked it up. "Hello, this is Curtis."

"Curtis, I just got your message. It was a wonderful time, wasn't it? What did I catch you doing this morning?" she asked.

"Not a thing. I just stepped out of the shower before you called. To be truthful, I was thinking about how nice it would be to have you here watching the sun come up with me."

"I would love to be there, Curtis. You have such a way with words to reach a woman's heart. When I start work today, I'll be able to look at my weekend schedule, so maybe we'll be able to find a way to spend some time together again real soon. That's provided, of course, that Delta hasn't assigned you a flight schedule this weekend."

"I'm still flying reserve, Kate, so any possibility of that happening is very slight as the regular bid captains want to fly their maximum hours. That's how they qualify for the big bucks. Anyway, I have a lot of vacation time coming, so you should consider my schedule available."

"That's really great. I'll leave you a message later today once I talk to the boss about where my cold cases are headed. I'm really sorry, honey, but some guy made me so tired that I'm running behind schedule, so I must go and feed the other man in my life before I go to work. Channing has been looking for his food for some time now. It's important to keep him on friendly terms now that he has competition for my time," she said, laughing. "Love you, Curtis."

"Love you too," he said. After Kate hung up, Curtis reached for his Dockers and his St. John's Bay polo shirt. When he finished dressing, he walked into the living room and sat down. It was still early in the morning, but it seemed like he had been up for several hours. It always had been difficult for him in recent years to sleep no matter how many hours that he had spent in bed. It had been this way for him for as long as he could remember. Not so much from nervousness as a desire for heightened preparation for what the day had planned for him. His brain was constantly thinking ahead, planning and refining the plan. That is what he believed had made him a better pilot than most as he always was finding the errors and fixing them before they happened. Leaning back in his La-Z-Boy, Curtis thought about the world that he lived in. A world that by most standards wasn't even remotely normal for a man his age to be enjoying alone. Getting up from the rocker, he walked over to the picture window and opened the drapes. He glanced admiringly at the large front yard and the numerous evergreens, which followed a careful designed straight line to his man-made fishing pond decorated with brown and white rocks that covered the banks on all four sides. An ivy-covered wooden bridge crossed over the center of the pond, allowing guests to walk across and view the several species of fish swimming and enjoying the water. Reaching to the right of the large picture window, he found the switch that illuminated the four installed field lights that shined down upon the pond area. Turning the switch on, he was satisfied that all the floodlights were in working order, so he turned them off and stared at the bridge.

He could picture Kate waving back at the house, wearing her finest wide-brim antebellum hat and mauve-colored gown as she held her parasol in her other hand to shade the morning sun. Was he assuming too much? After all, it was unlikely that a *Sports Illustrated* beauty like her would not have countless other men that would be aware of her besides him. But it was he, not some imaginary man, who had held this woman last night, so as they say, possession is nine-tenths of the law, and he was not about to give up his obvious advantage. Turning from the window, he walked into the kitchen to prepare his morning coffee and think about his next visit to Funston. If there were any other men, he was not going to wait for them to pick the flower of his choice—at least not without an effort on his part to make certain that she understood how much he really loved her. Pouring himself a cup of coffee, he wondered why he had chosen for so long to remain alone in Lift Bridge. He had a good career as a Delta captain, and his investments over the years provided him sufficient income to purchase one of the two or three most expensive properties in the area, matched only by the town banker and the owners of the Lindbergh lumberyard. As a pilot, he had travel the world and met his share of attractive women, many who had expressed their interest in ending what they felt was his needless desire to be a bachelor, something that actually was never part of his long-range plans.

His parents were the original reason why he had chosen to stay in the town that he grew up in, but now they had all but settled into their Florida Keys home, spending only a few weeks a year in Lift Bridge each summer. Worried about their only son, they use this time to try and introduce him to more than one of the town's available ladies, in particular female members of their adopted summer church, but Curtis had politely shown little interest. In fact, he had little interest in the church other than pleasing his parents by attending those Sundays he was in town. As a favor to his parents, he had accepted the request of the church's council to visit Funston and search for the history of his parent's church, and now by some strange manner of fate, he had met Kate. Pouring himself another cup of coffee, he thought back to the recent night with her just a few days ago. He couldn't dismiss how good the physical part of their relationship had been (Why couldn't he call it sex?), but that alone was not what he was feeling today. His life now had changed and seemed so complete because she was the woman that he had been searching for to fill his life and would remove his loneliness. When he was alone, as he had chosen to be for most of his adult years, he never paid much attention to what being alone really meant. Now today he found himself standing in his kitchen with his mind many miles away in a little town called Funston. The windows have become her eyes. The long-screened porch had become her mouth. The window watches you back, but never truly puts its arms round you or pulls you close. He suddenly began to realize that you give your life to bricks and mortar with little or no real meaning. Those many material things that he once cared about now seemed so unimportant because what he wanted now an desired was miles away, and he had no idea if this woman would want everything that he did. Over the years, he had managed so often to tell himself that he was managing just fine. And the truth was, he had managed just fine. He looked out the kitchen window for a moment at his Cessna aircraft now parked at the end of his lot. It was the symbol of what and who he was, a professional pilot. His friends openly admire the fact that he flew the wide-bodies as the captain for a major airline, but yet he wondered if that was enough, because after all, the woman that he loves might still be living with the ghost of her dead husband, let alone the admiring eyes of the competition in Funston. She had made no secret that her husband had been a kind and good man, and it was clear from her conversations that he once loved her deeply. "Truth was," he thought, "you never believed that it would happen, but it had. When you left her last night, you knew something was different. Since that first weekend when you held each other on that pagoda, you contemplated all the hours you have sat attentive and alert on the flight deck of the planes you had since flown and how recently you have found yourself growing less enamored of the white magnificence of those clouds that you once enjoyed flying though from thirty or thirty-five thousand feet. You remember the past moments when you would skim across the surface of those great clouds and begin to descent underneath them and how you would feel more like you were ridding the bottom of an ocean than a jet. Now that feeling has been replaced as you spend your hours alone trying to establish the needed courage to face rejection if that could become her choice about what you have in mind." Putting the coffee cup down, Curtis walked to the back door and stepped outside and glanced upward to the sky, as he had so often done in the early mornings. Today he watched the midday sun coming in through the break in the clouds as he waited for that call from Kate that would schedule his next trip to Funston. "Without a doubt," he thought, "a lot must be going through her mind as the pressure to bring closure to two high-profile murder cases weigh heavily on her mind, plus wondering if she has disappointed the memory of her dead husband by making love to another man."

Walking down toward the Cessna, his thoughts moved to the coming next two weeks when he would move from being a reserved captain to full-time. This change had been a day that he had been looking forward to when his schedule flights would finally be a triple-seven heavy, or the Boeing 777. He had been preparing for that, already knowing the flight deck by heart, even though he never had flown the wide-body before. How often he had pretended to sit straight in his seat, hands on the yoke, feeling the plane lurching forward, jerking just like a roller-coaster car at first until it reached its assigned altitude. But this was a dream, the training still in front of him, but the opportunity about to happen. "And yet you now only care if the woman is part of your future life." Curtis continued to circle the Cessna, prechecking the plane for his next flight while contemplating precisely how to begin telling this policewoman that he wanted her to be in his life when he felt the vibration of the cell phone on his waist. The sudden sound of the phone accepting the message told him that he failed to answer it in time and he swore to himself. Looking at the call identifier, he noted the phone number was Kate's cell phone, and his heart skipped a beat knowing he had missed the opportunity to talk to her. Dialing his mailbox, her voice appeared. "Sorry, I missed talking to you, Curtis, but it's been hell this week. Hope you understand and forgive me. You said you might have time this weekend, so if that's the case, I'm off this Saturday and would love to see you. Give me a call and tell me when you can arrive, if it's possible. Miss you."

"This Black Friday has now found some sunshine," thought Curtis as he left a message that he would be arriving at the airport around 9:00 to 9:15 a.m. on Saturday.

C H A P T E R   2 9

Closing In

Thirty minutes later after feeding Channing, Kate was dressed and going over her notes about her visit to the Gilbert Funeral Home. She was bothered about the mysterious benefactor that had stepped forward to pay the expenses for Gayle Browning. Here was a woman that had few, if any, relatives that her church knew about, yet someone had stepped forward and paid all her funeral expenses. Certainly these things did happen, but the curiosity that the stranger had demonstrated about a ring suggested some kind of close relationship other than just someone trying to do something for another person. "Why else," wondered Kate, "would he shown such an interest in that ring?"

Looking at Channing, who now appeared ready to go outside, Kate mumbled to the dog, "I think Bergman did kill his wife, big fellow," as if the dog could understand her. But the real question she continued was, did he kill his mistress also?

Opening the back door, she let Channing out and watched as he found his favorite spot near the back of the fence line. "What a dog life, not having to worry about your mess," she thought. It had been a brutal last few days for her with continued pressure coming from her bosses, along with that state's Attorney Underwood woman demanding answers that still were escaping Kate. Channing, now finished, ran back to the house and went scampering to his rug on the kitchen floor. Kate was exhausted, but she had work to do, so she went into the kitchen and made herself a cup of instant coffee. She was carrying the mug into the dining room with her notebook when her cell phone rang. Kate placed the mug on the table and answered it. "This is Detective Heller."

"Detective Heller, this is Gilbert. My brother asked me to give you a call regarding a Ms. Browning. He said you needed to talk to the person who prepared her for the viewing."

"Thank you for calling me back, Mr. Gilbert. I won't take up much of your time, but it was important that I talk to the undertaker who handled this lady and dealt with the family, so that's why I requested to speak to you. As you may have been told, the circumstances of Gayle Browning's death is still currently being reviewed, and this is just part of the investigation."

"We prefer the term funeral director, Detective Heller. It's a family business of two brothers and a sister, and we all are registered funeral directors with the state. It just happens that all the cremation requests are handled by me. In the example of Ms. Browning, she had no immediate family present, although her church friends were here in abundance. My guess was she had close to over seventy-five people paying their respects. She was such a beautiful woman to have died so early in life," commented Gilbert. "We are, of course, not medical examiners, so I don't know what I can help you with, although my brother indicated that you have requested a description of the individual who paid for our services. Is that correct?"

"Yes, that's correct, Mr. Gilbert."

"Ethics are very important to the Gilbert business, Detective Heller. The man requested that his contribution be strictly private. Usually information such as your requesting would require a court order, but since he wouldn't leave a name, I suspect that we are not violating his desire of confidentiality."

Gilbert couldn't see Kate rolling her eyes while trying to avoid providing her true feelings about this particular Gilbert who came across as a person who would usually enjoy talking down to people. Instead she simply replied with a smile in her voice, "I'm not a lawyer, Mr. Gilbert, but my guess would be that you are correct. However, you certainly have every right to consult your attorney should you feel uncomfortable about answering my questions."

The phone was silent as Gilbert paused for a moment to consider his answer. "As I specified, he indicated that he wanted to be an anonymous benefactor to the woman, so obviously I wouldn't have any record of his name. This is not as unusual as you might think, Detective Heller, because quite often many families just don't have the resources to pay for a funeral, and upon learning of another's plight, suddenly someone comes forward but doesn't want the immediate family to know. Pride can be very powerful, Detective Heller. In any event, Ms. Browning had that benefactor who took care of all costs."

"I understand that he paid cash, even provided extra money in the event your charges exceeded the usual cost for the cremation," commented Kate.

"Yes, that's true, but we didn't need the extra amount, so we contacted her former congregation. It's my understanding that the remaining funds were used it for a memorial in her name."

"Do you remember anything about the benefactor, Mr. Gilbert?"

"You mean other than being a man, Officer?"

"Yes, say, for example, how he was dressed, his height, weight, or color of his eyes? Some people like to wear jeans, others not so," she said.

"By the way he talked and handled himself, I would say he was a professional person. His mannerism suggested to me that he could have been a lawyer, a corporate executive, someone who was very used to being in charge."

"What was his physical appearance, Mr. Gilbert?"

"He looked like he was the type of man who spent a lot of time in health clubs. Very tan, about six feet tall, maybe 185–190 pounds. He was the type of man who enjoys being dressed in designer clothes."

"Why do you say that?" asked Kate.

"Well, he was dressed casual but seemed to favor the Polo-brand jacket and pants. He also wore excellent shoes."

"Age range, Mr. Gilbert?"

"I'd say around forty-five, forty eight."

"Is there anything else that you can remember, Mr. Gilbert?"

"Only that he asked several times if the lady had been wearing any special jewelry when her remains were delivered to us. I told him she wasn't, but he did seem to be concerned about some type of valuable ring. We always remove any valuables, Detective Heller, and return them to the family unless they specify differently."

"But what about someone like Ms. Browning, who has no immediate family, Mr. Gilbert?"

"In that case, we secure the items until notified by the county as to what to do with them. Right now we only have the items sent to us by the medical examiner, which was only a box containing the clothes that she was wearing plus her shoes and an inexpensive watch, nothing more. Is there any more questions, Officer? As I have several more families to deal with today. One of our directors is sick today, so I'm doing double duty," said Gilbert.

"One more question please. Does your funeral home maintain security cameras that would cover the parking lot or surround the building?"

"Yes, but usually those involved in crime don't consider a funeral home as a prime source of revenue," remarked Gilbert.

"Yes. That's true again, Mr. Gilbert, but I was thinking more of an opportunity for me to be able to see if you would have film on him leaving the building or, say, the type of car he was driving. Everything helps, Mr. Gilbert, in a police investigation, as I'm sure you understand."

"I'll check that date for you, Detective, and see if we still have a separate tape. Sometimes we record over tapes, so I'm not sure that it will do you any good."

"Do your best, Mr. Gilbert, that's all the Funston Police Department can ask for. Well, you've been extremely helpful, so I think that's all I'll need today. If you can think of anything else, I'd appreciate a call," said Kate, thanking him and hanging up. Sitting down, she thought about Gilbert's comments regarding this mysterious benefactor. First, she doubted that Bergman had any connection to paying for the cost of the arrangements since the Gilberts would certainly have recognized him from past visits during other church member's funerals. The ring was a puzzle, unless the man had purchased it for her and now wanted it back, either due to its value or the concern that it could be linked to him. Kate made a note to call the hospital and medical examiner to see if anyone could remember her wearing one, and if so, where the hell was it now? Checking her notes, she glanced at the list of banks that she had brought up on the computer. The church secretary, Laura, had indicated that one of the women in the choir had commented about a beautiful ring that Browning had been wearing, and she had admitted to the woman that she had received it from some guy named Perry, a banking executive.

"Wait a minute," thought Kate. Gilbert had just told her that the benefactor was some type of professional guy, like a lawyer. Someone who was used to giving orders, like maybe a banker, thought Kate, picking up her printed list of banks again. "Jesus," she thought to herself, "this town has fourteen banks and countless branches." It could take hours to track down a Perry, if in fact he had really told the woman his right name, which probably he hadn't if he was married and just using the dead woman. Still many men were notoriously stupid when chasing skirts. Getting up, Kate started to toast herself a raisin bagel and poured herself some orange juice since it obviously going to be a long afternoon. Looking at her watch, she suddenly remembered that she was to meet Curtis at the airport tomorrow morning. They had agreed to see each other on Saturday, and she been so tied up in this damn case today that she had almost forgotten. "What the hell is wrong with me, Channing?" she yelled at the dog as she again checked her watch and noted that if she worked hard, she still had a few hours remaining before she would call it a day.

Putting the list of the banks in front of her, she dialed the first one on the list. Three hours later, her frustrations increased as she had worked herself through one receptionist after another, countless human resource people, and half a dozen part-time employees at each bank on her list with no acknowledgment of anyone named Perry. Finally after the eighth bank, a young receptionist had told Kate that they had a chief financial officer whose first name was Perry. To her disappointment, Perry turned out to be a woman, causing Kate to wonder if he could ever be found before she lost her mind, patience, or both.

Taking break for a moment, she went into her bedroom and removed from her closet her favorite cream-colored Isadora ruffle blouse. Taking off her police uniform, she stood in front of the six-foot mirror and admired her body. Tall for a woman at five feet ten inches, she carried her one hundred twenty-seven pounds well. Turning to the side, she noted that marriage and the last three years had not changed the voluptuous suggestions of her healthy woman's figure. Moving her eyes up from her hips to her breasts, she put on the blouse and buttoned it to the neck. Satisfied, she walked back to the closet and selected her Marlin fit gray striped trousers. Now fully dressed, she stepped back from the mirror wondering if Curtis would really like the outfit as much as she did at this moment. She had often dressed up for her dead husband, and the best that she had heard from him was that she looked nice. On their last night together before he had left her life forever, she had purchased a silky black see-through negligee. He had made love to her for less than ten minutes before falling asleep, without saying a word about the negligee. Still Kate had loved him and, until Curtis, never considered any other man could have treated her better than he had. Well, Curtis was changing her mind. Removing the outfit, she hung it up in the closet, deciding to take a hot shower and read a little while before going to bed.

C H A P T E R   3 0

Missing You

Flying was his life, so the sight of geese and ducks flying below him didn't cause any special anxiety. A pilot's safety is often measured in understanding that you often share the same airspace as that of the birds, and since most migratory birds are attracted by open fields and grasslands, you attempt to stay away from those areas, especially when flying below 3,000 feet. Like any aircraft of this size, his $488,000 Skylark Cessna was not immune to the damage that could be caused by an 8- to 12-pound goose hitting the nose, the trailing edge of the aircraft's wing flaps, or the engine itself. Smiling, he thought that in the case of being hit by a bird that size certainly did matter. A tiny bird like a sparrow would not be able to cause any real damage, but at this altitude, there would be pelicans, cranes, and other-size flying bowling balls.

Curtis checked his airspeed indicator, which registered 145 KTAS. His altitude of 2,950 feet should have him well clear of the Canadian honkers, which roamed this part of Michigan in search of cornfields. He checked his watch and smiled at the thought that about now the woman he was falling in love with was getting ready to meet him at the Funston airport. He imagined her sitting in the passenger seat next to him. It was then that he saw the book on the seat *Fate Is the Hunter*. He had forgot to put it back on his bookshelf. The book, written in 1961 by Ernest K. Gann, was his favorite because it was an autobiography of the life of a former pilot who had flown old DC-2s and DC-3s. The book's popularity would later cause it to be made into a movie, although as he could remember, the author would become angry because it didn't resemble the original story. Reaching for the book, he tossed it onto the back two seats of the aircraft as he refocused his attention back to the open sky. Suddenly he heard the soft bang, then another, and then a third one. "What the hell was that?" wondered Curtis. He knew, but denial often comes easy. Reality with a pilot comes faster.

When his twin-engine Cessna hit the flock of birds, his heart sank for a moment. "You can handle this," Curtis reasoned. "It's happened before, but why now?" he wondered when his life was about to come together with the woman he was falling in love with. Then his professionalism training kicked in as the aircraft suddenly rolled fifteen degrees to its starboard side. In this area of the world, he remembered that the birds should be crows (lots of crows), seagulls, ducks, red-wing blackbirds, and unfortunately, stray geese. The geese were what concerned Curtis most because they were dangerous feathered objects traveling forty miles an hour. At least every other year, some pilot was almost decapitated by a goose crashing through his windshield. But for only the luck of God, no plane had gone down yet. Since his Cessna was powered by free rotating blades, Curtis knew that the hit would not find the birds disappearing into the metal and glass of his aircraft engines, but he knew that the blades of his engines could be affected. Curtis continued to climb as his plane wobbled briefly to its side, but he noted that the trajectory remained firm, as did the air speed. Neither engine showed any sign of reduced power or potential flameout, so the conditions look good, rationalized Curtis.

For whatever the reason at this moment, Curtis thought about Chesley Sullenberger and how he was able to land his aircraft in the cold Hudson River and save all those lives. The man turned out to be a hero, using his experience as a fighter jock with twenty-seven years' experience to the limited sixteen years that Curtis has logged. Arguably a lot of difference, but Curtis knew his skills were exceptional, especially when challenged as he was now. His Cessna began to level off, but he continued to search the land below for possible emergency landing areas. Before him already loomed Cottonwood

Lake sixty-miles from his home. The Cessna continued through the cerulean-blue sky toward Funston, with Curtis watching the terrain and his cockpit light indicators for any signs of trouble. And while radio communication seemed furthest from one's mind, he knew that it was time to contact the Funston tower and alert them to the fact that he had encountered a bird strike and that they should be prepared for a possible emergency landing. The decision was not an easy one since he knew that in a small town like Funston, any plane emergency would be major news on any radio or television outlet.

"Funston Tower, this is Skylark triple seven, over."

"Roger, Skylark. We have you on radar. What do you need?"

"Just stand by," Curtis responded as he remained focused on the instrument panel and his air speed.

"This is Funston Tower, acknowledge if you need assistance."

"Funston Tower, this is Skylark triple seven. I encountered a bird strike, but there's no indication of any damage to the Cessna. Everything appears fine. You can do me a big favor if you would have someone check to see if a beautiful woman is waiting for me in the business aircraft terminal. She's a Funston police officer and may have picked up on the developing problem over the local police band radio. There's absolutely nothing for her to worry about."

"Roger that. You must be talking about Detective Kate Heller. She's every guy's number ten in this town," said the male controller laughing. "We'll make sure she gets the word, Skylark. And let me just say that you are one lucky fellow to have someone like that waiting for you, fellow."

Kate had gotten up early after taking a shower for the third time since last night. Why, she was not sure, any more than understanding why her heart was beating rapidly either. It must have been from plain nervousness or anxiety over missing Curtis. Adrenaline coursed through Kate. She had to get control of herself. She was not a schoolgirl, but her actions seemed to suggest something else. Turning on the local Funston twenty-four-hour news, she listened to an array of endless political opinions and minor claptrap about the expansion of a new highway direct to downtown Detroit. "Who the heck cares about Detroit?" she said to Channing, now watching her get dressed.

"The whole city is nothing but gangbangers killing each other. The place makes Gary, Indiana, look like a honeymoon destination compared to the burned-out sections of Detroit," she reasoned.

Kate remembered her now-deceased parents telling her how they used to ride their bikes on a Sunday through downtown Detroit over to Belle Isle Park. It was described by her mother as five miles of the most beautiful scenic shoreline one could ever see. Her dad would join in on the story of their Sunday bike rides, looking at her mother, saying, "Tell her about the submarine races," while her mother would look away smiling. It took her girlfriend to break the news to her about those submarine races since her parents chose to keep the secret to themselves. "Then again," she wondered, "how does one explain to her daughter that Dad and Mom were fooling around in the back seat of a car?" Reaching for her gray striped slacks, Kate checked the fit of her slacks in the bedroom mirror before she sat down on the bed and put on her newly purchased white Adidas walking shoes. Turning her attention back to finishing dressing, she started to put on her blouse while listening to the radio station's sports report discussing the decline of the Detroit Pistons basketball team. As she was checking the blouse to assure it didn't expose too much cleavage, she stopped and froze when the announcer mentioned that the airport was tracking a private plane on approach that had encountered a bird strike. The announcer was uncertain of the situation but encouraged everyone to stay tuned to the station for further updates. Kate, trying to assure herself about the odds against this being Curtis, grabbed her undercover .38 Special, tossed it into her handbag, and walked briskly down the hallway and out the door to her car.

In less than ten minutes, she had arrived at the Funston Airport and parked at the private section designed for business travelers. Leaving her handbag in her car, she activated the door locks and walked in to an empty terminal building and looked out onto the airfield.

"Detective Heller," said the voice waking through the door marked Private.

"Yes?" said Kate.

"I'm Sandy, the airport dispatcher. We got a call from the pilot of a Cessna that will be landing shortly and wanted us to tell you not to worry. He said everything was fine, just had a soft bird strike."

"Did he give you his name?" asked Kate.

"No, just told the tower that a Funston police officer would be waiting for his arrival and that he didn't want you to worry."

"But he never gave his name?" asked Kate again with an obvious worry on her face.

"No, but using his exact words may give you all the clue you need," said Sandy smiling. "He said to check on that beautiful woman waiting for him. Those were his exact words, Detective Heller. That must mean something to you, Detective Heller," said Sandy, snickering.

"Yes, it sure does. Yes, it sure does." Turning to the window, Kate thanked Sandy and watched the sky. Within five minutes, she observed the smooth glide of the Cessna making a perfect landing, using only about half the runway before taxiing toward the terminal and shutting its engines down. Wiping the moisture from her eyes, she waited patiently as Curtis gave instructions to the waiting maintenance crew, then turned and walked briskly into the terminal building. Seeing her smiling face, he walked to her, kissed her, and then whispered in her ear that they better leave before someone snapped their picture or wanted an interview.

"It wouldn't be a good day for the male population," he said, "to read that some other man may have picked the town's prettiest flower."

"Did you say 'may have'?" questioned Kate.

"Well, you know what I mean," replied Curtis.

"Maybe you better spell it out somewhat clearer before the day end's, Mr. Patterson," she said holding hands as they left the terminal building.

Sliding into the car, Curtis reached over from the passenger side and pulled Kate to him and kissed her hungrily.

"Wow, you did miss me," she said.

"More than words can say, Katherine."

"Oh, it's Katherine now?" she said, teasing Curtis.

"Only on special days, just to let you know how much I love to say your name."

"All my life, Curtis, people have called me Kate or Katie. You're the first that has called me Katherine since my father. We'll leave it special just between us," she said. Putting the gear handle in drive, she pulled the Civic out of the airport onto the expressway. "Was it scary?" asked Kate.

"You're talking about the bird strike?"

"Yes."

"No, actually, I was more scared when I saw you in the terminal waiting for me. I've hit birds before, so it's all about your previous pilot training when that happens. However, in the art of falling in love with a woman, I've had little training."

"I think you're doing very well, Curtis, from my past experience with you."

"I'll take that as a compliment that I'm at least beginning to learn. Tell me about that outfit you have on today. Is it new?"

"Yes," she responded, now uncomfortable, not quite sure where this conversation was headed, but keeping her eyes on the road. "Do you like it?" she asked, taking a chance on his answer.

"It's gorgeous. You are a natural stunning woman to begin with. Then add to it that ruffled blouse alone that you're wearing today only enhances the fact that you have the rare ability to wear fine clothes and elevate that attractiveness to raw sensuality. It's unfair to all the men in Funston that here I'm the chosen one to be alone with such a beautiful creature."

Kate changed lanes and entered the street that would bring her to her townhouse. "That's quite a compliment, Curtis, one that any woman would love to hear from that special man, but remember, I've dressed up for you today, not anyone else, so if as you say that raw sensuality exists in your eyes, it is only for you. You're only the second man that I've ever dressed up for, Curtis. The first one used the phrase that I 'scrub up nice.' That was at the time a nice compliment. You, on the other hand, can make me blush, but in a nice way."

"Sorry, I'd didn't mean to embarrass you, Kate."

"Don't apologize. A woman wants to feel wanted. Like the time on the pagoda, Curtis. I could tell that your body wanted me, but you didn't try to go any further, although admittedly I would have let you despite the fact that we could have been discovered. That's being wanted, not used."

Curtis was about to respond, but Kate had changed lanes and was pulling up to a seafood take-out restaurant. "You stay put, flyboy. Today's my treat," she said, getting out of the car. As she entered the small restaurant, he noticed the newspaper rack. Getting out, he put the three quarters in the slot and removed the paper while returning to the car to wait for Kate. Turning to the sports page, he checked the standings of the Detroit Red Wings and was about to read about the recent trade of their star defenseman when Kate came out and jumped into the car. As she was pulling back out into traffic, she smiled and said, "Ah, my raw sensuality has now taken second place to the sports section already?"

Looking at her, Curtis paused for a moment before saying, "Don't underestimate my true priorities when it comes to you, Officer. This man would never ever sit at a table or while in a car read a newspaper while he could be looking at your nipples bursting through that ruffled blouse."

"What did you say?" she yelled in shock.

"I'm having fun with you, dear, just funning with you. Everything is where it should be," he said laughing as she playfully punched him on the shoulder.

Pulling up to her townhouse, he got out of the car carrying the seafood and the paper up the stairs as she was already opening the door. Entering, they were greeted by Channing, who smelled the seafood but turned away.

"Guess he's not a fish lover," commented Curtis.

"No, he's an Alpo meat lover," said Kate. Walking over to Curtis, she spoke softly into his ear, "Why don't you take the seafood and put it on the table while I fix Channing his dinner, or would you like to venture into my raw sensuality first?"

Not believing he heard right, he pulled his head from her whispering lips while hearing her laugh as she said, "Now who's blushing, Mr. Patterson?" she asked, walking into the kitchen.

After they had eaten, Curtis got up and invited Kate to join him on her couch. "That was perfect. I've always liked seafood. They have some great seafood at Fisherman's Warf in San Francisco when I have a stopover there. But they don't have the excellent company that I'm with today," he said, reaching in his pocket and pulling out a small box.

As she stared at the satin box, a sudden moment of anxiety started to surface. Kate wasn't certain where this was heading, nor was she certain if she was prepared.

Curtis, becoming sensitive to her developing anxiety, reached over and put his hand on hers and said, "Relax, dear Kate. While I might be inexperienced in finding the right woman to love, please understand that I do have the ability to recognize fear in others. Before you open this box that I have for you, I want you to listen to me for just a moment. More importantly, so that you understand I would love to take you up on that little offer that you made in my ear earlier. However, that's not why I flew in to see you today. Sure it would be a lie if I didn't honestly say I've been dreaming of that ever since I had returned back to Lift Bridge, but again, that's not why I'm here with you today. Remember earlier today I told you that the fear that I had was not in the bird strike that caused some initial concern, but rather you were my fear, and for a very good reason. You see, life doesn't always present the opportunity to find that one special person in their life that they have been searching for. This little box is my gamble that you might feel this man is worthy of being with you for the rest of his life. If you're scared or unsure because it's too soon, I will understand."

Her heart beating, Kate tightened her grip on the box but hesitated in opening it up as she looked directly into his eyes, tears now beginning to form. Looking back down at the box, she took a deep breath and slowly opened it. She froze as she gazed upon the array of moon-accent diamond stones with the yellow sapphire in the center.

"Oh my god, Curtis, it's gorgeous. I've never seen any ring more beautiful in my life."

"I hope not, since it was created only for you, the woman I love and want to marry," said Curtis.

"You mean it has no duplicate?"

"No," he said simply. "You happen to be only one of a kind." Getting up, he pulled her up with him and put his arms around her while kissing her neck. Now facing her forward, he drew her tight against him until she felt his familiar body and his hands now surrounding her waist. "You have time, Kate," he said while putting his head against hers. Pushing back against him, she took his right hand and moved it gently to her breast.

"I don't need time, Curtis. The answer is yes. I love you too." She turned around and put her arms around his neck. "While I understand why you are here today, you have to understand that your future wife has a right to her feelings also. I don't want you to leave and go back to Lift Bridge right away," she said as she took his hand and led them both into her bedroom. "Now tell me more, Mr. Patterson, about that raw sensuality."

Curtis woke up when he heard Kate's voice. At first he thought that he was dreaming and tried to shake the dream from his head, but he couldn't because she was talking to someone.

"Jake, this is Kate," she said softly, trying not to wake Curtis.

Curtis, opening his eyes, could hear the other male voice yelling back.

"It's Sunday, for Christ's sake," he said. "Where the hell are you, Detective Heller?"

"I'm in bed reading the newspaper," she said while watching Curtis wake up and look at her. Putting her finger on her lips, she signaled him to be quiet as she continued, "How come I'm the last one to know about the new spider bite victim?" she asked.

"What goddamn spider bite victim are you talking about?"

Curtis, now fully awake, turned over, smiling at Kate and at the same time rolled over and put his lips on the inside of her open thigh.

Smiling back, she mouthed the words, "I'll change my mind."

Now getting up with a look of faked sadness, he walked into the bathroom and closed the door and started the shower. Returning her conversation back to Jake, Kate said, "The spider bite that this guy over at Funston Hospital is apparently dying from. It's all over the news, and we don't know anything about it? Let me help a little then. His name is Perry Sinclair, and he's in critical condition according to the article. Although it's probably a long shot, my cop intuition is telling me that it might be connected to the Bergman situation."

"You're kidding me," said Jake. "What makes you connect him to the Bergman case? Do you by any chance have the scoop of the century packed in your sexy lingerie that you're wearing in bed? As I remember, Bergman left town sometime back and is living in Wisconsin."

"Look, Jake, I'm not carrying any scoop in my lingerie, you pervert. The guy's name just recently came up as someone that Gayle Browning might have had an interest in before she died. Do you or do you not have any information that you're holding out on me?" she asked.

"Not a bit," he said. "Do I need to know anything more about this before our Monday meeting with Captain Wagner?"

"Yes, Sergeant. You need to write this down in order that you understand. First, I don't wear lingerie to bed. Never have, never will. I'm the type of woman that wears nothing. Second, this case is making me grumpy, so don't take anything personal," Kate admonished as she hung up the phone. Hearing the water in the shower still running, she walked into the bathroom and opened the shower doors. "So you started before me," she said as she joined Curtis in the shower.

Driving to the airport, Kate talked about the paper that she had found on the table that he had purchased while she was getting the seafood. She told him about her visit to Bergman's former church and how the dead organist had mentioned to a member of the choir about some banker by the name of Perry, who had given her a ring that was now missing. Now the guy was in the hospital from apparently being bit by some spider.

"So you think he may have been bit by the same type of spider?" asked Curtis. "I thought that you had ruled out that a brown recluse spider had killed her?"

"I have, but this is too weird for me not to follow up on this story." Pulling up to the terminal, Curtis drew Kate close and gave her a deep kiss."

"I hate this part," she said. "It's not fair that we live so far apart."

"It drives me crazy too," said Curtis, "but I'm carrying a lot of your love back with me for the next few days. Say, that's a beautiful ring that you have on," he said as he walked toward the terminal building.

Glancing down at the ring and thinking about their last moments together in the shower, Kate knew that this separation wasn't going to work much longer for either of them. She then watched as he started the plane's engines and moved toward the runway. In a few minutes, Curtis lifted off the airport toward his home away from her. Crying, she started her car engine and headed to the hospital.

The Hospital Visit

Kate pulled up to the visitors' section of the hospital and shut her Civic down. As she exited the car, she checked to make certain that she had pinned her detective shield to her belt buckle. She had decided against changing into anything else than what she had worn to the airport. It was Sunday, she was a detective, and this was the best that the Funston police department was going to get today.

Great generals shone on the battlefield, most senators and congressmen excelled at bullshit on their playing field, and Kate Heller knew that she had few equals when it came to tenacity. She was smarter and better prepared than almost any cop she'd gone up against, and she truly believed that her work ethic and mental reasoning were second to none. Therefore, her jeans and matching light-blue shirt should do the trick, she thought. "Best-dressed detective on the force," she laughed to herself. When she strode through the emergency swinging doors of Funston General Hospital, she was radiating the confidence that a hawk has when spotting the young chicken in the farmer's field. The physical demands of the coming week would almost seem a relief in comparison to what she expected to be waiting for her within these walls. Looking around for the information desk, she heard the exchange between some young doctor and what appeared to be an unhappy mother. "Whatever's ours is yours," the young doctor replied to the apparent frustrations of the mother. "Your primary care physician will receive the lab report and contract you directly. It shouldn't be much longer."

"Can you do some more checking?" the mother asked. "It doesn't add up, Dr. Mitchell."

"I'll do what I can," he said as he looked at his watch in hopes that he could find some reason to escape her persistence.

Kate turned away from the ongoing conversation in hopes of finding someone who could help her. Then she spotted the young girl standing next to an information booth.

"Good morning," said Kate to the candy striper volunteer, who looked to be all of fourteen years old. "I'm Detective Heller of the Funston Police Department. Could you please direct me to the senior duty nurse or who I might talk to regarding one of your patients?"

As the candy striper turned to look for assistance, a middle-aged woman wearing a stethoscope approached both her and Kate. The woman had that look of being in charge and took Kate back to her first encounter with Sister Agatha when she was in Catholic grade school. The look that said, "Just accept and don't push it."

"Good morning, Officer. I'm Mrs. Maggie Olson, the head nurse for the morning staff. What is it I can help you with?"

"Mrs. Olson, you have a patient in the hospital by the name of Perry Sinclair. He was admitted two days ago. It's important that I have a word with his doctor since the matter involves a current active ongoing police investigation. Is his doctor in the hospital this morning?"

"He is, but I can't guarantee that I can reach him. You see, Mr. Sinclair is in very serious condition in our critical care unit. My guess is the doctor is with him along with other staff members all trying to control the situation."

"And what situation is that, Mrs. Olsen?" asked Kate.

"That information, Detective Heller, I need to leave for discussion with Dr. Alan Ogden, his disease specialist that has arrived here from Wisconsin. As a hospital, we are required by the federal government to follow the rules of HIPPA or lose our tax-exempt status. It's silly, I know, but in truth we sometimes can't even release information to the spouse. The rules today, Detective, put handcuffs on medical people to release even the most basic information."

"Fair enough, Mrs. Olson, but I'd appreciate it if you try and track down Dr. Ogden. I'll wait until he's free, but I must see him before I leave this hospital. By the way, what actually is the doctor's specialty?"

"He's a top infectious disease doctor that we had to fly in by helicopter. Regretfully our hospital was not equipped to deal with this situation, nor did we initially have the means to stabilize the problem that Mr. Sinclair faces. Now if you will excuse me, I'll go direct to the critical care unit and see if I can locate the doctor. It may take a while, so please have a seat. I'll call you if I can't find him or send him down to see you if I do."

"Thank you, Mrs. Olsen, I'll be right over in the waiting area doing some paperwork," said Kate. Watching the head nurse walk toward the elevator, Kate thought the nurse provided some interesting comments for someone so guarded. She knew that bringing in outside help would be something most hospitals would try to avoid before admitting that they were in over their heads. "This is the same hospital that handled the Browning woman's autopsy, and they didn't need any specialist to determine the cause of death in her case." She wondered if the chief administrator of the hospital was now having second thoughts about the previous case of a spider bite.

Kate was still secretly furious over the arrogant Dr. Patel not willing to reconsider his initial judgment that Browning had died of a brown recluse spider bite, but it would seem that the Funston medical team had something else with Sinclair. While she was waiting, she sent Curtis a text telling him her ring was beautiful. She concluded her message by telling him they needed to discuss the wedding plans the next time he was in town as she was anxious to be his wife. As she finished writing down several questions that she would need to talk to Curtis about, the strange voice startled her.

"You are Detective Heller, I take it?" asked the doctor.

"Yes, and you must be Dr. Ogden. I appreciate you taking the time to see me, Doctor. I wouldn't have bothered you, but your patient Perry Sinclair has a particular interest to me regarding an ongoing case that I'm working on. You see, several months ago, this hospital performed an autopsy on a deceased woman, a Ms. Gayle

Browning. Like Mr. Sinclair, she was also bitten by a spider, but regretfully she died at her home."

"Under most circumstances, death by a spider is most unusual, Detective Heller. What type of spider supposedly bit her?" asked Ogden.

"The medical examiner of this hospital, a Dr. J. Patel, stated that it was a brown recluse."

"Oh really?" said a surprised Ogden. "That would be most unusual to die from that type of spider bite since the brown recluse is more noted for causing the affected area to sometimes, in extreme situations, require amputation, but causing a death? Now that's something very unlikely based on national health statistics. You're sure, Detective Heller, those were the actual findings?"

"Yes, I read the report myself."

"Well, I'm on loan to this hospital, so I try to avoid getting into any political squabbles, but rest assured, Detective, that few doctors have the medical background to actually distinguish the difference between a mite or tick bite from that of any spider. Anyway, so that we can both get on to our work, what is it you might need to know about Mr. Sinclair's illness that I might be able to share with you?"

Kate couldn't help but notice that Ogden and Curtis were about the same height, although Curtis was somewhat more rugged look-ing and about twenty-five pounds heavier. "What's is his condition, and have you been able to determine the cause of his illness?" asked Kate.

"As you know, Officer, I have to be very careful discussing any-one's medical issues. The government has put serious restraints that can even affect our ability to practice. What I will say to you is he can use a few prayers to relieve his pain, but I'm confident the antidote will win the day. He was, in my opinion, attacked by a Phoneutria spider. The venom is toxic to the human nervous system, especially to a man. In some examples, like that being experience by Mr. Sinclair, it will cause prolonged painful erections that can last several hours. The worse cases can prove lethal, although that's actually rare."

"Sorry, Dr. Ogden, but that type of spider I've never heard of."

"It's more common name is the Brazilian wandering spider. Phoneutria is what the medical field refers to it as. Others just call it a banana spider, but it's one in the same."

"You must have been fortunate to have seen the actual spider," commented Kate as she wrote down the name in her notebook.

"You obviously know something about this subject, Officer, since under lab conditions is really the only way for its proper identification? The paramedics brought in the dead spider, and I put the Phoneutria, or banana spider, under a microscope. It has many names, I'm afraid. There is no doubt about this one that I can assure you of. His cousin is very common in certain parts of this country, but the Brazilian spider is a rare find, although because of the international market now bringing into this country more types of foods, it has resulted in some unwanted guests."

"In truth, I've actually seen this type of spider myself, Dr. Ogden, in a controlled environment in the home of a professor of entomology. He actually kept them in glass fish tanks with a secured lid."

"My guess is you're referring to Professor Davis, since he's usually my supply source for any antidote and background information on this type of spider. Hospitals rarely store the antidote because few cases ever come up that need it."

"Obviously, Doctor, we've met the same professor," said Kate. "Do you know if Mr. Sinclair's wife is in the hospital? I need to interview her as part of my investigation."

"No, she should be home as I encouraged her to get a few hours of rest. I told her we would call her should his situation change," said Ogden. "Now if you would excuse me, I must get back upstairs and see how he's doing, Detective. I don't want to be impolite, but he's not having a walk in the park over this thing."

"I understand, Doctor. Here's my card should you feel that I need to know anything else. Again, thank you for this cooperation. I'm only a Christmas and Easter Catholic, but I will say a prayer for the Sinclair family. Please keep our conversation private to Mrs. Sinclair, because her husband actually knew the lady that died, and she may not be aware of it."

Looking somewhat puzzled about her comment, Ogden said, "I think I understand, Officer," shaking her hand, "but you need to consider doing something about that church attendance and going only on Christmas and Easter. Incidentally, that's a beautiful engagement ring, so one day you might need someone to bless your future marriage." He entered the elevator.

Kate watched the door shut before turning away and heading out of the hospital. "He's really a nice guy," she thought, getting into her car, but the religious stuff was most unusual for a doctor since the majority of doctors that she ever met didn't seem to put much stock into religion. God, she was tired. No doubt it was due to Curtis. She smiled, put the car into drive, and headed home. She noticed that the sky had become faded denim blue. The trees were now giving the first hint of how brightly they would appear when it turned fall in a few weeks. Although she knew very little about Dr. Ogden, she could tell that he would maniacally approach his work in order to discover any elusive evidence necessary to identify what had caused Sinclair's current problem. Something that he had said about the spider's name stuck in her head, but her exhaustion prevented her recall ability to function as it normally would.

C H A P T E R   3 2

Return Visit

"Glad you had the time to come along, Elmer," said Jack. "Dr. Ogden was scheduled to join me but has been called out of town regarding a sick patient in Funston, Michigan, and with Pastor Bergman having requested a few days off, I thought it would be the time for me to look over the parsonage. As you heard from Ogden, there remained a few concerns from the report that was submitted. Don't misunderstand, Elmer, the inspection was fine, and don't read anything into this revisit, but some things have come up that we can't discuss. When we're able to talk about it, everything will be much clearer." Jack now made the final turn that followed the dirt road leading to the entrance to the parsonage grounds. Looking at Elmer, he felt the need to explain a little more before they arrived. After all, Elmer had belonged longer to the congregation than him and, besides the two men that Jack and Ogden had assigned, had actually had done a good job.

"I've advised Pastor Bergman that we needed to do a reinspection in order to satisfy all insurance requirements and the church council. As we did before, we gave him the opportunity to join us and be here when we did this, but he declined, saying it wasn't necessary. He was even told that we would delay this inspection until his return, but once again, he said that it wasn't necessary. In other words, it's important to me that should this subject ever come up, that it be understood we respected the pastor's privacy."

"What are you looking for, Jack?" asked Elmer?

"To tell you the truth, Elmer, I have no idea. Alan and I just have an uncomfortable feeling about what might be going on at the place, nothing more."

"What makes you think that way?" asked Elmer.

"It's something that has been just recently brought to our attention about the pastor's former life in Funston, where he had previously served before becoming our pastor. But as I said, we can't comment on that at this time. My guess is that the pastor will discuss it shortly and clear up any and all questions. That's all that I can comment on, Elmer, so please be patient. I know that this is hard to do, but we just have to be careful, but I will give you a little information."

"The talk is that he had problems before coming to us," said Elmer. "It's my understanding that his wife had been hurt in some kind of home invasion about two years ago. Elsie Cutter said her daughter had read about it when she had traveled to Michigan to visit her kids last year."

Jack, now trying to decide how to answer those comments, replied, "Yes, that's true, but to the best of my knowledge, that information hasn't been released to the congregation yet, Elmer. The pastor has not officially confirmed any rumors. It's something, as I just mentioned, that we have to be very careful about until he says something, since to do otherwise is an invitation to have the district come down hard on us for interfering with the pastor's private life." Now seeing the parsonage, Jack said, "Well, we've arrived, partner. It's time to get to work."

Pulling the car up to the entrance to the parsonage, Jack stopped the vehicle and shut off the engine. "Let's get this over with, Elmer," said Jack as he got out of the car. Both men now walked up the cement steps and stood on the porch.

"Looks like he forgot to lock the door," commented Elmer as he turned the doorknob and the door opened wide.

"Anyone home?" yelled Jack.

"I just think he forgot to close it," said Elmer as he walked inside and stood in the living room. "It looks just the same as how Ed and I left it."

"Well, I'll have to remind him, Elmer, about the door being open, because there's a lot of things in here someone could steal that are both his and also belong to the congregation," said Jack as he walked toward the master bedroom. "Look here," he remarked.

"What?" asked Elmer.

"He even left his computer on. Look at all those stupid-looking spiders on his screen saver, Elmer," remarked Jack as he sat down on the leather computer chair.

"Yeah, Ed and I seen the spiders before. He must like bugs. That's the only thing we could come up with when we first looked at his computer. Since I'm not against any law to like spiders, we considered it his business, not ours. If it would have been pornography, we would have reported it."

"It is his business, and we're not here to interfere with that, yet it's also our concern to satisfy ourselves that any members of the congregation that might visit him at the parsonage are comfortable. You know that twice a year the church has activities here. In early March the Easter egg hunt, and later in July the woman hold their annual thirty days of prayer." As Jack continued to talk to Elmer, he reached inside the wastepaper basket to retrieve a piece of disregarded paper to write a reminder memo to talk to Bergman about the unlocked door. Looking at the paper, Jack noticed that it contained a list of names underlined in red. "Elmer, do we have any new members by the name of Gayle Browning or Laura Staple?"

"None of those names ring a bell, Jack, but you know how it works. The pastor always follows up on those that sign our Sunday register for future potential members. Those might be just candidates to join our church or acquaintances of his."

"What about a woman, Kate Heller, from Funston, Michigan. He's written her name down also?"

"No, maybe just a family friend," said Elmer.

Spinning around in the chair, Jack focused on an eight-by-ten-inch hanging picture of four guys with golf clubs standing next to an autographed picture of Tiger Woods. Getting up from the chair, Jack walked over to the framed picture and looked closer. He could make out Paul Bergman, but the other three he failed to recognize. Funny, he thought, as many times as they had invited the pastor to go golfing, he had always declined, saying he never played golf, but there he was posing for a picture with one of the world's most recognizable golfers. Placing the picture back in its original spot, he then returned to the desk and removed the small papers containing the names from the wastepaper basket. Sticking the scraps of paper in his pocket, Jack turned away from the computer and began moving throughout the rooms of the parsonage, rechecking all the electrical sockets and the bathroom plumbing.

"Elmer!" he shouted. "Do you remember checking the water heater and furnace?"

"They were both all right, but you can recheck them if you want. They're located down near the guest room. The tags indicated that the water heater is less than four years old, and the furnace is listed as six years old."

"Jack, that picture of the golfing buddies."

"Yes, I put it back."

"That's not what I meant. It wasn't here before. There was just a picture of a woman playing the organ. He must have replaced the picture."

Walking back to the bedroom, he pulled the golfing picture off the wall and turned it around. "Just like I thought," said Elmer, pulling the frame apart and finding the woman's picture hidden inside the frame. He handed it over to Jack.

"Very nice-looking woman, Elmer, nice indeed, but I've never seen her before. Again, nothing that is our business," he said, replacing the picture on the wall.

"Everything looks good in the house, Elmer. Let's walk down and take a look at the attached shed and garage. Then we can wrap it up and call it a day."

Jack reached the shed first and was beginning to unlock the door when Elmer walked up beside him and was holding an empty, fired rifle shot casing. "Probably someone doing target practice," remarked Jack.

Walking inside, they stood in the middle of the large room, taking in what appeared to be more of an arranged living area than a storage room. The snow blower and lawn mower occupied a corner of the room, but looked out of place with the new couch and two easy chairs.

"Is that the gun cabinet over on the right side near the wall, Elmer?"

"One of them," said Elmer. "Ed and I spotted it the last time, along with the sealed vault to the left of it. The gun cabinet we took a peak at, but it looks like it has a new lock on it now. The steel vault, you'll never get in since it has a special locking device. My guess is he stores the real firepower in there, plus other personal items," said Elmer.

"I didn't think Pastor was a hunter," said Jack.

"Most of the guns were rifles, not shotguns, plus a few pistols. At least the ones we could see."

"Why do you think he has all these firearms?" asked Jack.

"Again, we decided that it was not ours to question his hobbies," said Elmer. "Besides the rules were we were to inspect, not question his private interests. You have to admit, Jack, that Pastor keeps a clean house and shed. There's nothing out of place. Even his workbench has all the tools hung up."

"Look at the painting hanging on the west wall, Jack," said Elmer.

"What about it?" asked Jack.

"It's the same woman that is on the picture in the parsonage, isn't it?" asked Elmer.

"By God, you're right, Elmer. Isn't that strange? Although in this one there's a young girl also."

"Well, I've seen enough, Elmer. It looks well cared for, so we can lock up and hit the road. That's new," said Elmer.

"What's new?" asked Jack.

"I never saw those fish tanks before. It doesn't appear that they have any water in them, said Elmer as he walked up to them and looked inside. "Matter of fact, all they have in them is a grass bed."

Jack walked up and looked inside and was about to reach down and feel the grass when Elmer walked up behind him and took his hand and pulled it back.

"What's wrong?" asked a startled Jack.

"I don't like it, friend. Pastor is using these tanks for something besides keeping fish. For all we know, he could have damn snakes for pets under that grass. Let's wait until he gets back and ask him before we go hunting under that grass bed."

"Okay," said Jack. "Then since we're done, let's lock up and get back to town."

During the ride back to town, they spent the thirty-minute ride to Elmer's house speculating about Paul Bergman. Finally unable to hold back any longer, he said, "He's got to be one of the strangest men of God I've ever encountered. The whole parsonage and what's inside all feels very creepy to me."

"Look, think about this. Have you ever belonged to any congregation that hasn't had some type of pastor controversy? If he warns against sin, he is a crank and is meddling in other people's matters. If he suggests changes for the improvement of his church, he is autocratic and wants to be a dictator. The guy can't win, Jack, period. If he dresses neatly, some in church will call him a dude. If not, others will call him a slouch. I've been here most of my life and have seen at least eight pastors come and go. We had a Pastor Lance Overstreet before your time that tried to please everybody, and people thought that he was a plain fool. The elder board had a talk with him in an attempt to slow him down, which resulted in another group in the church going after him because they thought that he didn't practice what he preached. See what I mean, Jack. Bergman may seem weird because we're looking to find weird," Elmer said as he burst out laughing.

"Sounds like we have the making of a movie, Elmer," said Jack. "But I hear what you're saying, old buddy. The problem here at Trinity, though, seems to be a movie plot that isn't going to work out."

"You're gonna tell me why?" asked Elmer.

"Yes, Elmer. You got me convinced," said Jack. "Those fish tanks weren't there to store mice or some domestic pet. Pastor uses them to collect his spiders, and the real question on my mind is for what?"

CHAPTER 33

The Wife

After a minute or so of watching the morning commuters come and go into the building, Kate glanced one more time at herself in the Honda mirror then opened the car door and crossed the street. This was not going to be an easy interview with Perry Sinclair's wife. No woman wants to hear about her husband having his hand in another woman's cookie jar. Kate walked through the revolving doors and looked for the building's list of tenants. As she was studying the board, she smiled watching a young woman who appeared to be exchanging the last kiss of the morning with a well-dressed-looking lawyer who was having a most difficult time removing his hand from his wife's or girlfriend's behind. The first thing that had hit her was how damn attractive these people were and how young. Many of them in the building could have been cast members for any Broadway play. The men hunky in that image of "I don't think I have to shave" look, while the women were mostly icons of sheer beauty, all glowing with health and confidence. Why this bothered her made no sense since she was very attractive with the self-confidence that radiated the feeling that "You don't want to play porker with me."

Finding the name of the company she was looking for, she adjusted her leather briefcase containing not a single item in it outside of her badge and sidearm, except, of course, her trusty ballpoint pen, notepad, and small tape recorder. Kate Heller squeezed her thirty-two-year-old body into the elevator and pushed floor 14 and took a deep breath. She had purposely dressed in civilian clothes so as not to alarm Barbara Sinclair's coworkers, who would be curious about the arrival of a policewoman to visit their office manager. Kate had called and made the appointment, having indicated that she needed to talk to her about her husband, but felt it was better that they do it away from her daughter, who was already undoubtedly worried about her father being in the hospital. As she exited the elevator, she patted the side of her pinstripe skirt while adjusting her matching jacket. She felt so different wearing the crisp white blouse and black leather shoes with the three-inch heel. She no longer felt like a police officer but rather a partner in a law firm.

She walked into American Life and moved directly to the receptionist desk. "Good morning, my name is Kate Heller, and I have an appointment with Ms. Sinclair." She watched as the young college-age girl appraised her, trying to determine if she needed to hurry or not.

"Please sign the registration book," said the perky-looking receptionist, "while I notify Mrs. Sinclair that you are here. Would you like me to get you something to drink while you wait?"

"No, that's not necessary, but thank you anyway."

As she stood waiting, Kate noted the wall with all the award plaques displayed. She walked over and scanned each of the ten awards. The first three of the ten plaques listed membership into the million-dollar club. All three had the name, Barbara Sinclair. "Very impressive," thought Kate. One award was placed at the top of the rest, with Sinclair's name on it, indicating membership into the Diamond Crown Room Club or what the company called the Five-Million Dollar Circle in sales. "Hmm, quite a saleslady," thought Kate. She couldn't help wondering if Perry might have felt the competitive spirit of their marriage being a good thing or not.

"She's ready for you," came the receptionist's voice. "Follow me. I'll take you back to her office."

After what appeared to be about a hundred-yard walk, past countless cubicles occupied by well-scrubbed-looking college kids, Kate found herself standing in front of a large office. "Have a seat next to the small desk in the corner," said the receptionist. "She'll be here in about five minutes."

Sitting down, Kate looked the office over, which appeared to be almost eight hundred square feet in size. A large mahogany desk with an apple computer at one end and a vase of flowers at the other made up the work station of Mrs. Sinclair. No pictures displayed. "That's interesting," she noted. She also observed that in the opposite far corner were three expensive chairs. "Probably used during a beatdown session or evaluation time when the boss could make you feel all equal, even though, of course, you were not and probably would never be. That's the purpose of this small desk," she thought, "but with a somewhat different approach. Here, the quest could feel that they were actually working partners without the overpowering desk. Here you could feel that the boss was really interested in what you were trying to sell her even though it most probably would never happen. If the sale was possible, the receptionist would have placed you at the mahogany desk." From where she was seated, Kate could see out the large picture window with a view of the big lake and the many expensive sailboats now being sailed on the last days of summer.

"Nice view, isn't it?" said Barbara Sinclair walking into the room. "Shall we move over to the chairs in the other corner?" she asked.

From the tone of her voice, Kate could well understand how Barbara enjoyed the feeling of being in control. "Funny how power always wants to control the meeting," thought Kate. It reminded her of her first boss, who made sure that everyone who was in his office always sat on chairs directly across from his desk that were designed to have you look directly up at him.

"If you don't mind, Mrs. Sinclair, this chair is fine."

Pushing a button on her office red phone, Barbara called the front desk, saying, "Hold all my calls, Megan, and make sure I'm not disturbed." Satisfied, she then turned to Kate, offering her a smile. "You indicated that you needed to talk to me about my husband?"

Right to business, thought Kate. No good morning, how's the weather, or nice suit you have on. "Yes, but first may I ask, how is Mr. Sinclair doing? When I had visited the hospital, his doctor had indicated that he was encountering several challenges."

"He's resting comfortably, or at least he was this morning. It was a terrible experience for all of us, but especially for him, as I'm sure that you understand. You've met Dr. Alan Ogden, I've been told. Without him, Perry would never have made it."

"Yes, Dr. Ogden seemed to be a fine doctor," said Kate. "Has Dr. Ogden indicated if there will be any permanent damages to his system?"

"You must be referring to the poison in his system from the spider. Dr. Ogden said that some men have become impotent, but it's not certain at this time if Perry will face that problem. I guess we'll cross that bridge when the time comes."

Somehow Kate thought that the bridge was going to be more difficult than she was anticipating. "Could you tell me, Mrs. Sinclair, how your husband first got bit by this rare spider? I'm sure Dr. Ogden has mentioned to you how uncommon it is for the Brazilian wandering spider to make its appearance in this country."

"Yes, he did, and it was that damn fruit basket that someone sent us. I knew something was wrong when the return address was phony. Our daughter was home when the basket was delivered by some stranger. Both Perry and I were at work, so Mary called her dad to ask if she could open the damn thing before we got home. It had some sticker on it that said 'Open immediately.' He then called me because he knew that I would be home first. When I knew that I wouldn't be home fast enough, I gave Mary instructions to wait until I got there before she opened it. Somehow I became concerned about the contents because we couldn't understand who had sent the box. It didn't have a name on it, just a return address. Looking back on it, I'm glad that we had that conversation. Otherwise, our daughter might have died from that spider biting her. I had her read the return address back to me, and since there was only an address on the box with no name of the sender, I decided to stop at the location on the way home and check it out since I was somewhat familiar with the street. It turned out to be a jewelry store, not any company that specialized in gifts or fruit baskets," said Barbara.

"Was there some special reason, Mrs. Sinclair, that you felt the need to check out the location other than you having some recollection about the street?"

"I'm afraid that I don't understand the question, Detective Heller."

"Well, we all receive misdirected mail and on occasion an ordered book by someone else, so it just seems unusual to me that you felt the need to check out the sender's address, that's all," offered Kate.

"No reason, just that it was on the way home and not much out of the way."

"What was the name of the jewelry store?" asked Kate.

"It's called Rogers and Sons Jewelry Store. From what a clerk told me, they have been at that location for over eighteen years. They had never heard of any company sending fruit baskets from their area."

"Have you or your husband ever purchased any jewelry from that store, such as a ring or watch?"

"No, neither of us had ever been to that store." Kate could see that Barbara continued to run that question through her head but said nothing more.

"When I got home, Mary started looking at the basket and spotted some type of bug in the fruit, so we decided to wait until Perry arrived. He didn't think that it was any big deal, so he opened it because Mary and I were frankly afraid to do so. It was awful, the way that spider just came out from under the fruit and attacked Perry. You know, we all grow up thinking that bugs and spiders run from us, but that goddamn thing had its mind on coming after one of us from the moment Perry let it out. It hunted us, for Christ's sake, not the other way around, Detective."

"That's the nature of the Brazilian wandering spider, Mrs. Perry. They do not create a silk trap like most spiders and wait for hours but rather hunt down and attack their prey. Did your daughter recognize who delivered the fruit basket?"

"She only said that it was a car, not UPS or the mailman."

"Did you ask her what type of car, or maybe would she be able to describe it?"

"No."

"Has your husband any enemies that you know of, Mrs. Sinclair?"

"That I find an unusual question, Detective. Are you suggesting that the spider was sent to us for the purpose of doing harm to our family?"

"No, it's just the type of question that police often ask, Mrs. Sinclair. Again, do you have any enemies that you are aware of?" asked Kate. "Both you and your husband are successful business professionals. That sometimes causes jealousy."

"This all sounds rather stupid, Detective," said Barbara.

"No, it's not really stupid at all, Mrs. Sinclair. In the business world, you achieve success through recognition awards from your sales skills. My rewards come from apprehending those that try to harm society. In my professional opinion, that fruit basket was not sent to you as a thank you for past services or even just from a friend. That gift had a special meaning of harm to your family, Mrs. Sinclair, to your husband, you, or maybe even your daughter." Reaching in her briefcase, Kate pulled out a picture of Gayle Browning and slid it across the desk to Barbara.

"Who is this?" she asked.

"I was hoping that you might know her, or have met her at some social event, maybe at the local food store or some political event. Maybe sold her some insurance or, for that matter, was in your congregation."

"No, I never have ever seen this woman. What did she do?" asked Barbara.

"Look again, Mrs. Sinclair. Did she ever attend any women's fundraisers that you might have met her at? Maybe she filled in as a substitute teacher, possibly an organist at your church, or that you just casually bumped into someplace?"

Barbara now looked more closely at the picture. The woman was young and beautiful, that was apparent. "Again, Detective, I can assure you that we have never ever met. In my business, it's important to recognize faces. That's an asset in making our sales goals and yearly salary. I really don't understand what she has to do with Perry being bit by a spider. Look, I'll say it one more time. I meet a lot of people each week and during the year in my business. Faces are something that I remember. I can assure you the woman has nothing to do with our family."

"It's all in the eyes," thought Kate. If she's lying, the moment had arrived. "The woman in the picture is dead, Mrs. Sinclair. She was also bit by a spider, only not as lucky as your husband."

"I'm sorry to learn that, Detective, but I must be slow this morning. What does her death have to do with this family?"

Kate's eyes bored down on Barbara as she looked directly into Barbara Sinclair's eyes, choosing her words carefully, yet knowing there was no easy way to do this. "Mrs. Sinclair, your husband and the dead woman knew each other. They knew each other very well. I'm the lead detective assigned to review the circumstances surrounding her unfortunate death several months ago, by which was determined to be the result of a spider bite. Because of that and my investigation with her former church where she was an organist, your husband's name came up."

"Perry's name came up? What in heaven's name for?"

"That I can't comment on at this time, other than to tell you that your husband and Ms. Browning knew each other, and this will soon reach the news media because of the unusual circumstances of spiders biting both victims. One person died under unusual circumstances, while the other almost died under additional unusual circumstances. This is a small town, Mrs. Sinclair, and news travels fast." Kate retrieved the picture, put it in her briefcase, and started to get up from her chair. "Look, Mrs. Sinclair. Your husband has been through a lot. I've decided not to interview him right now regarding Ms. Browning, but in the days to come, I will. He has become part of my investigation, and he has a right to legal counsel should he wish. At this time, understand that he's only a person of interest to me, not a suspect or being charged with anything regarding her death. Still he might have some information that will help me close the file on Ms. Browning, so the day is arriving when I'll need to talk to him."

"Are you suggesting, Detective Heller, that my husband was screwing that dead woman?"

"No, Mrs. Sinclair, I'm telling you that they knew each other, and that her name and your husband's name have come up in my investigation of her death. I'm telling you only that when he's feeling better that you both need to discuss this matter while I continue to do my job." Walking to the door, Kate stopped and turned back to Barbara Sinclair. "Try and encourage your husband to give me a call in the next few days. I do need to talk to him because truthfully he may have some answers that might save lives. Thank you for your time, Mrs. Sinclair. Call me anytime if you need to talk about anything."

Kate walked out of the office to the elevators and pushed the button that said Lobby. Exiting the professional building, she walked directly to her car, entered it, and took a moment to clear her head. Starting the engine, she pulled out of the parking area and headed back to her townhouse, speculating about Perry Sinclair. Clearly he had not murdered Gayle Browning but nevertheless was part of what was going on. She was back at her townhouse in fifteen minutes and took another fifteen minutes to get into the house, lay her briefcase on the kitchen table, and get into a pair of light khaki slacks and a short-sleeve white shirt and then feed Channing. She then removed a pair of fluffy white slippers from under her bed and paused for a moment to look in the mirror. Kate liked clothes, as did most women. They were, she thought, the chosen symbols of a person's individuality, or lack of it, and not a small matter to be overlooked. There also were uniforms, and it paid a woman to understand that the uniform put her on an equal with many of the people she had to deal with each day. Take, for example, Mrs. Barbara Sinclair, who wore only the most expensive designer clothes. "Well scrubbed up," as her deceased husband would have said. In addition to her intellectual range, she liked to look good, and she had today. Kate felt somewhat sorry for the woman, and yes, Perry, because the coming days were probably not going to be filled with the best Victoria Secret clothing that money could buy or that her husband would have liked to see his wife wearing.

CHAPTER 34

Captain Wagner

It was a clear, warm Monday morning when Kate parked her little red Honda civic with sixty thousand miles on it in a lot two blocks from police headquarters. Certainly it didn't make sense when she now had her own parking place adjacent to the front door, but today she didn't want to advertise that she was meeting with the bosses. She especially didn't want to have to deal with Cpl. Howard Singer, who in his own mind felt that she had stolen the detective promotion from him. The fact that he was the noted womanizer in the precinct didn't help matters either.

It was ironic, actually, that she had been assigned to review the Bergman cold case, along with the Gayle Browning death, when one considered her experience level with the Funston Police Department. Howard has spread the rumor that Captain Wagner had fallen victim to pussy fever in promoting her over him when everyone knew that it was his turn to get the gold shield.

As she walked the two blocks, she double-checked to be certain that she had her detective shield attached to her belt buckle and her regulation Smith & Wesson .40 cal. firmly in her Fletch pancake holster. Unlike her male counterparts, Kate preferred to keep the high ride holster and weapon hidden instead of on the outside of the police jacket. She liked the design, which contoured to the natural curve of her hip, keeping the molding on the front side of the holster for significantly more comfortable carry. Since she was the first woman detective, no regulations had been created that specified her attire. Male detectives often wore old jeans and the latest designer polo shirt unless meeting someone important. Undercover detectives could be counted on to wear clothes that often had seen better days. Kate had decided to play it safe and continue to look like a woman, not a hooker.

Thus she arrived at the front steps to the building at 7:30 a.m., wanting to make a good impression while at the same time avoiding any obstacle to her first real serious meeting that she considered important to her career. Walking into the building, she stopped in the police building's kitchen to get coffee, hoping to see someone from her old shift, but found no one. She filled a cup, took a sip, found it to her liking, and then trekked down to the hall to Captain Wagner's office. As she got closer, she saw that the light was on, but Wagner was not in his office.

She walked in and placed her briefcase on the floor near the middle of the table that had obviously been set up in Wagner's large office for a meeting. Reaching inside her briefcase, she removed the legal pad and placed it on the table with her notes regarding the Bergman case and that of Gale Browning.

"Oops," Singer said, walking into the office. "This must be the wrong location for my meeting this morning. Sorry, Detective. I guess we're alone though. I happen to see you come out of the kitchen and walk down this way, but I got temporarily distracted watching that incredibly muscled ass as it moved back and forth walking itself down the hallway. You must work out." He raked his thick black hair back with his fingers.

She looked over her shoulder. "Nice of you to notice," Kate said, trying to hold her temper and not get angry before her important meeting.

"It would be hard not to," Singer said. Did I ever tell you, Detective, that you need to celebrate that new promotion by putting your hand on a real hard club, one that you wouldn't ever want to let go of?"

Kate started to get up when, to her surprise, Captain Wagner walked up behind Singer and slapped his hand down hard on Singer's shoulder.

"What the hell!" snapped Singer, ready to push back until he realized it was Wagner.

"Tell me, Corporal Singer, how long will it take you to change into a street uniform to help the school crossing guards, because, hotshot, that's where your next assignment will be while I prepare your exit interview. Aside from being a disgrace to your uniform, the fact is insubordination to a superior officer happens to be grounds for dismissal a corporal."

"Wait a minute, Captain, you can't do that without approval from my union rep."

"Oh really?" said Wagner. "And just what is that union rep going to do for you when Detective Heller files her sexual harassment suit against you? One that I will personally cosign on her behalf. Now get the hell out of my sight before I actually get upset and shoot your ass for impersonating one of my officers." Singer turned and walked away.

"Thank you, Captain, but I was about to handle Corporal Singer myself."

"I know that, Detective Heller, but it's my job to flush the grime off our uniforms before they soil the rest of us. I will be filling the proper charges this afternoon, so he won't be bothering you or anyone again," said Wagner. "Now if you are ready, Detective, I would like to hear some good news about the Bergman and Browning files. At noon, I have to meet with our state's Attorney Underwood on a number of subjects, and this is one that she will most likely bring up."

For the next two hours, Kate brought Wagner up to speed on Bergman, Browning, and now Perry Sinclair. She then had added her dealings with Patel, along with her feelings about his misdiagnosis regarding what had killed Browning.

After listening to her report, Wagner sat back in his chair for almost five minutes before he addressed Kate. "Detective Heller, you may need some help as I see it. Too many balls in the air is not a good thing for any of us, and it would appear that's what you got. Besides, all work and no play isn't good either. I see that you're wearing the Hope diamond on your left finger, or if not, its sister."

Kate found herself blushing a little but recovered enough to say, "Thank you for noticing, Captain. He's a Delta pilot, and we've just gotten engaged, but the wedding won't be too far behind."

"Well, good luck to you both," said Wagner.

"Thank you, sir. I have a suggestion, Captain Wagner, one that might tame the tiger and avoid you having to hire another police officer. It will allow Singer to keep his job, provided, of course, you have enough confidence that it might work."

"What do you have in mind, Detective?"

"Assign him to me if you can spare him for a few weeks so that he can help me with the Bergman and the Browning cases as needed. I will put him on a short leash and no second chances. He has a wife and kids and, aside from being the office jerk, has a reputation of being a good cop. If you agree and he accepts, my only request is that I speak to him first before he starts the new assignment."

Wagner thought about this for a minute and said, "Somehow I get the feeling, Detective, that Singer would be better off if he accepted my offer before he accepts yours. In any event, I'll be telling him that he's assigned to you and that it would be in his best interest to make an appointment to see you before I change my mind. You're dismissed, Detective Heller, but let's see some progress on those cold cases, Detective."

As the day progressed, Kate found herself more and more concerned about her visit this morning with Captain Wagner. She had filled him in on where she was with the investigation of Gayle Browning and Paul Bergman, and to her surprise, he had appeared satisfied that she was moving in the right direction. He had agreed with her assessment that Perry Sinclair was probably more of a loose-zipper suspect than one who actually did Browning any harm. Who sent the spider in a fruit basket into the Sinclair home was admittedly a remaining puzzle, along with the missing ring. Connecting the brown recluse spider bite to that of Browning, he considered a lost cause forever due to the cremation of the organist. Wagner had gone out of his way to praise her work, but somehow Kate felt like the manager of the Chicago Cubs baseball team who just received a vote of confidence that everyone else in the city would assume was the kiss of death to her career unless he brought in a World Series championship to a city that was a hundred years overdue.

Turning her car south, she headed directly to the shopping center and the jewelry store where Barbara Sinclair had stopped in her confusion to determine who sent the fruit basket. Certainly someone could have written the wrong address on the box and that would be it, nothing more. At the same time, Kate wondered if the address held a bigger meaning.

It took her less than twenty minutes to reach the outer area of the shopping complex and only five minutes more before she was pulling up to the Rogers and Sons Jewelry Store. Kate could tell just by the building that this was a store that only catered to those interested in fine jewelry. The building was of expensive-grade stone, with the front window advertising only upscale watches and diamonds. Walking in, she was immediately greeted by what appeared to be a woman about twenty-seven or maybe twenty-eight.

"Looking for something special, miss? Maybe something to compliment that beautiful ring that you're wearing?"

"Thank you for the compliment, but my name is Detective Kate Heller from the Funston Police Department. While I would rather be looking at all your beautiful jewelry, today this is an official call regarding a past visit by a woman whose husband is currently in the Funston Hospital."

"I'm Angela Rogers, the owner's daughter. I hope that we didn't provide any reason for this unfortunate situation with the woman's husband."

"No, nothing like that, Angela, just the fact that someone used your address when sending the family a fruit basket that unfortunately was the cause of him having to be admitted to the hospital. The details are part of a police investigation, so with regret I can't talk about it. Let's just say the contents of the basket contained more than fruit, which caused him to need medical attention. Maybe you would locate the owner of this store so that I can have a few private minutes with him?"

"If you wish. Just have a seat anywhere, Detective. I'll locate Dad for you," said Angela.

"Thanks, but I'll just look at all your beautiful jewelry while I wait for him."

Kate noticed the men's Rolex watches first then kept moving down the glass cases until she saw several varieties of men's wedding bands. She was bending over to get a better view of one that caught her attention when Angela returned. "Dad asked me to bring you back to his office. Please follow me, Detective Heller." Angela then walked over to what appeared to be just another part of the room until she pushed on the wall and a hidden door opened, allowing them to enter Rogers's private office. When the door closed, she secured it with a thick sliding metal bar. Kate then followed her through a second door, where Rogers was waiting while examining what appeared to be a diamond necklace.

Getting up, Rogers walked over to Kate and reached for her hand. "I'm Simon Rogers, the owner of our little store. Angela has indicated that you wished to speak to me alone?"

"Yes, Mr. Rogers, I'm Detective Kate Heller of the Funston Police Department. I just needed to speak to you for a few moments regarding a lady that recently visited your store regarding a gift basket that she received from somebody using your store address. Although I recognize that the basket wasn't sent by your store, the lady's husband is in the hospital under some unusual circumstances that makes me feel that some connection does exist, but frankly I don't understand what."

"You may leave us alone, Angela," said Rogers, noting that his daughter was still in the room.

"Certainly, Father," responded Angela. "I'll be in the main showroom should you need me." She then left the room.

"Mr. Rogers, I'm currently the officer investigating regarding the death of a woman who died of a spider bite, and as strange as it might sound, this woman is connected to another person who now is in the hospital from another case of being bit by a spider. In the last case, the victim received a fruit basket from this address, which contained the most deadly spider in the world. My guess is they used this address for some reason, but I don't understand why. It could have been done to throw the family off as to who really sent the basket or to deliver some subliminal message to the recipient that I can't figure why. I assume that it's not your practice to send thank-you gifts to good customers when they buy expensive jewelry?"

"Well, if we did, Detective, and we don't, it wouldn't be a fruit basket containing any spiders," said Rogers laughing. "Sorry about making light of the terrible situation, Detective, but your story, if not coming from a police officer, borders on the absurd."

"Yes, I can understand how ridiculous this must sound, but as we speak, a man continues his personal struggle to regain his health, and a woman he knew has ended up dead. My job is to work with this puzzle and find some meaning, which is why I'm here, Mr. Rogers."

"Maybe the spouse found out that the ring wasn't for her," chuckled Rogers.

"What did you say, Mr. Rogers?

"It's just an inside joke, Detective Heller. I said what if the spouse found out that the ring or jewelry wasn't for her. We have it happen all the time where some husband or wife buys something for their lady or male friend and it's found out about, and the gift causes rethinking about the engagement, the wedding, or the current marriage."

How could she have missed it? thought Kate.

"Mr. Rogers, I need you to back-check your sales records for a Mr. Perry Sinclair, a Paul Bergman, or a Ms. Gayle Browning. I'm looking for a red ruby diamond ring with two stirrup-shaped loops that cradle a red stone. It probably was bought as a gift by one on those two men for Ms. Gayle Browning. I'll leave you my personal phone number until you've had a chance to check your records."

"Your card won't be necessary, Officer Heller. That ring would have meant more than a gift, Detective Heller. That happens to be one of our specialty rings that sells for over twenty thousand dollars, closer to twenty-five thousand with certain type diamonds. By the way, I've been admiring your engagement ring, which was obviously designed by one of our competitors. Its craftsmanship and unique-ness suggests that it's one of a kind and probably worth upwards of sixteen to eighteen thousand dollars, maybe a little more due to the yellow stone. Only a policeman would dare wear it due to its value and attractiveness. I point out the price only because if the red ruby ring was purchased by Mr. Sinclair or Bergman, it was a very serious investment and meant the same thing as yours, Detective. It would have meant that someone intended to marry the woman he was giving the ring to. Those rings are not just given after a night at the opera," he said. Now pushing his intercom, Rogers asked for Angela.

"Yes, Dad."

"Angela, I need you to run a check on the sales of our ruby stirrup ring, the one that sold for about twenty thousand dollars. We only sold about seven of them, so it shouldn't be hard to find. You may start your search the name of Sinclair or Bergman, possibly Browning," said Rogers.

"Give me a few minutes, Dad."

"Well, we'll see what we can come up with, Detective. My personal guess is someone would have been most upset if their spouse purchased something of that value for someone other than them. You know, the custom of the ring has a long history to it. It originally was worn only by wives, until it changed in the twentieth century when husbands started wearing wedding rings. Its modern custom began in Europe, but the tradition dates back to ancient Rome. Its original stated intent was that it be the last gift before you get married. Our ruby stirrup ring was designed to be a modern engagement ring, so my guess, as I stated, was that the person who purchased it had marital plans in mind. That yellow sapphire on your ring must have a special message to the person who gave you that ring, Detective. I must consider the possibility of creating one for our special clients also," said Rogers. The sound of the intercom brought Rogers back to attention.

"Yes, Angela?"

"The ring, Dad, was purchased by a P. Sinclair. He had it insured to a Ms. Browning. She actually came in to have it sized."

"Thank you, dear," said Rogers as he disconnected the intercom. "Did you hear her?" asked Rogers?

"Yes, and I certainly appreciate your cooperation, Mr. Rogers. Since this is an ongoing police investigation, I will ask you and

Angela not to comment on this to anyone," said Kate. "Also I would like a photocopy of the sales receipt, if you don't mind."

"You have our word, Officer Heller," said Rogers. He was about to get up when his personal line rang.

"Hello, Angela? She said what? Please come back here before the detective leaves. Thanks. Detective Heller, my daughter has just discovered something from one of our other employees. I've asked her to come back here and tell you directly," said Rogers.

Kate was wondering what this was all about when Angela appeared in the room.

"Dad, when I started the search for who purchased the stirrup ring, I asked Rhonda to help me. Actually I didn't need her because it didn't take long for me to find the records before calling you back. After I told you about the ring, she came up to me and mentioned that she remembered some man coming into our store pretending that he wanted to buy a matching ring for himself that he had gotten for his wife. She said that she brought up the records of the sale since only one ring of that type had been sold during the last year. She had started to refer to him as Mr. Sinclair, assuming that he was that person. She indicated that he seemed very nervous and had asked her to verify the address that she had on file because he was going to probably put the ring on payments and wanted to make sure we had the correct information. According to Rhonda, he told her that he needed a little time to think about it and left the store but never returned. She now thinks that she was duped and that he wasn't Perry Sinclair."

"Is there anything else she told you about the man?"

"No. I asked her if she could describe him, and she said no because it was too long ago."

"You have security camera, I assume," said Kate.

"Sorry, it was too long ago. We record over the tape after one week," said Rodgers."

"Well, this extra piece of information has been very helpful," said Kate, addressing both Angela and her dad. It's obvious that more than Mr. Sinclair was interested in that ring. Giving both of them her personal card, Kate asked them to call her if they could remember anything else about the ring or if anyone came in attempting to sell it back or trade it in on something else. Shaking both their hands, Kate followed Angela back out through the hidden door and left the jewelry store.

She had barely entered the car when she felt the tickle from the vibrator on the cell phone attached to her belt.

"Hello."

"Detective Heller, this is Corporal Singer. Captain Wagner has asked that I give you a call regarding my future."

"Yes, I know, because I've requested that you be assigned to me for the time being. Are you familiar with the Bonnie and Clyde Restaurant?"

"Yes, I've eaten there several times over the years."

"Good, then meet me there tomorrow morning around 9:00 a.m. I'd like to discuss your future with this police department."

The Meeting

Kate always liked to arrive early. It was part of her DNA that called for her to evaluate anything before the target knew that it was being hunted. She remembered the early morning bass fishing trips with her dad. The Red River was just another river flowing through the outskirts of Martindale, Illinois, her hometown. Everyone that lived in Martindale knew that the Red River was home to northern pike, perch, bluegills, and largemouth bass, and while the locals would on occasion experience a fair day fishing, few considered it to be more than a place to wet your lures. Her dad, however, was a different story and would come home with ten or more bass and be the envy of every fisherman in town. Although they tried to get him to share his secret, he would not bend, only to her. It happened one morning at 1:30 a.m. when he woke her up and took her to the Red River, and they came home with twenty-six largemouth bass. "You see," he had told her, "the bass arrive early as they hunt the minnows swimming near the shore. While man thinks early is at 5:00 a.m., the bass have set their clock for 2:00 a.m. and particularly like the full moon."

Thus it should have come as no surprise to those who knew her that Kate would arrive at the Bonnie and Clyde Restaurant a full sixty minutes early and sit in the back of a parking lot between two Ford Explorers waiting for Corporal Howard Singer. Yet to her surprise, she spotted Howard's red Mustang arriving a full thirty minutes before their appointed time, but he didn't circle the lot as she thought he would do looking for her Civic. Instead, he parked his

Mustang and walked up to the front door and started to lean back against the wall, one ankle crossed over the other, looking half-asleep and thoroughly relaxed. Reaching in his jacket pocket, she noted that he pulled out a small notebook and started to read its contents. Darn if the guy hadn't prepared some advanced notes and was looking them over.

She was impressed. The guy had initially looked like he had perfected the art of falling asleep on his feet, something she had thought only doctors could do, and he ended up being prepared for their meeting. Starting her car, Kate circled to the back entrance, locked her car, and proceeded up the back steps into the heart of the restaurant and laid her briefcase on one of the tables in the far corner of the dining room. Motioning the waitress over, Kate asked her if she would notify the police officer out front leaning against the building that his party was inside waiting for him.

"Let's see how Howard handles the fact that his future boss has arrived first," she snickered to herself.

In a few short seconds, Howard was walking back to the table looking baffled that she had beaten him to the restaurant.

"Good morning, Corporal Singer. Did you have a difficult time finding the restaurant?"

"No, it really wasn't that difficult. It's still fifteen minutes before you told me to be here," he said, trying to determine how she beat him to their meeting.

"I never suggested that you were late, Corporal Singer, just asked if you had a hard time finding the location." Kate looked over to where she had last seen the waitress and signaled her to come over to the table.

Arriving, she spoke to Kate, "Do you both know already what you would like, or would you care for a menu?"

"In my case, I'll just have the continental breakfast," said Kate.

"Make mine the same, but tomato juice, cold," said Howard.

Writing down their order, the waitress disappeared towards the kitchen area.

"Do you have children, Corporal Singer?" asked Kate.

"We have two, one boy, twelve years old and a girl, fourteen going on twenty-four," said Howard. "Besides that, it's just my wife, Patty, and I. She's finishing her post doctorate."

"What field will she be practicing in?" asked Kate.

"She's securing her doctorate in archaeology. She's into biblical research, hoping to unlock secrets that could alter the course of history," said Singer sarcastically. "When she's not in class, she helps out her dad at his at his religious store. He sells Bibles, tapes, books, and other items that church people are interested in."

"You seem less than excited and supportive of her choice of studies," commented Kate.

"Let's just say, Detective Heller, that the mysteries of the Old Testament are not my idea of how to spend time with your wife. I actually am proud of the fact that she wants a career. It's just the choice of her occupation. When you do archaeology, the study of these lost treasures, it often prevents you from being home for dinner. Then other times she could be gone for months at a time. I see from the diamond ring that you're wearing marriage is on the horizon for you. Congratulations. I regret not being more aware of your engagement," said Howard.

"Yes, he's a pilot for Delta Air Lines, and like your wife who will be potentially digging for lost treasures in foreign lands, mine will be gone for endless days to Europe. Well, it's for better or worse, they say, so we both will need to adjust to the new careers of our spouses. And speaking of adjustments, Officer Singer, how do you think that you will adjust to having to work for a woman, if only temporarily?"

"Well, I certainly don't have much choice," he said while laughing.

"Actually you do, and it might be in your best interests to think about it, since I'm not going away anytime soon. There will be new rules, Corporal Singer, some that you might not like, besides having to put up with my muscular ass, as you referred to it as."

"I deserved that, and can only offer my apology," said Howard.

"Apology accepted, and no second chances on that one, Corporal. But let's talk about your appearance today, for example. Those that report to me will be required to wear their protective vests at all times while they are on duty. If you don't care about your safety, maybe your wife does." Kate noticed that Singer was looking at her chest to determine if she was wearing one herself. "It's there, Corporal, and it's damn uncomfortable for a woman, especially those of us that the boys like to refer to as carrying a big rack. Second rule is that my team members only carry authorized sidearms approved by the commanding officer of the Funston Police Department. Therefore, leave your .500 S&W special at home in your gun cabinet. We both know that we can tame the beast with a .40-caliber here around Funston, and besides, the elephant gun that you have in your car delivers a kickback so heavy that my guess is you haven't practiced with it anyway. Third rule, and please pay close attention to this one. There will be no second chance that involves sexual harassment. Enter that arena again, and you're going to face charges, understood?" Kate watched Howard's eyes as he considered his choices.

Howard measured his words when he responded. "Nothing that you have indicated is unfair, and even if it was, you would still have my cooperation, Detective. You have my word and appreciation for what you have done to help continue my career. I know that only I can save it for the future, but you have my word that everything is understood."

"Very well, Corporal Singer. Today's a new day for both of us. Starting now you are to patrol the heavy industrial complexes and school zones, but be available for special assignments needed by me regarding my two cold cases involving a Pastor Paul Bergman and a deceased mistress of his named Gayle Browning. I will bring you up to speed on these cases in the near future. I hope to meet your wife in the days to follow. When my future husband, Curtis Patterson, flies in sometime in the next week, all four of us need to go out to dinner together. Speaking of food, here comes our breakfast, so from this moment, Howard, let's forget about the past and concentrate on moving your career forward."

Later as she pulled away from the restaurant, Kate thought that the breakfast meeting had gone very well. It would be undoubtedly be hard for a guy like Singer to reduce his testosterone level because he knew that he was a good-looking guy and half the women in

Funston seemed willing to let him put it to use. Still, he seemed willing to accept her new rules, and for at least today, it was a good start. As she saw the entrance to a roadside rest stop, Kate pulled her car into the car's only section and shut the engine off. Picking up her cell phone, she dialed Curtis's cell phone number. Looking at the schedule he had given her, she realized that he should be back or arriving soon. He had told her over the phone two days ago that he needed to see her soon, even if she could only spare a few hours. She knew what he meant, because the hunger was there for her also. She listened to her phone as it continued to ring his number. "Pick up the phone, Curtis," she said as it continued to ring. Finally it went into his answering system indicating that he would call back as soon as possible. Smiling, Kate said into the answering machine, "Remember the last time, Curtis, when after making love to me, you leaned down and kissed me and said, 'Are you okay?' Do you remember what I said? 'Oh, yes, it's all good.' I'm thinking about that all good, Curtis, and miss it. Call me when you get this. Love you. Kate."

Leaning back against the car seat, Kate thought about the last time when she had used her hands to stroke him, driving him crazy. When her lips had reached his stomach, she could feel his indrawn breath. She had moved lower, and he had told her he was about to lose control, and he then had suddenly rolled off the bed, telling her he'd be right back, and he had returned in seconds. This time he wasn't gentle as he had taken her shoulders and whispered in her ear that he could see the passion in her eyes wanting him and knew that she was ready for him. She remembered that moment as he entered her forcefully, and that she had cried out as the sensations began to build. She had dug her fingernails into his shoulders. Neither one of them could talk, for the mating ritual was consuming them both. Curtis had made it last longer than the first time so that she would climax before he did. When she lifted her hips to take him deeper inside and cried his name, he had then buried his face in her shoulder and found his own release. Waking up from the momentary dream, she put the car in drive and pulled slowly out into traffic.

As Kate was driving to her townhouse, she continued to review in her mind all the reports that were given to her regarding the death of Gayle Browning. The detective originally assigned to the case, a Detective David Lopez, had retired during the last six months and had indicated that there was no sign of foul play. The deceased was found on the floor while apparently trying to reach the phone on her nightstand. All the prescription bottles that had been found had been bagged and turned over to the medical examiner at Funston Hospital. The report had indicated that the doctor had concluded that she had died of the brown recluse spider. Reaching for her cell phone, Kate called the switchboard of the Funston Police Department and asked if they had an updated listing of former Detective Lopez's phone number. They did, but it appeared to be his original number since there were no apparent changes on file. Thanking her, Kate dialed the number that was on file and waited.

"Hello," replied the young child's voice.

"Is your dad at home?" asked Kate.

"He's outside painting the boat. Do you want me to get him?"

"Yes, would you please tell him I'm a police officer where he used to work and I need to speak to him."

Kate heard the phone being dropped on the counter and the voice yelling, "Daddy, someone is on the phone!" A few moments passed, and she heard the voice.

"David Lopez, who's calling?"

"David, this is Kate Heller from the Funston Police Department. We met at your retirement party. You had put your arms around me and whispered those encouraging word that all rookies want to hear. It went something like this. 'Remember, rookie, the first rule of wearing that badge: things will always get worse.'"

Laughing, Lopez said, "I remember you well, Officer Heller. Boys being boys, we had a bet that you would be married within six months."

"Well, you would have lost that bet, David, since I didn't get married that quick, but I'm getting married to a Delta Pilot in the next few weeks."

"Congratulations. Some of us also thought that you would climb the ladder pretty fast. How did I do in that case?"

"Better. It's Detective Heller now, thanks to Captain Wagner and the support of many guys like you," answered Kate. "I happen to read the report that you left on me before you retired."

"You are very kind, Kate, but my guess is you earned everything through your outstanding work. Detective positions are given only to those that have made the grade, nothing more," said Lopez. "You being the first female police officer that the department has ever hired presents a special responsibility to see that the door is opened for future opportunities for women. Those that follow will be measured by your work."

"Thanks for the compliment, David. I was just there at the right time."

"I doubt that, Kate. Word has it that you are working on an old case of mine, which is probably the reason for this call. Nothing much there, I'm afraid. It was just a simple case of being bitten by a bad spider, or so I was told."

"It's getting a little more complicated than that, David, since the deceased woman was a member of that same church where the pastor was accused of trying to murder his wife. His wife, as you probably have read about, has also died recently after months of being in a coma. She was, if you remember, found in her garage with a cord around her neck. She passed away not too long ago."

"Well, isn't that something," said Lopez. "So what has this all got to do with you now, Detective Heller?"

"Please call me Kate. They have me revisiting both cases to determine if anyone has missed anything. The papers have picked up on the past cases and think that the Funston Police Department might be operating like Barney Fife. The matter gets worse as the new assistant district attorney for the county tends to agree with their observation."

"Good Lord, Kate, anything else?"

"Yes. We have another case of a spider bite ongoing at the Funston Hospital. The guy's name is Perry Sinclair, a CFO at one of the larger banks in Funston. The interesting twist on this one is that he was seeing Gayle Browning at the same time as the pastor. You can't make this stuff up, David."

"You're kidding me."

"It's all true, David. I bet you're glad to be retired now. The deceased lady organist was given an expensive ruby stirrup ring with a value over twenty-two thousand dollars by her secret boyfriend, who is now in the Funston Hospital, but the problem here is that he was apparently bitten by a different and more deadly spider. This one is called a Brazilian wandering spider, and people die from that bite. Let me get more to the point. David, by chance, did you find any indication that Ms. Browning had received any packages prior to her death, such as a fruit basket or some other type of gift? This is how the spider arrived at the current guy's house. Also, did you remember anything about this ruby ring?"

"No, and we did a clean sweep of the place. We even came back later after it was determined that she was bitten by the brown recluse to see if we would locate it. Image, if you will, police officers setting spider traps. Small wonder people laugh at us. Well, you can pretty much guess how that turned out. We ended up looking like fools since the chance of finding a spider of any kind was equal to finding that needle in the haystack. She was pill crazy, though, along with having several types of anti-itch creams. I put that stuff all together and sent it to the medical examiner, plus the broken piece of some type of service pin. She was not wearing any rings that I remember."

"Service pin, David? That part I don't understand."

"It was on the floor near her body, but it was nothing, Kate. It could have been there for days, maybe months. I just happen to run across it when I was on my knees looking for the damn spider. It wasn't actually even a pin, just a piece that looked like a question mark."

"You mean something with a hook on the end?"

"Yeah, that's it."

"Is there anything else that you can remember David?

"No, as I said, it was just a simple matter of a spider bite. There is no smoking gun, Kate. It is what it is," said David.

"The ring has the interest of someone, David, because of its value being well over twenty thousand dollars. Somehow I have the feeling that finding the ring may well find us a killer. Listen, if you think of anything, please call. In the meantime, enjoy your retirement, and keep the phone off the hook."

"Appreciate that, Kate. Good luck on that marriage," said Lopez as he was hanging up.

Kate had just laid her phone down on the seat of her car when it rang. Not recognizing the phone number, she said, "Detective Heller."

"Detective Heller, this is Perry Sinclair. My wife indicated that you wished to speak to me. I'm still at Funston Hospital and will be here for at least another full week. They are just watching my progress, but I'm willing to see you if you can make it to the hospital."

"I would like to do that, Mr. Sinclair, but I must caution you that I'm working on a murder case, so you might want to talk to a lawyer first before agreeing to see me."

"I don't need a lawyer, Detective Heller, since I've committed no crime against Gayle Browning. She was just a close friend."

"Then I'll see you later today since I need to visit the medical examiner at the hospital also. I should be over to see you later this today, maybe around 2:00 to 2:30 p.m."

"Fine," replied Sinclair, "I'll be in the patients' lounge at that time waiting for you."

Kate called Curtis one more time and once again reached his voice mail. She advised him that she would be home this evening and that he should call her right away since she was worried about him as he had indicated that he would be home earlier today. Kate then checked her notes and found the provided phone number of Dr. Patel, and to her surprise, he picked up the call."

"This is Dr. Patel."

"Doctor, this is Detective Heller. I need to have a few more minutes of your time regarding Gayle Browning. You have my word that I won't overstay my visit since it's understood that your time is limited."

"Be here by noon if you can, Detective Heller. I have to leave the hospital by 1:00 p.m. today for my downtown office."

"I'll be on time, Doctor. It would be helpful if you would have the inventory of the items that you received regarding Gaye

Browning. I'm particularly interested in a small broken piece of a service pin that was found on the floor next to her body."

"That I'm unaware of," said Patel. "I believe the only thing that we had received at my office were prescription bottles. Now I have to run since I'm being paged."

It was turning out to be one of those days, thought Kate. Dealing with Patel was like having a hangover, which she hadn't experienced since her college days, when one stayed up all night with your friends trying to pass those final exams before summer break. Undoubtedly Patel believed in his assessment that Browning died of a brown recluse spider bite, but he was dead wrong, just proud, and besides, who was going to challenge his results as he was the chief medical examiner for miles around? And of course, she couldn't request a second opinion because Gayle Browning was cremated. How convenient, thought Kate, slamming the palm of her hand against the steering wheel.

Gaining control of her emotions, she pulled her Honda up to the small blue door at the back of the hospital. She knew from past visits this was the entrance to the morgue and probably where she would find Patel. Getting out of the car, she walked up to the door with its frosted glass pane and looked up, smiling at the security camera directly above her head. "Who in the hell are they worried about, for God's sake? It's not like someone is going to sneak in and steal a dead body." As soon as she opened the door, the smell hit her immediately, the way it always did in this part of the hospital. What did her first boss tell her? "Oh, Kate, it's nothing more than the smell of death. Since you're not married," he had told her, "you don't have to worry about bringing home the smell that always found its way to your clothes even though they try to cover it up with Trigene disinfectant." The smell lingered as she walked down the hallway and entered a small office and introduced herself to the assistant pathology technician, Neil Tyson.

"Hello, I'm Detective Heller to see Dr. Patel."

Tyson, looking her up and down, responded with a courteous and efficient manner.

Kate had seen that look many times. *Zoccu a fimmina avi, l'omu u disa.* "What the woman has, the man wants."

"Yes, he's expecting you," said Tyson. "Follow me please."

"The technician with his cheery-looking smile and swarthy good looks must drive the college girls nuts," thought Kate, smiling.

Walking at a brisk pace past the isolation room, Tyson moved through the postmortem room, where two naked women corpses were laid out, and marched right into a large conference room in which Dr. Patel was seated. The room, like the entire facility, was built around a gloomy environment. It had an octagonal table with six black chairs around it facing two large blank chalkboards on the wall. No pictures graced the room or had flowing water fountains or a brilliant painted sunset. "After all, this is not the Sandal Hotel Resort," she reminded herself. In their place was a massive round clock in a stainless-steel frame that announced the time, now 11:45 a.m. Without getting up, Patel indicated for her to have a seat across the table from him while he offered her tea or coffee.

"No, thank you, Dr. Patel, I'm good."

Still not looking at her, Patel questioned, "Well, what do I owe the pleasure of your visit today, Officer Heller?"

"Murder, Dr. Patel, murder, and just for your records since we last met, it's now Detective Heller."

"Well then, Detective, my congratulations on the promotion, but my report stays the same, so you best find the spider and advise him of his rights," Patel said. "It would seem to me that proving murder could become a real challenge. I've already filed my report that the woman died of a brown recluse spider bite and nothing more," responded an angry Patel.

"My guess, Dr. Patel, is that you have identified correctly that the Browning woman died of a small arachnid bite, but just have the wrong little animal. It's a common mistake even with the most experienced doctors, so I wouldn't feel bad. It's my opinion that Gayle Browning died as a result of being bitten by a Brazilian wandering spider, one much more toxic than that of a brown recluse. I would like to see your official report on your conclusion," said Kate.

"Are you calling me a liar?" asked Patel.

"No, of course not, but let me ask you a couple questions, Dr. Patel. Does your report indicate that the spider's venom introduced red blood destruction? Second, when you first examined the body, did you find the original skin lesion?"

"I found the skin lesion on her neck, and since she was dead, I'd seen no value in checking for any red blood destruction."

"Are you aware, Dr. Patel, that most doctors, including those with an internal medicine specialty, often mistake a spider bite with that of a mite, tick, or other insect? That, in fact, most doctors overlook the more serious conditions that cause that skin lesion, such as diabetes, resistant staphylococcus, or even lymphoma?"

"I'm not the average doctor, Detective Heller, and I've been doing autopsies for over twenty years. I don't make mistakes."

"I don't question your competence, Dr. Patel, but let me ask you what I consider a fair question. How many other brown recluse spider bites have you examined that have resulted in death to a victim, like Gayle Browning?"

"None, but that doesn't prove anything. There's always a first, and Ms. Browning is a first," replied Patel.

Looking at the clock, Kate noted the time of 12:28. Unfortunately, Dr. Patel, I can't dismiss the possibility of murder that easy, and since Ms. Browning has been cremated, certain things are forever sealed. Even if one accepts your conclusion that she died of a brown recluse spider bite, you have made that determination without benefit of actually putting that fiddleback spider under a microscope. No, Dr. Patel, the conclusion in the Browning death stands on weak legs. In the United States, there averages only one to two deaths each year by a brown recluse spider bite, and those deaths usually are children, not adults. As you may be aware, Doctor, this hospital currently has a patient admitted due to being bitten by the Brazilian wandering spider, the most dangerous of all spiders. That person had a relationship with the individual that you performed an autopsy on that you say died as a result of a brown recluse spider. The coincidence is most striking, and since I don't believe in coincidences, something tells me that there is still much to be learned about what actually happened to Ms. Browning. Wouldn't you agree, Dr. Patel?"

"Are you about finished, Detective Heller? As I must get to my regular practice?" Reaching under his desk, Patel pulled out a box.

"This box contains your request for the prescription bottles and ointments that accompanied Ms. Browning, plus that little piece of metal that makes no sense to me. If you have any further questions of me, I would suggest that you contact my attorney," said Patel as he handed Kate a card. Getting up, Patel indicated that the meeting was over as he picked up his messages and started for the door.

"Oh, Dr. Patel, I might have to take you up on that offer."

Turning, he looked directly at Kate. "What are you talking about?"

"In a few minutes, I'll be visiting a patient currently in this hospital who I just mentioned was bitten by a Brazilian wandering spider. That patient survived because the doctor was able to put the spider under a microscope and determined that it was a Brazilian wandering spider, or more commonly referred to as a banana spider, which leads me to believe that's what actually killed Ms. Browning. Since that will be hard to prove without a body, it may well come down to my having to find the person who actually I believe introduced the spider into the Browning home. On the other hand, Dr. Patel, I may just have to use the evidence that the deceased happened to leave us before she died. When this evidence is presented to the District Attorney, it's likely that that this matter of the spider will take on some clarity for all of us. When that happens, we all will spend some time in court, Dr. Patel."

"Why wasn't I notified of this other case?" asked Patel. "And what evidence are you talking about, Detective Heller?"

"Why you were not notified about patient Perry Sinclair is something that you will need to review with the hospital administrator regarding the Brazilian wandering spider evidence. That is best explained by the time period that we live in, Dr. Patel. You see, Gayle Browning actually took a picture of the spider that bit her with her cell phone camera. Please give me a call, Doctor, if you think of anything else that might be helpful in this case." She brushed past him, walking down the hallway toward the main entrance. Kate knew that it wouldn't be long before her conversation with Patel would find its way through out the hospital, so she found the nearest receptionist desk and asked for the floor and room number for Perry Sinclair.

The elderly volunteer smiled and checked her computer for the information and said, "He's on the twelfth floor, room 218A. You'll find the elevators just past the cafeteria, Officer. Have a good day."

Kate looked down the hallway and could see several hospital people waiting their turn at the elevator, so she walked the short distance and entered the closing door before it hit her. She remembered how she once tried to stop an elevator door with her hand, and the sliding door had broken her watch crystal, costing her a cool hundred dollars to replace it. She reached over a nurse and punched the number 12 button and felt the acceleration. As it turned out, she was the lone rider to the twelfth floor and discovered that the nurse's station was within sight after she exited the elevator. Walking up to the administrative desk, it was easy to tell that the staff was engaged in paperwork, cell phones, and internet surfing but not paying much attention to any help needed at the desk. She was about to yell for assistance when the man marching toward her appeared to be a doctor, and an uptight one at that.

"Who are you?" asked the immaculately dressed doctor.

"I'm Detective Kate Heller from the Funston Police Department, and you are Dr.—?

"I'm the chief of surgery, Dr. Eugene Feinstein. This is my ward, Detective Heller, and is there something that I can assist you with?"

Kate observed that the doctor chose to carry his stethoscope dangling from one of his pockets instead of around the neck. Wearing a pale-green long-sleeved shirt with black pants, he looked ever the part of a casually dressed businessman attending some seminar. "Yes, you can, Doctor. You have a patient, Mr. Perry Sinclair, on this ward who I'll be interviewing shortly in reference to an ongoing investigation. If you have a room that I could use, it would be most appreciated. If not, we can use the visitors' lounge."

"You are aware, Detective Heller, that this man is just recovering from serious issues as a result of a spider bite?"

"Yes, Dr. Feinstein, and it's his experience with that spider bite that remains central to my investigation. You can be certain that my interview will be brief."

Kate watched the doctor struggling with his decision as he tried to decide how much authority on this matter he was willing to concede.

"You can use the empty conference room, but I must limit your time to no more than thirty minutes."

"Thank you, Doctor. I believe from my previous visits to the hospital that the conference room is all the way down the hallway and to the left. If you would be so kind, please have one of your staff members locate Mr. Sinclair and send him down to me."

Glancing at his Gucci sports watch, Feinstein acknowledged her request, turned, and headed down the hall.

Kate, entering the conference room, took the seat at the end of the long table and placed her notes and small tape recorder in front of her. Within a few minutes, Sinclair entered the room, and she could tell that he was very nervous. Getting up, Kate motioned for him to have a seat at the other end of the table.

"Mr. Sinclair, my name is Detective Kate Heller, and as you can see, I'm going to record this interview with your permission. But first, tell me how you feel and if you still are willing to talk to me without your lawyer being present?"

"Actually I feel much better today. Dr. Ogden got the physical thing under control, which was a living hell while it lasted. You know that warning about taking Viagra and what can happen is no joke, but having it happen because of a spider bite is worse because it seems to last forever. But as I've said, Dr. Ogden solved that problem, plus in administering the antidote, he was able to put me out of any danger."

"I'm happy to know that your health is returning, Mr. Sinclair. About needing that legal counsel?"

"I won't need that," said Sinclair.

"All right then, Mr. Sinclair, let me begin asking a few questions," said Kate as she turned on the tape recorder."

"Don't you have to advise me of my Mirada Rights first?" asked Sinclair.

"Miranda Rights are given only to anyone who has been arrested or facing arrest," said Kate. "Remember, as I've stated, you have every right to have a lawyer present if you wish.

"Why don't you start asking your questions and we'll see how it goes."

"It doesn't work that way, Mr. Sinclair. I'm in the process of recording you now, so remember what you say could possibly be used against you."

"Okay, but if I feel uncomfortable with your line of questions, the interview will cease until I obtain legal counsel, right?"

"Fair enough, Mr. Sinclair. Are you feeling well enough for this interview to continue, or do you need more time to rest?"

"No, everything is fine now, so ask your questions. I have nothing to hide."

"Were you aware that Ms. Gayle Browning was also sexually involved with a Pastor Paul Bergman of Trinity Lutheran Church?"

"Yes, she admitted the affair to me but said she was going to break it off. She had indicated that she was beginning to be afraid of him."

"What was she afraid of, Mr. Sinclair?"

"That, she wouldn't tell me. All she ever said was that he was becoming creepy with his hobby, but when I pressed her about the hobby, she would always change the subject. The paper had said that she had died of a brown recluse spider bite. Is that true?"

"I don't know for certain how she died, Mr. Sinclair," said Kate. "That's one of the reasons why I have been assigned to reexamine the circumstances of her death. What I do know is that you need to have a long talk with your wife before some reporter gets to her first. This is a high-profile situation that now involves you, a pastor, and an organist who was sleeping with you both. His wife is dead, the organist has died, and you could have died. These things just don't go away. And one more thing, Mr. Sinclair, just so you understand the complete picture."

"Yes."

"I don't believe that the spider just happened to be in that fruit basket. My guess is someone put the spider inside, and thus we can't be sure if you were the actual intended victim of what I believe to be the Brazilian wandering spider."

"What do you mean?"

"I mean that anyone in your family could have been the intended target, not just you."

"But I'm the one who had the affair. They didn't do anything."

"It doesn't matter, Mr. Sinclair. Always remember that you took something away from another man or woman. That person is unhappy and may have wanted to inflict pain by going after your wife or daughter.

"You mean someone like Pastor Bergman?"

"Not necessarily, especially if she had other intimate friends that she was seeing besides you two."

"I just don't believe she was like that, Detective Heller. Besides, we had an understanding."

"What understanding, Mr. Sinclair? An understanding because of a ruby ring? That was a very impressive ring that you bought Ms. Browning. Few men will pay upwards of twenty-two thousand dollars for a ring just for an overnight stay. She may be attractive and good in bed, but I doubt that would justify that expenditure. So what went wrong, Mr. Sinclair? Did you present her with the ring as a suggestion that you were going to marry her, and then you found out that she was still playing lights out with Bergman or some other guy? Did it suddenly dawn on you that a woman who has no regrets sleeping with two married men might be so inclined to want to taste the fruits of a single man as well? That would certainly get me upset, Mr. Sinclair, especially after buying her a ring that cost more than some people make in a year."

"I don't like where this conversation is going, Officer Heller. Maybe I do need to seek legal counsel after all."

"Maybe you do, Mr. Sinclair, if not because of me, but to prepare yourself for your wife, who is going to wonder where and how you got the money for that ring that she didn't know about. And of course, there's the matter of the funeral expenses."

"What funeral expenses? I don't know anything about funeral expenses," said Sinclair.

"Ms. Browning had no family, as you are aware of, Mr. Sinclair, yet some mysterious benefactor paid for the entire funeral with cash, as was the case with the ring, which incidentally has gone missing. But you know that, of course, since you've been trying to locate it, haven't you? What you don't know, of course, is that you're not the only person who has been interested in that ring, and therein is the rub, Mr. Sinclair."

"What do you mean, Detective Heller?"

"What I mean is someone may have found that ring, Mr. Sinclair, and is really pissed at the person that gave it to Browning. The good news is that I actually do believe that you didn't kill Gayle Browning, but the bad news is that the killer is looking for revenge, and he or she might not miss the next time."

Getting up, Kate pushed the stop button on the recorder and said to Sinclair, "Have a good talk with your wife. I've already met her, and she seems like a good woman who cares about you, so do yourself a favor and protect your family. That's all for today, but I will be back, Mr. Sinclair, so it might be a good idea to hire that attorney."

As Kate drove away from the hospital, she couldn't help but feel a little sorry for Sinclair. The man wanted to play, and now he was just beginning to pay. She wondered if maybe she had been a little too hard on him. Not really, she concluded, when one considered that she had followed the rules of what good cops are made of. "Never fight angry, which will make you lose your senses," she had always been told by her father. Retreat and plan is always a good strategy. Then aim for the head, because in any fight, a man with a broken nose will almost always retreat. She had bloodied Sinclair's nose and in the end being scared may save his family. There is a reason why people do not hug porcupines, Kate thought as she continued her drive. Sinclair was pathetic. The man had a young daughter and an attractive wife, but still Perry Sinclair had been thinking with the wrong part of his anatomy, and his wife, Barbara, was now going to have to decide if her porcupine was worth the risk of another try at their marriage. Well, they say good girls go to heaven, and Barbara certainly fit that bill, but Perry Sinclair? "Focus on the task at hand, girl," came the imaginary voice as her speedometer inched up to seventy. Time passed unnoticed by Kate. Once her mind was fixed on a project, she lost time of the clock. She'd have to be careful of this when Curtis became her husband, since it was obvious that he would want some of that time, as she would his. Since the death of her husband, work had been her drug of choice, but now she had Curtis. While she enjoyed her time off, nothing invigorated her more than poring over past cold cases and the competition of the gun range while going up against her male counterparts. Corporal Howard Singer had been the team leader on the firing range for over five years straight before she beat his top score by ten points. She remembered his shock when he had asked. "So how long have you been working on this, rookie?"

"Working on what?" she had asked.

"Being the best?" Singer grinned at his remark while looking at her chest and had moved closer to her and had said, "It will take more than having good tits and an ass to move up the ladder here."

Kate chuckled and at the time had stared back at Singer, then turned to the crowd that had begun to circle her to offer congratulations. "Hey, everyone, thanks, but where I grew up, the winner always gave the former champion a second chance, with, of course, an added caveat."

"What's the caveat?" Singer had asked.

"The current champion is allowed to select her choice of arms."

"Hell, that's no problem. Go ahead and pick it," he had said.

With that, Kate had stepped up to the range box and, with her left hand on her weapon, put all eight shots into the three-inch circle of the target. Turning to Singer, she had said, "Sorry, I neglected to tell you that I'm ambidextrous." Singer knew he was beat and just walked away, to the catcalls of his peers. Now today she was his boss, a detective, and they had as they say buried the hatchet. She couldn't help but laugh out loud.

Pulling up to her townhouse, she grabbed the small box that Patel had given her, locked her car, and entered her home, to the welcoming excitement of Channing. "Hey, Channing," she said while rubbing his head. "You act like this is Christmas every day I come home. Lucky me, I guess, huh!" Wagging his tail, Channing followed her into the kitchen until he found his doggie bed and settled down. "Be patient, big guy, and let me change my clothes first, and then I'll get you something to eat." Taking the small box, she laid it on the kitchen table, along with her cell phone. Walking into the bedroom, she hurriedly undressed and turned on the shower. After allowing the warm water to calm her tired body, Kate stepped out of the shower, dried herself off, and sat on the queen-size bed, head in her hands, then stretched out on the bed and fell asleep.

Curtis finally called her at eleven. Reaching for the phone, Kate picked it up on the second ring.

"Hello, this is Kate."

"Hi. I took a chance you might be up. Sorry, sweetheart, that I didn't call you earlier, but a passenger got sick on the last leg of the flight, and we had to make a special landing in Cleveland. The poor guy suffered a terrible diabetic attack, but we made it in time." His voice sounded heavy with exhaustion.

"Curtis, it's all right. You don't need to apologize. We both have the type of careers that will cause things like this to happen. Besides, police officers learn to take good notes."

"What notes, Kate? I don't follow you. What are you talking about, dear?"

"Notes that remind me what my future husband might need to do to make up for this oversight and making me worry."

"And that would be?"

Kate whispered seductively, "———."

"Good Lord, you sure can talk dirty late at night," said Curtis.

"Just imagine what you have missed, Curtis, by not being here. But those words are not dirty. You just happen to always make me feel like a woman should feel with the man she loves."

"It sounds as if your work schedule might still open this Friday and Saturday?" questioned Curtis?

"Friday for sure, with Saturday looking good. Can you make it?"

"I'll be there," said Curtis, "even if I have to swap trips. But tell me, how has your week been?"

"I'm beginning to make some headway in understanding what killed the church organist, although I'm still having a hard time finding a believer with the medical examiner. Like most doctors, they believe that they are infallible in their conclusions and don't want to let go of their opinions."

"Your mean the god complex is in place with him?"

"Yes, but he also doesn't like women," said Kate.

"That's very common with foreign doctors native to India, Pakistan, or the Arab countries, Kate. Women are to be seen but encouraged to remain silent in the presence of their men. I bet as beautiful as you are, he probably didn't even glance at your magnificent body, did he?"

"Doctors have little interest in that, Curtis. They see the female anatomy all day."

"I thought you said that he was a medical examiner. Those bodies wouldn't be as appealing as yours, Kate."

"He's got his own practice, Curtis away from the hospital. He sees a lot of live patients. However, he did give me the prescription bottles and ointment that the woman was taking, plus a broken pin. I haven't had a chance to look at yet, so I don't know what more they will tell me other than the organist was concerned about her spider bite and was trying to self-medicate the developing problem. It wouldn't have done much good in this case because, if I'm correct, she was bitten by the most dangerous spider of all. In that case, it wouldn't have matter what she was trying to do since the end result would have been the same without an antidote."

"The banana spider, right?"

"How did you know?

"You've forgotten that I took the course in college. The little bastard, unlike other spiders, hunts you. He doesn't build spiderwebs like the typical spider to lure his prey into the web. They spend all day looking for their victims."

"Yes, I know. I have another one in the hospital right now who is recovering from being bitten by that species. We know that for sure because the dead spider was brought into the hospital, unlike the case with the organist. In that example, there was no spider that could be examined, and since she was cremated all we had left was the opinion of the medical examiner. That was until now."

"You said until now. What do you mean by that, Kate?"

"We got lucky. The deceased organist actually took a picture of the spider on her cell phone before she died."

"Does Patel know this?" asked Curtis.

"He does, although I'm sure that he still feels that his reputation will win the day. All that will make little difference when I arrest her killer, though."

"That's the spirit, Detective Heller. It sounds like Funston's newest and prettiest detective has just about wrapped the case up. Should I start making plans for the honeymoon or wait another week?"

"Well, you might be just a little biased about my ability, but I love you for your confidence in me. Anyway, my love, we could talk about this all night, but I know that you are as tired as I, so I'm going to let you get some sleep."

"Fair enough, Kate, but leave me a message when you look at that pin. Somehow, and I don't know why, but that might be the big break you've been waiting for. Love you and good night."

CHAPTER 36

The Good Shepherd

The evening rush hour had come and gone, but the cars and trucks were still rumbling past her townhouse, making sleep impossible. Fortunately, sleep was the furthest thing from her mind as she thought about Curtis, spiders, and Paul Bergman. Lying alone in the bed of her former husband, she had a sudden rush of guilt as she remembered it was the same bed that just a short time ago had found her in the arms of Curtis. She pulled the sheet up higher, gripping it tightly in her fist, and wondering for the first time if she was jumping the gun. Was this happening too fast? The step that she was about to make was huge.

How could she know that it was right? What the hecking time was it anyway? "Damn it," she mumbled, as she turned to the side and glanced out into the darkness, with the only light being that of a half moon. A few stars shone brilliantly in the patch of sky that Kate could see through her bedroom window. She turned over and looked at the alarm clock that told her it was 4:30 a.m. "My god," she said to herself, "it's almost time to get up, and I just got to bed." Rolling over, she buried her face in the pillow and turned on the small radio she kept under her pillow. It was a habit that she had kept all her life as a born news junky. Sometimes it never got turned off, especially if the Red Wings were playing that night. They can keep the Tigers and the miserable Lions for all she cared, but the Red Wings made Detroit the Hockey Town, USA. This should be interesting with Curtis, she thought, since she knew he was in love with the Black

Hawks and proudly wore the Indian Head whenever he could. She had to admit that they had the better uniform, but hardly a match for the Wings when it came time for the playoffs. She listened to the local *Funston News* and was pleased that there was no mention of the latest citizen bit by a spider. Once they locked on to that, her days would be a living hell. Tossing the pillow aside, she got up from her bed knowing that there was not a chance that she could fall asleep with all the things on her mind, so she walked out to the kitchen and started the coffee pot. Grabbing the shampoo, she washed her hair in the sink and wet dried it with a towel and sat down at the kitchen table. She was still pondering her future with Curtis as she looked at the small box on the table. Tired as she was, there seemed to be little reason to put off examining it since there was little chance that she would be slipping back into bed as much as she would have liked to. She made a mental note that she would start looking for a new bed that would be her wedding gift to them both. That might help her sleep better, she thought. Reaching for the box, she opened the top up, noticing the extra-strength Bayer aspirin bottle, which still contained about twenty-five caplets. Putting it aside, she picked up the hydrocortisone cream, 2 percent, rash relief (almost all used up) and a brand-new box of Benadryl allergy tablets. Kate studied the array of medication, and it became clear that the woman was fighting off something that had gotten control of her health. Probably the first signs of the spider bite taking hold. The only other bottle in the box was a sample bottle, which the contents indicated contained seven capsules of something called Jalyn, which she didn't recognize. Opening up the bottle, she noted that there remained five capsules, so she must have taken at least the first two trying to fight off the oncoming storm. Then she noted the tiny box marked Pin, which she opened and found an inch one-half-size gold-plated shaft about the thickness of a paper clip. Only in this case, it had a rounded hook on the end. Drinking her coffee, she studied it for a full ten minutes, trying to recollect where she had seen that shape before, but in the end nothing came to mind. Walking into the bedroom, she pulled her outfit for the day from the closet, turned, and saw Channing still fast asleep in the corner by her bed. "Well, my protector," she thought, "one of us has to earn a living today."

Now just after dawn and fully dressed, Kate dialed Curtis's number. She was beginning to find these one-way chats, his voice mail, always listening to her respectfully, not something that she hoped would last much longer. She longed for the comings days when she would find him with her in the morning, but this was for the moment the best they could do.

"Good morning, Curtis. Wish you were here. Well, less than ninety-six hours, my husband-to-be, and then we'll see each other. Be safe. Love you." Picking up her notebook off the dresser, she returned to the kitchen table and started to review her notes. Based on what she knew about the murder of Bergman's wife, she felt that it was somehow linked to the Gayle Browning's death and the recent spider bite of Perry Sinclair. Confused as it was, there was one thing, though, that was perfectly clear to her. That the Bergman case was getting cold because the jury had acquitted him and the focus of him being a killer had moved away from his door. The answer for that was logical since people who got away with murder, or at least thought that they had, tended not to stick around. They moved else-where, and most often the local police department in order to track them down had to travel to find them. With resources what they were and budgets being held tight, many cases found themselves col-lecting dust in some detectives' file drawer. Kate highlighted Paul Bergman's name in yellow. As she studied her notes on the church secretary, something came to mind that the secretary had said to her regarding some donation made in her memory. What was it she tried to remember? Turning back to the page on her conversation with the secretary, she found the amount $1,500. "Very generous," she had underlined at the time of the call. What was the family name? Turning to the next page of her notes, she noted that the name was Mr. and Mrs. Phoneutria. Hmm, where had she heard that name before? Getting up, she walked to her bedroom where her briefcase was, opened it up, and pulled the spider book that the professor had given her. Returning to the kitchen table, she sat down and turned to the page on the Brazilian wandering spider. There it was in bold letters: PHONEUTRIA. It was another name for the Brazilian wandering spider. The killer had been so brazen that he had sent money in for her memorial and at the same time told the world how he had killed her. All along she had remained convinced that Dr. Patel's conclusion of a brown recluse spider death was self-serving and devoid of any real evidence, and this clearly proved it along with the cell phone picture. Reaching on the floor, she retrieved her purse and located the business card of Dr. Alan J. Ogden, the infectious disease physician that had treated Perry Sinclair. He had been adamant from the beginning that it was unlikely any brown recluse could have killed an adult human because its established track record on deaths were almost nonexistent in the last several years, and he had been right. Looking at her watch, she noted that it was only 7:32 a.m., hardly the time that any doctor would be in his office, so she decided to leave him a voice mail message and request that he return a call. Dialing his phone number and expecting his answering service to pick up, Kate was shocked to find that he answered the call.

"This is Dr. Ogden. Who's calling?"

"Dr. Ogden, good morning. This is Detective Kate Heller of the Funston Police Department. We met at the Funston Hospital when you were treating a patient by the name of Perry Sinclair. You gave me your card in the event that I had any further questions."

"Yes, I remember you were investigating some outstanding past criminal case. Has something happened to Mr. Sinclair? No one from the hospital has called me if that's the case."

"No, Doctor, I was just attempting to leave you a message in hopes you could spare a few minutes to help me on the subject of the Brazilian wandering spider. I must admit that I never expected you to pick up on your office line at this time of the morning. Please tell me if you would need a better time for us to talk?"

"Detective Heller, this time is fine. I deal with a lot of AIDS patients, most of which prefer that their sessions with their doctor remain private. This type of illness still remains socially unacceptable to the majority of society. I happen to be in early today for that type of appointment, and I just finished with the young man a few minutes ago. As it happens, I have a full half hour open now before anyone else comes in the office, so give me your questions."

"Doctor, one of the cases that I'm working on involves a woman who died of a brown recluse spider bite. I believe that I brought up the subject with you when we met, and that you felt that such a death was highly improbable, something that I had also felt based on other information that I had received from a local professor of entomology, a Prof. Joseph Davis, who you have also met before. As it turns out, the Perry Sinclair case which you treated and the woman who he was having an affair and later died are linked, Doctor, plus a second woman's death prior to hers, who I can't comment about. What I need to know, Dr. Ogden, is can a person generally survive a Brazilian wandering spider bite long enough to go out and get a prescription and self-treat the bite? The medical examiner released to me all of the prescriptions and ointments that she was taking to combat her illness. The ointments were Hydrocortisone, Benadryl, something called clobetasol propionate cream 0.05%, and a sample bottle of seven capsules of Jayln, in which five remain."

"You have an interesting assortment of medication, Detective Heller, to say the least. First, the Hydrocortisone, Benadryl, and the clobetasol propionate cream would all suggest the type of medication that most doctors would recommend to treat an insect bite or small spider bite that would cause a rash, itching, or general discomfort. The clobetasol propionate cream is often what my colleagues prescribe when they are unable to solve the rash or itching on the first visit, and as you already know that most doctors can't tell the difference between a spider bite and that of a tick or mite. If the deceased woman had been bitten by a brown recluse, its released venom would create slight pain at the site of the bite plus high-level itching. The real problem usually takes eight to ten hours for the developing muscle, joint pain, and vomiting. Now the Brazilian wandering spider can cause death in forty-five minutes without an antidote, but here's what we must remember. Its bite is horribly painful from the beginning for everyone, but men pay a particular harsh price because the venom causes as it did in Mr. Sinclair an unwanted erection that remains for hours. Still, it's important to remember that only 33 percent of the Brazilian spider bites actual contain any significant amount of venom. It's possible that her bite was slow acting. Then you have the wild card, Detective Heller."

"What wild card? asked Kate.

"The Brazilian Wandering Spider, which is also called the banana spider, has a North American cousin that also finds its way into homes. This one is less dangerous but nevertheless causes discomfort, irritation, and sometimes a fever. It leaves a nasty-size welt but little else."

"So no one can be totally sure what actually bit her is what you're saying, Doctor?"

"That's true unless I had a good look at the tissue in the area of the bit, but as I remember, you said the body was cremated."

"Yes."

"Well, that pretty much removes any opportunity to determine the species. I'm sorry, Detective, that I can't be of more help, but there is one thing that is perfectly clear, Officer Heller."

"What is that, Dr. Ogden?"

"The Jalyn pills were not hers."

"What do you mean, Doctor? They were found with the rest of her medicine."

"It doesn't matter, Detective, since Jayln is a pill that is used by a man, and not to treat spider bites. The drug is relatively new, so some doctors might not even be aware of the brand name at this point. It is used to increase the flow of the urine in men who have been diagnosed as having an enlarged prostrate. I actual prescribe it myself to many of my male patients who are dealing with benign prostate problems."

"So the man would have been in his fifties, sixties, or seventies, correct?"

"Not necessarily, Detective Heller, because I have a number of male patients in their thirties who have urinating problems," said Ogden. Prostate problems, while generally affecting older men, are not exclusive to that age group."

"What do you think that means, Doctor?"

"Nothing special, other than one of the men she was seeing probably was having difficulty urinating without the pill. His problem, however, doesn't prevent intercourse, unless he had additional medical concerns."

"Well, Doctor, the investigation has some good news despite the victim having been cremated."

"Is that so, Detective Heller?"

"Yes, before the lady died, she actually took a picture of the spider with her cell phone camera. My people blew up the picture and tell me that there's no question that it is the Brazilian wandering spider. I'm going to send it over to you for a second opinion."

"I'll be glad to look at it for you. Also, remember that the other creams you mentioned could have been used for other things besides insect bites."

"Well, Doctor, you have once again been generous with your time and most informative. I appreciate your assistance. Hopefully I will not need to call on you again so soon."

"It's no problem, Officer Heller. Have a blessed day."

Surprised again by Ogden's reference to Christianity, Kate couldn't help but ask, "That's the second time, Dr. Ogden, that you have introduced God into your conversation, and I always pictured most physicians being soft on religion."

"Many are, Detective Heller, but some of us actually do belong to a Christian organization. "When you treat as many people as I do, it never hurts to have the big guy on your side. Good day, Detective, and good luck on your investigations," he said as he gently hung up the phone.

Kate took a few minutes and studied her conversation with Dr. Ogden. Picking up the Jalyn bottle, she wondered which of the men, Bergman or Sinclair, had left his capsules with the Browning woman. As Ogden had said, it made little difference. Then again, why couldn't the woman have had a third male interest? If she did, then it could be something that she needed to look at. One should never limit the possibilities.

As she tossed the bottle back in the box, she paused and thought for a moment. Where does evil come from? It was clear that the

Browning woman was a magnet that attracted Rev. Paul Bergman and Perry Sinclair, both married men. The popular theory is that men can't keep it in their pants and hunt for women like the virginal-appearing Browning because it's what they do regardless if they wear a white collar around their neck of have a business card like Sinclair carried. Forgotten of course is that not all pure-looking women on the outside wear chastity belts, as was the custom of a knight's lady when he left for the Crusades.

Kate remembered the stories about film actress Grace Kelly, who was the blueprint for purity, yet had willingly found herself in the bedrooms of Clark Gable, Bing Crosby, William Holder, and Oleg Cassini, before becoming a princess. No, someone had killed Mrs. Bergman and Gayle Browning, and what did the great Detective Harry Bosch say in one of Michael Connelly's many books? "Everybody counts, or nobody counts." So the question remains, had she counted or unearthed all the men in the life of Browning that existed that might have wanted to do harm to a number of people? Kate wrote herself a note to check to find out if either Bergman or Sinclair had prostate problems. She wasn't sure what it would mean, but it was just another stone she would have looked under. If neither of the man had a need for such a pill, then things might turn a little interesting. Evil, she believed, often stayed dormant with a person for years, waiting to make its appearance. How else could one explain how one child can grow up in a home, abused and not loved, yet survive and be a loving spouse, while another uses their childhood environment as an excuse to murder and rape and expect society to make allowances for their actions while committing the crimes at age twenty-seven.

Time was beginning to rush past her like the Empire Builder Train, and Kate felt like the track, beaten and worn down by a case that was going nowhere. The telephone rang, and like a person unwilling to have one more problem facing her, she picked up the phone slowly. "Hello."

"Kate, err, Detective Heller, this is Corporal Singer."

Surprised to be receiving a call from Singer, she answered, "Yes, Howard, what can I do for you?"

"I was hoping that you would be in the office today, as I would like an opportunity to speak to you direct, not over the phone."

"They haven't given me my own office yet, Howard, so if this is a private type of conversation, why don't we meet at Kluckers in about an hour. We can have lunch and do business at the same time, and then nobody will be asking either of us questions."

"That's fine, Detective Heller, and thank you for making the time. See you there in about forty minutes."

Kate wondered what was going on with Singer as she gathered up her notes and put them in her briefcase. The usual villains, traffic and more traffic, delayed Kate from arriving at Kluclers ahead of Singer, as she noted his parked red Mustang near the front door. Seeing that the diner was unusually crowded, she decided to park behind a nondescript two-story building, from which she had been told was the location that ran the small empire that promoted the town's most notable former citizen that had ranked as the world's second tallest human. Kate laughed every time she thought of the town's crazed love affair with the former gentle giant. The building's current owners maintained a perfect manicured chemical lawn, as required by Wally's estate. As she walked to the entrance of Klucker's diner, she noted a maroon Mercedes was pulling up to an open slot not far from the front of the diner. Long fingers protruded from the driver's window holding what appeared to be an open bottle of Jim Beam. As she passed the car, the driver obviously noted her uniform and pulled his hand with the bottle back in the car. Deciding that this was not the time for an arrest, she continued her walk through the double doors into the restaurant. Removing her sunglasses, she looked for Singer but was unable to spot him at any of the tables.

"Well, good goddarn, if it isn't Funston's newest and best-looking Detective," offered the voice of the restaurant's most charming waitress.

"Molly Ann Walker, you still look like every guy's hope and dreams," said Kate. "How many hearts have you broken since the last time we'd seen each other?"

"You should talk, Detective Heller, by the size of that diamond ring on your hand. It looks like you have landed Prince Charming. Anyone I know?"

"You met him once, Molly, for a brief moment, and yes, he's actually is that guy on the white horse and all. He's flying into town this Friday, and I hope to be able to bring him over to see you."

"Kate, if my memory serves me well, Funston has no airport that I've been told that allows commercial aircraft."

"It doesn't, but he has his own aircraft, so he'll be landing at the private section. He's a captain for Delta Air Lines, and you actually met him several weeks ago."

"That's the guy? Wow, we have to have some serious girly talk woman," said Molly.

"Sorry, Molly, not today 'cause I'm on the business clock now. I'm looking for another police officer that should be in here someplace, but I can't find him."

"You must be talking about Howard Singer. He's in the men's think tank. Nice-looking cop but has come on too strong in the past. He's sporting a wedding band today," said Molly with a wink. "He's got the back booth over near the piano. He appears not to be a player today, so you won't be bothered or have to shoot him, if you know what I mean."

"I'll talk to you later," said Kate, walking over to Howard's booth and sitting down. As she was waiting for Singer to return from the men's room, she noticed that Mr. Jim Beam had come in and sat down near a booth in the front of the diner. She also noticed his jacket had opened when he sat down, revealing what appeared to be a shoulder holster. "Strange," she thought on both accounts. First, the guy looked more like a church worker than someone on the bottle, and second, why the iron? she wondered.

"Oh, there you are, Detective Heller," came Singer's voice. "You must have just got here. Bet you got caught in the traffic?"

"Sure did, Howard, and while we're not in the office trying to impress the brass, remember that you can call me Kate and I'll call you Howard, unless you want me to feel more important than what the situation calls for. Rank is important to acknowledge, but not away from the office with me, but I appreciate your concern."

With a somewhat relaxed look on his face, Howard said, "Will do, Kate, but if I slip accidently, please remember that I'm my father's son."

"You have my curiosity piqued, Howard. What does that mean?"

"My dad used to always say, 'Remember, son, should you ever be at a meeting or cocktail party with your boss, and you begin to have informal conversations with him or her, never ever forget that tomorrow morning, that person is still your boss.'"

"My dad was very similar," said Kate, "only he spent his extra time advising us girls that we should always remember that the promises your bosses make to you about promotions are always going to change the next morning when he wakes up besides his wife."

Both Kate and Howard laughed together as Molly approached the table. "Can I get you guys anything to drink before you order?" she asked.

"You first", said Howard."

"Make mine a lemonade, said Kate."

"Cherry Coke for me," offered Howard."

"I'll be back in a few minutes to take your orders. The special for the day is the homemade beef stew," said Molly.

Kate looked at Howard and the feeling that she was getting was that he was tense. It was clear that he didn't want to spoil any chance this meeting might provide but didn't know what to say or how to begin the conversation. She knew that she would have to break the ice. "Life is short, Howard," she said. You can't waste life's opportunities, and I can't be supporting the best field police officer now assigned to me if he is hesitant to step up to the plate."

"You're talking about me, Detective Heller, I mean Kate?"

"Yes, Howard, I was talking about you. So take your best shot, and I promise you that I won't do my left-handed trick on you today."

Howard smiled, remembering the day she beat him on the pistol range.

"Part of the reason why I requested this meeting, Kate, was that I wanted to release you from the burden of requesting me to join your team. Certainly the fact that you saved me from street patrol is most appreciated, but after the sexual suggestions that I made about you, I didn't think it was fair for you to start your detective career with this liability."

"Oh, that muscle-ass comment and how I needed to put my hand around a real club?" she said, watching Howard's face turn crimson red. "Think nothing about it, Howard, that's long gone as being important to our relationship. The truth is, women like to be admired for having the appearance of being sexy to a man. Your problem that day was that you were trying too hard to be the alpha-male type when you don't have to be, Howard. Your size thirteen shoes should be enough for any woman who is interested to imagine, if she wishes, and I don't. Strong men don't need a marketing campaign. Besides, that ring on your finger suggests to me that someone else has a stake in you first."

"I don't know what really to say, Kate, other than I'm sorry about that day."

"Apology accepted, Howard. What was the second reason you wanted to meet with me?"

"To let you know that if you needed any help on the cold case you're working on, I'd be glad to assist you. The budget is tough, and I didn't know if by volunteering my time, it could help you from not having to go to Wagner. I'd be glad to do it on my own time."

"There will be no need for me to go to Wagner as you have already been volunteered to me if I need assistance and you'll be paid for any extra time that you put in. And somehow, all things considered, it would appear that it will be sooner than later."

"Does that mean you are close to cracking the case, Kate?"

"Ever hear of Leonard Cohen, Howard?"

"No, was he in law enforcement, Kate?"

"Not at all, just a guy who once said, 'There's a crack in everything, that's how light gets in.' The light is beginning to get in, Howard, so it shouldn't be that much longer."

"Say, you two ready to eat yet?" came the voice of Molly.

"I'll take the homemade beef stew," volunteered Kate.

"Make mine the stir fry with chicken," said Howard.

"Should be up in about fifteen minutes," replied Molly as she walked the order to the kitchen.

"Don't look right now, Howard, but what's your take on that guy sitting at the table as you came into the diner? He's the one with the Heirloom sports jacket, wearing Armani jeans and leather boots. As you are thinking about this before you look up, consider the fact that under that sports coat is a shoulder holster. I spotted him earlier in his car with an open bottle of Jim Beam, although he's unaware that I've noticed anything."

As Howard moved his head up slowly, the dusty afternoon light slanted through the high venetian blind windows, causing him to squint as he located the person Kate had been commenting about. The man didn't appear to notice Howard's glancing as he continued to write notes on his expensive, leathered portfolio. Recognition usually came quickly to Howard, and there was little doubt that he had seen the guy someplace. "Maybe ticketed him," he thought.

"I'm seen him before," he softly said to Kate, "but darn if I can't recall where. If you want me to check him out, I'll be glad to do it."

"No, that's not necessary. He's not causing any trouble. Just makes me a little curious. Must just be the cop thing in me."

"Well, here comes lunch, and I'm hungry," said Howard.

Throughout the dinner, their food tasted good, and the talk remained business, until Howard commented in a low voice, "I think he's a lawyer, as I remember. I had stopped him for blowing a red light about six months ago. The reason I remember was that he had come out of some church where I was parked waiting for speeders and got him doing fifteen over the limit. He had told me that he was visiting his brother who was a pastor and didn't know the area. I let him go with a warning. If you need, I can find out his name by checking my records in my car. He had an easy plate to remember. One of these vanity deals that said Twin-2. I figured that he was one of those misplaced Minnesota Twins fans."

"Maybe it wasn't that, Howard. Maybe your speeder was visiting his twin brother, or the plate could be referencing a lost loved one in the twin towers of New York on 9/11. Anyway, let's forget it as he's minding his own business, and besides, I have to be moving along. Captain Wagner has me on his radar regarding this special assignment. Say, I remember that your wife worked for her dad at a religious store. I wonder if she could help me identify where this may have come from," she said, reaching inside her jacket and pulling out the small piece of gold one-and-one-half-inch piece of metal, with the hook on the end."

"Sure, I'll give it to her tonight. Where did it come from?"

"It was found on the floor next to the body of the dead organist that I told you about. Nobody seems to recognize what it is," said Kate. Getting up, she said, "I'll leave first so that the guy up front doesn't worry that we're trying to make him. I've already signed the credit card for our lunch in advance before you arrived, so don't worry about the bill. I would like you to call me if you find out anything about the metal hook," said Kate as she walked away from the table toward the door before suddenly turning around. "And oh, and by the way, Howard."

"Yes," he said as he watched her eyes moving up and down his body.

"Nice bulletproof vest that you're wearing today," she said, while continuing her walk toward the front door.

CHAPTER 37

The Break

Walking into his house, he heard the sound of the microwave running. "Hey, Sue, I'm home. Where are you? In the kitchen?" asked Howard.

"Yes, I just got home about thirty minutes ago. Would you do me a favor and grab two cans of cream corn from the cabinet for me? I'm just finishing the potatoes and ham."

Walking in the kitchen with the corn, he asked, "Where are the kids?"

"Junior is still at basketball practice tonight. Coach Feller is dropping him off home later tonight, and Monica, well, you know your daughter. She's doing an overnight at the Hazleton's. The girls have put together a sleepover to prepare for their final exams. Of course, you and I know that they will stay up half the night talking about the boys in school, not the tests."

"Well, that's natural," said Howard. You probably did the same thing when you were her age."

"No, actually we invited the boys over when we had sleepover for tests. We didn't think much of those T-shirts that those other girls wore that said, 'Good girls go to heaven.' We rather liked the ones that said 'Bad girls go everywhere.'"

"You are, of course, kidding, Sue. I thought all along that I married one of the good girls."

"When supper is over, and Junior is safe and sound, maybe you would like to see where bad girls really go?"

320

Howard, now smiling pulled his wife closer to him and said, "That I've always wanted to know, but remember, Sue, I'm a slow learner."

"Well, keep those thoughts Howard, but for now why not wash up and supper should be in about ten minutes. By the way, how did the meeting go with your new boss?"

"It went very well. As a matter of fact, she was very interested in your college major and the work that you do at the religious shop for your dad."

"Oh, she was? Somehow I must have missed the memo that your new boss was a woman."

"She's really a nice person, Sue. I'll be working with her on two special cases she's been assigned. She's engaged to a Delta Air Lines pilot, and they should be getting married in the next two months."

Reaching in his jacket pocket, he handed Sue the little shaft of metal that Kate had given him.

"What's that?" asked Sue.

"It's something that my new boss asked if you would look at. It was found at the site of one of the victims she's currently reinvestigating. No one seems to understand what it is, and she thought that maybe you'd take a look at it an offer an opinion. Remember many months ago a local pastor was accused of trying to murder his wife? At the time, he was having an affair with the church organist who later died of a spider bite. I believe this has something to do with those two individuals, although I can't be certain."

"Oh, I remember now, Howard. He was the one who got acquitted by that jury of dunderheads who bought his line of bullshit."

"Yes, but I wish you wouldn't use that language, it so unfeminine."

"Well, honey, I don't want to spoil your image of me, especially since we have that pending date to learn about how bad girls behave, but that Pastor fooled twelve adults with a sob story as I remember and now is as free as a bird. Why don't you be a helpful husband and put the hot dish on the table while I take that small little shaft of gold metal that you gave me and check it against my new promotional magazine. Something makes me think that I've seen it before when it wasn't broken off its original pin or clasp." Walking into the den, Sue opened up the drawer where she kept her latest promotional material for her father's religious store. When she found the right magazine, she returned to the kitchen and laid it by Howard's chair and finished setting the table.

"Smells wonderful, Susan. Is there anything I need to get before I sit down," asked Howard.

"No, let's just eat and discuss the magazine a little later," said Sue.

"You know, Sue, it's nice to eat at home for once. It seems that we're always eating at some restaurant, and I've always like you're cooking."

"That's a sweet comment, Howard. Thank you. I can't remember the last time that you ever said how much you like my cooking, so maybe we'll do it more often now. Where did you eat lunch today with your boss? It was today, wasn't it?" she asked.

"Yes, we met at Kluckers. You and I have been there before so you know that it's nothing special, just a place to eat. She wanted to discuss the cases that she's working on and to advise me that I'm on loan to her until she has closure on them." Howard watched Susan as she pushed her chair away from the table and began to collect the dishes. He hoped that the questions would cease since he didn't want to explain that he had requested the meeting with Kate and the real reasons for it.

"Is she good-looking?"

"I would say so, and is probably no small reason why that Delta pilot has given her a ring the size some Arab king could only afford. The guy is taking no chances, Sue, as he owns his own plane and flies in to see her regularly from what I understand. She's actually a neat person and has even suggested that one weekend when he's in town that we all go out to dinner."

"Well, that I would like to do. That will give her an opportunity to meet your very bad girl," she said with a wink.

Howard watched Sue as she stretched to reach the top shelf of the kitchen's cabinet to put away the clean glasses. No matter what else was going on, even if his workday had been a living hell, if he was dead tired from jostling with drunks or punk teenagers, even if Sue was bitchy causing the two of them not to be on speaking terms, she always had the same effect on him. One look at her, and he wanted her. The fire between them was mutual. And she was just as attuned to him watching her as he was looking. She turned after putting the glasses away, and Howard could see her eyes glinting and a warm flush starting to tinge her cheeks.

"Howard," she offered, her tone half-teasing, half-seductive. "Your son is going to be home soon, so do your best to hold on to that welcome home look."

He walked up to her, gently wrapping his arms around her, pulling her against him, ignoring her warning, and said, "I like the sound of the word *home*, Sue. It feels right, and so do you."

"You feel right too," she said, slipping her hands under his polo shirt, hiking it up as she whispered, "Let's not start something that we can't finish. Rain check, for God's sake, before I can't stop."

That was a long, awkward pause before Howard said, "You're right, honey, we'll catch up later."

"Did you put your handgun in the safe?" asked Susan.

"I never forget that, darling, with the kids in the house, plus I put the trigger locks on them also."

"You are a careful husband, Howard. That's one of the things that I love about you," offered Susan. "Let's take a look at this magazine now and see what we have for your boss."

As they both sat back down at the table, Susan moved closer to Howard and opened the magazine to the page that listed religious items. "That's what we're looking for," she said. "Items for that special church worker." Putting her finger on an item called Shepherd Staff, Pins and Clasps, she smiled saying, "Gotcha."

"What do you mean gotcha?" asked Howard, looking at her.

"You're the future detective, my husband. Can't you see it? It's right in front of you, Sherlock."

Pausing for a moment Howard studied the Shepherd Staff pin and understood what his wife was saying." The Shepherd pin consisted of a man standing behind two sheep holding a long shaft with a hook on it. The piece that Kate had given Howard was probably the end of the long shaft and was the hook used to gather the sheep. "Who buys these pins, Susan?"

"Sometimes teachers, teacher aides, often just pastors. Yet some of our best customers at Dad's store are parents who buy them for their sons who have become pastors or priests. Sometimes the men buy themselves the pin. The cost ranges from fifteen dollars for the cheap version to almost one thousand dollars for those made of pure gold. I'd say as a guess that the small piece that you gave me is pure gold and is on the high side of the figure. Remember, though, that sometimes it's only a tie clip, and the cost is much lower. One thing is for certain, Howard. The person that is wearing that pin is unhappy about the broken piece or maybe doesn't know that it is broken."

Howard picked up the magazine and remembered Kate's request to call her with any information. "Susan, we usually don't bring our work home, but I need to call Detective Heller about what you found out. I'll only be a few minutes, but something tells me this is the call she's been hoping to receive. According to her, our captain has been putting a lot of pressure on her to come up with some lead on these two cases."

"While you take care of that, I'll prepare something for your son. If you have time and you're off the phone, maybe it would be a good idea to thank the coach for bringing him home."

"I'll do that, Susan. If I'm not off the phone, just have him sit for a few minutes, and I'll find a way to free myself."

Going into their bedroom, Howard dialed Kate from his cell phone.

"Kate Heller, who's calling?"

"Kate, this is Howard. You asked me to call you if my wife could identify that small gold metal shaft." He could tell by her silence that she was waiting for more information before she was going to speak. "Susan believes that it is part of what is called a Shepherd's pin. You know, the type of pin that one wears on their suit jacket proclaiming they are the Shepherd of their flock. She said it's a common item worn by a priest, a pastor, or maybe even a general church worker."

"Do you have a picture of it?" asked Kate.

"Yes, there are several in the latest magazine that she has. I'll make sure to bring in the magazine, but something tells me that examples of it would be all over the internet."

"Good work, Howard, and make certain to thank your wife. I hope sometime I'll have an opportunity to meet her and thank her personally. Not that this means anything for certain, Howard, but one of the suspects to both murders that I'm reinvestigating happens to be the same pastor that was once accused of attempting to kill his own wife. You know, Pastor Paul Bergman, the guy that has left the city and is now a preacher at another church in Wisconsin. While he was the pastor of the church here in town, he also was also intimate with his church secretary, the organist who died of a spider bite."

"No kidding. Will it be possible to interview him in the future?"

"That will be a problem, Howard, since he's out of our jurisdiction, and all we have is circumstantial evidence. This one I'll have to do some more thinking on before asking Wagner to go out on the limb over. Regardless, you did your job well, Howard. Get some sleep, and we'll talk about it tomorrow. Thanks again and have a good night."

Howard walked out into the kitchen and found Sue putting all the food away. "Say, I thought that you were preparing something for Junior?"

"Coach Fletcher called while you were on the phone with your boss and said that he was taking the team out for a pizza so not to expect our son until about 10:00 p.m., so it looks like you have this bad girl all to yourself for the next couple hours."

"Which room shall we initiate first?" he asked, now unhooking her bra and letting it drop to the floor."

"That's a tough one." She wriggled out of her slacks, kicking them aside, and stood there in only a thong. "I think over the years we've already initiated them all, several times over. One of them, in case you've forgotten, produced Monica. All right then, how about right here?" He lifted her onto the hall table, shedding the rest of his clothes, and stripping off her thong in a few hot, fast motions. He moved between her legs, pushing her thighs apart, and wedging himself between them.

"Here is good." Sue's voice was breathless and her eyes held that familiar hunger that over the years had driven Howard crazy. "In fact, here is great." Her words ended in an aroused whimper as Howard reached under her, lifting her against him. "I'm a very bad girl, Howard, just so you know," she said, wrapping her arms around his neck and rubbing her body against his.

"That's what you told me, but I love this bad girl," he said.

"I hope so because this is my ovulation period, and I'm not protected, Howard."

He looked at her and smiled as he angled her, his erection nudging her, pushing slightly inside to see how ready she was. She was, as Howard said, "Bad girl might pay a price tonight."

An Undesired Rendezvous

"You want me to do what, Kate?" he asked as he leaned back in his leather swivel chair recliner.

"Take your future wife to church this Sunday morning. To be more specific, a Lutheran church located in Silver Valley, Wisconsin."

Curtis thought about her request before he carefully acknowledged it. "Wasn't this the weekend that we were going to select your matching wedding ring?" Trying to conceal his mild disappointment, he continued, "I have this continued vision of you being my bride soon and waking up to you next to me."

"We're going to do that all, Curtis, and very soon. It's just that my favorite guy has an airplane, and that I thought that with a little bit of female encouragement, he would be my escort to a Sunday service in Silver Valley. It's been years since I've visited the town, Curtis, and I understand that it's quite romantic by the lake downtown. We'll look at the rings on Saturday, spend some time together, and fly over to Silver Valley on Sunday Morning. The service doesn't start until 11:00 a.m."

"Kate, you're smiling, aren't you? You know perfectly well that I'm aware that a Pastor Paul Bergman is the pastor at that Lutheran church. He's the same guy that you told me was acquitted of murdering his wife, and the one that was having an affair with the church secretary?"

"Golly, Curtis," she said, almost bursting out laughing, "if I didn't know better, I'd swear that you were the detective, not me. Yes, he's the one. I just need to get to know him better if I'm going to solve this case. My captain has given me an extra day off and wants me to relax this weekend, and frankly where better can a person relax than going to church with the guy she's marrying?"

"Kate, this is shameful on your part. I want you to know right up front that this sweet talk will not work when we're married," said Curtis laughing. "Anyway, you're in luck since I've got off three days before my next trip. I'll see you at the airport about 8:00 a.m. this Saturday. Have a good day today, dear heart of mine," said Curtis as he disconnected the line.

Getting up from his chair, Curtis walked into the kitchen and put his cold cup of coffee in the microwave oven and heated it while he pulled the plate of cold chicken from the refrigerator and put it on the table. Walking over to the kitchen window, his eyes caught the Cessna, a dream plane for any pilot, and the signature of his chosen occupation. He then spotted the plump groundhogs sunning themselves on the grass without a care in the world. His thoughts of his trip to see his future wife was suddenly interrupted by the sound of the microwave indicating that his coffee was heated.

For the briefest of moments, Kate felt a tad bit guilty pulling Curtis into her plan, but then it again demonstrated the difference between the two men she had loved in her life. Both outwardly were strong, although Curtis was more giving without making her feel guilty. Certainly Curtis was much taller and seemly educationally deeper than her former husband, but both men created the presence that made other men reconsider any foolish attempts to hit on her when they were around. She would, however, have to make it a point not to tempt fate with Curtis, because the steel of his character might be hidden, and she preferred that it stay dormant.

As she sat in her new office, Kate pondered the information that she had received from Howard regarding the Shepherd staff. Actually it could only prove that Bergman had been visiting Gayle Browning, which she already knew was going on. That was provided that it was even his personal shepherd pin. The fact that it had been found on the floor only meant that someone had accidently broken it while in the house or that Gayle Browning had found the piece, laid it on her dresser, and during the last moments of her life, had left the piece as her last message identifying him as the cause of her impending death. The possibilities were endless and frustrating. Maybe it was time to review where she was with Wagner since she had seen his personal car out in the lot when she came in.

As she approached his office, Kate saw that the captain of police was behind his large desk signing papers. Without looking up from his work, he motioned for her to have a seat in front of the desk. She noted that the greeting appeared cordial, somewhat subdued, and a bit overall formal compared to her last meeting. After a full thirty seconds, the captain looked up at her. He smiled and said, "What do I have the pleasure of this morning? A new detective who wants to complain about her small office with a used desk along with no wastepaper basket. Maybe it's because you now have come to the understanding that you're here at my pleasure."

"I understand that."

"You understand what, Detective Heller?

"That I'm here at your pleasure. And to be blunt, I intend to live up to your confidence in me. My intentions are to not let you or the department down, Captain."

"You won't, Detective Heller, because if I would have thought for a moment that would be the case, I wouldn't be giving you the extra time that you've had to bring closure to these files. Obviously, I checked you out extensively before promoting you, as I had concerns about your, shall, we say style, err, qualities that you were bringing to this promotion. You understand what I mean, Officer Heller?"

"Yes, I think that I do, sir. You were worried that my being a woman might not measure up to what was needed to find the bad guys," she said while smiling directly back at the captain.

It took him a few seconds to determine that his new detective was having fun at his expense, but Wagner recovered and continued with the exchange between the two until they understood each other. "Your past word and present has been very good, but no assignment is guaranteed, Detective Heller, so consider yourself on probation for this period of time. You and I both need to determine if this marriage is going to work. We are doing a lot of good things, Detective Heller, and I won't let anyone f——, err, screw it up. Do you understand what I am telling you?"

"I think so, sir. All you want is results from your officers and the truth when you ask questions."

"Yes, Detective, but why does your answer leave me with concerns, and sometimes leave me feeling that you're like that Radar character on *MASH*? I've been where you are, Detective Heller. Have been doing this long before your parents bought you that first prom dress, so tell me, rookie Detective, how come after you gave the right answer, *results*, did you add the extra *truth* to your statement?"

Kate moved restlessly in her chair trying to figure out how to answer his question and still move her investigation forward. It didn't take me long, sir, to include the statement *truth*. I need your help, sir, and by telling you the truth, you may give me the needed help and allow me the ability to close these two cases sooner, or by not telling you the truth, I will still solve the case, but it will take me long."

"You understand math as I do, the shortest distance between two points is a straight line. Take your best shot, Detective. You've got fifteen minutes before I have another damn meeting with the Underwood woman, who spends more time with me than my own wife."

"You authorized me some extra time off to rest, Captain, and I appreciate your consideration. As you may be aware, I've recently gotten engaged, so this extra time off is special to me and my future husband. He has his own plane, so we are going to attend church together in Silver Valley this coming Sunday. Here's where the truth comes in, Captain. The church happens to be where Pastor Paul Bergman is the minister. You know, the pastor who was originally thought to have strangled his wife, but the jury had acquitted him. He is the pastor whose mistress was the organist at the same church and who later died mysteriously. Well, strange as it might seem, Captain, and as complicated as it is, that organist was seeing another man besides the pastor, and he most recently almost died the same way she did, by a spider bite."

"Are you telling me, Heller, that you think that all these deaths and incidents are somehow all connected to Pastor Paul Bergman?"

"He's my person of special interest at this point."

"You know that we have no jurisdiction to question him or, for that matter, even suggest to him that he's a suspect?"

"Understood, Captain, but one never knows if my father can't help me reach the top of that hill."

"What's your father got to do with it?"

"He had two favorite sayings, Captain. 'Sometimes you need to have someone help you carry that pail up the hill.' In this case, that's you, sir. The second part of his advice was that I was to remember that eighty percent of every job is just showing up. Just by my future husband and I going to his church or showing up, it's possible that we will learn something just by being there. There's no expense that the department has to cover on this trip since it's just a small prevacation for Curtis and myself."

"I still am somewhat confused, Officer, as to my role in this 'pail moving up the hill' example."

"I want the original cold case box on Mrs. Bergman stored in the basement," said Kate. The gatekeeper in charge doesn't want to release the evidence box without his squad leader's approval. I've tried twice, but no luck."

"Are you asking me to step in an authorize that original cold case box that you're having trouble getting, or are you suggesting that you're being ignored because you are our only female?"

"I'm not suggesting anything, Captain, other than that you have stronger spiritual leadership qualities than I do. Besides, the original investigating Officer was killed in a car crash, and many of the officers that worked with him at the time that he was here might be sensitive towards someone trying to overturn his original investigation."

"You will get your box, Detective, and when you go to church, watch yourself. We are doing a lot of good things here, Detective Heller, much of which can be undone in the eyes of the community if we resort to some of the old ways. Again, do you understand what I am telling you?"

"Yes, I do."

"Next week Friday, Detective, we graduate a new class of young cadet officers that will help out our regular squads. I would like you to be there."

"Yes, sir."

"I just don't want you to be there. I want you to see the dedication in our young people faces. I want them to see you as the example of what they can become. I want you to speak to the class and talk to them about results and truth. Think you can do that, Officer Heller?"

"Yes."

"I also want you to schedule a krav maga class for the new graduating class."

"Captain Wagner, how did you find out about that part of my background?"

"That's why I'm the captain and you're the detective. I've known for some time that you were qualified in contact combat, and it's time that our new officers were familiar with this self-defense technique used so effectively by the Israeli Defense Forces. Now if you will excuse me, Officer Heller, the Wicked Witch of the West awaits me."

Forty Days of the Word

Their time on Friday night had been everything that two people in love could have hoped for. Curtis had arrived shortly after 7:00 p.m., and Kate had picked him up at the airport, and immediately they had driven to her townhouse. The topics of the evening had turned immediately to Kate's matching wedding ring, which they agreed would be picked up in the morning, and Curtis's special announcement that he was now a full-bidding captain.

'What does being a bidding captain really mean?" she asked.

"All airline pilots are subject to the cock and bull of seniority, whether they like it or not," Curtis said. The system was originally established to ban favoritism and to provide some basis for assignment of bases, routes, flights, and pay. Its great fault, as in any seniority system, is the absolutely necessary conclusion that all men are equal in ability."

"Sort of like in a police department where just because you're a man and have worn a sidearm for ten years, it automatically means that you're going to be the best officer at overcoming the bad guy?" questioned Kate.

Laughing, Curtis said, "Yes, you got it." So in the world of aviation, the dullard and the genius must both live with the ostrich philosophy that one man can fly as skillfully as another. Yet it must exist, because in truth, it is a protection of the weak who are everywhere in the greatest number."

"So what you're saying, in effect, my dear husband to be, is that the public is still better off to have a bunch of those ten-year guys with sidearms than one super cop with a skirt that can shoot better?"

"That I would like to pass on, Kate, but the truth of the system is that it holds down the fire for greatness when you have to stand in line. In my case, what it means is that I'm now a full-bid captain who will get the least-attractive schedules, like Mason City, Iowa, while senior captains receive Paris, London, and Munich, Germany, flying the wide-body jets. It will change in time, so patience is the answer for now, but at least the money improves."

"While I've run out of patience, Curtis, so let's go to bed and forget about company business. We have a full weekend ahead of us, and I don't want to miss a moment of it."

In the center of downtown Funston, across the street from the Exxon station, stood the Frank Brothers Jewelry Store, where Curtis had purchased his special ring for Kate. She had heard about the store from friends, but most had felt that since they specialized in designer jewelry, most budgets couldn't handle the prices, so Kate had decided that she would purchase her earrings where she could afford it. "How did you locate this place?" asked Kate? "Especially since you live in Lift Bridge."

"A passenger on one of my flights left a copy of their magazines, so I grabbed it and put it in my briefcase. The magazine indicated that their specialty was designing custom rings that weren't duplicated, so I sent them what I had in mind, and the rest is on your finger today."

"My mother warned me about men like you," said Kate. "Guys that send flowers, open car doors, agree to spend Sundays in a church, and put expensive jewelry on their fingers. She said that most want something, and that they usually get it."

"She was right, Kate, but in my case, I keep it," he said while touching her hand.

Curtis pulled Kate's car over to the curb by the jewelry store, got out, and walked around and opened Kate's door. Together they walked into the store and up to the ring counter. A well-dressed woman who had been polishing rings turned into their direction, and when she looked up, her eyes went straight to Kate's and held for a piercing instant before shifting away to look at Curtis, only this time with a smile.

"Yes, may I help you? My name is Madelene."

"Hello, we're here to pick up my fiancée's wedding ring. It should be listed under Captain Curtis Douglas. Here's the receipt should you need any information," said Curtis. "The receipt and papers for the insurance should have been made out in advance to Kate Marie Heller," Curtis said.

Madelene, looking at the receipt, excused herself and indicated she would be back within a few minutes. It took only three minutes before she returned with the ring box and insurance contract, which she handed to Kate for her signature.

"You must try on the ring, dear, before we leave the store," said Curtis. "Make certain that it fits."

Opening the box, Kate couldn't believe her eyes as she looked at the cluster of diamonds that surrounded the wedding ring. She put her hand to her mouth and gasped with tears flowing down her cheeks. Now shaking, Curtis helped her slide the ring on her finger. "I've never ever seen anything so beautiful, Curtis. I just don't know what to say."

"It's really simple, my dearest. You say it fits and that I love you, nothing else is necessary."

"Oh, yes," she said excitedly, "it fits, and I do love you."

"Well, Madelene, it looks like my future bride is happy, so we'll be on our way. Thanks for your help," he said as they left the store hand in hand. Now getting in the Honda, Curtis pulled away from the curb and said, "Let's find a nice place to eat and talk about our future. Sunday morning will be here before long, so let's make the best of our time together today."

Sunday morning had come fast, and they had just reached their cruising altitude when Kate had leaned over and spoke as she held ring finger for him to see. "It's so beautiful, and the fact that you actually designed it for me makes it even more special. You didn't have to do this, as I told you when you gave me the engagement ring. You could have presented me with a simple wedding band, and I would have been yours. It's difficult to explain how I feel just at this moment. No, it's really easy. I feel like I'm your princess," she said as she held the ring out in front of him. "I know that a woman should not say anything about cost, but these diamonds must have come from Queen Elizabeth's collection. Why did you have the insurance policy made out in my name rather than yours? After all, they were bought with your money."

"The rings represent my love for you, not my ownership of you. If you change your mind, they are yours since they would then have no meaning for me as items or money. Love for me, Kate, happens only one time. You are my dream walking, and the rings make me very happy. Hopefully they will always sparkle like your eyes as they did last night when I made love to you, was it three times?"

"Your math is not your strong suit, Curtis, unless you're not counting this morning at 4:00 a.m."

Smiling he said, "Excuse me, dear, while I call in our final approach to Silver Valley Municipal Airport."

"Silver Valley Tower, this is Cessna 711 on final approach for runway 14R."

"Cessna 711, winds North-South 5–7 knots, visibility 12–14 miles. Your traffic is a Fokker, one o'clock three miles Eastbound."

"Approach tower, this is Cessna 711, I've always wanted to say this: I've got the little Fokker in sight."

"Roger that, little Fokker," replied the tower.

Curtis watched his approach with the greatest solicitude, for if there is one deep-rooted, ever-present fear known to all pilots, it's the hanging sword of a potential midair collision. No other prospect except the rare examples of structural failure equals that of a sudden appearance of an inexperienced novice appearing in your airspace.

Kate, listening to the exchange, almost had tears running down her face with laughter. Turning to Curtis, she watched out the cockpit window as the plane's wheels softly touched the paved runway. It took less than five minutes for the Cessna to taxi over to the hangar area and their waiting rental car. While Kate ran inside in search of a restroom, Curtis gave his credit card to the maintenance crew with instructions to top of the fuel tank and to do a general checkup for their return flight. After running his card through the charge card machine, Curtis walked inside and found Kate waiting for him. Grabbing her hand, they both walked out and got into the Lincoln Town Car.

"Do you have the address, Kate, or should I do a map quest on my cell phone?"

"I've got it all written out," she said as she placed the directions on her lap. "It's actually real easy since we're already on Hartford Avenue, which runs right into Highland. The church is directly on Hartford and Highland, so we can't miss it. It's a big old stone church fully a block long with vines all around it."

"Where did you get all the information, Kate?"

"It's all on the internet, like everything is. Everything, Curtis, including the names of the last three women you dated. They even indicated your lack of experience," she said with a sly grin.

"Well, the internet has a lot of catching up to do, don't they?" Looking at his watch, he said, "Hey it's only nine fifteen. Maybe we should get something to drink before we visit the church. I can give you a fifteen-minute update on what it is to be a Lutheran, and you can tell me what your plan is," said Curtis.

"Well, put your Lutheran hat on, Curtis. There's a McDonald's restaurant only three miles down the road."

Kate, not much of a church person, listened to Curtis explain the basic Lutheran philosophy and found it not much different than her own Catholic upbringing. Each church has its own mystic avenues to walk, but by and large the stairs to heaven were the same, built around fear of the Lord, the guilt, and the individual penances that you must pay in order to enter the gates. Kate fully understood that Curtis was a stronger believer than her, and that she had to move with caution on this subject even though he had admitted troubling feelings about his current church. Her plan, she had explained to Curtis, was really simple. To have them both concentrate on visual observations. It was through visual observations that most things were solved, because whether it be an office, store, or something as simple as a congregation, something was always present that told the entire story. She had remembered the first time that she had tested her theory on the subject when she had visited her doctor for her annual checkup. Always nervous about the visit, her idea was that she must learn to understand the doctor as much as he understood her medical records when she came back for the next visit.

The trick was to take in every little item in the individual's office, such as noticing the personal pictures on his desk, wall, and cabinet. The magazines in the office would usually be a dead give-away about the person. In the case of her doctor, she had learned that his interest heavily favored golf, private planes, hunting, and fishing. These things represented his world that you needed to learn to talk about if you wanted to learn to relax in his office. So the idea today was simply to study the pastor and learn about his world. She went on and explained to Curtis that she had been the first arriving police officer the day that Bergman's wife was found on the garage basement floor. There would be a slight chance that Bergman might recognize her, so she might leave from another exit without shaking his hand, as was the custom at most churches. On the other hand, since that day that she had found his wife, she had changed back to her natural blond hair color from her auburn color on that day. The truth was, she was wondering what he would look like after almost two years. Glancing at her watch, she nodded to Curtis that it was time to leave. Once again, like new lovers, they walked hand in hand to their Lincoln, with Curtis opening her door and kissing her cheek and saying, "Let's go get them," as they pulled out of the McDonald's lot.

Kate looked at Curtis and said, "Why did you say them?"

"What do you mean?" asked Curtis.

"You said them, not him."

"It's just a figure of speech, nothing more, Kate. Mind if I ask you a question about the day that you arrived at the Bergman house?"

"Of course not, there's nothing that I wouldn't share with you," she answered.

"You just talked about visual observations being so important to understanding everything about a person, correct?"

"Yes."

"What did you learn that day?" asked Curtis.

Kate thought back to that day when she first arrived at the scene and met Bergman and viewed his wife laying on the garage floor with a cord around her neck. "That he was lying about his involvement in his wife's assault."

"What made you think that?"

"He was more nervous about his story than actually caring about his wife on the garage floor. These are things that at the time you can't prove, Curtis. It's just there, and your experience tells you that, nothing more."

"Anything else that you noticed?" asked Curtis.

"Yes, the cord around her neck was not a rope or clothesline, not even a belt. It looked more like some ornamental ribbon or scarf. I actually forgot about it when they assigned a senior detective to the case. This whole cold case has started to get me down, Curtis. You're the only bright spot that fills most of my days. When you get a promotion such as I did recently, you want to take over your new assignment and hit the street running. Instead in my case, the captain assigned me to work on these unsolved cases, specifically one dealing with the unfortunate death of the organist. Bergman was having an affair with her, and most people still believed to this day that was the reason why he attempted to kill his wife." She was about to continue her story when Curtis spotted the all-brick church with its main entrance facing Hartford Avenue. Pulling up to the curb about fifty yards away from the double doors, Kate and Curtis watched as the first members started to drift in. "It's a beautiful old church, and from the date imprinted on the front bell tower, it's over a hundred years old," said Curtis. "Take a notice of all those stained windows. There has to be fourteen in the front alone. What do you think of that huge bell tower? I bet the bell must weight over five hundred pounds alone."

"It's a beauty all right, Curtis, but my guess is that unlike a lot of modern churches, this bell is rung with someone pulling on a rope tied to it rather than it being electrical. The church is also not keeping up with the changing times since I don't see any handicap parking or lift elevator to bring the older folks to the top," said Kate. "Also notice the back door. It looks like that's the entrance for the pastor and the church officers to come and go from. They probably bring the flowers in the back also. Well, maybe it's time to slip in before the main crowd arrives. If you don't mind, let's sit in the last two rows in the back, unless they seat us."

"That's fine with me, Kate, but let's find a place on the left side, where the pulpit is."

"What's the pulpit?" she asked.

"In most churches, they have a lectern where laymen often read from, and the pulpit is where the pastor preaches from. The pulpit is usually fancier and has a raised platform. That's where you will see Paul Bergman."

As they exited the car, they noticed that the front doors were now being fully opened by an attendant, who appeared to be welcoming all those who were now entering the church. As they walked up the steps leading into the church, they were greeted by a well-dressed family of four. Although the family had on their name tags and shook their hands, nobody inquired about their names as they walked up the remaining carpeted steps that led into the church. At the top, Kate noted that two well-dressed men in business suits sought them out and introduced themselves as elders of the church.

"Hello," the older one said. "I'm Carl Unger, and you folks must be visiting us for the first time?" For a moment Kate was temporarily petrified not knowing what to say. Then to her delight, Curtis took over.

"Mr. Unger, we're Curtis and Kate Patterson from Michigan. We just happen to be visiting the area for a few days and were delighted to find a church of our faith in Silver Valley. One doesn't often have an opportunity to see the natural beauty of a Lutheran church such as yours anymore. The last time my wife and I had the pleasure of visiting such a church was while we were in North Dakota. Yours is much older, I see, having been built in 1890."

"Yes, that's a long time ago, Mr. Patterson. In another three years, we will be celebrating having served the Lord for 125 years. I've been here long enough to have worked with six different pastors. I even met my wife here. Well, please go inside, folks. We have open seating, so sit anywhere you would like."

Walking inside, Kate found seating near the back and enter the wooden pew followed by Curtis. She whispered in his ear, "I really like the part about being Mrs. Patterson, but North Dakota, that you will need to bring me up to speed on." Looking toward the altar, she saw two large screens on either side. "They must be going to show a short movie," she said to Curtis.

"No, my guess is they have the order of the service appearing on each screen. Many churches are now going digital and will even communicate with you on their church service using Facebook or Twitter. Look they're beginning to put the order of service up there now."

Kate watched as the first frame appeared with a picture of Pastor Paul J. Bergman in his plain black vestments with the tagline, "Build one another up in love." She was taken back by his new well-trimmed beard, although showing some white hair. She glanced at Curtis and wanted to comment on something but noticed that he had his pen out and was making himself a note. The second screen showed what appeared to be the order of service for today, something called the Forty Days of the Word. Settling back in their seats, Kate and Curtis watched the church begin to fill up.

Looking at her watch, she observed that the time was exactly 11:00 a.m. All talking had ceased when the main church bell started to ring, followed by the organ music. Still no pastor appeared. Odd, thought Kate, as she wondered where he was. When the bell ceased its ringing, the door directly behind the pulpit opened, and Bergman appeared sitting down on a red velvet chair praying for what appeared to be for almost three minutes. He then stood up and announced that the first hymn would be "How Great Thou Are." As Kate scrambled looking for the hymnal book, she found that Curtis placed his hands over hers and whispered, "Wait and watch." Then to her surprise, the organist did the introductory, and Pastor Paul Bergman began singing to the congregation in an angelical voice, to which she couldn't ever remember hearing anyone ever doing so well. His voice was accompanied by both screens now alternately filled with images of Christ on the cross, soldiers fallen on the battle field, stairs leading to heaven, an American eagle, and Jesus on the crucifixion cross. The

hymn was actually beautiful, and she could tell that it was a favorite of the members. As Bergman entered the last stanza, he encouraged all to stand and join him. Curtis watched her emotions, himself
caught in the moment of what was happening. As they were sitting
down, he put his arms around Kate as Bergman now walked up to
the altar and began the order of service. Kate found that Bergman
could captivate his congregation as well as sing to them.

During his sermon, she admittedly was confused about the
Forty Days in the Words connection to the Lutheran Church. The
journey, as he called it, was for each to come together and understand
that God had never meant that Bible study was to simply increase
your knowledge but that each of us needed to become "doers of the
word." The most interesting part of the sermon to her was that this
six-week commitment to the study of the Word was not put together
by the Lutheran Church, but rather the salesman for this high-profile
program was Rick Warren, a well known Baptist minister, who ran
his Saddleback Church out of California. Kate knew some things
about his ministry that made her uncomfortable since in recent years
she had heard that he had branched out beyond his original conser-
vative reputation to peacemaker between the radical Muslim groups
and the Christian faith.

As she started to tune out the sermon, she glanced at the church
bulletin, which listed some of the officers of the congregation. One
name in particular caught her attention, a Mr. A. J. Ogden.

It was obviously just a coincidence, if one believed in such a
thing. Curtis seemed to be caught up in the service as he was intently
watching the screen for its next written instruction. Communion
came next, which reminded her of her early Catholic days, and the
ritual that followed, which always made her nervous, being afraid
that she would drop the wafer. She nudged Curtis, shaking her head,
indicating that she wasn't going to participate in the ritual today. He
returned a smile to her indicating that neither was he as he patted her
hand. Kate watched as the usher approached their pew and motioned
for Curtis and her to come forward. She looked at Curtis, who was
signaling the usher that they were not attending. Moving on to the
next row, Kate watched what appeared to be tables of six approaching

the altar. None of the Communion participants looked familiar to her as they passed her pew. The service ended sixty minutes after it started, with the Bergman walking down from the pulpit and standing directly in front of the congregation.

"I have a few items today that I need to cover regarding coming events. Jack Koehler, our chairman of the congregation, is seeking volunteers to help with our fall picnic. Those that are interested may call the church office this coming Monday. Also, there will be an elders' meeting Monday night at 7:30 p.m. Finally we want to welcome all our guests today and invite each of you to join us next Sunday again. As you're leaving today, please say hello and give me the opportunity to meet each of you individually. Please enjoy the good weather that God has granted, and God willing, I'll see each of you next week," he said as he walked down the aisle and positioned himself at the end of the church. She watched as the ushers began to start at the front of the church dismissing the members.

Curtis leaned over to Kate and asked her if she wished to leave through the back entrance or follow the crowd out up front and greet the pastor.

"Let's follow the crowd," she said. "It's doubtful that he would recognize me since I never officially interviewed him, just met him briefly at the time of his arrest."

Being the second to the last pew when it became their turn, Curtis allowed Kate to walk ahead of him as they exited their row.

As she approached Bergman, she said, "You have a beautiful voice Pastor, and I enjoyed your sermon very much."

"Thank you, said Bergman. You must be a visitor to our church this morning, I take it, or have we met before? You do look familiar."

Curtis had stepped up and joined Kate. "Pastor, good morning. I too loved your sermon on the Forty Days in the Word. This is my wife, Kate. We are the Pattersons. I'm Curtis, and we're visiting relatives this weekend."

"Are they part of our membership?" asked Bergman.

"No, they happen to be members of a Baptist church, while we're Lutheran," said Curtis. "They are going to be sorry when I tell them about the Baptist ministers involvement in the message today."

Bergman studied Curtis before saying, "Pastor Warren has promised to send two of his people to join in on our last Sunday of the forty-day program. He would have visited himself, but since the Lutheran Church is doing this with over four hundred Lutheran churches, he probably felt showing favoritism wasn't the right thing to do. Well, it was nice having you two here today." He then said, "Please enjoy the sunny day folks and come again," as he started to greet the next couple.

Walking down the steps, they held hands and continued their walk over to the Lincoln and entered their car. Curtis looked over to Kate with a grin that caused her to burst out laughing.

"Do you think anyone guessed?" asked Kate.

"That we were on a fact-finding mission or that you were not my wife?" asked Curtis.

"I'm sure they knew that I was your wife, unless you just had the habit of putting expensive diamonds on the hand of every woman that you take to church."

"No one in the congregation showed any signs of being suspicious about our intent, and I doubt that the Bergman was concerned about anything," said Curtis as he pulled away from the curb and headed back to the airport.

"That I'm not so sure of," said Kate. "When Bergman finished with the last members, I noticed that he watched us going to our car."

"Well, Kate, you are a beautiful woman. It probably means nothing."

"I hope so," she said. "I noticed that you were writing something down during the start of the service," Kate commented.

"Yes. Remember the opening picture of him in his black vestments?"

"Yes."

"I couldn't be certain, but that looked like a Shepherd's pin that he had on his shirt. Maybe you'll want to blow up the picture to be sure."

"We'd have to have that picture first," said Kate.

"My darling detective must be tired playing her wife role. We probably can get it off their website. It's likely that they'll have their Sunday service on it for at least a week."

"You're right. I'll bring it up tonight at home. I also think it's a possibility that one of the officers listed on the bulletin is, in fact, Dr. Allen Ogden, the guy who I met at the Funston, Hospital. It's a long shot, but if you remember me telling you the hospital did have to bring in a specialist from out of state to treat Perry Sinclair, the guy who was also mixed up with the church organist."

"And how will knowing that he was one in the same help you?"

"I'm not sure at this point, but one never turns their back on any possible clues." They were remarkably quiet during the flight back. Occasionally Curtis would affectionately put his hand on Kate's leg but avoided any more serious attempts to bring back the memory of their Saturday evening. Kate had made just enough movement with her leg to let him know that his caress was welcome, but she too restrained the moment for what it was. This was the part that they both disliked knowing that soon they had to once again be without each other.

As they were taxiing up to the Funston private business terminal, Curtis noticed the two mechanics waiting to help Kate down from the Cessna. "Looks like you'll be all right, sweetheart. Let's pick a wedding date real soon. I know that you probably want to wrap this cold case up first, but frankly being without you for days at a time is not something that this love-starved puppy can continue to handle much longer."

"I know, Curtis. I feel the same way, and it's never ever been this way before in my life." As he watched the sadness in her eyes, he pulled her close and kissed her passionately.

She then walked down the aircrafts steps and direct to the terminal building. Turning, she blew him a kiss as he engaged the Cessna and continued toward the runway.

CHAPTER 40

Exposure

Kate looked at her watch. It had been over seven hours since Curtis had left the Funston Airport in his Skylark Cessna for Lift Bridge. She remembered when he waved goodbye that he had that sexy grin that made her insides melt. This was a man she was looking forward to living with even though she understood that living together was going to be a biggie. It meant relinquishing another piece of her freedom and lowering that protective wall that she had built around herself since the death of her husband. He was worth it. They were both worth it. Putting on one of Curtis's oversize Delta sweatshirts, she combed her fingers through the layers of her blond shoulder-length hair and then walked into the kitchen as she poured herself a glass of Chianti. The wine wasn't meant to be savored. Pausing for a quick sip, she heard or thought that she heard the sound of stones being walked on outside her kitchen window. Turning off the kitchen light, she looked through the window for any sign of movement. There were none. Walking back to her bedroom, she looked into the early darkness of the evening, and again saw nothing moving in her backyard. "I must be just overly tired from the weekend," thought Kate as she returned to the kitchen to finish her wine.

Then her cell phone rang. Scooping the phone off the table, she flipped it open. "Hello, my love, you're home."

"Not home, Kate, just entered Lift Bridge. You're my home, and we need to do something about that soon. I thought about that the entire way back. And don't read me wrong about this. I understand that your career is equally important to you as mine is to me. This is about being in love with you, not requiring anything other than finding the best way that we can be together, regardless what it takes."

"I know how you feel, Curtis. Love is too wonderful to allow us to live so far apart. Let's start thinking about the wedding, and real soon." There she heard it again. "Curtis, please wait for a minute. I need to check on something." Walking once again over to the kitchen window, she looked outside for any sign of an animal or anything that could be outside walking on her stone walkway. "Hey, I'm back. I just thought that I heard something outside, but there was nothing."

"Where's your gun?" asked Curtis.

"Oh, it's nothing to worry about, Curtis, but just in case, the gun is always nearby, so don't worry. Since this is your first marriage, and the only one that you will have," she said laughing, "you might like a church wedding, but I'm open to whatever would make you happy, dear."

"Let's talk about that the next time I'm in town, but I feel strongly that the most important thing is that we be together soon. I love the idea of calling you my wife, Kate." She then heard the doorbell ringing at Curtis's house.

"Honey, it's Randy, the owner of the airfield that I land on. He must have heard me come in and is coming over to talk about my trip. Probably wants to know when we're getting married. Got to hang up, Kate, but I love you."

"Love you too," she said as she laid down the phone.

The call had come in unexpectedly from Bergman's brother. They had not seen each other in several months. He remembered how the last visit almost cost him some money since he had been stopped for speeding, but the cop, upon hearing that he was visiting his brother's church, had let him off with a warning. He had just gotten in his car and was heading home from a night out with his lawyer friends, celebrating the winning of his most recent court case, when he picked up his cell phone.

"Peter, it's me."

"Hi, Paul, what's up with my favorite man of God?"

"I need you to do me a favor," came the slurred, alcoholic voice of Paul Bergman. "I need you to send a message to a policewoman who is messing around in my life."

"Shit, he's been drinking again," thought Peter. His statistical alcoholic point sounds like he's at least point one-four. "What do you mean by a message, Paul?"

"Like the message I sent for you when the lady you were banging threatened to call your wife five years ago."

"As you remember, Paul, she still divorced me anyway."

"Doesn't matter, I still did the job for you, or have you forgotten that you owe me one?" said Paul.

"Jesus, Paul, you're a pastor, and I'm an officer of the court. We can't keep this crap up every time something goes wrong in our life."

"Last time, Peter, and we're all even. You'll never ever owe me a favor again," said an obviously drunk Bergman.

"All right, tell me what I have to do. I don't want to know what's going on, just what I have to do, Paul."

As quietly as he could, Peter walked down the cobblestone pathway that ran alongside the townhouse. The structure was built on short-enough footings, which put the windows just at the right height for him to see in. He was halfway to the rear of the house when suddenly the kitchen light was turned off. Had he made a noise? He cringed from the possibility of being discovered and hoped that the bitch didn't have a dog. Now the ten thousand dollars that Paul had given him for doing the job didn't seem as attractive as it once did, especially knowing that she was probably armed and he was not. He could hear his heart beating as he crouched behind the two large receptacle cans and waited. After five minutes and seeing no activity coming from inside the house, he slowly inched to the back of the building and the woman's bedroom.

The loud voices made him freeze. At first he couldn't understand the blue glow coming from the wall inside the house until he realized that the noise and glow were from a television inside her bedroom. The location of the room with both its windows facing the backyard probably provided her with understood false security as she probably thought that it would be virtually impossible that anyone would be able to look in. As he raised himself to view the inside of the bedroom, he could see a faint light coming from the adjoining bathroom. Looking closer, he noted that the windows were open about two inches each, which allowed him to hear the movement of the shower door and the running water. This added luck he assumed would give him just enough time to enter the bedroom and subdue the unarmed policewoman while she took her shower. As he tried to push the windows open, he became frustrated that the gliders would not budge. It probably indicated that the woman wasn't entirely comfortable with the window's overall security. She undoubtedly had been smart enough to put wooden blocks as the other end to prevent their movement. Reaching in his pants pocket, he removed a small glasscutter and a three-inch rubber suction cup, which he screwed onto a small wooden handle. Placing the rubber suction cup firmly against the window and holding onto the handle, he began to cut a large square opening that would enable him to reach in and unlatch the security lock and free the jammed window. His entry path almost completed, he abruptly stopped when he heard the water being turned off and the shower doors being opened. Backing away from the window, he silently swore because it was impossible for him to now remove the rubber suction cup without breaking the partially cut glass. His remaining hope was that she wouldn't turn on any extra lights or notice the window and just move to another room, giving him enough time to finish his work. Crouching lower, his eyes caught the woman's white antique dresser, which was serving as her resting place for what he determined was an M&P 357 Sig. Pistol and a box of Hornady TAP-FPD personal defense bullets. He imagined she was well trained to use the weapon, and his concern heightened for his own safety as he was unarmed with the exception of an H&K five-inch tactical blade knife. He knew that his odds of surviving a direct confrontation was slim if his presence was exposed. Sweating the possibilities of being faced with his exposure, to his horror, the woman suddenly walked into the room wearing a pink bathrobe and headed over to the dresser.

Thinking that she has somehow heard him and was now going to pick up the gun, he considered bolting and making a run for it when to his surprise she reach down and opened the second drawer below the weapon and removed a sheer white nightgown. Laying the nightgown on the bed, she then walked over to the closet and proceeded to remove her robe and hang it up. Naked now, he could see through the window that the woman was stunning and obviously confident of her body as she paused in front of a large six-foot mirror and examined her figure. Appearing satisfied with what she saw, the woman walked back over to the edge of the bed and slipped the nightgown over her head and sat down. Picking up the remote control on the bed, she shut the television off, which probably indicated that she was about to leave the room. He watched her as she appeared to be staring at the pistol in deep thought about something. But what? With her back to the window and never once looking in that direction, she continued sitting on the bed just looking at the weapon and the dresser for what appeared to be a full five minutes without showing any signs of moving. What the hell was going on? he asked himself. Then it suddenly came to him as he saw the two framed silver picture frames next to the pistol. She was looking at the pictures on the dresser. Relaxing now, he continued to watch her for several more minutes when suddenly she stood up and walked out of the room. As he considered his next move, he listened carefully, now hearing the sound of another television being turned on. The prize he once thought about had changed since he had first started his attempt to get into the house. The idea of his finding out what she might feel like with her hands tied and at his mercy had suddenly shifted. His original expectations of entering the room and having some fun with this woman then killing her had clearly changed back to just doing the job that he had been paid to do and stay alive. In this business, he thought, you had to think with your right head, or you might end up being the one planted in the ground. She was getting on his nerves not knowing what she was up to. He waited a few more minutes before he inched back up to the window. Looking into the room, he was able to see through the bedroom door that led down a large hallway, which he thought probably ended at the entrance to her living room. Still no movement or sign of the woman, but he could clearly hear the sound of a television and the now-familiar smell of freshly cooked popcorn. Obviously the woman had heard nothing and was settling down to an evening of *Desperate Housewives* or some other junk that woman liked to watch.

Well, he was through waiting around, so he moved back to the window while locating his glasscutter once again. Putting his hand on the suction cup handle, he retraced his initial cutting pattern while pulling gently on the glass until it easily came loose. Satisfied that he had made no noise, he gently set the glass on the grass while removing the suction cup, unscrewing the handle and putting it in his pants pocket. Moving back to the large hole in the window, he reached inside to release the latching lock when suddenly the unmistakable sound of Chelsea Dagger coming from his cell phone filled the evening air. "Jesus Christ," he cursed, as he quickly removed his hand and reached for his cell phone to cut off the sound.

Expecting the woman to appear at any moment, he moved away from the window and quickly raced back down the pathway until he reached the driveway. Seeing no one, he ran across the street directly to his parked car. Briefly turning, he looked back at the house and listened for any sound or lights being turned on, but saw no activity. In fact, the house looked dead, and he wondered if she had fallen asleep and that he had missed his chance in his panic. Still in his mind, the damn cell phone ringing represented too much danger, and he didn't trust his luck to hang around and be shot. He was not going to test his luck by going back. He was out of breath, and his heart was pounding. Now inside the car, he attempted to gather himself and recover from the near disaster. He knew that there was going to be hell to pay from Paul for not accomplishing his mission, but he didn't care. He had taken the precaution to wear gloves, so there was little chance that even the best labs could pick up his fingerprints on anything. Clearly he was showing signs of rust because even an amateur wouldn't have forgotten to mute his phone. Years ago this wouldn't have happened, but now like an old retread tire, he was about ready to have a blow up. Reaching in his pocket, he removed the irritating rubber suction cup to put in the glove compartment. Unable to locate the little wooden handle just added to his frustration. He sat in the car for a long time wondering if it had fallen out of his pocket before he turned the key and drove off.

She was swimming with sharks, and she knew it. Who had she been kidding, she thought, thinking back to the noise outside her kitchen window. She knew better from the start without even seeing him.

Now Kate had heard the cell phone and the fleet movement of someone running down the side of her home. Her only disappointment had been that he had not entered the house and found her waiting for him. She knew what happened tonight wouldn't have taken place if she had picked up Channing from his overnight boarding house. Before she had spent the weekend with Curtis, she had decided to take Channing to Becky's Bed-and-Breakfast kennel. It really wasn't a kennel, but more like Disney World for animals, as Betty had a 24-7 staff that made sure the animal was treated to a stay like they were on vacation. In truth, the first time Kate had used Becky, she had felt a little jealous when she had picked up Channing because he had enjoyed himself so much he had showed signs of not wanting to leave and come home. Tomorrow she would pick him up early, and there would be no second mistake like tonight.

Thinking back, she had been uneasy from the first moment that she finished her shower and had entered the bedroom. Why, she was not certain, but the feeling was clear that she was being watched and stalked similar to an animal. When she had hung up her bathrobe in the closet and returned to the bed, she had checked to see if her pistol was still on the on the dresser, and it was, but minus the loaded clip. That had been a serious mistake since it was her habit to leave the loaded clip with her shoulder holster on the kitchen table. Minus the clip, the gun was nothing more than a weapon with a single bullet in the chamber, not something you wanted in a situation that she might face. She had sat on the bed contemplating her next move while attempting to convince herself that her mind was just playing tricks on her. While thinking about her situation, she had looked to the left of her pistol on the dresser to the pictures of her mother and father, now inserted in the recently purchased seventy-five-dollar silver-framed holders. It was the one-inch-wide mirror-like frame around the picture that had given him away. As she had continued to gaze at the pictures, the mirror-like frame had caught his movements and her attention. Although she then knew that someone was at her window, she was unable to distinguish much more. She then made the quick decision to get up from the bed and walk out of the bedroom down the hallway into her guest room, where she stored her Nighthawk, the Para-Ordnance .45 ACP, with the loaded 10 rounds of ammo, and it's tritium night sights. At the same time, she picked up her Steiner binoculars with night vision, walked into the living room and waited for the uninvited mouse to come looking for its cheese. It was while in the living room she had heard the sound of a cell phone playing the Black Hawks' fan-favorite song, "Chelsea Dagger." The rallying sound could be terrifying unless you were one of the twenty-two thousand fans attending the game and listening to the organ blasting it out after a Black Hawks victory.

Her initial fear had now been replaced with the training motto that was stamped on her holster, "Fear no evil." Kate had been brought up and told over and over by her now-deceased father, "It's not whether you win or lose. It's how bad you beat the guy in second place."

"Well, buddy," she mouthed to herself, "you picked on the wrong house tonight." It was then that she heard the racing of feet down her driveway. Her initial instinct was to meet and greet her guest, but her training had once again kicked in. She had no idea if there was more than one intruder and was thus unwilling to give up her advantage that existed in the house she was familiar with. Instead she followed the sounds out onto the street, where looking through her side front window, she saw a man standing and momentarily looking at her house before he got in the car. Placing the night vision glasses up to her eyes, she was able to see what appeared to be a well-built white man. Focusing on the license plate, Kate was not surprised to find that the occupant had duct taped over the numbers. He had, however, forgotten the sticker on the rear window that said "Matthew 16:18–19." At this point, it hardly mattered because Kate had no idea if it meant anything or not. She had decided not to call for backup, but rather she called the personal cell phone number of her new support staff, Corporal Howard Singer, and see if he was on duty. He was just finishing a late supper when he had picked up her call on the first ring and following her instructions had arrived within ten minutes without benefit of sirens or flashing lights. She met him at the door.

"Thanks for coming, Howard, and sorry to bother you on your free time."

"Glad you called me. I didn't see anything suspicious coming down your block. You indicated a possible break-in attempt?"

"Yes. It happened as I was finishing taking a shower. I had just come back in my bedroom when I accidently spotted him watching me when I had sat down on the bed after putting on my nightgown."

"What did he do when he noticed that you were on to him?"

"He didn't know that I had seen him, Howard. You see on my dresser are two picture frames that have mirror-type edges all around the frames. I was looking at the frames that contain pictures of my parents when I saw his image appearing on the frame. I then left the room and armed myself with another pistol that I keep in the guest room."

"So did he make it inside the house or not?"

"No, his cell phone tripped him up as it went off, so he got spooked and ran back down the side of the house to his car that he left parked on the street."

"You're certain that it was a man?"

"No question about that since I picked him up with my binoculars as he entered his car."

"Did you get the plates?"

"No, but I can tell you that he was white, about 190–200 pounds. He had covered his plates, so I couldn't pick up on anything there, but his rear windshield had an interesting sticker."

"What did it say?"

"Matthew 16:18–19."

"Oh, he's Catholic boy, huh?"

"Why do you say that?" asked Kate.

"Matthew 16:18–19 is the biblical verse that all good Catholics consider the Holy Grail of their religion. I spent twelve years of my life attending grade school and high school, plus four years at Norte Dame, learning never to doubt the significance of that verse. Then after college, I married the original owner of the patent leather shoes."

"Howard, honestly I don't know what you're talking about, but before you leave tonight, we must talk about it. First though let's look the house over and make sure that everything is secure. I just don't understand what the motive might be for invading my house."

"It could be quite simple, Kate. From what I can remember you telling me, and what I sew driving up to your house, your bedroom is in the back of the house facing a large section of open land. As we both know, attractive women like yourself living alone are a magnet for bad guys looking for a little fun, if you know what I mean. Remember that the guy might not know that you are a policewoman and not a female duck without wings ready to be shot and eaten. Do you even know if he actually attempted to enter the house, or was he just a peeper?"

"Let's look. I haven't examined anything yet," said Kate.

Both Kate and Howard walked down the hallway and entered her bedroom. Howard then noticed the ten-inch cut square. Walking over to the window, he took his flashlight and shined it out the cut open hole on to the ground.

"See the glass on the ground, Kate? My guess is he was trying to reach inside and clear the security catch so that he could find a way to move your glider window. I see that you had it blocked at the end so that it couldn't move. Have you had reasons to be concerned before tonight?"

"No reasons, it was just a trick that I learned when I grew up living in a bad area."

"There isn't any sign that he cut himself, which surprises me in a way since he was in a hurry according to you when his cell phone went off. Did you recognize anything from the ringtone?"

"Yes, I could distinguish that it was the 'Chelsea Dagger' song. I've always hated that darn thing because it can scare you to death if you're not prepared, plus it's the Chicago Black Hawks' signature when they win a game. You'd think that the Hawks would be more creative like our Red Wings."

"While not every team has access to baby octopuses, Kate, to throw on the ice like our Red Wing fans do," said Howard. "You know, I kind of like the 'Chelsea Dagger' song, especially since the group's leader named the title of the song after his wife, Chelsea."

"You sure know a lot of superfluous information, Howard," commented Kate.

"Wait until you get the Catholic Church overview and the patent leather shoe story," said Howard. "I think that I'd like to go outside and grab that glass on the ground. It may have some prints on it. Why don't you check all the other rooms to make sure everything is locked up tight?"

"Good idea. Howard, why don't you walk around the perimeter of the house and go across the street, where he had parked his car right under that elm tree. Who knows, we may get lucky, and he dropped something."

Howard followed the path starting at the front of the house to the rear of the building. Kate's bedroom had two large windows that were low enough to the ground that it was easy to see in with a little help. The help on this night came from the little kneeler bench that Kate undoubtedly used for her flower bed. He had put it up against the wall of the house to look in and cut the glass. As he was walking over to the window with the hole in it, he found the glass on the ground that he had seen while in the house. Howard carefully picked the glass up and proceeded to retrace his steps back to the front of the house, where he laid the cut glass on the porch and then crossed the street to the elm tree. Reaching into the pocket of his Notre Dame jacket, he found his spare flashlight and began to search the ground near where he thought the car would have been parked. His search found nothing, but then again he didn't expect that he would. Shutting off the flashlight, he started to return back to Kate's house when he spotted the wooden dowel on the curb below the grass line. Looking at it, he could tell that it was some type of small handle, but for what? he wondered. Putting it in his pocket, he crossed the street and picked up the glass and reentered her house. Walking into the kitchen, he found Kate making a pot of coffee.

"What did you find?" asked Kate.

"The piece of glass cut from your bedroom window, plus a piece of wood. It wasn't too far from where the car would have been parked. Actually it was on the street, just below the elm tree out there. I almost missed it."

Putting the coffee pot down, Kate picked up the wooden dowel and examined it. "Did you notice the printed name on the wood, Howard?"

"No, what does it say?"

"It says Jake's Lumberyard. I can't help but wonder what the dowel was used for?"

"Then we have the magic question: where in hell is Jake's Lumberyard?"

Pouring each a cup of coffee, Kate said, "Jake's Lumberyard is in a small town called Martin, Michigan. Now what about Matthew 16:18–19?"

"It's that part of the New Testament that covers Saint Matthew and, as I mentioned, the part that the Catholic Church clings to. Matthew 16:18 opens with the statement, 'And I say unto thee, that thou art Peter, and upon this rock I will build my church.' To a Catholic, Kate, it identifies Peter as the first pope and thus the Catholic Church as the one and only true church. It is the second part of his statement that adds more flavor to the first part. In Matthew 16:19, Jesus adds, 'And I will give unto thee the keys of the Kingdom of heaven.' That suggests to me that your visitor may be connected to a church."

"You surprise me, Howard," she said while sipping her coffee. "You know a lot about the Bible."

"You mean for a guy that made those sexual remarks to his boss?"

"No, that's old news, and we've moved beyond that, remember? It's just that most men won't show that side of themselves, and in the last day, two men I know have stepped on out on that subject. So do you believe it, that the first pope was Peter and the Catholic Church is the true church, Howard?"

"What I believe is that Peter was singled out as special to Jesus, and that the rest is open to individual interpretation." He was about to continue when his cell phone rang. "Hello, yes, everything is fine. We are investigating the crime area. Detective Heller wasn't hurt, and I should be home in about an hour," Howard said as he hung up.

Kate smiled before she said, "Your wife?"

"Yes, she worries a lot. Where was I? Oh, yes. Most good Catholics don't doubt the significance of the scripture, just understand that man has a tendency to take a chicken feather and make it into a chicken coop."

"But not you, I take it?" remarked Kate.

"I'm a policeman like you. It's our nature to ask questions and challenge those who hyperbole as part of their makeup. Take my comment about it possibly being a Catholic who visited you tonight. The fact is that it could just as well have been anyone who believes in the good book, but especially clergy. You see, the Holy Grail of the Protestant Church is what is called the keeper of the keys. If you ever visited, say, a Lutheran church, you would have heard sometime during the service the pastor saying, 'By the power invested in me I forgive you all your sins.' That's the keeper of the keys that most pastors believe was said in Matthew 16:19, specifically intended to suggest that Jesus had them in mind when he proclaimed, 'And I will give unto thee the keys of the kingdom of heaven.' So you see you can read into it what you want."

"What do you read into tonight, Howard?"

"I'm still stuck on my original theory. The window peeper sees attractive naked or somewhat-naked woman and begins to have these fantasy ideas, but botches the break-in through fear caused by his stupidity of his not shutting off his cell phone. What's your take?"

Picking up the cut glass from the window, she said, "Peeper was carrying a glass cuter and suction cup. As you can see, Howard, a portion of the glass has a round image of a suction cup left on the glass. That wooden dowel appears to me to be possibly the handle to the suction cup, which he took with him. I bet that the piece of wood you found was the handle that fell out of his pocket and was inserted in the rubber cup. No, my theory is sex might have crossed his mind but wasn't the primary reason on his mind."

"So are you thinking that his real reason was your fortune or your life?"

"There is no fortune in this house, Howard."

"Maybe there's a connection to the cold cases you're working on?"

"If so, there's some good news in that. It would probably mean that someone feels I'm getting too close to finding out all the answers. Anyway, tomorrow I'll file the normal report, pick up Channing, and have security lights put in around the house. You need to get home now and put your wife's mind at ease. I need to call Curtis and do the same or shame upon me to think he will forgive me for not keeping him posted on my life. That's the problem, Howard, when you have a spouse. It's more than just about us. They will worry all the time. I know that I do when Curtis is flying one of those wide-bodies in bad weather or traveling across the mountaintops somewhere over Colorado or Salt Lake City. I appreciate you being there for me tonight, Howard, as a police officer and a friend. What about those patent leather shoes and your wife?"

"Frankly, it's a little embarrassing now that I think about it," said Howard, "considering what we've been through on this subject, but maybe you can see your way clear to just recognize it as something juvenile and nothing more. The term comes from a movie by the same name making fun of the adolescents. Catholic boys growing up trying to get an edge on the Catholic girls they were trying to hit on while in class. You see, the girls all wore these type of shiny shoes that were notorious for reflecting a peek up their skirts when you sat next to them in class."

"You did that, Howard?" she said laughing.

"Sure, but unlike many of the other Catholic girls, my future wife, Sue, didn't play the game as others did in those days," said Howard. "She was a true Catholic good girl and always wore panties."

"Oh my god, Corporal Singer, you were a piece of work in those days."

"I was, and it's taken a long time to turn the corner in my case. Fortunately some of us get help," he said while looking at Kate with a smile on his face. "Well, as you said, it's time to make my wife comfortable and head home."

CHAPTER 41

The Box

Kate walked in, hung her police jacket on the coat rack, and turned facing Channing as she shut the front door. "You are supposed to be happy coming home, Channing. Your own bed, bowl, and water dish await you. You should have been here last night instead of enjoying yourself at the doggie hotel." Channing looked about as happy to be home as a cat looks being the guest of honor at a dog pound. Kate knew in a couple days her canine would once again adapt to being her protector, but for now depression had set in. Becky had done it once again at her doggie heaven kennel, where the animals were treated like they had arrived for a Sandals Club Vacation rather than an overnight animal boarding house. Heck, the woman even offered a first-class overnight, which allowed the preferred animal its own private room with a couch and chair. Becky staffed the building 24-7 in order to allow each dog to go out at least once a night, all for $150 per 24 hours.

Kate watched as Channing sniff his dog dish, and then look up at her as if he expected something more than just his premium beef cut dog food. "Well, big fellow," she thought to herself, "that's all we got for now." It had been a busy morning already with picking up her dog and visiting Mickey's security systems. Mickey being a former Funston police officer had taken early retirement and started his own security and private detective agency. His reputation was good, and his prices were discounted to police and firemen who needed his service. Kate had explained the failed break-in attempt without going into any more details than necessary. Mickey had several package programs that fit almost any budget, so she took the Gold Package that he recommended. He told her that his team would install the system by the close of the day, which included two door sensors, nine window sensors, one motion detector, and three rotating security cameras placed to cove the rear of the house that would cover the backyard and sides leading up to the street. Kate agreed to the one thousand and fifty-dollar price gladly and went home.

Now she lifted the murder box from the floor up and onto the kitchen table once again. She was anxious to read the now-deceased officer's report on the attempted murder of Pastor Bergman's wife. Although Kate had arrived at the scene and found her with the cord around her neck, the official investigation had been assigned to a Detective Redmond, who had died within the year of the investigation from a suspected heart attack. Lifting the top from the murder box, she pulled out the contents and organized them on the table. She could tell that the larger file was from the evidence archives accumulated from Redmond's investigation, while the smaller one was from the original investigation. Somehow she felt that the key to the series of events that followed, including the death of the organist and the circumstances of Perry Sinclair, were all part of a common thread that would lead to the murderer. The initial report filed by Redmond had indicated that he had gotten there soon after Officer Heller and had moved quickly under the suggestion of Rookie Heller to determine where the husband was prior to finding his wife convulsing near death on their garage floor. Reading on through the report, Kate noted that Redmond had credited her with fast action in attempting to control the wife's breathing while at the same time calling for the paramedical team. As it turned out, Redman wrote that Bergman had lied about his whereabouts that evening in an attempt to cover up his ongoing affair with the church organist. The couple's young-adult daughter had been fast asleep in their upstairs bedroom and had slept through the entire event until the father had come home and woken her up. Redmond went on to say in his report that Bergman's church had moved swiftly in asking him to step down as their pastor, resulting in him locking himself in a nearby hotel hospitality suite. A security guard at the hotel later found him unconscious, empty pill bottles, and a long rambling note blaming the Funston police for not believing his story that he had nothing to do with the circumstances of his wife's attack. The report concluded with his arrest and charges with the crime. Kate read the report over and over trying to understand how any jury could have acquitted this man, but they did. The only conclusion that one could extract from the apparent reluctance of the jury to convict the man were newspaper articles that indicated that Bergman's continued confessing that his only guilt was letting his wife down and not being there when his family needed him. As one jury member has stated, "Trying to understand this man was impossible." Bergman himself even testified that the case was like murder. She wrote, "With everyone wanting to solve it, including himself."

She continued to look through Redmond's report trying to determine or see any indication that the organist had been interviewed. There was none, nor any indication that the detective or anyone had visited the Lutheran Church Headquarters in Detroit to understand how it turned out that Bergman had managed to be transferred to Silver Valley soon after his wife's death and that of the church organist. Kate got up and retrieved a small container of peach yogurt from the refrigerator and sat back down.

Turning back to the Redman report on the investigation, she noticed that Redmond had included a general remark on the bottom of the report, as almost an afterthought. Redmond underlined in yellow, "The suspect had said that he had a lifetime battle with the 'demon inside his soul.'" Redman had recorded his own personal feelings by writing and circling, "Bullshit."

Redmond had removed any misunderstanding of how he felt by concluding his overall feelings of the investigation by stating that it was his opinion Bergman intentionally, knowingly, maliciously, and brutally attempted to strangle his wife and then attempted to cover up his actions with a false alibi. That alibi had been that he was doing late-night research at the Funston Junior College. Still no records of his every being at that college on the night his wife was fighting for her life could ever be verified. Getting up from the table, Kate poured herself another cup of coffee and sat down.

One hour later after taking a short break, she heard the low chime from her computer, so she got up and went to her bedroom and checked her email. She studied the screen for a few moments before answering. It was from Howard Singer, her partner in crime as he put it, wanting to know if she had contacted someone to secure her home. If not, he would be glad to take that responsibility off her shoulders. Kate responded and told him everything was all right and that it had been taken care of and sending him her personal thanks for his concern. Returning to the kitchen table, she picked up one of the crime scene pictures and studied it. It clearly showed the cord around the victim's neck that had eventually sent her to the undisclosed nursing home, where later she had died. Taking a large magnifying glass from her kitchen drawer, she focused on the victim's neck and the cord. It was the same as she remembered and not the typical clothesline cord or small cinching rope used to secure canvas covers to a trailer or boat. Probably didn't mean anything, she thought, other than it wasn't the type of cord most people would have laying around the house. "It would be nice if Bergman's daughter was close by so that I could interview her regarding all the questions that keep coming up, but all indications were that she moved out of the area soon after the death of her mother." Well, some people just don't want to be found. The pastor was able to find a way out of Funston along with his daughter. Both had taken measures for different reasons and in the process had dragged the branch behind them to confuse anyone attempting to follow their trail. When people run, pondered Kate, they're just running, and they don't care about what they have left behind. What's important to them was that they felt that they had left their past behind them and the objective was to keep moving away from it. She continued to think about the cord and wondered where it was and why it wasn't part of the evidence. There seemed to be no mention of it beyond it just being around the wife's neck. She took the magnifying glass once more and studied the rope. "Where the heck have I seen that before?" she wondered to herself.

Kate picked up a second picture taken from a greater distance that focused on the dying woman's body but also presented an over-view of Bergman's garage, which seemed to be used more for the storage of general junk than a shelter for one's cars. Clearly the couple seemed to throw few things away, including what appeared to be two large twenty-gallon fish tanks. On the table taken from the box was a plastic bag containing a silver necklace with what appeared to be some type of charm on it, or maybe a vessel of some kind? Kate held the translucent light-blue vessel up to the kitchen light but couldn't determine if it contained anything inside. Placing it down on the counter, she pushed back her chair back and closed her eyes for a moment trying to remember what was bothering her so much from the appearance of this little charm. "Think, woman, think," but nothing came to mind. The sudden ringing of the doorbell and the barking of Channing returned her to the current world of reality. Getting up, she walked to the front door, now guarded by an anxious Channing. Opening the door, she was greeted by a tall, young representative of Phillip's Glass Repair Service.

"Sit down, Channing," commanded Kate, with the dog quickly obeying.

"Hello, I'm here to see Ms. Kate Heller?"

"Yes, I'm her," she said noticing the nervousness of the young man as he observed her sidearm. "I'm with the Funston Police Department, and unfortunately someone tried to break in and messed up my window last night. It's around the back. And don't worry about the dog, he'll be all right."

"You mean someone actually tried to break in the home of a policewoman?" commented the bewildered repairman. "What about your dog? Hell, he looks mean."

"Well, someone did break into the house, as you'll see from the back window. The mean dog that you're looking at was on vacation. Please don't ask. It's a long story.'"

"The dog on vacation, well, a new one, lady. Well, I'll take care of the window, and it shouldn't take very long. I probably can manage from the outside, but will you be home for the next hour should I need to come back inside?"

"I'll be home for quite a while as I'm doing my office work in the kitchen. Just feel free to come in anytime you need. The dog won't be barking anymore, so don't worry." Kate smiled as she watched the kid pick up his tools and quickly move around the side of the house. "Channing, you behave yourself," she warned as she walked back to the kitchen.

Sitting back down at the table, she picked up the paper bag containing the victim's underwear and socks plus a pair of black patent leather shoes. Thinking back, she now remembered what Howard had said about his wife's patent leather shoes. He couldn't help but look down at her polished police black oxfords. "Not a chance, boys. These are too dull."

She asked herself, "Did Bergman strangle his wife that eventually led to her death, or was he just an innocent pastor with a loose zipper, something not so uncommon with those wearing the vestments and collar?" There were but two possibilities. Either he was a pastor disgraced for the crime that he did not commit or now living with, perhaps, the shame of attempted murder for which he was not convicted. The man could sure sing and preach, a great sermon. That she now knew firsthand and, by his admission to a jury of his peers, was capable of telling lies. Rubbing her eyes in an attempt to starve off the developing headache, she then reached for her purse containing her small bottle of Bayer aspirin. As she pulled the bottle out, she noticed the folded church bulletin where Curtis and her had visited to observe Paul Bergman. Laying the bulletin on the table she proceeded to get a glass of cold water and downed the two aspirins. Hearing the movement in her bedroom, she walked down the hallway into her bedroom finding that a new glass pane had already been installed. Jesus, the guy was fast, she thought.

"Just finishing the job, Ms. Heller," he indicated as he was latching the window and was demonstrating to her that it would slide without catching. "Here, why don't you try it yourself," he offered.

Kate slid the glider window until it was firmly in place and then locked the mechanism tightly in place. Reopening it, she gave the repairman the thumbs-up sign. "Works like a charm. Come around up front, and I'll write you a check," she said.

"The boss said no charge," Ms. Heller."

"Thank you, but I prefer paying."

"He thought you might say that, so he asked me to have you just stop in someday in the future and he would give you a bill at that time, but today no charge or I'll get in trouble."

"That's fine, but please tell him I'll see him before the week is over," said Kate.

Picking up his tools, the repairman disappeared around the corner and headed back toward his truck, while Kate walked back to the kitchen where she sat down and reached once again for silver necklace containing the vessel.

Holding it up to the light, she noticed that what at first appeared empty, she now could tell that it contained a white fluid but was sealed so tight as to not leak out. Interesting, she thought, since whatever fluid was inside would require the owner to smash the glass vessel. Opening her purse, she put the vessel inside. As she was about to close her purse, she noticed the church bulletin on the table from the Silver Valley Lutheran Church. Picking it up, she turned the page until she found the listing of the church officers. It was probably nothing, but again she saw the name of A. J. Ogden, who was listed as an officer of the church. "It couldn't be the same guy, could it?" she wondered. Could this Ogden be the doctor that she had met at the Funston Hospital? Walking over to her computer desk, she searched for information on Silver Valley Lutheran Church. The website produced several different listings. Finally she was able to access the official web page that listed the church staff and a link that produced each Sunday service for the benefit of all members who were unable to attend. When she clicked on that part of the menu that listed the church staff, Paul Bergman's picture appeared, plus individual pictures of the church council. For this picture, Bergman had dressed in a suit, as did all members of the council. She noticed the Shepherd Staff pin on his lapel right away. It clearly was intact, with the shepherd hook prominent and unbroken. Returning to the link that covered each Sunday service, she clicked on this past Sunday's sermon. Once again Pastor Bergman appeared with the introduction to the Forty Days of the Word service. In this photograph, he was wearing a simple black dress shirt. On his lapel, like in the other picture, was the Shepherd pin, but this time without the Shepherd hook. "Had it broken off? Impossible to tell without blowing up the picture," she said to herself. Kate was about to close the website when she noticed another link that was called Sunday News. Clicking it on, it became clear that this page was used to review prayers for that particular Sunday, plus the following week's events, birthdays, those with medical concerns, and new visitors. The mention of Curtis and Kate Patterson from Funston, Michigan, appeared. Had they mentioned anything about where they lived? She knew that she hadn't, and she had been with Curtis all the time. Who would have known besides Bergman? Maybe, just maybe, he was Dr. Alan Ogden. If so, they were allies in the Bergman mystery and probably didn't even realize it. What did Thomas Jefferson say about something like this? "The moment a person forms a theory his imagination sees in every object only the traits which favor that theory."

"My whole case against Bergman seems to be one large fire, and just when one thinks that the solution is right around the corner, the lucky prick finds someone who is willing to spray champagne on it. Rocking back and forth in her computer chair, she knew that she had missed something, but what was it? That cord around Bergman's wife. It was no cord. It was a sash, she reasoned, now getting up from the chair and going into the kitchen to retrieve the picture. Kate picked up the photograph and put the magnifying glass on the picture of Bergman's wife one more time. She now knew what it was. It was Bergman's white sash that he kept around his waist. He had used it when they had the argument over where he had been. "But it really didn't matter, did it?" she thought, since he couldn't be tried for the same crime twice. Putting the magnifying glass down, she held the picture up one more time and now focused on the fish tanks. It was either the fish had all died, the family had just got tired of the continuous cleaning, or they were used for something else, maybe spiders? Kate looked for Ogden's phone number.

CHAPTER 42

Life Changes

"The cemetery is quiet, but aren't they all?" she said to herself. "That is, unless it's a cemetery where blacks bury their dead." Those cemeteries were often visited by relatives throughout the year, especially on Mother's Day, Father's Day, and special holidays like Memorial Day. African Americans seemed to have a tendency to honor their dead, and they had no difficulty with others knowing it, while Lutheran cemeteries and Catholic cemeteries, which heavily favored whites, were most often visited out of necessity or guilt by those that happened to find their way to these places. Today, Kate had found her way, and the cemetery was quiet. Low, moody clouds eclipsed any trace of the early-morning sun. But it really didn't matter what the weather was like today, or for that matter, that she was the only car parked adjacent to the section reserved for fallen war heroes. It was the same ritual each month, and she had been doing this for nearly three years. Looking at her watch, she noted the date was the eighteenth. The time on her watch said 9:25 a.m.

That was when her husband had been killed by the Iraqis on his first tour. And now it was time when her life needed to change. Whoever originated the phrase "Time heals all wounds" was wrong, or at least it had been wrong until Curtis came into her life. There were some wounds that nothing could heal. They remained open sores that feasted as the years and months crept by. Someday she would talk to Curtis about these sores, but the time was not now. She made her way across the cemetery's manicured lawns, first passing a headstone announcing the resting place of General Vincent "Rusty" Olsen. Even in a cemetery, rank has its privileges of location, thought Kate. As she walked past headstone after headstone, she noted that each had their own story. Reaching his simple white stone, it read, "Capt. William Heller. Born 1975. Died 2010." She stood reverently before it. The familiar gripping pain constricted her chest. It never got easier. It never would, but not just because of his sudden death, but because of many other things that one day she would talk about. She knelt, running her fingers over the white stone, tasting for a moment her own tears as they glided down her cheeks. His whole life extinguished in one heinous, senseless moment by a stranger thousands of miles away. She took the bouquet of red, white, and blue flowers and placed it on his grave. She presented it this way each month like it was a sacred gift, rather than a crumpled tangle of stems that they would become in a few days. She bowed her head, letting the grief and the guilt consume her. She didn't pray. She couldn't because somehow it didn't seem right. That she would also have to ask Curtis about it someday. Spying the nearby cement resting bench, she sat down and began to think.

Even in a cemetery, she couldn't remove the cop in her. She thought about Bergman and Sinclair knowing that they held the key. Was it Aristotle who had once said "The least initial deviation from the truth is multiplied later a thousand fold"? Looking up at the sky, she watched as the low-lying clouds, now black and bloated, abruptly split open as slit by a scalpel. The brilliance of the lightning flash told her that she had about five minutes before the rain arrived. Walking at a brisk pace, she just reached her car before the area was covered by a torrent of slanting rain. Inside the car, Kate could hear the *tat, tat, tat* of the rain on the roof of her car. She rubbed her eyes leaned back and returned her thoughts to Bergman. He was clever and somehow had recognized her when she had attended the Sunday service with Curtis, but how? She had done her best to change her appearance, but now she was convinced that it didn't work. What had he noticed that changed all that? There was only so long that you could act like a fool, even when you were in a car by yourself without another soul around for miles, and Kate was beginning to feel like a fool having been identified by Bergman.

She started the engine and turned the wipers on high trying to shoo away the rain from the windshield so that she could see out at least a little. "Damn," she thought, "if it doesn't slow down, I'm going to ruin these shoes I'm wearing today." Then it suddenly hit her, something so simple that she had overlooked it when Curtis and her had visited Bergman's church. It was the shoes, the goddarn shoes. You could learn a lot from shoes. Most undercover or beat cops usually go for big, comfortable things appropriate for walking and standing all day. Knowing that they would be doing a lot of walking that Sunday, she had worn her standard cop shoes for comfort, and Bergman had obviously picked up on it. "Too late now," she thought as she pulled away from her parking spot and moved passed the cemetery guard shack onto the highway. The road back to Funston was dangerous enough with all its road construction warning signs, let alone the rain making travel, much like traveling over polished ice. She turned the radio on and listened to her favorite classic rock station that played songs mostly from the eighties. She knew from her monthly travel to the cemetery that she should be home in another fifty minutes, so she started singing along with the music she knew and humming those songs she didn't. The less than hour drive back to her townhouse had went reasonable fast. As she was pulling up to the house, Kate waved to her neighbor, parked her car, and entered through the side door of her house to the welcoming excitement of Channing looking for a handout. "Just relax, big guy," she said as she went to the refrigerator and removed a piece of leftover ham and fed it to him. Now happy, Channing walked over to his spot near the kitchen door and flopped down on his dog bed. Seeing the blinking red light on her answering system, Kate went over and hit the play button.

"Detective Heller, Dr. Ogden returning your call. My office manager indicated that you needed to talk to me. Why don't you use my cell phone number? It's easier to reach me, and in most cases, I always pick up. Talk to you later," he said then hung up. "Damn, I forgot that I even left him a message," thought Kate while shaking her head. Reaching in her purse, she pulled his business card and found his cell phone number and dialed it.

His voice mail kicked in. "Hello, this is Dr. Ogden, I'm sorry that I can't speak to you now, but I'm with a patient at the present time. I will call you back if you leave your phone number."

"Dr. Ogden, this is Detective Heller. I'll be working out of my home office for the next four hours if you have an opportunity, please call, Detective Heller."

Whatever else might have been missing from the evidence box that Captain Wagner had provided her regarding Bergman's wife, it certainly wasn't for a lack of notes submitted by the now-deceased detective. Although his handwriting was cramped, it was neat and meticulous, filling about forty small pages. His method seemed to favor recording what he found and digested and then to summarize them before moving on to the next item. That way, she guessed, was his attempt to catalog his raw findings along with his conclusions before moving on to the next item. The focus on all forty pages was that Bergman was more than a person of interest, but rather he was the interest, period. He was a good detective, thought Kate, as he took all fragments of what he was looking at and put them all together and wove them into a solid and reliable narrative. His notes called attention to the cord around her neck. He had made a crude drawing of her neck, which seemed to indicate two cords without an explanation. Kate was puzzled by the drawing since it didn't seem to make any sense. As she was looking at the drawing trying to understand his unwritten message, her kitchen phone rang. "Kate Heller," she said.

"Detective Heller, this is Dr. Ogden returning your call."

"Doctor, we talk so much, maybe you should just start calling me Kate."

"All right, that sounds good. Kate, what can this old country doctor do for you today?"

"Help me catch this killer, Dr. Ogden, nothing more than that," she said. "I would like to have one of my associates drop off at your office a small necklace with a tiny inch-and-one-half small vessel attached to it on a chain. This item was around the neck of the victim that I'm now investigating as a possible murder case. Inside the vessel appears to be a liquid that maybe you can help me identify. I will provide you with a legal authorization to break the vessel if needed in order to have the contents tested. I don't want to chance this going through an outside lab because somehow I think that this little item may hold the key to the murder cases that I'm working on. Would you consider looking at it for me, Doctor?"

"Kate, you have piqued my interest. How will it be arriving, may I ask?"

"It will be hand delivered to you by a Corporal Howard Singer, who works for me. His instructions will be to remain in your area until you have it tested."

"Well, it shouldn't take long since I have a full lab at my clinic and three lab technicians."

"Thank you, Dr. Ogden. Just give Howard your customary fee, and you'll be reimbursed for your time right away."

"That won't be necessary. Just give me honorary mention when you solve these cases," he said laughing.

"That will not be a problem, Dr. Ogden. I have one more thing to satisfy my curiosity please."

"What's that, Kate?"

"I visited a Trinity Lutheran Church in Silver Valley with my fiancée in the last week. The church bulletin listed a head elder by the name of A. J. Ogden. Could that by any chance be you, Dr. Ogden?"

"Guilty as charged. We're you visiting us on business or pleasure, Kate?"

"Now this part gets tricky, Doctor, since you already know what I'm involved in. I will answer your question with the understanding that you can't share our conversation with anybody."

"You have my word of strict confidentiality, Kate."

"My visit was actually business. I was at your church as part of an investigation involving your pastor, Paul Bergman, who was, as you already know, once a pastor of the Lutheran church in Funston, Michigan. I have some issues with him regarding my ongoing investigation of his past relationship with an organist of that same church.

I wish that I could share more information with you, but because it's an ongoing investigation, the law prohibits me from doing so."

"I don't know what to say, Detective Heller, regarding your business visit, other than I'm shocked about Pastor Bergman being any type of suspect. Like any Christian church, you can always find a group of us wanting to replace our minister because it's the nature of churches to always being searching for the next Billy Graham."

"Well, we know that is unlikely to happen, Dr. Ogden, but what you can do to help me in my investigation is to not say anything about this conversation to anyone until my work is complete. Officer Howard Singer knows less than you about my visit, and for good reason, so I would appreciate that you not bring up this subject. If my suspicions prove correct on what I believe is in that vessel, then closure to my murder cases is not far behind. That's all I can tell you now, Doctor. Anything else would compromise my investigation as I'm sure that you understand, but I appreciate everything that you're doing to assist me."

"You're welcome, Detective. Oh, by the way, have you set a wedding date yet?"

"Not yet, Doctor, but we're moving in the direction of resolving that issue very soon. Curtis lives in Lift Bridge, and although he is a pilot and can fly in on his scheduled days off, we want to be together every day, not just once every other week."

"I'm familiar with the town, Kate. The village father years ago decided to put a lift bridge there because the Black Hawk River flowed through the town, and the local politicians felt that the bridge would allow the river to be a navigable waterway for commercial boat traffic. As it turned out, river trade never materialized. The state of North Dakota has one in Fairview, North Dakota, but in their case, I read that the bridge was built in order to accommodate rail traffic. Like their sister in Michigan, the need for it never supported the dreams of what it was intended to be used for. Anyway I'll take a look your mystery container and give the results to your partner."

"Thanks again, Doctor," she said, laying the phone back in the cradle.

Ogden's nurse Stacy had been standing in the doorway for almost a minute, and he could see the reflection of her in the darkened window of the computer screen.

"Stacy? I was mile away. Did you need something?" he asked.

"No, Doctor, it's just that I noticed your light on back here, and I thought you would have left by now. If you continue to work so many hours, your beautiful wife is going to change the lock. Maybe you should just pick up the work tomorrow and get some rest. You look pretty darn tired, Doctor."

"Stacy, I can always count on you to make me feel that I'm not the doctor of this clinic, just another man needing a woman to watch after me, besides my wife, of course. But I thank you. All men should be lucky enough to have so many people watching out for them. I'm going to be leaving now and will be back in the office about 10:00 a.m. tomorrow. The first patient isn't scheduled until eleven, but in the event a police officer by the name of Howard Singer shows up and delivers a package for me, please lock it up right away. You won't know him since he's from Funston, Michigan. And I need one more favor, Stacy.

"Yes."

"You are not to ask him any questions, just accept the package and let me know that it has arrived."

"I bet it's a gift for Betty," she offered.

"Well, in this case, you would be wrong, but you've given me an idea," he said, now turning the lights off and locking his office door. Reaching for his cell phone, he placed a call to Betty.

"Hello, Alan," she said. "What is happening in the world of medicine?"

"Nothing special, just wanted to find out if you would like to go out for dinner tonight. We haven't done that in a while, and some things have been going on today that we could talk about and enjoy a night out at the same time."

"Well, I have always enjoyed a good mystery, Alan, and it's one less cooking night for your wife, plus the doctor's buying as usual. Where will I meet you?"

"Let's try Fox's Pub near the waterfront in about an hour and a half," said Alan.

"I'll be there after a quick stop at home to change," said Betty as she hung up.

When Alan arrived at Fox's Pub, he saw Betty's car and pulled in right beside it. Locking his door, he then walked inside the restaurant. Betty had picked a table near the largest window overlooking the small man-made pond, which was now filled with white geese and a few ducks of various species. Seeing Alan, she waved and raised what appeared to be a large glass of wine. Walking over to the table, he picked a chair nearest his wife, gave her a warm kiss, and sat down. Unable to hold back his building frustration, he said, "Something is going on with Paul Bergman, and it has me worried, Betty. I got a phone call today from a Detective Heller from the Funston, Michigan, Police Department. You may remember me telling you that I had met her some time ago when I was treating a patient at the Funston, Hospital, for a Brazilian wandering spider bite. At the time she happened to be investigating my patient's relationship with another woman, who had died of another spider bite. She was trying to see if there was any connection and had a long conversation with me. You cannot talk about this to anyone, my dear."

"Yes, I remember, Alan, but if my memory serves me correct, that woman died from another type of spider? Wasn't she an organist?"

"She was and actually an organist at the same church that Bergman had served as their pastor. The same church that you recently visited and found out that his wife had passed away. It's a small world, Betty."

"You've got to be joking, Alan," said Betty.

"I wish that I were, but it's all true. That detective mentioned that she had recently visited our church during the past week as part of her continued investigation on Bergman. But there is much more to this, Betty, and somehow I believe Bergman is at the center of it. She didn't so much as say that, but she's sending me a vessel that was found around wife's neck connected to a necklace. I'm afraid that I already know what it contains."

"But his wife is dead? What does this have to do with the organist and the guy in the hospital?" asked Betty.

"I wish that I could tell you, but unfortunately much of this is as big a mystery to me as it is to you tonight. Look, would you like to take a few days off and join your husband on a trip over to Funston?"

"Are you thinking about going against the rule not to interfere with Bergman's last place of business, Alan? You said so yourself that this type of thing can cause us a lot of trouble through the district president's office."

"I don't intend to cause any difficulty, but we have to be sure about this man, and we will make this just an overdue vacation, but who knows what we'll find. Even a blind squirrel can once in a while find a peanut."

"Well, always remember that more than one blind animal has found themselves on someone's dinner table for being too curious. It appears to me that Bergman might be dangerous. Well, let's talk more about this after dinner Alan. You invited me to dinner tonight, and I intend to take you up on this rare opportunity to enjoy a night out."

"Fair enough, my charming wife, and besides, it's been many years since I've gotten you drunk."

Alan woke up to the bright sunshine coming through the window. He could hear the doves in the yard welcoming the morning sun and probably enjoying the sunflower seeds that he kept below the bird feeder for them. It had been a wonderful evening with Betty as they had enjoyed the typical five-star food and service of the restaurant. Later their lovemaking had made Alan so tired that he had apparently overslept. He looked at the alarm clock, now indicating that it was half past ten. Turning over, he reached for Betty and found an empty bed. Sitting up, he tried to ignore the headache as Betty walked into the room bringing toast, juice, and a small glass of champagne.

"Wow," she said, "you look like you could use a doctor, Alan."

"Not a doctor, my wife, just a refill of male testosterone, which seems to somehow be escaping me."

"You did very well last night, Alan, for a man your age," she said smiling. "Although I must admit you used to do it very well for most of the night, when you were thirty," she said, winking.

Drinking his juice, Alan then reached for his cell phone on his nightstand.

"You're not working today, Alan, remember?"

"No, but I want to get a hold of Jack before he heads out to goes fishing, as he usually does on Saturday. The fact is, he probably is already at the lake since he likes to head on out before the rooster crows. We need to talk about things with Pastor Bergman regarding his wife and other concerns that I have. I thought it would be a good time after church on Sunday, when he usually goes back to his country parsonage."

"You and Jack had better be careful with that man," said Betty. "There's something there that just doesn't fit right. Anyway, while you talk to Jack, I'm going back to the kitchen and finish cleaning up," she said as she kissed him.

As Betty walked out of the bedroom, Alan left a voice mail for Jack about his desire to visit Bergman on Sunday, indicating that he only had to call back if his plan was not possible.

Putting his phone down, Alan walked over to the bedroom window and looked out. Morning didn't always make the neighborhood look any better. Today nothing was stirring and was as close as anyone gets to absolute stillness. It was a Saturday for sleeping, thought Alan.

A Lonely, Unloved Calling

Bergman sat on his barstool, shoulders slumped, his vestments damp and disheveled. It had been just an hour since he had arrived at his parsonage in the woods, and he was already craving his next drink. If they could only see him now, he thought. Some things stayed the same, while some things changed. The situation here in Silver Valley sucked. And he was a prisoner to it. Even the booze wasn't enough. He was drowning, and he no longer gave a damn. First his wife, and then the death of the woman he had fallen in love with. Gayle Browning had been a unique and talented woman, and he missed her dearly. He shrugged into his casual clothes while throwing his vestments on his bed. The clock in the hallway chimed three thirty as he opened the front door and walked down to the parsonage shed. He wondered why everyone called it that since it served as an extended guest room as well as storage area and workshop. Walking inside, he locked the door and surveyed his belongings to ensure that nothing was disturbed. He had assumed that by now at least four individuals had openly inspected his house and storage area and that there would be telltale signs of their intrusion into his life.

Yes, he had encouraged their desire to inspect his property as part of their stated requirement of the constitution of the church, but he knew that was not the real reason. They just didn't feel comfortable with him, especially Betty Ogden, who had been on a crusade since his arrival to block his ministry from ever getting started. As he circled the large room, surprisingly everything still appeared in order. Satisfied he walked over to his light-brown leather couch and sat down. Reaching underneath the couch, he touched the listening device that he had mounted against the frame. Like the first device at the parsonage, this unit had been placed in such a way that none of the church snoopers would have ever found it, or the small tape recorder that had captured every word said. He glanced up at the large Victorian painting of the mother holding her infant daughter. It was an elegant painting that had produced countless hours of enjoyment for him as he marveled at the artist's skill that created this masterpiece of Gayle Browning, his former mistress. The picture presented the innocence of a time long since gone. Bergman focused on the left eye of the child with her head resting against the woman. The child was, of course, the creation of the artist and had no connection to Gayle. The painting was just high enough on the wall that only he could tell that the child's eye was the lens of a camera. "Thank you very much, Radio Shack," laughed Bergman. Leaning back against the leather couch, he pushed the button that released a foot extension on the end of the couch that offered Bergman the opportunity to fully stretch out. Time had been kind to Paul Bergman. His short brown hair was a bit grayer, but he was still lean and fit, his face still seriously handsome. Images flashed through Bergman's mind as he recalled the day his wife had confronted him about the pictures that she had found in his car glove compartment. She had borrowed his car to pick up clothes at the dry cleaner and had opened the glove compartment looking for the receipt and had discovered the pictures that Gayle had given him of their lovemaking in the church balcony. Angry, she had waited up for him and had heard him coming home from his late-night meeting. Confronting him in the garage, she had screamed and swore at him wanting to know why these naked pictures of him and Gayle Browning were in his car. Before he could answer, she had rushed him and banged her fists against his chest. He remembered how her anger intensified as she grabbed his clerical collar and ripped it off his shirt. She had called him a phony bastard as she had yelled and sobbed while fighting him. Angry, his right arm had clutched tightly around her neck as he had thrown her to the basement floor. But as she continued to yell and struggle, he had reached for the sash around his clerical garments in a frantic attempt to restrain her. Thinking that his weight had overpowered her he released his grip in an attempt to tie her hands with his sash when his wife's teeth sunk deep into the exposed skin of his wrist. She had twisted her head ferociously from side to side like a mongrel trying to free the last piece of meat from another dogs attempt to steal its food. "My hand, you bitch," he had said as he place the sash around her neck and pulled it tight.

As he was thinking about that day three years ago, the unmistakable sound of a car caught his attention. Getting up from the couch, he walked over to the small window facing the parsonage and saw A. J. Ogden's silver Corvette. Within seconds, Ogden and Jack Koehler had emerged from inside of the car and were walking up to the front door of the parsonage. "What the hell do they want on a Sunday afternoon?" he wondered. Obviously they would know that he was at home since his car was parked in its normal spot. He watched them as they rapped on the door and finding no answer had walked around the house looking for him. His hopes faded that they would leave when noticing that Jack was pointing to the parsonage shed and started walking in that direction, with Ogden following him. Removing himself from the window, Bergman realized that he had little choice but to greet them and see what was on their mind. After all, someone could have died, he thought, and they were just coming out to tell him about it. It might be nothing and he was concerned for no reason at all, he thought. Opening the door, Bergman walked outside and waved to the two men.

"Hey, fellows, what do I owe the pleasure of this visit to? Are some members complaining that I extended beyond the normal sixty minutes for my sermon? If so, what they need to do is listen to a good Baptist minister, who is usually good for an hour and a half."

"No, nothing like that, Pastor," responded Alan.

"Shall we go inside, or would you like to stay outside?" asked Jack.

"Actually neither, if you don't mind. The weather is so nice, why not just sit over there by the picnic table," offered Bergman.

Alan looked at Jack somewhat puzzled, but they both joined him at the picnic table.

"Well, what is on your mind?" asked Bergman, not offering either any refreshments.

Deciding not to ease gently into the question, Alan decided to be direct. "We understand that your wife has died in the last three months. Is that true?"

Somewhat surprised, but measuring his words carefully, Bergman said, "Yes, that's true, but it was a private matter. As Jack can attest to, I requested personal time off a while back. It was to deal with my wife's funeral."

"But you said nothing to us at that the time, that it had to do with your wife, or even mentioned it to the congregation," said Jack. 'We find that more than unusual, Pastor, since as a Christian church, our mission is to help each other in a moment of grief."

"As I said, it was a personal matter, and I intended to announce it to the congregation before the end of the month," commented Bergman. "You both should understand that issues involving a pastor's illness or personal matters relating to his family can cause some members of the congregation as well as its officers of the church to begin rethinking that pastor's call status. In the end, many of us become guarded in sharing this information. A pastor's life in a congregation can have a very short shelf life, if you are following my concern," offered Bergman.

"What I'm following, Pastor, is that you feel under certain circumstances it's permissible to withhold information. Sort of like that of a physician, who withholds information from his patients that he has several malpractice lawsuits filed against him. To admit anything could cost him dearly in his practice. Maybe like the CEO of a major corporation who doesn't want his board of directors to know that he really never did graduate from Harvard? Am I following your logic, Pastor?"

"You're being typically unfair, Dr. Ogden, and mixing apples with oranges. A pastor's career can be ended if he's not careful. You and I both know that, and if you've forgotten, any district president would support me on that," said Bergman.

"Well, we think that you should have said something, Pastor," said Ogden. "Ours is a very Christian, family-oriented congregation that prays for each other, and by you not sharing your grief with us it seems very unusual for a pastor hired to promote that very thing to his sheep. Neither Jack or I should be viewed as King Ahasuerus in the Old Testament. You needed not be in fear like then, that we carried the golden scepter that could cause your death. But make no mistake, honesty is always the best policy in the Christian world. We feel that this type of paranoia characterized by delusions that honesty could cause you to lose your job is not a healthy condition for our pastor. Was your wife ill for very long?" asked Alan, "or do you consider that question also a violation of your rights regarding confidentiality?"

Ogden's last question and current tone took Bergman somewhat by surprise, so he decided to give them some information to see just how much they really knew.

"Mrs. Bergman had been hurt in a home invasion incident and had been under the care of health professionals for some time," lied Bergman. "Her injury caused her to enter into a deep coma that she never recovered from. With regret, her situation took a turn for the worse, and she passed away at the nursing care unit that she had been staying in. Gentleman, as I'm sure you do understand, the recalling of these events remain difficult for me. It's not my intent not to be forthright, but the rules under confidentiality are just as sacred to a Pastor as it would be to a layman, so please no more questions regarding Mrs. Bergman."

"We apologize, Pastor for any discomfort that we have caused you with these questions commented Jack. We both hope that you will share as much as you can with the Congregation in the near future to avoid the obvious questions that will arise. You know how laypeople are with gossip. Do you need any more time to take care of your family matters?"

"That's very kind of you, Jack, since I've used up all my allotted vacation time this year. Would you speak to the council and see if they can authorize three more personal days? That should be enough to finish my business in Funston. Our home has been on the market for over two years now, but as I'm sure that you understand, it's almost impossible to sell one's home without giving it away."

"So your daughter is not living in it now?" asked Ogden.

"No. Since the death of my wife, she's moved away from the area and is now married living in Oregon. She has her own family now, so the contact has been limited."

"In addition to Elmer and Ed from the trustee board who initially inspected the parsonage, I want you to know that I followed up on their inspection, Pastor. It was a routine follow-up and part of my job to just provide a complete overview for our council and nothing more."

"Yes, you actually did mention that fact to me, and as I indicated that was acceptable with me," said Bergman. "Did you find anything wrong?" he asked.

"Nothing wrong, Pastor, with the parsonage. You have done a splendid job of maintaining both buildings. We noticed that you're an avid gun collector, although none of us can remember you being interested in hunting."

"Hunting is not for me, gentlemen, since that would involve killing animals, which I'm personally against. The firearms are a private and personal collection, and to be honest, few have ever been fired. When I was a young boy, I always wanted to own firearms but couldn't afford them, so when I got married, this just became a hobby designed to make up for what I couldn't have as a child. I hope that answers your curiosity."

"It does, Pastor," said Alan. "Do you have any idea where Ed Preston has gone?"

"Ed? I had no idea that he even left, although I must admit now that you bring it up, that I haven't seen him in over three weeks."

"Tell us about those empty fish tanks in the parsonage, Pastor, and why they have straw beddings in the bottom. Are you using them for some other types of pets?"

"They are strictly fish tanks, Alan. I put the straw in them to absorb any moisture when they are not in use. I'm afraid of mold building up," said Bergman.

"Well, Jack, I think that we can let Pastor enjoy the rest of the afternoon, don't you think?" Now getting up from the picnic table chair, Alan said, "Let's get home before Betty gets nervous and sends the law out looking for us. Thanks for your time, Pastor, and your cooperation on the required inspection process." Shaking his hand, they returned to their car and pulled onto the dirt road.

As Alan and Jack left the parsonage compound, they drove in silence for over five minutes, not saying a word. Finally Alan spoke up. "I don't like it, Jack."

"You don't like what, Alan?"

"Well, first of all in case you missed it, our pastor had the strong smell of alcohol on his breath. Second he clearly didn't want us in either the parsonage or his shed. Third, the idea that his wife's death is his own private matter and his insistence on us respecting this confidentiality is ludicrous, if not the actions of an insane man."

"Now, Alan, he was on his own time off, and he wouldn't be the only pastor to ever suck on the orange juice."

"No, Jack, he wasn't on his own time off. The fact is, Friday is his day off, while Sunday is a full workday for him, and we both know it. We also have closed our eyes to each Saturday where we allow him to remain at his parsonage to do whatever he desires. You want me to buy the idea that his home is off limits, well, I'll concede that point. But his wife's death remaining private is a crock of buffalo chips, period."

Jack remained silent while Alan kept his eye on the road. Finally the silence was broken. "Well, Dr. Watson," he said in a mocking tone. "Do you have a hypothesis?"

"Jack, I expect better than that from you as the president of this congregation, but more importantly as my friend. We have a problem, and it deserves our attention," said Alan.

"My apologies, Alan, you are right. It's just so difficult to grasp what is going on with this guy."

"Apology accepted, Jack. Here's my unproven theory, so just hear me out. I believe that Pastor Bergman's current baggage was fast-tracked to us from his former congregation under the full knowledge and cooperation of his district president in Michigan. In the Catholic

Church, if we were dealing with a priest, it would most likely have something to do with some type of perversion, little kids, or some lawsuit filed against a priest's behavior, but in this case I doubt that. In most examples, a simple call to his former congregation would clear up a lot of things, but as you and I both know, such outreach usually results in a congregation being put in the penalty box forever should they ever need a future pastor. The Lutheran Church runs its local business with the hammer-on-the-thumb approach and dares you to cross that line. Should you stray from their business model, the next pastor that you would ever receive would be, like, well, forget that since you would never receive a pastor. I have the sinking feeling, Jack, that Bergman has a ton of secrets at his former congregation. Maybe even put his hand in the cookie jar, and that's why we got him."

"You mean stole money?" asked Jack.

"No, I'm referring to more serious things Jack. Our church had an outside visitation from an off-duty police officer in the last two weeks. I haven't talked about that because she asked me not to discuss it with anyone. Following that visit, that officer requested something from me that involves my physician skills. This came up because we had met weeks ago when I had provided assistance to a patient admitted to the Funston General Hospital that involved a case she was working on. It's complicated, Jack, but she has placed me in a position that doesn't allow me to say much more. I'm going to ask you to trust me on this one, Jack, but I somehow feel that we need to know much more about our pastor Bergman. So much that Betty and I are going to take a few days off and tour Funston, Michigan."

"That's where Bergman was a pastor before he came here," said Jack.

"Yes, but we won't be visiting his congregation," replied Ogden. "I want to meet with my detective friend and see if she will provide a beacon of light on this very dark problem that I think we have."

"I would say those are pretty strong assumptions, Alan, without proof."

"Then let's get the information the honorable way," said Alan.

"How's that?" asked Jack.

"Behave like a politician," said Alan. "She asked for a favor, and I granted it. Now it's time to call in that favor and see if she is willing to put our minds at ease regarding our pastor. A lot has gone on in Funston, Alan, and that's where the secrets are buried. We owe it to our members here that they have nothing to fear from his ministry."

"What makes you think that we have anything to fear, Alan?" asked Jack.

"It's very simple, Jack. He lied to us back there at the parsonage when he said that the fish tanks were just being stored and kept from collecting moisture by the use of that straw as a bedding. Remember that favor that I did for the policewoman?"

"Yeah, but you never mentioned exactly what it was."

"She's sending me a sealed vessel that Bergman's wife wore around her neck to see if I can test the contents and determine what's in it. I believe she already knows what's in it and she just wants me to confirm it, Jack. Somehow I feel that what I'm going to find is an antidote against being bitten by the Brazilian wandering spider."

"I don't get the connection, Alan," said Jack.

"His dead wife must have somehow found out his little hobby of keeping this deadly spider for pets, and he removed her fear by providing her with an antidote, just in case one got loose. And those fish tanks in the shed, Jack, with the straw bedding. Don't be fooled. Those are for his pets, and it wouldn't surprise me if they contained spiders, the deadly kind, Jack."

"God, Alan, I hope that you're wrong," said Jack, watching his house beginning to appear in the distance.

"I do too," said Alan, pulling up to the colonial home to let Jack out.

The Doctor's Office

His office was busier than it usually for a Monday morning, thought Ogden. "Have I missed an appointment?" he wondered. As he entered his office from his private entrance, he could see in the reception room a woman trying to control the coughing coming from her daughter, who was now holding a hanky over her mouth. A baby nearby was throwing blocks from the toy box at what appeared to be his older brother. Funny, thought Ogden. "Say, Stacy, what do we have out in the reception room? I didn't think that my appointment schedule had anything on it until one this afternoon. It looks like that young girl has a very bad cold."

"Sorry, Doctor, my fault. I remembered that you were going to be in around ten this morning, so I had Mrs. Applegate and her kids wait for you. I didn't promise her an appointment, but her daughter seemed to have something going on. Fire me if you have to, but I'm just a softy when it comes to kids being sick," said Stacy.

"Well, you can save your job if you can bring me a cup of coffee into my office. Give me five minutes to go over the mail, and I'll see your patient."

"That's great, Dr. Ogden. I have one more thing, please. What's that, or shouldn't I ask?" said Stacy, pointing to the package. "Your police officer arrived with that package you were expecting, but once he found out that you would be coming in until around ten, he preferred to go down the block for some coffee. He said that he would be back shortly."

"That's fine, Stacy. I'm sorry, but that package is a private matter for the police. Put the family in room number two. I'll be in there in about five minutes."

Half an hour later, Ogden had finished with the Applegate family and was walking out of his office when Stacy indicated that Officer Singer was in the reception room. "Please send him into my office," replied Ogden. In the next few minutes, when he walked into Ogden's office, the first thing Ogden noticed was how well Singer's uniform seemed to fit him. "The man's conscientious about his appearance," thought Ogden. He liked the officer already, since in his mind, neatness suggested a well-organized and dependable person.

"Dr. Ogden, thank you for seeing me," said Sinclair.

"You're welcome, Officer. Can I get you something to drink? My next patient isn't scheduled for another twenty minutes."

"Thank you, Doctor, but I just had some coffee down the street. I see that you have the package that I left for you from Detective Heller? I assume that she has already had a discussion with you on what she hopes that you will do with whatever is inside?" said Sinclair.

"Yes, she has, and I take it she discussed it with you also?" said Ogden.

"Not actually, but she said we would go over it together when the results came back from your lab."

Opening up the sealed package in front of Sinclair, Ogden removed the chained necklace with the small vessel and walked over to a large microscope that rested on a small table away from his desk. Putting the necklace and the vessel on the table, he laid the vessel directly under the microscope. After about three minutes, he removed the vessel and locked it in his safe.

"Very interesting contents, Officer Sinclair, but of course we must wait for the official report from my staff, but it seems unlikely that the results will be any different than my own visual observation. You're not curious, Officer Sinclair?"

"Certainly, but I work for Detective Heller, and I trust she will tell me what I need to know when she's ready."

"I like you, Officer Sinclair, because you have all the right answers. Integrity is lost in our new society. Actually, your Detective

Heller had called me earlier today and felt that I should share the results of my findings with you. As she put it, there so should be no secrets between her and her partner, especially should something happen to her."

"She put it like that, should something happen to her?"

"Yes, just like that, so my educated guess is that she is working on something that carries an inherent danger to all those involved in its investigation. The contents in that vessel, Corporal Singer, are in my opinion an antidote for a spider bite. I just recently injected that particular antidote into a patient at Funston Hospital. Something tells me, Officer, that it would be wise for the Funston Hospital to stock that antidote until Detective Heller brings closure to her murder cases. See that gun on your waist, Officer?"

"Yes, but what about it, Doctor?"

"You, sir, would stand a better chance at surviving a bullet from that weapon than a bite from the most lethal spider that this antidote is intended for. You all need to be careful with this one," said Ogden. "Anyway, I'll have the results for you in short order. My wife, Betty, and I will be visiting Funston in the next week and hope to see your Detective Heller."

"I'll let her know, Doctor. And thank you for the advice. We'll watch our backs. Well, my time is about up, but I will be in town for the next couple days since Detective Heller has asked me to hang around a while until you have actually tested the contents in the vessel. I brought my clubs along so I'll kill some time on the links and maybe even do some fishing. This is my card, Doctor, which has my cell number on it. Please call me when the results are ready for me to pick up." Singer shook the doctor's hand and walked toward the front door.

Ogden looked through his window and watched as Singer climbed into his car and pulled away. Dialing Stacy's extension, he waited for her to pick up.

"Yes, Doctor?"

Stacy, would you bring back the file on Perry Sinclair. He's a patient that I treated some time back when I visited the Funston Hospital."

Laying the phone down, Stacy found the Sinclair file and walked it back to Ogden's office and handed it to him. "Thank you," said Ogden. "Would you hold my calls for a while as I'll be on the phone and need time to concentrate. And please pull my door shut for now."

As she left the office, Ogden began to review the Sinclair file. His interest focused on the microscope viewing of the saved dead body of the Brazilian wandering spider. The report indicated that the remains were that of a female spider, one still containing silk bundles, or egg sacs. Ogden paused for a moment and thought about that. The little lady was undoubtedly not in a good mood when she attacked Sinclair. Ogden knew from his experience on this type of deadly spider that the male spider, upon mating with the female and depositing his sperm, usually made a timely departure soon after, because the female's normal predator instincts returned in short order, and his life was in danger. Looking closer at the magnified picture, it was clear that it was a female since the male spider had swollen bulbs on the end of their palps, and these were not present. Leaning back in his chair, Ogden started to understand why the contents of the vessel were so important to Detective Heller or, better yet, to the wearer of the necklace. The necklace was the insurance policy against being bitten by the spider. That meant, thought Ogden, that Bergman was purchasing these spiders for purposes not intended to be just for pets. Suddenly he thought back to the inspection of the parsonage that had been done by Elmer and Jack. Turning around in his chair, he reached for his book covering the five most dangerous spiders in the world. Pulling the book from its shelf, he opened the page to the Brazilian wandering spider and read the section covering its required care. The spider seemed to have a verity of insects that it enjoyed eating to include termites, ants, and general bugs that it trapped. Mice and small rodents seemed to attract its attention also, but these like humans seemed more to serve its predatory nature. Turning the page, Ogden then noted that the maintenance of this particular spider required a large fish tank with a bedding of straw where the spider could hide undetected. This was certainly not the type of animal that you wanted to meet in your house, under your bed, or arriving in a fruit basket, as was the case with Perry Sinclair. Above all else, hunting and killing were where they shined. In the bug world, the Brazilian wandering spider would be truly equivalent to a wolf or shark.

Leaning back in his chair, Ogden tried to put the pieces together and find logical reasons and answers as to what actually existed at the parsonage. All these things regarding the pastor's wife, his lover, and now Sinclair could be just one big coincidence and nothing more than a tangle of love affairs gone bad, not outright murder with a spider as the weapon of choice. Yet it could be Bergman just got himself involved in a situation with his wife's death and he couldn't control the situation. In that example with a mistress, that could place his ministry in jeopardy, and the anger of Sinclair stealing the affections of Browning, the dominoes just really started to fall. Maybe when Betty and he arrived in Funston, Detective Heller would have some of the missing answers that would alleviate this developing feeling that Bergman had brought evil to their church rather than a pathway to salvation.

Abnormality

She had been trying to sleep after Howard's call, which had informed her of the contents of the vessel, but it had been impossible. She had been lying on the bed, thinking about what he had confirmed for most of the evening, before she had finally closed her eyes from exhaustion. At eleven thirty she was woken up suddenly from the flash of the security lights going off in her backyard and shining in her bedroom. Reaching for her pistol, she walked over to the bedroom window looking down at the bare and gray yard below. The grass near her tree was the only splash of color that she could identify. Opening the window, she could hear the wind blowing the branches but could see no other movement. As the security light went off, her eyes became better able to scan the entire yard, producing only a faint glimpse of a rabbit eating clover in the grass. Channing, hearing her movement, had come into the room showing no signs of anything other than a concern about losing his sleep. After about five minutes, she secured the window and returned to the bed while keeping the pistol within reach as she drifted back to sleep.

The panic attack hit her before four in the morning as she felt that her entire room was contaminated by lurking arachnids with eight legs and numerous eyes. She found herself thinking about them all and trying not to think about it at all at the same time. Kate had bad dreams before, but nothing like this. In checking the bedspread and pillows, it still couldn't remove the feeling that somehow they had been crawling on her while she was sleeping. Jumping out of bed, she went directly into the shower and scrubbed herself from head to foot trying to get the feeling off her. Not trusting her silk pajamas, she put them in a black garbage bag and sealed it. At half past five, she was so tired she physically couldn't do any more, and sleeping was impossible. Kate contemplated taking the day off or even calling in sick or just take a drive over to the forest preserve with Channing. She knew that Curtis was on an overnight somewhere in California, so the chances of reaching him were slim. And even if she did, what was the great new Detective Kate Heller going to tell him? "'Hi, honey, I wish you were here because frankly spiders scare the shit out of me'? Well, deal with it, Kate," she thought. "Put your big-girl panties on and get back to work. Otherwise, Wagner may have to find another detective to solve these cases." In the end, she put on her uniform and walked into the kitchen to prepare for what she knew would be a full workday.

"It's time to refocus," she thought as she sat down at the kitchen table and looked at all the items she had received reluctantly from the cold case files. Dr. Ogden's confirmation that the liquid in the necklace's attached vessel found around Bergman's wife's neck as being the antidote for the Brazilian wandering spider bite only confirmed her growing suspicions. It didn't prove that Bergman had murdered his wife. What it did suggest was that Bergman had a connection to the deadly spider, which had almost killed Perry Sinclair. Her problem was that she was unable to connect this with the organist death positively because that goddamn stubborn autopsy report by Dr. Patel insisted that the bite came from a brown recluse, and of course, that spider didn't kill its victims. If only she had the actual spider, then she wouldn't have to rely on second opinions that could be taken apart by lawyers.

She rubbed her forehead in frustration and said out loud, "This will not go unpunished, no matter how smart you think you are, Bergman." She looked at the time. It was already quarter to nine. She reached for her phone on the kitchen table and dialed the Gilbert Funeral Home that had handled the Gayle Browning cremation.

"Gilbert Funeral Home, can we help you?"

"This is Detective Kate Heller of the Funston Police Department. Is Mr. Gilbert available?"

"Which Mr. Gilbert are you looking for? We have two."

"It would be the Gilbert that handled the funeral for Ms. Gayle Browning."

"If you would hold on for a minute, I'll see if he's in," said the receptionist.

Kate waited patiently, hoping she would find the right one in the office.

"This is Mr. Gilbert," came the voice. "You wanted to speak to the individual who handled the Browning funeral. I believe that we have spoken some time back, Officer Heller?"

"Yes, that's true, but I have a follow-up question, Mr. Gilbert. One that deals with the deceased's personal effects, which I believe that you said you retain for a period of time?"

"Yes, by law we are required to retain them for several months, and then we can dispose of them as we see fit. Usually we send the clothes to Goodwill or some organization such as that. Any expensive items that we have, our policy is to hold a little longer and then wait for some church-sponsored event that they hold to raise funds for. Things like summer vacation Bible studies or their food pantry fund-raising events. I think that we may have covered these procedures the last time that we talked, as a matter of fact."

"You did, Mr. Gilbert, but in my business it never hurts to double-check conversations when so much is at stake. Have there been any requests for the remaining items of Ms. Browning?"

"In her example, she came to us with only her clothes, shoes, and an inexpensive watch, so as you can see, there was very little to maintain, but nevertheless those items will be handled in accordance with the states requirements. It is funny, though," said Gilbert.

"What is so funny?" asked Kate.

"Well, there was some interest in a missing cell phone. First we had the question about an expensive ring, if you remember, and then the question about a missing cell phone."

"Who called asking about a cell phone?" asked Kate.

"He didn't leave a valid return phone number, but because of his insistence, I even called the Funston Police Department to see if they had retained it through their investigation. They said they had it and would retain it until their investigation was completed."

"Really?" replied an astonished Kate.

"Yes, that's what they said, so when I tried to call the gentleman back, I discovered the phony phone number."

"Well, as usual, Mr. Gilbert, you have been most helpful. I must confess that I'm as puzzled as you on the matter of the cell phone, but should you receive any further interests regarding Ms. Browning from any source, I'd appreciate you giving me a call direct."

"We will do that, Officer Heller, and best of luck on closing this case," said Gilbert. "It will make us all feel a lot better when this unusual situation is put to rest. No pun intended, Officer."

"Can anything else possibly go wrong?" she wondered. "No sleep since going to bed last night and now this nutty cell phone deal." She was about to reach for the Bayer aspirin when she heard the rain. Looking outside her kitchen window, she could see the ash-gray sky and the developing cloud cover. In the distance, she saw the flash of lighting. Counting to five as she used to do when she was a child, she reached four when the clap of thunder sounded. Then shortly she saw another flash, and started to count. This time it reached three before the clap of thunder sounded. She called for Channing, who raced to the door and outside, seeming to understand her excitement over the impending shower. Looking up from the open door to her outside light fixture, she watched a spider weaving its web. A drop of the new rain now beginning to fall clung to a new web that stretched from the light fixture to almost her kitchen window. "Channing!" she yelled. "Come inside now!" She watched the dog race to the door and inside, out of the falling rain. The breeze picked up, and she could see the stress that it was putting on the web that now seemed secured to her window. Why won't the darn thing break? she wondered, not fully realizing the strength of the spider's web. Then she screamed as she saw the spider coming down, plump belly moving from side to side as it ignored the rain and began to weaving a new strand. Kate, unable to watch the show any longer, pulled the curtain shut and once again sat down at her kitchen table and reached for her notebook to write down her conversation with the Gilbert Funeral Home. The ringing of her cell phone was a welcome sound from the past few minutes of watching a spider. "Hello, this is Detective Heller."

"Kate, this is Howard. Just calling to see if you have anything I can help you with? One can get mighty bored ticketing speeders and just driving through neighborhoods waiting for trouble when I know that you are doing the heavy lifting with the Bergman and Browning cases."

"I'm glad you called, Howard."

"You are?"

"Yes, pride can only go so far, Howard, and to be frank, sometimes a man might be able to do a better job than his boss can," said Kate.

"I doubt that," replied Howard. "You've got the detective shield, and I'm learning from you, not the other way around."

"You've come a long way, Howard, in the area of diplomacy, and I appreciate your comments, but here's what I need your help with. The boys down the precinct are playing games with Wagner and me regarding the evidence that they have collected on the Browning death. My guess is they are still worried that I'm looking to make one of our own look bad in the reopening of the Browning case. Wagner ordered them to send to me all the collected evidence they found at the time of her death due to the spider bite, and they did send all of it, with the exception of one small item that seems to be in their custody yet. Howard, I need you to pay them a visit and assure them that they have nothing to fear, but I want that cell phone that they have in their possession that they forgot to include in the items that Wagner sent to me. You can tell them no hard feelings and that I'm not going to mention this to Wagner, but I need that woman's cell phone sooner than later."

"Kate, consider it done. I'll give you a call later today and let you know how it went."

"Thanks, Howard," she said. "I'd hate to have to come down there and shoot one of the little bastards," she said, hanging up.

Satisfied that she had severed her pride from her investigation and given Howard an opportunity to assist her, she took two slices of honey wheat bread and put them in her toaster, while pouring herself another cup of coffee. Looking at the window again, she noted that the spider had finished its morning work of setting the web trap for unsuspecting bugs. Her eyes caught the struggling gray moth as it struggled in vain to free itself from the dangling web. As it jumped around trying to dislodge itself, the spider came down from the upper right-hand corner of the web and moved slowly toward the moth. As the spider watched its prey attempting to escape, Kate could almost feel that the spider had no sense of urgency since it had already caught its victim and appeared more satisfied watching the fear displayed in the moth than actually eating it. She sighed watching the hopelessness of the trapped moth. Mouthing her verbal support, Kate encouraged the moth to put its foot on the gas. The job required concentration. There was no room for existential worrying or thoughts of alternative escapes. This was all about basic survival.

Bergman had been in his own web not too long ago but had found a way out and now undoubtedly feeling safe. Kate smiled because she knew that relaxed sheep were always easier to slaughter. Wherever he was, she knew that he was not sleeping well either, probably having dropped into the abyss where few ever recover from. Bergman certainly was smart enough to understand that she was on his trail, finding out by now that he had been out of line in every way there was. He had been where he shouldn't have been with someone he shouldn't have been with, eventually killing her with something that he should have kept in a safer place. But he was getting away with it. He was playing the game and winning, probably fooled into believing that he was at the top of this game.

CHAPTER 46

The Web

It was a warm summer morning, and by the light of the rising sun, it suggested that the day would turn into a scorcher by noon. As he looked out the living room window, the landscape with its earthy glow transformed the parsonage into the ultimate prize location for any pastor and his family. The problem, of course, was that he didn't have any family, and the officers of his church now had their doubts about him continuing his residency in this paradise. As he pondered this dilemma, he heard the unmistakable sounds of coyotes coming from the wooded area near the gatehouse, as he liked to refer to it as. Actually it was a shed and was called such by the officers of the church and the few members of the congregation that visited the parsonage. Walking into his bedroom, he picked up his .45 cal. Nighthawk and moved into the kitchen. Reaching up into the cupboard, he removed a bottle of old Vodka and topped off his coffee cup. Taking a drink and now satisfied, he opened the parsonage door and walked out onto the porch and looked down at the gatehouse.

If properly developed, the brain is capable of processing an astonishing amount of different information at the same time while under pressure. However, one's body often, unable to truly multitask, resorts to gross motor skills to survive. Even as Bergman understood that officers of the church were closing in on what mysteries existed in his life along with learning about his involvement in his wife's death, Bergman clearly recognized that his greatest danger remained with the Funston Police Department and a female detective by the name of Kate Heller. With a backdrop of fear surrounding the tenacious reinvestigation of two suspicious murder cases by the newly promoted female detective, he knew that it was only a matter of time before she found a way to come calling once again in his direction. He decided not to wait for her anticipated arrival but rather take advantage of the recent approved time off he had been granted to attend to his remaining personal affairs that still remained in Funston, Michigan. While thinking of this, he looked toward the far end of his yard near the gatehouse and spotted the darting gray body of a large coyote approaching the outer boundary of the shed. Making sure that his weapon was chambered and the safety was off, he walked down the porch steps and circled to the back of the parsonage and continued his movement down the tree line out of sight of the animal towards the shed. When he was within twenty yards, and in back of the structure, he carefully moved around the building to the front and surprised the coyote. The animal flinched, having sensed Bergman, but he was much quicker and squeezed off two shots keeping the Nighthawk custom front sight eye level of the animal. The 180 grain slugs found their mark slamming into the coyote's shoulder, shattering sections of the animals front leg in the process. It dropped like a sack of wet sand, with the animal unable to move. Walking over to the dying small wolf, he fired another shot into its head. "See one, think two," Bergman whispered his mantra as he turned and fired two additional quick shots at the charging second male, dropping him within ten feet from his shoes. Putting his Nighthawk in his holster, he walked the remaining distance to the parsonage shed to secure the necessary tools to bury the two coyotes. The animals had made the mistake of underestimating his skill level and had approached his property, as they often had done in the past, and today paid for their foolishness.

While some men killed for pleasure, some on the other hand like Bergman were blessed with a higher cause and actually enjoyed the power of holding another's life in their hands and watching the fear set in before their death. Such was his pleasure an almost holy one, he thought smiling to himself as he visualized Kate Heller and his planned trip to Funston. How would she react when he had her in his gun sight? Like most woman, she would probably try to nego-tiate her way out of the situation if he gave her a chance. She was after all beautiful and a prize for any male. As she looked at the gun, he imagined her suddenly feeling a thump deep inside her chest as she tried to figure her way out of the trap. Hell, she could even have a fatal heart attack as she measured her last moments. Bergman paused at the thought. Maybe he should ask Dr. Ogden what a fatal heart attack felt like. He laughed out loud as he thought about the foolish-ness of such a question and Ogden's obvious answer. "Nobody knows what a fatal heart attack feels like, Bergman," he would say. "There are few survivors to tell us."

After burying the two coyotes, Bergman walked back up to the parsonage and packed his pair of running shorts and two black T-shirts, plus the additional clothes that he would need for the next four days. Checking his watch, it noted that it was 11:30 a.m., which gave him a full six to eight hours to drive the remaining distance from Silver Valley, Wisconsin, to Funston, Michigan. Picking up his cell phone he placed a call to his church secretary to remind her that he would be gone for several days.

"Trinity Church," responded the unfamiliar voice.

"This is Pastor Bergman. Where is Debra this morning?"

"She had to make a dental appointment, Pastor, so I'm filling in for her until she gets back. This is her daughter, Candy."

"Oh, yes, Candy," now recognizing her voice. "You're on college break, correct?"

"Yep, and I'm going to enjoy these next two months, Pastor."

"Good for you, but I need you to leave your mother a message. She already knows that I'll be out of town for the next four days, but I was just calling to let her know that I'll be on my way shortly and she can call me on my cell phone if she needs anything. I've arranged for Pastor Schmidt to cover for me should an emergency come up. He'll check in with your mother sometime in the next twenty-four hours."

"I've written all that down, Pastor. She told me that you were going back to Funston, Michigan, on business matters. It seems like everyone is visiting Funston, Pastor."

"Really, who else is going besides me?"

"Maybe I said the wrong thing." said Candy.

"That's nothing to worry about, Candy. Pastors keep everything confidential," replied Bergman.

"Well, I understand Mr. and Mrs. Ogden have left for the area also."

Bergman remained silent for a few seconds before responding, "Well, maybe the doctor is attending some convention in that area and Betty is joining him. In any event, it's unlikely that we will meet up. Just please make sure that your mother gets the message that I'm on my way. Other than that, enjoy you summer," he said, now hanging up.

Bergman didn't like what he had just heard. Alan Ogden, and especially his wife, Betty, had been a pain in the ass ever since he had accepted his call to this town. Most of his life, people had underestimated him and paid the price. Even in seminary school in St. Louis, while out on the town during a weekend break with a girlfriend, he'd whipped the ass of some bike-riding dude who made a pass at his girl, actually broke the guy's right kneecap with a well-placed right heel. The poor bastard had figured him as a seminary student and an upstanding representative of the Jesus crowd, probably thinking that he would act like a gentleman and just cave. Bergman thought back to the guy's scream at the broken bone, ripped ligaments, torn cartilage, and a future world of visits to the orthopedic ward. No, the Ogdens better reconsider their intended mission to Funston since they were well past their prime in dealing with him should that have crossed their minds. As he finished packing, he carried the suitcase out the parsonage door and opened up the trunk and deposited his baggage inside. Closing the lid, he got into the car and drove down to the gatehouse. Walking inside, he returned in five minutes carrying a sack containing a quart mason jar. Getting back inside the car, he laid the jar on the passenger side of the car and pulled on to the gravel road in order to exit the parsonage grounds.

After three hours of driving, his hands felt like claws from gripping the steering wheel, but at least the temperature had started to change with an increasing brisk wind that now seemed to follow him into Rockford, Illinois. The heat was gone, now replaced with the lingering gray clouds and endless tollbooths that collected their nine-ty-cent penalty every fifteen to twenty miles to support the unneces-sary road repairs that kept the politicians and unions happy. Unlike Wisconsin, the roads of Illinois seemed to suffer from a strategy of using inferior materials that resulted in countless repairs every year to keep the union men working and the votes coming in for the pol-iticians that depended on their votes. Checking his watch, Bergman noticed that the time was 4:00 p.m., so he placed another call to his office.

"Trinity Lutheran," responded Candy.

"Candy, this is Pastor. Your mother is still out of the office?"

"Yes, the dental work took a little longer, so she just went right home. I'll be leaving in another thirty minutes since it's been real quiet around here. There have been no calls, Pastor, so as we say in college, 'You're good to go.'"

"Well that applies to you also, Candy, but before you leave, I was wondering if your mother mentioned who the Ogdens were staying with?"

"To my knowledge, the Ogdens are not staying with anyone, Pastor. Mom booked them at the Windham Hotel, near where Mrs. Ogden is attending her business conference. She said it's off the riv-er's edge in Funston and where all the money exists."

"It sounds to me like they will have a great time. Unfortunately, it's miles from where I'll be, and in my case, it's where the money is not, if you know what I mean."

Laughing, Candy said, "Well, make the best of it, Pastor, and maybe I'll see you when you return."

"That's a deal," he said as he hung up.

Watching for any highway patrolman, Bergman eased forward on the gas pedal until his speed reached seventy miles per hour. The additional acceleration caused the mason jar on the passenger seat to jiggle and move to the edge of the seat. Reaching over, he pushed it back against the cushion, but in doing so noticed that the spider had appeared out of its straw bed and was now attempting to climb to the top of the jar. He could sense the arachnid's frustration as it reached the top and the air holes but couldn't escape its glass cage. Turning back to the highway, he picked up the sign that indicated that it was under hundred thirty miles before he would cross into the outer edge of Michigan. Finding the channel for old-time radio programs, he turned on the station and was delighted to find that *Gun Smoke* had just come on. He had always liked that Western program and particularly enjoyed William Conrad playing the part of Marshall Dillon. It had turned out to be a perfect June day, now in the midseventies, and the closer he got to Michigan also increased the number of old big trees, which were fully leafed and fluttering alongside the road. Outside the car, the farm fields were active with last-minute farming and spraying. Being back close to Michigan had sharpened his memories of better times, complete with the threatening episodes of his fighting the legal system and the Funston Police Department. But now that he was about to return, he felt that the past had been patiently waiting for him.

Now past six o'clock, Bergman began to look for the welcoming signs of Funston that would proclaim that it was the former home of the gentle giant Wally, once the second tallest human in the world. Why the town was in love with being the second best never ceased to amuse him, but that was their deal, and it had been going on for over fifty years. As he turned the bend and noticed the water tower in the horizon, he knew that he was only about seven miles from Main Street, Funston. It was then that he saw the billboard advertising the Windham Hotel. Reading further the sign indicated that it was off exit 22 and Skunk Lane Road. The first time he had heard about Skunk Lane Road, he had asked one of the older members of the congregation why they just didn't change the name to something like Happy Valley or any name that suggested a better reputation than that of a skunk. The member had told him that the name was something historic, going back to the 1600s, and while some had suggested a change the people who wanted to retain it were worth a zillion bucks and had made it clear that they wouldn't approve of any changes. Rather than risk upsetting the wealth of the town it was decided that they could call it Chicken Shit Lane if they wanted. Wally's welcoming sign appeared first, only Bergman noticed that the marketing folks attached to promoting the giant had added some hyperbole, now indicating that Wally just happened to be the tallest former lawyer in the world. Bergman passed the entrance to the park and school named after Wally and continued down the road toward the Windham Hotel. In about five minutes, he saw the large white marble building and exit 22. Turning off he drove another half mile until the sign indicated Skunk Lane Road. Turning, he proceeded down the road past the Windham property two more miles until the Hampton Inn Hotel came into view. He had been familiar with the moderate-priced hotel as he had once attended a pastor conference at the hotel. Pulling his car into the long driveway, he parked near the hotel and got out. Locking his car door, he walked the few steps to the two large doors into the lobby area. As he looked around, he found the registration desk and approached the female clerk.

"Hello, sir, can I help you?" offered the girl.

"Yes, would you have a king-size bed available tonight?" asked Bergman.

Checking her room chart, the clerk replied, "We have a king on the second or first floor, both are nonsmoking."

"I'd prefer the first floor," said Bergman, "provided that it's not near the elevator. That constant noise is hard for me to handle," handing his credit card over to the clerk.

Picking up his card, she said, "Sorry, no king available on the first floor, but the room on the second floor is close to the stairs, which leads to the back entrance, Mr. Bergman." Now swiping his card, she asked, "If that will do, we'll book you in it right now. Will you just be with us tonight?"

"That's hard to tell at this point. Do you have space tomorrow should I need it?" asked Bergman.

Looking at her computer, she checked the next few days. "It looks like the next three days are all open at this point, Mr. Bergman, but why not check tomorrow morning before you leave just to make sure. In the meantime, we'll put your bill under the door at about six tomorrow morning. We provide a complimentary Funston newspaper in the morning along with a light breakfast. Is there anything else we can help you with, Mr. Bergman?"

"Yes, I have friends staying at the Windham down the road. Would you have the hotel phone number available?"

Writing it down, she handed it to Bergman along with a diagram of the Hampton Inn's property, which contained two swimming pools and several hot tubs.

Thanking the clerk, Bergman walked back out the door and directly to his car. Inside he removed his phone from his jacket and dialed the Windham.

"Windham Hotel, can I help you?"

"Yes, would you ring the room of Mr. and Mrs. Alan Ogden please."

Hearing the clerk connecting the call, it was but a short moment before Betty picked up his call.

"This is Betty Ogden."

Smiling, Bergman disconnected the call. "Ah," he thought, "it's better to visit the vampire in her cave than inviting her into your house." Opening the car door, he walked outside. The very idea of Betty the bitch being just down the road brought sudden laughter from Bergman. An attractive, almost-naked redhead sitting in one of the many hotels hot tubs turned in his direction in an apparent attempt to see what was so funny. At another time, he might have ventured over to the lady, but not today. He wanted to get the lay of the land before he considered supping with the devil's disciples at the Windham. Walking through the parking lot, he found his way down to the river's edge and the cement pathway that appeared to lead around the edge of the beach in the direction toward the Windham. Hearing the pounding of joggers' feet, he looked to the left and saw a five-foot-wide parallel asphalt running track that continued in the same direction as the cement pathway. Clearly the town's fathers had been smart enough to connect all the properties and fine restaurants to satisfy the old money that lived in these parts. Turning around, he headed back to his car and opened up his trunk and removed the small overnight bag containing what little clothes he would need. Checking, he made sure that his Nighthawk custom pistol was in the bag. Lifting it out, he shut the lid and moved to the front of the passenger side of the car and reached in retrieving his mason jar.

Putting the jar in his canvas sack, he walked to the hotel though the side door and headed to his room on the second floor. Unlocking the door, he stepped inside carrying his overnight bag and mason jar. Putting his bag on the provided floor luggage rack, he walked over lifted the bedspread on the king bed and slipped the jar underneath the bed. The counterpane felt slightly damp, so he fiddled with the heater under the window until he could feel some warmth coming out of it. Sitting on the bed and tired from the long drive, Bergman thought that he would take a nap before doing anything else. He soon found out that the bed was awful. The mattress dipped in the middle, and the sheets didn't have that fresh smell. Placing a call to the front desk, he demanded that they change the bedding or provide another room. In the end, it took more than an hour for the maid to appear, but at least he could then feel as if he were sleeping on new sheets. After brushing his teeth, he decided to take that overdue nap. Bergman slept an hour and woke up looking up at the ceiling, having a sensation of something lost and something gained, but couldn't explain either feeling. Laying back down, he tried in vain to fall back to sleep, but the alarm clock in his head went off every fifteen minutes. Frustrated, he called room service for coffee. He was through shaving and showering before it arrived. He knew what was bothering him but had avoided confronting it from the moment he got into the room. Until he got it out of his system, there would be no sleep, no peace. Then blocking his phone number, he dialed the only number that he had ever permanently memorized in the last three years, which was the cell phone number of Kate Heller.

"This is Detective Heller."

"Do you miss me yet?"

"Who is this?" she asked.

"I asked, do you miss me yet?"

"Look, I'm a police—"

Bergman hung up and smiled, thinking about what would be going through her mind as she struggled to figure out who was calling her. Now he could sleep.

CHAPTER 47

Cell Phone Puzzle

Getting up early, Kate turned on Fox news and watched Don Imas doing his normal routine of putting down anything that moved while encouraging his normal cast of characters to fill in any blanks of nastiness that he might have forgotten. She remembered when he was the morning anchor at another station and wore a cowboy hat as his symbol of ruggedness, but Fox had apparently shortened the rope that he was allowed to dangle. Today he didn't look healthy to her, with his hair combed to resemble someone who got his finger jammed in an electric socket. Picking up her coffee cup, she took a small drink and whispered to the television screen, "Imas, your time on this earth could be measured by a stopwatch." Shaking her head, she remembered reading once that death was the great mystery of life and so much depends on attitude and prayer. "Well, Don, you've got an attitude problem, so my personal suggestion is that you spend a lot of time praying." Turning away from the television, she called for Channing as she walked to the side door. Opening the door, she pulled back out of the way as Channing flew by her as he raced across their yard and spotted by her next-door neighbors two crabapple trees, which had recently been pruned. Watching her dog smell the bottom of the trunk, it was not long before both trees had been watered, and Channing then raced back to the house like a bandit fleeing a bank heist. Kate knew that it was pointless to scold the dog and the fact was that Debbie, the owner of the adjacent townhouse and crabapple trees, took it in stride, suggesting that Channing's devotion to watering the trees added flavor to the apples. The chime from the grandfather clock in the living room made her glance at her watch, which indicated it was 8:00 a.m. In another two hours, Curtis would be landing at the Funston Airport for their planned weekend to talk about the wedding date. The idea that he would be with her for a few days was something that she was looking forward to, even if she would be working most of the time. Curtis had suggested that he stay at a motel until they were married since he knew that she often worked at home and would have people coming and going. Kate had firmly said that wouldn't do, and besides, she wanted her life out in the open. To pacify his obvious determination to protect her image, she had agreed to allow him to sleep in the guest room, provided, as she pointed out, that visitation rights remained.

She had just finished her shower when her cell phone rang. "Hello, Howard, what's happening with my partner this morning?"

"I have the cell phone that you requested and wanted to drop it off so you can look at it."

"That was quick. You didn't have any trouble with the men in the evidence section?"

"None, it's amazing what a dozen donuts will do to cure resistance."

"Did you look it over last night when you got home?"

"Not a chance, Kate. This is your case, and I thought that you would want to review it in your own way. When and if you want a second opinion, I'll be glad to give that, but you're the boss and need to evaluate things first."

"You keep buttering me up this way, Corporal Singer, and you'll make Detective tomorrow," said Kate. "I'll be home for another two hours, so if it's possible, drop the cell phone off before ten thirty this morning. I'll be gone after that as I need to run to the airport and pick up my guy, who's coming in for a few days. This is the week we talk about wedding stuff."

"Well, happy days are about to begin, Kate, so I'll be there in short order so you don't have to worry.

"Thanks, Howard," she said hanging up. Hurrying to her closet, she removed her favorite white slacks and silk red blouse.

Laying them on the bed, she opened up her bottom dresser drawer and found the package of new Candies panties and Vanity Fair bras. As she started to dress, her cell phone rang again. "What the heck is going on?" she wondered as she answered her cell phone. "This is Detective Heller." Waiting a few seconds, she repeated, "This is Detective Heller, can I help you?" Kate knew someone was on the line because she could hear the open line and noise in the background and what appeared to be the sound of two people talking in the background. Maybe it was a television in the background, she thought. She was about to disconnect the call when the caller said, "Do you miss me?" or something like that. She was about to question the caller when whoever it was hung up. What a strange thing to say, she thought as she continued dressing. Now dressed, she picked up her cell phone and looked at the caller identifier and noticed that the call had been blocked. Clearly the caller didn't want his or her phone number to be traced, but then again what crank caller would want to be identified? Finished she hurried into the bathroom to put on her makeup before Howard arrived.

It was less than thirty minutes since his call to Kate when Howard pulled up in front of her townhouse and pushed on her doorbell. Within seconds, Channing and Kate came to the door.

"Howard, come on in and have a cup of coffee with me," said Kate while Channing sniffed at his leg.

Walking in, Howard look at her and said, "You look gorgeous, Detective Heller. Can I say that without getting in trouble?"

"This is a time, Howard, that if you didn't say it, you would be in trouble." She laughed. "I just hope my new husband-to-be says something equally as nice."

Following Kate into the kitchen, he placed the cell phone of the dead organist on the table. "It's the basic US Cellular Samsung model, nothing fancy. You don't see many of these flip-open type phones anymore," said Howard. "Why were you interested in her phone?"

"Because the funeral director that handled her arrangements had indicated that he was contacted to see if it was sent with her when they received her remains. The caller had been so persistent on the subject that the funeral home actually called the Funston Police Department. They told him it was part of their evidence box."

"Interesting," said Howard, "but I still can't see how this will help you."

"I'm not sure either, but it's the old saying about leaving no stone unturned. One never can be sure about anything because it's sometimes the little things that bring closure. I'm not good at cell phones, Howard. How do I look at the menu on this one?"

"Here, let me show you," he said while taking the phone from Kate. "First you just flip open the cover like this. See where it says Menu? Then just press the Menu button down, and it will display all the services it offers," he said, handing the phone back.

Kate, holding the phone, then pressed the button, and it displayed the different categories of Phone Calls, New Messages, Easy Edge, Display Sounds, and Multimedia. Doesn't seem like there's much here," she remarked.

"There really is, Kate. Each one of those areas usually stores past or current pieces of transactions that the owner has done or, for that matter, who has been trying to contact you either by phone or text messages. Take that Send button. On many phones it will tell you about the owner's last list of calls, unless they've erased them."

Pressing the Send button, Kate remarked, "Nothing there, Howard. All it says is no recent calls. What does Multimedia mean on the phone?"

"That usually is the section for the camera. As I indicated, this is a basic model, but it has the camera and audio feature, which means you can take pictures, record sound, and even do a limited amount of things like a movie camera can do. When you're done, you can even send them to another cell phone. That why as cops we have to be careful because every time we stop someone who has a camera, the possibility exists that our work is being recorded, maybe even sent to the media or possible the person's lawyer."

Thinking about this, she looked at Howard. "I never told you this, but the church secretary has told me that the organist took pictures of herself and Bergman making love in the church balcony. My initial feeling was that the Browning woman would have removed them a long time ago. You don't think that we could be lucky enough to have them on her camera, do you?" said Kate, getting excited.

"That's a real possibility, unless she erased them," said Howard. "It's also possible she might have sent them to Bergman to view. You know, Kate, it's not unusual for couples to have sex tapes of themselves making love. Mind if I look?"

Kate handed the camera back to Howard, and he pushed the menu button, which once again displayed the list of the camera's services. He moved down the list until he reached Multimedia and pushed the button until it displayed the word Camera. Below Camera, he found what he was looking for. Howard then scrolled down to the words My Images. He then returned the camera to Kate and instructed her to press the Menu button one more time.

Pressing the button, she viewed a series of pictures of Bergman and Browning engaged in various positions of lovemaking. "Pretty self-explanatory, wouldn't you say, Howard?" letting him look at what she found.

"Explanatory regarding sexual activity, but in my opinion, not enough to pin a murder on him," said Howard."

"You're right. I guess my idea didn't pan out regarding the camera."

"Maybe, maybe not, since the camera's memory indicates that it has over 123 shots on this thing. You've got a lot more pictures to look at, Kate. Although one can't be sure it appears that she took many other pictures after these personal ones. Why don't you skip to the front and work yourself backwards? That way we can see the last pictures she might have taken before she died."

Now familiar with how the cell phone camera worked, she moved to the last image recorded and displayed the picture. "Take a look at this, Howard. What do you think it is?" asked Kate.

"It's a small metal box with a picture of a Chinese woman in a garden. See the Mandarin orange trees next to her? Maybe it was her favorite odds and ends box given to her by a friend. It's also possible that it's just a box that contained tea bags for her evening treat."

Filling Howard's comments in her memory bank, Kate pulled up another picture. It was just a simple picture of what appeared to be her small library of favorite books resting on a self near her bed. "It looks like she was a fan of James Patterson. She must have ten of his books alone," commented Kate.

"What happened to Sandra Brown, Elizabeth Gage, and all the other female soft porn writers?" asked Howard.

"Oh, you read them too." She winked.

"No, I just check them out for my wife at the library when I pick up the latest Nelson DeMille or Lee Child novel. Now, those two guys are captivating and masters at keeping the reader interested," said Howard.

"You need to read *Fifty Shades of Grey*, Howard, in order to really keep up with what is going on in women's minds. Before you ask, no, I haven't read it since I understand the prose is beyond what a good Catholic girl like I should be reading, but some of my girlfriends have indicated that every new bride needs the book on her bed stand."

"I thought you said that you weren't a practicing Catholic."

"I'm not, but once a Catholic always a Catholic. It's like riding that bicycle, Howard, you never really every forget how. Well, it does seem that these pictures are a waste of our time, wouldn't you think?" Looking at her watch, she said, "Shit, he's about to land in fifteen minutes. Howard, I got to run, or he'll wonder where I'm at. Look," she said, handing him the camera, "I want you to spend whatever time you need and clear the rest of these pictures. I doubt there's anything on her cell phone, but let's make sure. When you're done, take the rest of the day off and take that lady of yours to dinner. We'll pick this up on Monday as I've got to practice becoming a bride."

Howard took the camera and walked briskly out of the house with Kate in hot pursuit as she locked the door and ran to her car. As she was pulling away from the curb, she opened her window and yelled what he thought was, "I'm shutting the phone down tonight."

Howard smiled, picking up on Kate's meaning, and how the two were going to probably spend the next few hours.

CHAPTER 48

Pure Gold

Saturday morning was sunny and cool. Good hunting weather, thought Bergman, as he got into his sweats and black T-shirt. He began his jog along the riverfront, heading toward the Windham Hotel. He always did his best thinking while running, and today's first subject was Betty Ogden, who about now based on her past history should be on the jogging track. He knew that the doctor would not be accompanying her but rather sitting in the lobby reading the Funston paper. Betty was the golfer, while Ogden was the bird watcher. Betty could probably put a leech on a fishing hook, while Ogden would prefer seeing his fish at some aquarium.

As he picked up the pace, he switched mental gears and gave some thought to his recent call to Officer Heller. He could tell that the call had surprised and confused her just by her voice inflection. Getting her number had been easy since she had left her card with him the day she had arrived on the scene of his wife being attacked. Like most people who are homogenous in how they live their life, she retained her original cell phone number. Well, as the saying goes, life is all about keeping your friends close and your enemies closer, and this woman had demonstrated that she was certainly his enemy. He knew what he had in mind for Betty, who operated everything on a tight schedule that rivaled the split-second timing of the flying wallendas. She would require some luck. With Heller, it would not be about luck, since information provided by the Funston Police Department indicated the policewoman spent a lot of time working out of her home. Both were smart women, and he had a working knowledge about both, since each had spent talk time with him. One regarding the assault on his wife, while the other on church matters. "But words are just air," he said to himself as he glanced ahead on the track for any sighting of his target. "Faces are the key, since they always tell you more if you pay attention." Most people don't know, but it is the house that holds the darkest secrets, and someday he would be visiting Detective Heller's house.

Walking through the Windham's large sliding glass door, Betty and Alan entered a huge patio that was probably larger than most hangars used by airlines to overhaul their wide-body aircraft. Following Alan, Betty realized that her husband was going to hunker down near the swimming pool whose dimensions qualified as an NFL football field. "Alan, I'm going to hit the track while you watch the teenage girls impressing their boyfriends in their new swimsuits."

"Have fun, Betty. I'm actually going to read Bill O'Reilly's new book on the assassination of Lincoln."

"You've got to be kidding. That story has been told in a thousand books over the years."

"I know, but this one is supposed to cover more information never released before. Anyway, it will keep me busy while you work on your figure. When you're done, we can have some breakfast," said Alan.

"That's a deal," she said as she started jogging toward the river's edge while the seagulls scattered at the sound of her approaching footsteps. Betty, a beautiful woman, had only one imperfection, according to Alan, which he had mentioned one day while admiring her bikini panties.

"You know that wonderful body of yours could use a little color," he had remarked that day.

Well, the morning sun, which felt good on her skin, should help a little more today, thought Betty as she turned and headed in the direction of the Hamilton Inn. She had planned on an earlier start, but this morning she hadn't received any complaints from Alan regarding her lack of color or needing to work on her figure as he convinced her to spend a little more time in bed. She had been into her jogging for about twenty minutes when she spotted a small section of woods resting at the edge of the trees about a hundred feet away. Moving off the track, Betty spotted the picnic table almost at once and decided that the extra time with Alan had sapped more of her strength than she realized. "That's what you get for thinking that you're eighteen again," laughed Betty as she welcomed the opportunity to sit down for a few minutes. The location of the table gave her the opportunity to relax and be unseen by most that would travel the path. Without the morning sun, the darkness of the wooded area reminded her of horror novel writer Stephen Jones, who once had written the words, "Who knows the darkest part of the woods and the path from there to the pub." Betty had sat quietly for almost ten minutes when she noticed the jogger in the distance stop and tie his shoelace before continuing his aggressive jogging pace. "He acts like he's behind his schedule," thought Betty as the runner moved past her location without glancing in her direction. Betty watched the man and his fluid movements as he continued his rhythmic strides away from her area. Then he stopped again as if something had drawn his attention. He began to look around but not toward the woods. Something about him was familiar, but what it happened to be escaped Betty. Like many runners, he was wearing the typical jogging pants, sunglasses, and comfortable satin T-shirt. The small letters CSU on the T-shirt meant nothing to her as he once again broke into a full jogging stride. Getting up from the bench, Betty walked back to the track and continued jogging toward the hotel off in the distance. "I don't know what it is about that river's edge and cool-looking water, but it makes me more interested in a margarita than ham and eggs." Tired, Betty reached for her cell phone and called Alan.

"Command center, this is Alan."

"Alan, this is Betty. You need to put down your book and pick me up at the Hampton Inn. That little extra time you were granted this morning has exhausted me. Meet me out front near the entrance, and we'll go out and have something to eat."

"All right, Betty, see you in about five minutes," said Alan.

Alan got up from his poolside chair and grabbed his book and started to head to the front of the hotel lobby. He couldn't help but watch the young couple at the end of the pool, each drinking a glass of wine. Unaware or unconcerned, it really didn't matter to the younger generation as the girl set her glass on the edge of the pool, stood, and pulled off her yellow top. The guy stood and took off his shirt and removed his swim trunks. Alan paused for a moment wondering how far this game was going to be played. To his amazement, the girl dropped her khaki swimsuit bottom and kicked it away laughing. She stood there a few seconds, made a few gyrations, then threw her arms in the air, then said, "Ta-da!" and bowed to the man. It wasn't long before they embraced and kissed and their hands ran over each other's body. Alan had seen enough and continued his walk to the lobby and out the hotel's front door to his car. The drive down the road to the Hampton took about two minutes. Betty was standing outside of the hotel and got into the car as soon as Alan pulled up.

"Where to now, my jogging queen?" asked Alan.

"Well, there are no officially approved nude beaches in Funston to the best of my knowledge, but it has a lot of secluded forest areas that could provide us unofficially clothes-optional choices."

"I'm beyond the carefree mosquitoes make no difference to me part of my life, Betty. You're a beautiful woman, but remember that I'm a doctor and it's my responsibility to help you avoid any unnecessary illness." Alan continued his drive looking for a good restaurant but noticed that Betty seemed to be deep in thought. "Did I disappoint you in what I said?" he asked.

"No, I'm actually hungry. It's just that I saw something on my limited jogging today that keeps nagging me. I had to take a break from the jogging, so halfway through the run to the Hampton Hotel, I left the track and sat down on a park bench near the edge of the woods."

"So what concerns you about that?"

"Another runner jogged right past the area where I was sitting. He couldn't see me since I was near the edge of the woods, but when he bent over to tie his shoe, I got a good look at the back of his T-shirt. I had seen that shirt before, Alan, but until right now I had forgotten where and who was wearing it. The shirt on the back had the letters CSU."

"So what are you saying since the letters mean nothing to me, Betty?" Pulling over, Alan parked the car in a small windswept lot. Alan waited patiently for Betty to explain what he had obviously been missing.

"I believe the man on the track was Paul Bergman, and somehow he has learned where we are staying. I believe that he was stalking me."

"Please, Betty, don't you think it could have been someone else? After all, he's on our mind, and that's the reason why we took this trip, to find out some information on him."

"The letters, Alan, represent Concordia Seminary University, and he was out on that track for some reason, unless his being there was coincidental."

"You know, Betty, that I don't believe in coincidences."

"What do you believe in, Dr. Ogden?"

"Well, truth and justice are a good start. But when one deals with Pastor Bergman, it seems harder to find than a nickel at the bottom of the Funston River. You know, Betty, we could all have made a big mistake about this guy. We could be married to our feelings and we just don't want to recant or retract anything because it would make us a little less smart. You understand?"

"I understand, Alan, and I don't think that either of us is being stubborn or egotistical. You're a great doctor and a loving husband, but frankly I want to lead a more normal life, not chasing the questionable life of my pastor, who should be leading us to the gates of heaven, not to woods where Alice in Wonderland lives. He was on that track, Alan, and he was not there looking for lost car keys. He was on a mission, Alan, and one that involved us."

"Then we best give this some serious thoughts when we find that restaurant that I promised you, Betty."

As Alan continued driving looking for a restaurant, he spotted a sign advertising the Purple Gang Restaurant, "five miles south, next exit."

"Now that's an interesting one," commented Betty. "I hope that it lives up to its reputation."

"What reputation?" asked Alan.

"Well, since you're not from these parts, it requires a little history lesson from a Michigan girl."

Watching for the next exit, Alan asked, "Tell me a little about the Purple Gang. Educate your husband."

"Well, to begin with and simply put, it was a gang that got its reputation in Detroit around 1920. They were an organized group of young Jewish bootleggers and hijackers who roamed Detroit and Chicago, killing rival gang members who got in their way of making money during the prohibition of alcohol."

"Sounds like a fun bunch of guys," said Alan.

"They were so much fun, Alan, that they ended up killing over five hundred members of rival gangs."

"What happen to them?"

"Well, first let me tell you how they got their name, Alan. As I mentioned they traveled from Detroit over to Chicago and on the way would stop at sort of a halfway point in the little town of Albion, Michigan. One of the owners of a business in Albion gave them the name of the Purple Gang, because, as he described them to his friends, "They're rotten purple like the color of bad meat." Eventually like all good arrangements, the gang fell out of favor with each other and just self-destructed."

Seeing the exit to the restaurant, Alan turned off the main road and entered the drive to the eatery. "So like a marriage gone sour, they just divorced?"

"You got it, Alan. That's also happens when you have a tired wife and she hasn't been fed. The next thing you know, she's searching for some attorney."

"Well, we're here, Betty, so let's see if I can save this marriage."

Two hours later as they were in their car and returning to the hotel, Alan asked, "Well, did it work, Betty?"

"You mean did you save our marriage?"

"Yes, but before you answer that question, I'd like to make one more stop before we go back to the hotel. Remember how we used to park near the river on a Sunday afternoon after going to the movies?"

"Sure, but it's light out now, Alan, and we're a little old to be busted by Funston's finest," she commented as Alan had entered a dirt road leading to edge of the beach front. Stopping, he shut the engine off and put his arm around Betty. It didn't take long before she put her head on Alan's shoulder. They sat there awhile looking over the river.

Finally Alan spoke. "You are a tough lady, Betty. But even tough people can get overwhelmed sometimes, so I want you to understand that what happened to you on the jogging track is not something that I have taken lightly. Bergman has met his match if his plan was to hurt you, because he has to go through me first from this moment on. You know, Betty, we're good people, and sometimes evil likes to go after good people. What these folks fail to understand is that when shit hits the fan, we're at our best."

Betty nodded. They kissed again, and she marveled at how happy she felt, how safe. She'd experienced more than her fair share of male inadequacy in the past years of her life, and up until she had met Alan, that had only meant pain. But with her husband, it was different. Safe in Alan's arms, she could look back and see that most of her life before Alan had been spent under a dark cloud of fear, waiting for a man's jealousy to explode in rage.

"Penny for your thoughts?" said Alan.

"I was just thinking about how lucky of a woman I am," she said as she wrapped her arms around Alan's neck and pressed her lips lightly to his. "I think it's, as the young people say, time to get a room."

Starting the engine, Alan paused for a moment and turned to Betty. "Well, did you like our brunch this morning?"

"Yes, and I hope that you did also since it was most unusual, wouldn't you say?"

"Very much so, Betty, especially having the host and staff all dressed up in the 1920s clothing. By chance did you notice the European porcelain that was so delicate that you could see through it? And what did you think about the teapot? It was painted with pink roses and lined with gold? I wondered what that was all about."

"All that was part of the Purple Gang trademark," said Betty. "The porcelain and china was used often as gang barter and was how they paid their bills when hiring mechanics to fix the bullet holes in their Ford cars. If you noticed, all their staff wore badges with names of former gang members. We were served by Abe and Ray, who were playing the role of the Bernstein brothers. I'm told that the Purple Gang was friends with Al Capone, who used to travel from Chicago to Detroit to import liquor from them. They have such roots in history that they got name-checked in an Elvis Presley song. Remember 'Jail House Rock.' Next time it's played, listen closely. Here, look at the receipt they gave us today," said Betty, handing it to Alan.

Alan, looking at the receipt, noticed that it said the Blind Pig. "Why do they have that name when the restaurant is called the Purple Gang?" he asked as he was now pulling the car back out onto the highway.

"Remember that no one was allowed to sell any liquor in 1920, Alan, so each place selling the illegal stuff was called the Blind Pig. At one time, my parents told me that Detroit had over fifteen thousand blind pigs operating illegally," said Betty.

"That's really interesting. Somewhere between college and medical school, I've lost touch with a lot of history, but fortunately I have you," he said.

"That's so true, my dear, and always remember V. I. Warshawski."

"Who?" responded Alan.

"V. I. Warshaswski, the woman author who once said, 'Never underestimate a man's ability to underestimate a woman.' We actually are a world of information, you know."

The reminder of the drive back to the hotel reminded Alan of rush hour, or as he remarked to Betty, nose-to-butt cars. For whatever was the reason, drivers all seemed to be in a hurry to get somewhere, with the result that no one was getting much of anywhere. Finally the drive to the hotel came in sight, and Alan turned onto the entrance of the hotel and parked the car directly below the window of their room.

Getting out of the car, Alan and Betty walked back into the hotel and up the stairs to their room.

CHAPTER 49

Disappearance

Bergman couldn't understand why Betty was not on the jogging track. He knew her habits since the first time he had seen her jogging on a Saturday morning on a track in Silver Valley. When he had walked over and said hello, she had even had invited him to join her some future morning, explaining that this was her routine every Saturday. Well, regardless, he was going to follow his plan even if this had failed this morning. After all Hebrews 11:1 said, "Faith is the substance of things hoped for, the evidence of things to come." On the way back to his hotel, he called the Ogdens' hotel room number with no answer. "What can you do when things begin to fall apart?" he mumbled to himself. "Just don't panic," he admonished himself. "Panic isn't listening. Panic has no ears, only a voice that comes to you like the winds of anxiety." He was smarter than this troublemaker, that he was certain of. Reaching the hotel grounds, he entered the property through the back entrance and took the stairs to his room. Swiping his magnetic card into the door lock, he walked in. Securing and double locking the door, he quickly removed his clothing and was about to take a shower when he glanced at the bedspread and noticed that someone had looked under his bed. To his horror, the jar was gone. For God's sake, the mason jar was missing. Why? It made no sense. What if someone opened the thing? "Control yourself," he said. He walked around the room looking to see if the maid had placed it in another location as she cleaned the room. "Think this thing out before you assume the wrong thing." Taking a break from the developing concern, he walked into the bathroom and poured himself a drink into one of the provided Dixie cups. Throwing the cup into a wastepaper basket, Alan returned to the living room and picked up the room's phone and dialed the reception desk.

"Hello, this is Angie. What can I help you with?"

"This is Mr. Paul Bergman, and I was wondering if the cleaning lady for this floor is still on duty."

"No, I'm afraid she will not be working again until tomorrow morning. Is there something that we can help you with, Mr. Bergman?"

"I've seem to misplaced a mason jar that I had left on my hotel room dresser. It's nothing of real value except to my daughter, who always gives it to me when I go out of town. It's a father-daughter thing, if you know what I mean."

"What was in the jar, if I might ask, Mr. Bergman?"

"I really don't see why that matters. The point of this call is that it is gone. But if you must know, actually nothing, because the value is in the sentimentality, his voice registering irritation."

The desk clerk, picking up on the change in Bergman's tone, replied, "I'll try to contact the maid at home and see if she can remember seeing the jar. I'll give you a call personally and let you know what we have found out. In the meantime, if you would like, I'll send someone up to your room to help you look for it."

"No, that won't be necessary. I've been jogging most of the morning and need some rest. I'll wait for your call, if you don't mind. Bergman, now satisfied that his wishes were going to be honored, lay back on his hotel bed and tried to imagine the day ending better than how it had started out."

It had been 2:33 p.m. when Bergman had fallen asleep on the hotel sofa while waiting for a call from the reception desk telling him that the mission was accomplished, that they had reached the morning maid, and she knew what had happened to his mason jar. Now waking up, he glanced at the phone thinking that he might have not heard their call back. Of course, as he had expected, the call had never come updating him on their search. Why should it, he thought, considering the type of help now employed by most hotels in a nation now served by more foreigners than Americans. Picking up the hotel phone, he dialed the reception desk.

"Front desk, may I help you?"

"Yes, this is Mr. Paul Bergman. I was expecting a call from your manager. Is he available?"

"You must be talking about Abdul. He's the only manager on duty today."

"Okay, it must be Abdul. Would you put him on the phone please."

"Sorry he's gone home for the day, but he left a message saying that if you called to tell you that he couldn't reach the maid. He said that he regretted this and that there would be no charge for the room."

"What's your name, young man?"

"Jeff."

"Well, here's the deal, Jeff, and don't take it personally. I'm not interested in a fucking free room. Your maid has misplaced something very important to me, and I need to recover it before the Mayan calendar kicks in."

"Sir, I'm sorry, but I don't understand what the Mayan calendar is."

"Jeff, how long have you been in this country?"

"I was born here, Mr. Bergman."

"That's good, but it's now clear why our school system is ranked around seventeenth in the world. You see, Mr. Jeff, the Mayan calendar has predicted that the world will come to an end in the winter solstice, but don't worry about this coming winter since the death of this globe is sooner than you think. I suggest that you visit your local library and read Michael Drasin's book *The Bible Code*. You see, young man, the author found the hidden message in the Pentateuch, which happens to be the first five books in the Bible. Thus he predicted that a comet will crash into the earth in 2012 and annihilate all life. He was wrong, of course, but the point of this education lesson, Jeff, has been done for only one reason. I want that goddamn mason jar that your maid has somehow misplaced, and I want it now before the world does actually come to an end. Call Abdul and get him off his prayer rug and find that woman and that jar now, or I'll start burning up the phone lines to your corporate headquarters in New York. That, my friend, will result in the unemployment of at least two people, maybe three at this five-star hotel," Bergman said while slamming the phone down.

Bergman stood and walked around the sunlit room looking at every possible hiding place for the jar. The room was a wall of framed pictures representing every conceivable historical fact that made up the town of Funston. One picture even had the city's hero Wally as he appeared in a circus act long before he became billed as the World's Tallest Lawyer. Walking over to the window, he pulled back the curtains exposing the wooden frame that ran along the window. "No jar there," he grumbled, as he continued to circle the room, even opening up the provided closet safe. Where in the hell did she put it!" he yelled, picking up the hotel's copy of the Gideon Bible and tossing it at Wally's hanging likeness. Abdul, the camel jockey, was taking his sweet time, and being an impatient man of God, Bergman considered walking down to the reception desk and kicking a little ass as a shortcut through the obvious bullshit that everyone was feeding this guest.

The ringing of the phone startled Bergman. "Hello."

"Mr. Bergman, this is Mr. Fakhoury returning your call."

"Who?"

"Abdul Fakhoury, the hotel desk service manager. My desk manager has indicated that you were unhappy with my not returning your call. Didn't he mention that the hotel maid couldn't be located, and that to compensate you for your loss of the jar, that I authorized a free hotel stay?"

"Mr. Fakhoury, I appreciate your offer of a free hotel stay, but to be frank, you could offer me an entire week, and it would not replace the value of that jar. As I have stated a number of times to your staff and yourself, it's not the cost of the jar but rather it has a sentimental value because it's my daughter's and that she sends it with me when I go out of town."

"Could I call you back, Mr. Bergman, as I believe the maid is trying to reach me."

"Yes, call me back," said Bergman.

Hanging up, Bergman digested his call from Abdul Fakhoury and reviewed what he had said or didn't say. It distilled down to a few key facts. Either Abdul had never called the maid as he had promised to do from their original conversation or was now for the first time receiving a call from the hotel maid after being contacted by the on-duty manager. In any event, it had the smell of a conspiracy and cover-up. "But why would this be necessary?" he wondered. The usual reason was everyone was now afraid of losing their jobs.

Bergman heard the phone ring again. "Hello"

"Mr. Bergman, we have found your jar and the maid is bringing it in right away. It appears she thought that it was a throwaway item and took it home to be used later for storing pennies, sort of a kid's bank. We will, of course, fire Mrs. Gonzales. Please accept my apology for the grief that this has caused you. It should be here within twenty minutes, Mr. Bergman."

"You don't need to fire the maid, Mr. Abdul, just get the jar to me, and we'll call it even. I'll be in my hotel room for the next three hours doing paperwork. Thank you for your cooperation, Mr. Fakhoury." Bergman laid the phone down and began to worry. Did the maid open the jar? If so what, would he do?

Bergman stood again and began to walk nervously around the hotel room. Glancing at his watch, then the TV screen, which was now on Fox News, he couldn't help but notice that the anchorwoman was talking about the ten things that people fear most. Dentists were number ten, with dogs, thunder and lightning, airplanes, scary spaces all making the list. It came as no surprise that spiders and snakes ranked in the top tier. Glancing at his watch again, he heard the elevator door and the bell ringing its arrival on his floor. Soon the knock on the door came, and he opened it up.

"Mr. Bergman, I'm Jeff from the front desk. Mr. Abdul asked me to give you this item with his sincere apology," he said, handing Bergman the jar.

"Thank you, Jeff, this will make my young daughter happy that I've found her special jar. Please give my appreciation to your boss for his involvement in locating the missing item," said Bergman as he began to close the door.

The Secret

Howard sat down at his dining room table and considered what he had discovered on the Browning cell phone. The organist had taken a picture of the spider before she had killed it with one of her shoes. Then while struggling to deal with the advancing venom in her system, she had taken another photo of the aggressive spider, who clearly was preparing to attack her a second time. Browning had snapped a total of four individual pictures before she had crushed it with her shoe, to include showing the location of the bite on her left leg. What she did with the spider was not recorded. Howard clearly thought that this brave woman was attempting to tell the secret of her developing death, but she left one important item out. What did she do with the dead spider? Nelson De Mille had written in one of his great novels, "Everyone loves a mystery." So very true, because if they remain a mystery as he said, it becomes a career problem for that cop. At least that was how Howard remembered it anyway. Going back over some of the earlier photos that were on the camera, he wondered about the one that showed the books on her small bookshelf in her bedroom. Browning seemed to have a particular interest in the author James Patterson. Retrieving the photo from the cell phone camera, he looked close at all the titles, until he found the one he was looking for, *Along Came a Spider* by James Patterson. "Very clever woman, this Browning," thought Howard. Reaching once again for his cell phone, he dialed Kate. As promised, she had decided even his call would go into her voice mail.

"Kate, this is Howard. The secret of the Browning phone is no longer a secret. Enjoy your time with Curtis. We'll talk about this on Monday. It can wait, so don't call back."

The sun was setting, and the sky turned from a grayish dirty color to a solid black as the twilight lingered then made its irrevocable decision to die on the horizon. Howard had walked outside, as he often had done when struggling to make sense from something that confounded him. He looked up at the stars, as he had often had done when he had been a teenage boy. Finding the Big Dipper, which his science teacher referred to as the Great Bear, he tracked the dipper-shaped group of stars in the constellation called Ursa Major, and as often was the case recently, he reconvinced himself that the dipper shape was not changing. He had brought up his curiosity on this with his wife, who attributed his observations to his working too hard. His fascination with the sky dated back to the days when he and a group of his friends would sit for hours on the roofs of their homes watching for UFOs. He was about to go back into the house when he heard the soft rhythmic sound of the ducks coming over his house as they used this part of the valley as their fly pattern going into Lake Darling, located about a mile away. In a few months, hunting season would return, and Howard would join the many other hunters heading to the lake to intercept the arriving ducks and geese. Opening the front door, he walked down the hallway and was about to return to his computer when it suddenly dawned on him where the dying organist put the spider. Was it possible that in her last moments, sick with a fever and hurting from the bite, that she had done it? Grabbing the organist's cell phone, he once again brought up her last pictures and looked at the beautiful container with the pictures of the oranges on it. "Checkmate," he said.

He went inside and walked back into the kitchen and laid the cell phone down on the table. Not a regular drinker, tonight Howard poured himself three fingers of Marker's Mark. It was a night that he wished that his family were around instead of visiting friends out of state. Clearly he was bothered by what he had found, since the camera contained the evidence that Kate needed to identify what had killed the Browning woman. What it did not tell was who did it, but he had his own ideas that he would cover with Kate. Now finishing his second drink, he stretched his head from side to side until each ear touched each shoulder. He then swirled his glass and sent the last swallow to exercise his insides. At the kitchen table, his mind replayed the images that he had seen on the camera. It was clear that Browning had given herself to Bergman, surrendering to him body and soul. Their lovemaking, with the exception of taking place in the balcony of the church, had appeared to be warm and all consuming. The woman was beautiful, and Bergman clearly had wanted her, and she had responded as the sexual uninhibited woman she appeared to be. So if he killed her, what was the motive for taking the life of a woman he clearly appeared to be in love with?

CHAPTER 51

The Light at the end of the Tunnel

She saw the sun come up in the morning and thought she had been awake all the time. Curtis was in the process of leaving the bedroom and had stopped for a moment to kiss her good morning. She remembered that she had put her arms around him to entice him to come back to bed, but he had encouraged her to remain where she was as he was going to do a little early-morning running since he couldn't sleep. He had told her that he was happy that they had agreed on a wedding date and that he just wanted to share this good news with the birds and neighborhood rabbits and anything else he would meet. Kate had pouted for a moment but quickly smiled at his happiness and waved him on to have a good time. For about fifteen minutes more, she remained in bed then sat up and decided to check her email, trying to work out what she would do while Curtis was outside enjoying his exercise. She alternated between clearing her vast amount of email and spam, plus going to the bathroom and working in a shower between her computer work and still preparing for Curtis's return. Over and over, she tried to dismiss comparing her former husband and Curtis, but facts were facts. Curtis simply was dedicated to making her happy before he allowed himself the same opportunity, while her former husband, as good a man as he was, had a more self-interest toward life and, in particular, lovemaking. Her husband, handsome and funny at times, along with being charismatic, could make her feel special one moment, while suddenly changing his mood should she fail to satisfy his testosterone-fueled advances. Then he could become frightening and predatory when he would cast his ice-blue eyes in her direction. Curtis's attentions were more inclined to be nobler, gentle, and somehow infinitely more precious, and although his longing to touch her was always apparent, he waited for her invitation.

Drying herself off from the shower, she put on a new nightgown and sat back down at the computer. Her first impulse was to throw the remaining email away, empty the trash, and pretend it had never was sent. But in the end she, just couldn't just erase everything without looking at least at the sender's address. She had scanned about seventy-five emails when she recognized Howard's. Pulling it up, she noted that it was short and apologetic for even leaving her a voice mail on the weekend of Curtis visiting. What voice mail was Howard referring to? It was then that she remembered that she had told him that she was taking the phone off the hook, so he must be apologizing for sending her something. Well, true to her word, while she didn't actually take the phone off the hook, she had ignored any calls coming to her cell phone.

Reaching for her phone, she checked to see if any messages had been received. Now noting that she had two messages, she dialed her phone number. The first message was from a telemarketer asking her to support the Michigan State Police Fraternal Order of Police yearly drive to help widowed police wives. She put the message on save and pulled up the second message, which was from Howard. As she listened to his message, her excitement increased, since it was obvious that he must have found something. But what, he hadn't said. She stood up as she considered her next move, but before she could complete her decision, she heard Curtis coming in the front door.

"Where are you?" he called.

"I'm in the bedroom, just working the computer."

Walking into the room, he said, "You're just as bad as me, Kate. We just can't leave the work alone. I guess it's just the nature of being a pilot and a police officer. Oh well, at least in your case you turned off the cell phone, which says something anyway," said Curtis.

"I cheated," she said sheepishly.

"You did what?" He laughed out loud.

"I cheated, because Howard left me a message on the computer apologizing for leaving me a voice mail. While you were running outside, I listened to the message," she admitted.

"So what did it say?" He gave her a hug of understanding.

"He said the Browning cell phone and what it contained was no longer a secret. I haven't called him back yet as I was waiting for you. I already feel bad enough clearing my voice mail since we agreed no company work as this was the weekend for us to plan our wedding."

"Look, Kate, I think that you might have me confused with someone else. We both are trying to please each other, and that's what's going to make our marriage wonderful. At the same time, sometimes our jobs will require our attention, and in my case, I want you to understand that my love for you is not ever going to be affected by the sudden necessity of you not having to do your work. Now please make that call so we both know what's behind door number two." With that, Curtis left the bedroom and called for Channing to go outside with him.

Hearing the back door close, she dialed Howard.

"Good morning, Kate. With all due respect to the boss, I thought I encouraged you to enjoy your weekend and that you didn't have to return my call."

"Curtis is the one who encouraged me to call you, so everything is fine. Is your wife all right with doing work on the weekends?"

"She is, and anyway she's not home this weekend. She took the kids with her to one of her sisters, who are having a birthday party. It's out of state, so it's me and the dog. The pictures are very good, Kate, and I believe she was trying hard to tell us who killed her. Once you look at them, I'm sure that you will be happy."

"That's really good news, Howard. You said that she killed the spider after it bit her with her shoe? Was there enough left of the spider after she killed it for us to possibly identify what type it was?"

"Yes, and there's even a picture of where the spider bit her. They seem clear enough for someone who is an expert in this field that they should be able to tell you what type of spider it was. Remember that the woman took a picture of it before she killed it, so once it's magnified, it should be easy to identify. Do you remember the picture she took of her bookshelf?"

"Yes, most of the books as I remember were written by James Patterson."

"I looked at it closer this time. One of those books written by him was *Along Came a Spider*. In my opinion, there's a clue there, Kate, and she was trying to tell us something, but darn if I can tell you what it was. I thought that the clue might be inside the book, if it still exists."

"That's a good thought, Howard, but let me return to the spider for a moment. Did she take any picture that would tell us what she did with the spider after she killed it?"

"No, and that surprises me since she did everything else to help us. Wait a minute, wait a minute. Maybe she did and we're not thinking. Remember the can with the picture of a Chinese woman on it? We couldn't think what the small can was for. Like the book, if we can locate the can, it might answer a lot of questions. What's to say that she didn't toss the dead spider into the can? Find the can, Kate, and we may find the spider she put in it. Find the book, and it may have some written notes in it. Who was in charge of cleaning out her apartment?" asked Howard.

"That I'm not sure of, but maybe Captain Wagner can give us a hand on this one. You've done a heck of a job, Howard. Something tells me we're about to close this case very soon. Let's meet at the Funston Police headquarters on Monday and go over everything."

"Kate, before we hang up, did you set a date with your guy?" asked Howard.

"Yes. Two weeks from Monday right here in Funston. We decided on no big wedding, just a simple ceremony. Curtis has a house in Lift Bridge that's fairly large, along with a landing strip near his property. I'll tell you more on Monday."

"I'm happy for you, Kate, real happy for you. Good night."

"Good night, Howard."

Kate heard the door open and the racing feet of Channing heading to his doggie bed. "I'm still in the bedroom, Curtis."

"Did my bride-to-be receive some good news?"

"Yes and no. Howard found pictures on the organist's camera that almost identifies the murder weapon, which of course was always what I thought that it would be, a spider. He thinks that they are clear enough to determine its species. The doctor who performed the autopsy always insisted that it was a brown recluse, which I doubted because the venom from that spider is not potent enough to kill most people. On the other hand, if it's a Brazilian wandering spider like the one which attacked the second boyfriend of the organist, well, then, things should get real interesting for Pastor Bergman."

"So you think that Bergman killed the organist and tried to kill her second lover?"

"Yes and his wife also," said Kate. "The problem is, we still don't have the spider, although Howard has me convinced that the organist put it in a small metal canister."

"So he's found the spider and the can?"

"No, not yet, but we're working on it," said Kate.

"What about Bergman?" asked Curtis.

"What do you mean?"

"Well, just because he kills her doesn't mean that he couldn't have come back later before the police found her and took the evidence, does it?"

Kate looked at Curtis and smiled. "So Bergman has the spider?"

"Honey, I'm just a pilot, not a detective, but let's just say that he was the one who originally gave her that metal can. He may have taken it back fearing that it could identify him, and just maybe not even know what she had put in it. Wouldn't that be funny? Guy kills girlfriend with dangerous spider, and she finds a way during her last moments to return it to him."

"I think that you might be on to something, Curtis. Maybe after we find that box containing the spider, we will need to take our honeymoon to New York and reopen the investigation into the fatal crash of TWA Flight 800 that exploded in midair in 1996. Many people still believe it was brought down by a missile, not mechanical failure."

"Why do I get the feeling that I'm being made fun of?" Curtis laughed.

"You're not, sweetheart, it's just that the light in the tunnel seems to be getting further and further away no matter how many clues I stumble onto."

"Maybe you just need to look at the glass as half full, Kate. From what you've told me, no one has suggested that if you fail, that a transfer to North Dakota is a possibility. Besides you're going to be my wife in fourteen days, which guarantees you free air travel for life, a nice home, and a large closet to hang up those teddies."

"Come to bed, Curtis."

"I'm a little tired, but thank you for your interest," he said shyly with a smirk.

Kate stood up and ran her fingers through his hair while she said, "Keep me up a while longer."

Curtis suddenly found his lost energy and put his arms around her. This was something that he was certain would have a happy landing for both.

Little Things Mean a Lot

Rolling over, Kate smiled as she looked at a wide-awake Curtis. "Do you have any questions for me?"

"Like what?"

"Like what's going to happen next when the justice of the peace says, 'I now pronounce you man and wife'?"

"If I need to know anything, you'll always tell me, isn't that correct?" asked Curtis.

"Of course."

"Then the only real thing that I need to be absolutely certain of is that you will have no reservations about making our home in Lift Bridge, at least for the time being. You know that I would have gladly moved to Funston and commuted to my base city to preserve your career in a heartbeat. When you close this case, there's little doubt that you will be offered a promotion, so I truly understand the sacrifice that you are making Kate, but this does not mean that I consider my career more important than yours."

"Really, Curtis, the decision was not that difficult. If I'm as good as you feel that I am, then things will work out. What's to say that I couldn't develop another career? Unless I've missed something, there are not any private investigators for miles surrounding Lift Bridge, and I sort of like the idea of going independent. Besides, my partner Howard Singer needs an opportunity to become a detective, and in my opinion, he's got the right stuff."

"Well, I guess that settles it then. You finish the Bergman and Browning case, and you become the temporary retired first lady of Lift Bridge. What more could a new husband ask for while having his bride near him with her arms around him every day?"

"I wish I had the rest of the morning off to begin practicing my bride role, but Howard and Captain Wagner are expecting me in the office this morning," said Kate as she rolled the covers off herself and got out of bed. "You stay and rest a little while longer, or at least as long as Channing allows you before he wants to go out." Not waiting for an answer, Kate hurried into the bathroom and turned on the shower.

Finishing dressing, Kate walked back into the bedroom to look in on her knight in shining armor. Smiling she leaned over and kissed her fiancée on his cheek and quietly hurried down the hallway and out the door to her car. She reached the highway in less than two minutes only to find a developing traffic jam. "What in the heck," she proclaimed, only to see two Funston police cars speed past her on the restricted lane used for emergency traffic, followed by the blaring siren of an ambulance following the two black-and-whites. *Must be heading to the Funston Hospital,* she thought as she turned off the highway an onto a two-lane road that would take her to the station uninterrupted by the backup. The clouds overhead, which had been threatening since she had left the house, suddenly began to let loose. "What next?" she thought as she turned her wiper blades on full cycle. She could barely see the city's towering buildings pocked with windows as the charcoal clouds that stubbornly hung over the area prevented any clear visibility as they shielded the rays of the sun. The crisp air along with an accompanying light breeze was just enough to make her grateful that she had remembered her light police jacket. Picking up her cell phone, she called Howard to alert him that she was running a little late.

"This is Corporal Howard," came his official-sounding voice.

"Howard, this is Kate. The main highway into the office is jammed up, so I'm running about ten minutes late. Sorry about that."

"Yeah, I understand, so I'll see you there in a few minutes. Any idea what's causing the backup?"

"No idea, but two black-and-whites were leading an ambulance into the hospital. See you soon," she said laying the phone back on the seat. Kate was still thinking about an apparent emergency when she parked her car and hurried into the reception area of the station, now dripping wet from the rain that hadn't seem to let up.

"Hello, Daisy," she said to the receptionist. "Did Howard or Wagner arrive yet?"

"Wagner arrived just before you and went to his office. Howard isn't here yet, but I'll let him know that you have arrived. Should I send him to your office?"

"Yes, and take messages for me today since I should be in a meeting for the next two hours."

Walking down the hallway, Kate passed by Wagner's office, but noticed that it was empty. She continued down the corridor past another three offices until she reached hers. Opening the door, she turned on the lights only to be greeted with the noticeable smell of flowers. Looking to her left toward her console table, she smiled as she viewed the large arrangement of pink roses. Walking over to the flowers, she pulled the card signed, "Love, Curtis," and put it in her purse.

"Good morning, Kate," the voice behind her said, almost causing her to knock over the vase.

"Oh, I'm sorry, I didn't mean to scare you," offered Howard as an apology.

"God, they told me that you hadn't arrived yet. I guess that the wedding plans are making me come unglued. Anyway, I'm glad to see you're here. Maybe we'll have a few minutes to ourselves before the captain wants to see us."

"Sure, what would you like to cover first? And by the way, what in the world is that smell?"

"The smell is from the roses over on the table. Curtis is my flower man ever since we've met. He's already purchased more dozens of roses than my former husband had in the three years that we were married. But don't misunderstand, he was a good man, just didn't do the flower thing. Anyway, the reason why I wanted to speak to you is that in the very near future, I will be advising Wagner that I'm resigning from the Funston Police Department after I complete these two cases. Curtis and I have decided to begin our marriage in Lift Bridge rather than him having fly back and forth to see me. Before you wonder, yes, he did offer to put my career first, but it was my decision to move. In the future, police work will still be part of my life, but I've decided to follow a different path. You have a great career developing here, Howard, and I'm going to do what I can to make that known before I leave."

"I don't know what to say, Kate, other than I'm in complete shock. There's little doubt that in a short period of time you would have been given a command position. Needless to say I'm happy for you both," said Howard. "Thank you for your vote of confidence in me, but we all recognize how things work at our level. Mistakes have a habit of filling the largest section on one's résumé. Still I appreciate your words of encouragement."

"Thank you, Howard, but let's move on. We probably have very little time left. Now tell me what you think about that little metal box that you suspect holds the key to what we are searching for."

"Well, as I mentioned over the phone, it's my feeling that the organist knew that she was in trouble from the bite and used her last moments to try and help those that would investigate her death, although I'm certain she held out hope that it wouldn't come to that. When she killed the spider, somehow she realized that her assailant needed to be found in order to prove what happened and what did it. She must have had a lot of courage, Kate, to be thinking ahead as she did. In her dying moments, she discovered the metal box in her bedroom and put the spider's carcass in it. She probably figured that eventually the right people would find the box and open it and put two and two together."

"But why wasn't it found by our investigating officer and turned over to me like all the items were, except the cell phone? Something still is not right about this, Howard. The guys in the evidence room may be determined to protect one of their colleagues, but only to a point. It's one thing for them to feel that this female detective is messing around on the sacred ground of one of their buddies, but they still are police officers."

"I know, Kate, and that's why I believe that the investigating detective never found the can."

"Then who's got it?" she asked.

"That's the million-dollar question, but I have a guess, Kate." Howard was about to explain his theory when the receptionist stepped into Kate's office.

"Hey, gang, I'm sorry to break up this meeting, but Wagner wants me to give you a message with his apologies. It would appear that the dragon lady, or officially our new attorney general, wanted to see him at her office right away. That woman either enjoys chewing his ass or she just likes his company. Anyway, he said to tell you both that he has to reschedule."

"Thanks, Daisy, for the update. And by the way, I appreciate you putting the flowers in here. The boys can be brutal trying to make me explain how hard I had to work to earn them," she said smiling.

"You're welcome, Kate. Curtis does seem to be a thoughtful guy. You are one lucky woman. Tired-looking, maybe, but one lucky woman," Daisy said as she left the office laughing.

Kate, noticeably blushing, turned to Howard. "Don't say it, Howard, just continue with your thoughts on the metal box."

Howard, putting his hands up signaling surrender, didn't even smile for fear that Kate would pull her gun. "Well, as I started to say, the reason why the investigating detective never found the can was that it was removed by the killer before he arrived. It's my guess that the organist was visited by the killer first and that he had brought the deadly Brazilian wandering spider with him, probably in some other type of container like the metal box. You would know who that guy probably was if the doctor who did the autopsy had any level of competence."

"What do you mean, Howard?"

"It's my guess that Gayle knew her killer very well and probably had sex with him that day. It's also my guess that the doctor who did the autopsy was more concerned with establishing his opinion that she was bitten by a brown recluse spider and overlooked checking if she had engaged in sexual intercourse before her death. His sperm was the DNA and the fingerprint that you should have been given to help move this case along. Anyway, after having sex, they took a nap, giving the killer an opportunity to release the spider from the can into the bed. He leaves, giving the spider the opportunity to do its job, and comes back later to check on Gayle. Finding her dead, as he expected her to be, he then takes back the can, not realizing that she had put the dead spider in it and left. Pretty wide theory, but it's the best that I can come up with on short notice," said Howard.

Kate studied Howard for a few seconds wondering if he was serious or just making conversation. "You might be heading in the right direction on this one, Howard, but unfortunately as you know, Gayle Browning was cremated and we will never find that DNA, and let us not forget that she was playing slap and tickle with Perry Sinclair as well as Paul Bergman and maybe others."

"True, but find the metal box, and just maybe we find the killer," said Howard, not wanting to give up his theory. "We sure need to interview this unholy pastor. He's got the motive for killing his organist more so than this guy Sinclair. She had, after all, taken pictures of him doing the dirty deed, and his wife had found them in his car by accident, and I believe that this somehow led to an argument and her death as well. The man was drowning in his mistakes, Kate, and was covering them up as fast as he could. The jury bought his sob story regarding his wife, but his church organist was beginning to be a major problem to his career and of course at the same time was beginning to lose interest, having met up with her new friend Perry Sinclair, who from everything you told me really wanted to marry her. My guess is that she enjoyed his business card more than that of a pastor and all the benefits that come with his wallet. Bergman couldn't have been making more than sixty thousand a year at his church, while good old Perry was pulling in about one hundred fifty thousand dollars plus his investments. Money isn't everything, as we both know, but the divorce rate is very high in the ministry as wives and girlfriends realize that a pastor's salary doesn't get you passage on the *Queen Mary* cruise line."

"As you've said, Howard, it's not always about money with a woman. Sometimes it's about love, and Sinclair did want to marry her. Remember that he did purchase her a ring that was over twenty thousand dollars, that somehow has disappeared as well."

"Maybe, just maybe, when we find the metal box, the ring will show up as well," said Howard.

"Here's what I would like you to do, Howard. You have a better relationship with our guys in the evidence room, so I would like you cleanse this part of our investigation by having another talk with the boys just to make sure that they are not holding anything back. Later I want you to visit Dr. Patel and have a man-to-man talk with him regarding his autopsy and find out why he didn't attempt to determine if Gayle had sexual intercourse during the last hours of her life. My guess and yours is that he's more inclined to share things with a man than a police officer in a skirt. While you're doing this, I'm going to pay another visit on the Sinclair family, hopefully the husband if not the wife, maybe both."

Leaving police headquarters, she noticed that the sun was beginning to break through the gray pallor that roofed the city. The brightness, while still unable to bring full color to the hues of the grass, still managed to lift the spirits of an individual. Passing a tall eucalyptus, she rolled down the window and could almost taste the damp flavor of the tree. As she continued her drive to interview Perry Sinclair, she turned south onto highway 59 and followed her way to the bottom of the hill, until she stopped in the parking lot of one of Funston's spectacular river-front beaches. The sun now fully out reflected off the water creating a silvery shimmer. It was, she thought, a place that she must bring Curtis to visit before they went on their honeymoon. After all, newlyweds dream that their honeymoon will last forever. She felt that if they were together today right now, feeling as she did the dream would be a reality. Like the unfolding wings of a blue heron waking from a long day of rest at the river's edge, Kate knew that it was time to continue her journey. Unlike the blue heron, who would often walk the edges of the river in search of minnows, she needed to illuminate one of her own little fish. The time had come to abandon the pretense of coincidence and turn the law dog of her efforts in the right direction. Turning around in the parking lot, she pulled back out onto the highway and headed to Sinclair's bank.

More to the Point

It was a large bank, one of those that used an awful lot of security glass to protect its tellers. Kate never cared much for this type of operation, preferring instead the friendliness of the small bank and its tellers, who remembered your first name and would even take your coffee can full of coins to run them through free. Banking was much different today, with the financial institutions operating much like their brother airlines, who made more money charging for over-weight luggage than the profit from the sale of a ticket. The First Bank of whatever, Chase, and other money movers now nickeled and dimed their customers by charging a fee in some cases just to talk to a teller or imposing a penalty for those wonderful late fees, which were the greatest of all scams on the poor. Of course they weren't the only member of society that scammed the public, unless of course you felt that it was a fair exchange of business to charge a late-paying credit card holder a 28 percent interest fee on future transactions should you miss a single payment. It was only a few short years ago that society considered anyone charging another person a 10 percent fee was equal to being a member of the Mafia. Walking down the marble floor toward the personal banker offices, Kate diverted away from the cages and approached the service desk.

"Yes, can I help you?" asked the cheerful, high school-aged girl.

"Yes. Can you tell me if Mr. Perry Sinclair is working today?"

Looking somewhat nervous, she asked, "Mr. Sinclair, our senior vice president?"

"Yes. My name is Kate Heller, and if he's in, I'd appreciate you letting him know that I'm in the lobby, Ms., err, I'm very sorry, but I didn't get your name."

"It's Judy, Ms. Heller, and to be honest with you, usually Mr. Sinclair will only see someone who has made an appointment." Looking down at her calendar, she said, "I'm sorry, but your name is not on the list he's provided me. It's best if I schedule you for a future appointment."

"Judy, I neglected to give you my card," she said as she handed it to the young receptionist.

As she looked at Kate's card and weighed the possibility of facing the wrath of a senior vice president being upset or going up against the law, the decision was made quickly. Pressing the intercom, Kate listened to the conversation between Judy and Sinclair's office.

"Mr. Sinclair's office, this is Gretchen. Our instructions were that Mr. Sinclair was not receiving any calls this morning."

"I'm sorry, Gretchen, but I have a Detective Kate Heller from the Funston Police Department wishing to speak to him."

"Mr. Sinclair is on a long-distance call with our corporate office in London. I can't disturb him now, Judy, or there will be heck to pay," said Gretchen.

Kate wrote a note on a piece of bank paper and handed it to Judy.

"She says she'll wait, just let him know, please." Judy heard the phone being slammed down as she turned back to Kate.

"I heard, Judy, just don't worry, everything is going to be fine. Meanwhile as I wait, can I ask you a few questions?

"Sure, as long as I'm not in trouble."

"No trouble, Judy, just asking for a little help as I wait. How long have you worked for the bank?"

"Almost two years. They're pretty good about hiring high school kids, Detective Heller. If we do a good job, they keep us on for summer vacation relief when we go to college."

"Seems like a nice place to work, Judy. Does that computer of yours tell you who might be a bank customer? Don't be frightened, Judy, I'm not going to ask about anyone's bank account, just if they bank here, nothing more. If you're worried, I can get the information another way."

"These questions do worry me, Detective Heller, but let's give it's shot anyway," she said.

"Just between us girls, and this goes no further than you and I, could you tell me if Gayle Browning was a customer of this bank?"

"Was?"

"Was or is, it really doesn't matter, Judy."

Kate watched as Judy did an apparent search of the bank records. Amazing how kids of this time period can master these computers, she thought. Watching Judy's eyes, she could tell that something was puzzling her in what she was reading.

"Everything all right?" asked Kate.

"Yes or so, I think so," said Judy. "It says that she had a checking and savings account, but both are now cancelled."

"Well, there's nothing unusual about that, Judy. People often change their banks." Kate watched the girl, and she could tell that something else was concerning her but was hesitant to discuss what it was. Although she didn't want to put pressure on a kid, Kate knew that something was wrong, so she decided to play her Detective card. "Tell me what your computer printout says, Judy. I'm working on a serious police matter that could save future lives."

"It says that both accounts were personally cancelled by Mr. Sinclair, something that would be most unusual."

"Why?'

"Well, because that usually has to be done by our finance department since checks have to be issued when a person closes out the accounts. It's just not something that a senior vice president would normally be responsible for." Judy was about to say something else when her intercom buzzed.

"Yes, this is Judy."

"Mr. Sinclair will see Detective Heller now. Please find one of the floor mangers to escort her to the conference room on the second floor," said Gretchen.

"I heard it, Judy. Thanks for the girl-to-girl talk. Here's my card and personal phone number should you remember anything else we might need to talk about. You won't have to have anyone escort me since I've been here on business before. I happen to remember where the conference room was. Getting up, Kate shook Judy's hand and walked over to the elevator and pushed the second floor. Kate had always hated elevators ever since she was a child. As the door opened, Kate hesitated as she carefully made sure that the floor of the elevator was in place, having read too many stories about people entering an empty elevator with no floor. Satisfied she entered and felt the sudden lift of her enclosed box. At the second floor, the doors opened, and Kate walked out of the elevator and down the carpet floor until she reached the clearly marked conference room B and entered. Sinclair was sitting at the end of the table clearly annoyed. She noticed that he was not wearing his wedding ring.

"You know that this is going to cause talk among the staff, don't you?" said Sinclair.

"Why, Mr. Sinclair? You're not dating me. We are not carrying on any secret love affair like you did with Gayle browning. Sure, I'm a Detective, but that could mean only that I need to see you because of one of your banks customers might have my concern and nothing else. I won't take up much of your time, so I suggest that you relax and let me finish doing my job. Anything else will only draw unnecessary attention that you don't need. I'm here today not to accuse you of anything but actually to try and find a way to remove you from my radar completely. I see that you are missing your wedding ring today. If it means what I think, that's unfortunate, Mr. Sinclair, but in all honesty my sympathy goes out to your wife first, because she is the victim, not you."

"Can we skip the sarcasm, Detective, and get on to why you are here today."

"Certainly, Mr. Sinclair, it's about the murder of Ms. Gayle Browning."

"She was bitten by a spider, Detective, not murdered, even the papers said that."

"Yes, and as I recall you were also bitten by a spider, but you got lucky, didn't you? Both of the spiders were from the same arachnid family, or to put it another way the Brazilian wandering spider family. How are your wife and daughter doing, Mr. Sinclair? I'm asking only because we are still not sure that you were the intended target of the person that sent you the Spider."

"My wife and I have decided that it was best that I move out for a while so that's the reason for the missing ring. She hasn't filed for a divorce yet, but my guess is that it's only a matter of time. If my wife and my daughter are in any danger, I have a right to know, Detective."

"That I understand, but we can reduce this concern by you helping me answer a few questions."

"Do I need a lawyer?"

"We all will need a lawyer at some point in our lives, Mr. Sinclair. That's your choice, but I'm not charging you with anything yet."

"Ask your questions, Detective Heller."

"Did you have sex with Gayle the day of her death?"

"No, not even the last month of her life, but not because I didn't want to, of course. You see, I was having male difficulties, if you understand what I'm saying. My doctor had put me on a special drug called Jalyn to help me with an enlarged prostate. It has some side effects in the beginning, which causes in some cases a lowering of a man's testosterone. It also embarrassingly can, on occasions, prevent a man from performing, if you understand what I'm saying, Detective."

"Don't be embarrassed, Mr. Sinclair. I've been married once to a very fine man who unfortunately was killed defending his country and will soon to be a new bride to another fine man. I understand when a man can't salute the flag, if you know what I mean. So was your not having sex with Gayle causing any other problems that I need to know about?"

"No, but I was suspicious that she had resumed her intimate relations with Paul Bergman during that difficult period."

"What made you feel that way, Mr. Sinclair?"

"Little things, like small gifts."

"Not a twenty-thousand-dollar ring, I take it?" said Kate.

"No, more in the area of reading material and cutesy little metal boxes with candy in it. Sometimes she would leave them in open sight to make me jealous. That's not to suggest that she didn't intend to marry me. After all, she didn't return the expensive ring that I gave her, which said something, didn't it?"

"What it said, Mr. Sinclair, was that you were a fool. Women don't always return gifts of that value, feeling that the person that gave them the booty has been paid in full. It's your life, Perry, but it seems to me that you were outmatched in this relationship, but it wouldn't be the first time for a man, just maybe your first time. As I look at it, Mr. Sinclair, so far nothing has gone the way that you planned, and I imagine that's what your wife has already told you. Yet the good news is that I doubt that you had anything to do with the murder of Gayle Browning. The bad news, however, is the killer is still out there, and it's obviously the case that you've pissed him off and that he's into payback. A few more questions, Mr. Sinclair. Did you pay for the Gayle Browning funeral?"

"Yes."

"What did you do with that twenty-thousand-dollar ring that you bought her?"

"That I have no idea about. The last time we were together, she was wearing it. When she died, I tried to find out about it, but it just disappeared. Maybe your police have it or the medical examiner pulled it off her finger and just forgot to return it. It's also possible that Bergman has it since it appears to me that he was the last one to see her. What I do know is that the funeral home didn't see it on her when they prepared her for the cremation. My wife has found out about it and as you can understand feels some of the money that I used to pay for it was her money."

Getting up, Kate started to leave but thought better of it and asked, "How are you feeling outside of your marriage difficulties?"

"You mean the spider bite recovery?"

"Yes, it was my understanding that the bite can have some aftereffects."

"No, that part seems to be all right. Interestingly enough, you're the second person today who has asked me how I was feeling. Do you remember a doctor by the name of Alan Ogden?"

"Yes, we've had more than one conversation during the last month. That man saved your life, and I consider him an excellent infectious disease doctor."

"Well, he called me yesterday as he's in Funston vacationing with his wife for a few days. I must confess that I was very impressed that in this day and age that a doctor would take the time to check up on a former patient."

"He certainly is a special person, Mr. Sinclair. We should all be so lucky to have him as our physician. Did he indicate where he was staying?"

"No, he didn't, but my caller ID indicated that he was calling from the Windham Hotel."

Writing the information down, Kate said, "Thanks for your time. Remember to call me if you ever need to talk about anything. Oh, I have one more thing Mr. Sinclair."

"Yes?"

"You have a sweet young receptionist downstairs by the name of Judy. She cleared my call directly into your personal secretary. Now it's not my business to know who you choose to hire, or for that matter choose to fire, but I'd be very disappointed to learn that Judy would lose her job due to your private secretary finding fault with her doing her job." Kate watched Sinclair digesting her comments, but he elected not to respond. Thanking Sinclair, Kate left the conference room. As she got on the elevator, Kate checked the internet on her cell phone and found the phone number of the Windham Hotel. Crossing street to her car, she slid in and dialed the Windham.

"Windham Hotel, this is Sue."

"Sue, this is the Funston Police Department, and I need you to verify that you have guests by the name of Alan and Betty Ogden registered. You do! Thanks for your time, and please don't alert them to my call," she said, hanging up.

The Mechanism of Death

"I'm here to see Dr. Patel," said Howard to the attractive nurse.

"Yes, he's expecting you, Officer. Please have a seat, and I'll call you when he finishes with his patient."

Howard sat down and marveled at all the certifications displayed on the wall. Getting up, he walked over and started reading each one. "The Commonwealth of Massachusetts awards Doctor M. Patel certificate of appreciation for his work in Forensic Pathology." "Very impressive," thought Howard, as he glanced at the next certificate. "The United States Air Force awards upon Doctor M. Patel the Reservist rank of Major in the Air Force Medical Corp. Recognition as one of the top Medical Doctors in American Universities, Colleges, and Medical Schools." The list of certificates seemed endless as Howard took note of Patel's degree as an MD, internal medicine, and other subspecialties. Walking back to his cushion chair, Howard sat down and looked at the magazines sitting on the oak desk next to the chair. Most were typical of the standard doctor's office giving the impression to the patient that the professional that was going to review their health life was intellectually deep and well read. Picking up the *Sports Illustrated* magazine, Howard noted that it was the latest addition as were the copies of the remaining publications. No medial magazines, which struck Howard as interesting, but then again maybe Dr. Patel liked to keep that part of his world in his office. Howard remembered that any police officer worth his rank had to have a superior skill in visual observations since this trait separated one from the average officer. The office was clean and seemly to any first-time visitor, let alone the regular patients. In truth, one came away with the impression that you were in good hands with this doctor.

"Officer Singer."

"Yes," said Howard as he looked up at the tall and stunning woman wearing a stethoscope around her neck. The woman appeared to be just under six feet, with jet-black shoulder-length hair, with a face that suggested gentleness that avoided the often cynical look that appeared with many medical doctors.

"Good morning, Officer Singer. I'm Dr. Bridgestone, assisting Dr. Patel this morning. He asked me to bring you to his private office, so if you would follow me please."

Howard couldn't help but notice how young Bridgestone appeared to be considering that it took a minimum of eight to ten years just to qualify for a basic medical degree. Walking down the hallway, he guessed her age to be about twenty-six, maybe twenty-eight.

"Right in here, Officer," she said, now turning and walking back down the hallway. Howard was left to observe Patel's office, which contained at least three computers and an array of reference books that would fill a small library.

"Please come in, Corporal Singer," said Patel as he glanced up from his large walnut desk. "She does look young, doesn't she? Actually Dr. Bridgestone is in her early thirties and a fine neurologist and, due to her outstanding skills, soon to be a neurosurgeon. She's visiting today to meet with two of my patients who have concerns in that area. Please sit down, Corporal, and allow me to answer any questions that you might have."

Howard was amused at how the doctor had made a point to address him as corporal rather than by the traditional officer title used by most of the public when meeting the police for the first time. He surmised that the doctor was attempting to establish territorial control, with corporal being much lower on the food chain than that of a doctor.

"Thank you, Dr. Patel, for agreeing to see me on such short notice," said Howard. "While I was waiting for you to finish with your patient, I couldn't help but admire your professional certificates. If I may ask, could you help this neophyte understand just what a medical examiner is?"

"Certainly," said Patel. "Laymen will usually think the term means that I'm a coroner, but in the medical world, it becomes more complicated. What it really means is that I'm a physician with a specialty in pathology and subspecialties in forensic pathology. It's difficult to understand, Corporal Howard, but that's the best I can come up with."

"I think your explanation is fine, Dr. Patel. My guess is it's much like internal medicine, where doctors receive a general certification in internal medicine, with special qualifications with additional training in cardiovascular disease, critical care medicine, endocrinology, infectious disease, and medical oncology, just to name a few. If I'm correct, sleep medicine doctors now fall under the American Board of Internal Medicine."

Pausing for a moment and studying the police officer, Patel sat up straight in his chair. "Do you have a family member in the health field, Corporal Singer?"

"No, why do you ask, Dr. Patel?"

"It's just unusual for someone to be that familiar with the American Board of Medical Specialties. Anyway, it's just a compliment regarding your awareness of my profession."

"Thank you, Dr. Patel. In order that I not waste your time, I just have a few questions that follow up on a visit that you had not too long ago with Detective Kate Heller regarding your autopsy on a Ms. Gayle Browning. In review, she's the woman that died of a spider bite not too long ago."

"Yes, I remember the case well, and to be honest, I took strong exception to Officer Heller questioning my findings. After all, I'm not your average appointed medical examiner on this subject since I use 3-D imaging radiology and sometimes CT scans to view a dead body internally before I touch it with a knife. I found her method of questioning most offensive at times."

"Please accept my apology, Dr. Patel, for anyone on the Funston Police Department failing to recognize your outstanding qualifications. After all, I noted that you are listed in the *Castle Connolly Guide of America's Best Doctors*. Anyone that understands how a medical provider receives inclusion in this book should take exceptional care before calling into account the work of that particular doctor. If my understanding is correct, it is your peers that provide the opinions on your skill level that make it possibly to receive this recognition. Frankly a doctor whose name appears in that book is much like being selected to be on the all-star team in baseball. Detective Heller, in her own profession, is considered one of the stars of the future."

"Again, your understanding of my profession is most unusual, Corporal Singer."

"Detective Heller was recently promoted because she has become an expert at determining the mechanism of what kills or why something doesn't. That's how she uncovered the fact that Gayle Browning was killed by a Brazilian wandering spider, not the bite of a brown recluse spider. Please note, Dr. Patel, that I said *killed* because she is about to arrest the man who did this. You see, Doctor, the victim, Gayle Browning, actually left a picture on her cell phone of this spider that clearly identifies the small arachnid. She actually killed it with her shoe before the venom took her life and put it in a small container. Nothing is simple, though, Doctor, in police work, because we need two things to help us wrap up this particular murder, and that's the reason for my visit today."

Now appearing nervous, Patel asked, "What is that?"

"First of all, the container holding the spider that we believe killed the Browning woman is missing. That, of course, is not a concern of yours. However, what concerns Detective Heller and I is that the police report filed regarding the death of Gayle Browning suggested 'Death by suspicious causes.' What this means, of course, is that because the woman was young and that there were no signs of foul play, the detective at the time punted the ball. This report was directed to your office, Dr. Patel."

"What do you mean punted the ball, Corporal Singer?"

"It's an old American expression better understood by the term *pass the buck*. Since the Detective couldn't understand what killed the woman, he just noted it on his report for the medical examiner to do a complete autopsy. Did you do a complete autopsy, Doctor?"

Now showing the first sign of perspiration beginning to form on his forehead, Patel answered, "Of course I did. Detective Heller has a copy of my report."

"It must be the result of her being a woman, I guess," said Howard. "For some reason, she can't locate that part of your report that covers an examination for traces of prior sexual intercourse. As you know, Doctor, that fluid secreted by the male reproductive organs would be the DNA that could possibly identify the killer. Would you have your staff provide me with another copy of your medical examiners report before I leave?"

"That would be impossible, Corporal Singer, as all reports of that nature are retained at my office location at the hospital. Please tell your office that I will address this request and have it faxed to Detective Heller within the next forty-eight hours, if that would be acceptable."

"Your cooperation is most appreciated, Doctor," said Howard rising to shake the doctor's hand before he left. "One remaining question, Dr. Patel. On your certificate of internal medicine, it says that you received it in 1987d which means you've been a professional Doctor for over twenty-five years. That's a long time, Doctor, considering that one must go to school for almost ten years."

"Yes, it means that I'm pushing fifty-four years old," laughed an obviously unnerved Patel.

"That's young, Doctor, but still after all that time, one must get tired of taking those tests for board certification."

Howard caught Patel's glance studying his face line by line like Sherlock Holmes with a microscope. He was waiting for the question from Howard that never came as to when he had last taken the board certification test.

"Have a good day, Corporal. With regret, my time is limited," said Patel.

"Good day, Doctor. Our office looks forward to receiving your report regarding what you found when testing for sexual intercourse."

The Jar

"Jerkoffs," Bergman said as he closed his hotel room door and took the mason jar with him over to the light of the window, where he could hold it up and examine it better. Outwardly he saw no sign of any tampering, but then again with the spider buried deep within the bottom of the jar under the bed of grass and fine straw, it was anyone's guess. Placing the jar down on the edge of the windowsill, he decided to allow enough time for the spider to come to the top as he walked over to the hotel-provided refrigerator and removed a can of sprite. Pulling the small tab, he heard the fizzle of the pop as the contents attempted to escape their tin container. Taking a swig, he walked back over to the window and glanced down at the jar resting on the sill. The dilemma caused by the maid couldn't help but reminded Bergman of the passage in Revelation 16:1, "And I heard a great voice out of the temple saying to the seven angles, go your ways, and pour out the vials of the wrath of God upon the earth." His patience reaching the breaking point, Bergman reached for the jar and held it up to the light, gently shaking the container at the same time. Nothing! Raising the jar above his eye level was when he noticed the scratch marks on the sealer metal ring of the jar. Someone, unable to twist it open, had applied a tool to twist open the lid. "Good God!" exclaimed a now-frightened Bergman. "Someone has opened the jar and probably unwillingly let the spider out, and I can't do anything about it." The maid had become the modern-day version of Pandora, only instead of a box being opened, letting all human ills into the world, she has let the most dangerous spider out probably into her home. Taking the jar, Bergman put it into a plastic bag that the hotel had provided for dirty clothes and opened his room door and walked directly to the stairs. Following the staircase down, he exited the hotel and proceeded to a close unoccupied cabana nearest the Funston river shoreline. The small shelter provided just the enclosure he needed as he removed the jar from his plastic bag. He then checked his pocket to assure that he had brought the small vial of antidote. Satisfied, he dumped the contents on the ground, backed away, and watched. Spotting a broken umbrella handle, he took the handle and moved it over the contents on the ground until he was satisfied that the spider had not been in the jar. "Stupid woman," he softly shouted. Picking up the empty jar, Bergman walked back to the hotel. Entering the lobby, he decided to pick up a complimentary copy of the *Funston Daily Herald* at the front desk before going back up to his room.

Approaching the desk, he heard the receptionist say, "How creepy is that."

Thinking that she was talking to him, he said to the clerk, "I'm not sure I know what's creepy."

"You haven't heard?"

"No, is something going on in the hotel?" asked Bergman.

"No, not here. One of our maid's children is in critical condition at the hospital. They don't know if she is going to make it."

"I'm sorry to learn that," responded Bergman. "Had the girl been ill for a long time?"

"No, according to what we know, she must have been bitten by some small bug, or so her mother seems to feel. The poor woman just got into this country within the last year, and now she has this thing going on," said the clerk. "It's just so darn creepy being attacked by a bug."

"Someone is telling the story wrong," said Bergman. "Bugs don't attack people, maybe bite a little."

"Maybe so, but the Hernandez woman said her daughter said the bug had a big red mouth and just leaped on her daughter's arm.

Anyway, don't worry about your room being cleaned. We're bringing in a temporary replacement to clean the second floor."

As the hotel clerk began to check in a new family, Bergman took his paper and walked to the elevator. Getting off on the second floor, he moved down the hall to his room and opened the door. Finding the room dark and unable to locate the wall light switch, he moved over to the window and drew the curtains, letting the late morning sun light come in. Knowing that he had to think about what he just learned, Bergman walked into the bathroom and poured a glass of water, taking a long drink while attempting to sort out what the girl downstairs had just said. Returning to the window, he glanced down into the hotel parking lot and watched the activity of a hotel coming alive with departing quests. From his vantage place on the second floor, he could scan the countryside and the main roads coming into the property. The roads seemed to be engulfed with an endless supply of vendors, along with new arriving families and salesman. Bergman pulled up a chair and watched with fascination the coming and goings of this small village of continued motion. Psychologically speaking, it didn't take an expert to figure out that one day soon those tracking him would find him and he would go to jail. Well, maybe not jail, but one way or another put an end to his way of life. Certainly the nosey maid had moved the clock much closer to midnight than he had expected. If only his wife had not opened up the glove compartment in his car, both she and Gayle would be here today, but life was a constant what-if existence. What if Perry Sinclair would have not met Gayle at his bank, and what if the maid would have just thrown the mason jar away? "Maybe," he thought, "I could have avoided breaking all the laws of the church and the state. Then again fate is the hunter, and it has a habit of catching up with you." Berman remembered first meeting Gayle at the Silver Valley library and finding out that she was an organist, something every church never has enough of.

Without telling her his occupation, she had asked him about it later into their conversation.

"What do you do for a living?" she had inquired.

He had repeated her question with an answer that even surprises him today. "You know what I do for a living, Gayle? In my line of work, I'm forced to bend laws all the time." At first, he noted the shock on her face, but as he began to explain what pastors are required to do, it was the turning point in their new relationship. "You see, Gayle, as a pastor, your job is to promote the religion that as a pastor you were called to represent. Although that might sound easy, the fact is many people who come to you wanting to become part of that faith often are Baptists, Catholics, and Lutherans who have decided later in life to change religions and become members of the church that you were trained to represent. Sometimes it because of marriage, other times noting more than wanting something new. Thus as their new pastor, I often bend the laws of my church to accommodate them."

He was thinking back to that day and the hours and months that followed with Gayle when he noticed the police car pulling into the Hampton Inn parking lot. He watched as the car stayed in place for a few minutes before the police officer opened the door and got out. His heart skipped a beat when he recognized that it was a woman in plain clothes. Although she was still a good walking distance from the hotel and had her hair pulled back in a ponytail, there was little doubt that he had seen this woman before. Her suit did little to hide the fact that she was carrying a weapon underneath the lime-colored jacket. She was on a mission that he could tell as he watched her scanning the entire lot and hotel. Turning from the window, Bergman collected his remaining personal items, checking his overnight bag for his Sig Sauer P229 .40 cal. He removed the weapon and pushed the gun clip into the gun and put it in his windbreaker jacket. Having double-checked the room, he then opened the hotel room door and slowly made his way to the stairs. Checking to ensure that he was alone, Berman walked down the stairs and headed to the back exit of the hotel.

CHAPTER 56

The Certification

Patel waited until his last employee had left the office and then he walked down to the waiting room area and sat down. Putting his feet up on the leather cushions and his hands behind his head, he stared at the framed certificates and commendations on the walls with the pride of a man satisfied in his achievements. After his meeting with Corporal Singer, he had the uneasy feeling that one had when they knew that there were being watched yet was unable to ascertain the true threat. Uncertain what meaning existed from the policeman's visit, he began to read each of the certificates on the walls with the care of a surgeon examining CT scans while looking for a shadow on the film.

Patel over the years had taken enormous pride in his work both as a medical examiner for the Funston Hospital and in his state-of-the-art medical clinic that now employed eighteen people. There was good reason for this pride because Patel, unlike many of his doctor friends, played by the rules. Those rules were simple. Failing to understand that unnecessary greed and the stretching of the rules on reimbursement payments from the government was the quickest way to lose your medical right to practice. He had seen it often over the years where friends of his had engaged in submitting requests for payment for MRI and CT scans that had exceeded government guidelines. He had heard the conversations from fellow doctors who bragged about charging for Medicare procedures not done. Although the general public didn't understand, an individual physician may practice any kind of medicine with or without additional training, and many did. Well, not in his case, Patel said to himself. Twenty-five specialties are recognized by the American Board of Medical Specialties. Those awarded a DO degree are offered a broader opportunity of one hundred and six specialties under the aegis of the American Osteopathic Association. And then is the board certification of that specialty. Patel knew that board certification was an important factor to hospitals, and few doctors advanced without it. In fact, without it, a doctor was often left to swim upstream all by himself. While many doctors who were not board certified still chose to call themselves specialists, board certification within the industry was the standard used by hospitals and most to measure competence and training. Patel knew that the American Board of Surgical Medicine continued to not recognize the term *board eligible*, a term used by some doctors who have been out of medical school long enough to have taken the exam and had either failed to pass the test or just ignored it. Patel played the game required of his profession because the public and those that hired him understood the difference, and thus he always maintained his board eligibility requirements, which were expected of him every ten years.

Now he turned his attention to his silver framed medical doctor degree, his eyes moving to the left of the degree and focusing on the American Board of Surgery certification presented to him in 1991. His office walls had endless commendations that through the eyes of the typical patient visiting his office all suggested that their heath was in good hands. Distinguished Service Award, Outstanding Merit Award, Doctor of the Month by the Rotary Club, recognition not only as one of the best doctors in the city of Funston but one of the five hundred best doctors in the United States. But none of these recognitions were as important to Patel as his board certification as a surgeon. It also reduced his malpractice liability insurance. Getting up from his seat in the waiting area, he walked over to his framed certificate of board certification. Thinking back to the meeting with the police officer, he remembered how impressed he was that Singer knew so much about the medical profession. What had Singer asked? "How long, Dr. Patel, have you been a surgical doctor?" was the questioned asked because Singer was just fascinated with the industry, or was Singer hunting for something else?

Patel thought back to his earlier days as a doctor when he had graduated from Michigan State University Medical School in 1984 as an MD. He had fast-tracked his career and received his board certification in surgical medicine in 1987 as listed on the framed certificate. Single and the sole receiver of his parents' estate when they died in a tragic plane crash, Patel had put his medical career on hold and enrolled into the school of pathology at the University of Utah. Money had never been an issue since he had inherited over five million dollars following the suit settlement with the air carrier. After graduation and a two-year stint as the assistant medical examiner at Red River Community Hospital of Buck Town, North Dakota, he moved to Funston, Michigan, and bought a little health clinic from a retiring doctor. Yes, life had been good up until the autopsy on that church organist Gayle Browning. Taking the board-certified surgeon certificate off the wall, he returned to one of the waiting room chairs and sat down once again. He looked at the recertification date and noted that it had expired in 2007. He didn't immediately panic because he knew that some specialties didn't require recertification at all and that those doctors in other specialties such as internal medicine were grandfather prior to 1990. Heck, internal medicine doctors often referred to themselves as board eligible, a term that was not recognized by the ASMS. But what about surgeons, and how could he have forgotten? Taking his certificate, he walked back to his office and pulled his file on board specialties and turned to the page that covered the American Board of Surgery. As he read the requirements, general certification in surgery, with special qualifications in pediatric surgery and general vascular surgery and added qualifications in surgery of the hand, surgical critical care. He froze reading the last eight words: "Certifications are valid for a 10 year period." Now he knew the answer to his meeting with Singer when he had asked about how long he had been a doctor. It was not so innocent of a question. His heart skipped an extra beat as he knew what this meant. His days as a medical examiner would be over. While this would do little to effect his clinic practice, most hospitals that have admitting privileges could play hardball and, if they chose to do so, could refuse this privilege for him as a practicing surgeon. He was not in the specialty such as dermatology and psychiatry, where doctors usually conduct their entire practice in their office, and a hospital appointment was not as essential, or as good a criterion for assessment, as in his specialty. He knew the rule of thumb on this subject, as did every doctor. The best hospitals were usually quite careful about admissions to their medical staffs. The best hospitals were highly selective, so a degree of screening is usually done once every two years. How they have missed their credentialing of him since 2007 was as puzzling as his own failure to process the required paperwork for his continuation of board certification. Looking through his file folder, he found an application blank to begin the new process and laid it on his desk. The question was, would he be able to correct this oversight before the hospital timetable for new credentialing began? Spinning around in his office chair, Patel picked up his autopsy report on Gayle Browning that he has sent earlier to Det. Kate Heller. There was little that he could do about his initial conclusion that the death was a result of a brown recluse spider bite despite being advised by Corporal Singer that their evidence suggested that another species of arachnid had taken her life. But really, how would he have known, since until now no one had brought in the spider for analysis? Surgical mistakes and other medical harm contribute to the deaths of 180,000 hospital patients every year, but for Christ's sake, this was a dead body, why was he worrying? He had done everything else according to his pathology training, so the best approach would be to stop outguessing himself. Picking up his medial bag, Patel shut off the lights and secured the back door as he left.

The road meandered along the South Fork of the Funston River, a roller coaster of asphalt barely wide enough to accommodate two cars travelling in opposite directions. The sun was beginning to lower itself in the sky but had not yet reached the point that it had descended low enough that the rolling hills and trees would cast shadows across the road. Patel, depressed over his discovery, had hit the brakes more than once as he approached the sharp turns of the road that would take him home. Approaching the final turn, his eyes caught a young woman pushing a baby carriage. For an instant, his mind returned to the movie *Untouchables*, where a woman lost control of her baby carriage and it went down a long series of steps. Fear grabbed his throat. He jerked hard to the right on his car, strangling the steering wheel as his Mercedes's front right tire clawed the gravel as he left the asphalt. He continued on for another five hundred feet before he was able to gain control and pull his car off the road. Getting out of the car, he looked back in the direction of where the woman and baby carriage should have been, but nothing was in sight. Getting back in the car, Patel still shaking sat still for a few moments before he returned to the road. The incident had been taken as a sign to Patel. He had been given a second chance, and he would not disappoint.

CHAPTER 57

The Report

Kate looked at Patel's autopsy report, which had arrived as promised by Howard. The doctor had said she would get it to her within forty-eight hours, and Patel had managed it in forty-seven. "Maybe I'm too sensitive," thought Kate, "and it has nothing to do with my gender. Maybe the guy just is stressed running back and forth from the hospital to his clinic every day. Burning the candle at both ends can happen to doctors as well as us every day police officers who are getting married." She looked at the cause of death listed on the preliminary autopsy report section, and Patel had reported it originally as undetermined. In his line of work, undetermined is equivalent to a tie. And usually most ties don't make anyone happy, and Patel appeared to show his displeasure by bringing the wrong closure to the case by picking on the brown recluse spider. But now and then we all have to accept the fact that we have failed. His justification rested on the fact that the brown recluse spider was a known killer of humans, which it was. The problem was that deaths by this spider was almost exclusively young children, not a church organist in her thirties. Kate wondered why Patel did this job in the first place. She had looked up the salary of a forensic pathologist and by the standards of the medical community most were bottom feeders in the medical world, making in the range of $52,000 to $165,000, with the higher end holding positions in larger cites. Clearly a man like Patel who owned a clinic in the downtown area of Funston did the work because he liked it since money was not the issue. Kate had observed autopsies before, and she knew that there was a dedication to the job because as one pathologist had put it, "Every death should count, not just for the privileged." The basic procedures follow the same pattern with every medical examiner, so she scanned the report looking for those areas that she was familiar with. Cause of death, samples of tissues, body fluids, those external injuries as well as internal ones. Then were the required hair samples, from the head, pubic region, and swabs from the mouth, vagina, and anus. Kate noted that Bergman had written nonapplicable to that area of the autopsy, and she wondered why. Maybe Patel was rushed due to an unusual amount of autopsies that he had to perform that day? On the other hand, maybe the pressure came from those wanting the body to be released to tidy up the remaining legal affairs, collect insurance, or just wanting to arrange the funeral. She would not actually know until she had a final conversation with Dr. Patel. In truth, everything other than the question about the abbreviated autopsy seemed in professional order. She was about file the fax report when she noticed that Patel in signing his name didn't provide the usual supporting documents covering his specialty. Few hospitals permit doctors to practice unless they carry malpractice insurance. This not only protects the hospital but the patient as well, and regardless that this patient couldn't speak, it really didn't matter because lawyers had a tendency to sue everything and anything. Kate wondered about this oversight by Patel, finding it most unusual for a doctor not to follow the protocol and the basic hospital requirement for each physician to attach his current license applicable to his specialty, especially in view of the recent findings that most hospitals have less-than-outstanding safety scores. She made a note to ask Patel about this oversight but didn't consider it crucial to her investigation. She didn't look forward to another visit to his office, but there was no basis for requiring him to come in to the station. As Howard had said to her when he reviewed his meeting with Patel, "We can't force him to be friendly, but somehow I can't imagine him deliberately compromising his medical license with the police by lying about anything when we are asking him for information on murders. He's bound by professional ethics to give us any information that could be used to solve these murders."

She reminded Howard that Patel never volunteered anything. "How true," he had said, "but let's remember he's not obligated to tell us anything other than what he has written on his report. The remainder is up to us to ask the right questions." Hearing the sound of footsteps coming down the hall, Kate looked up as the receptionist walked in her office.

"Detective Heller, your guy called when you were in Wagner's office this morning."

"Daisy, you can call me Kate, for God's sake. Detective is only used when the brass is around. Did he leave a message?"

"Yeah, he wanted to know if you were still on the pill."

Seeing the shock on her face, Daisy said, "Gotcha, didn't I? Actually all he said was that he had taken Channing for a good run and he'll see you at home."

"You know, Daisy, you keep this up, and it will be back to Detective Heller. Anything else going on?"

"Nothing much except that young Mexican girl is still in intensive care."

"I must have missed that one, Daisy. Gang related or did she get hit by a car?"

"That's what's strange. The hospital isn't talking, and neither is her doctor. Everything seems on lockdown."

"Thank you, Daisy. If you learn anything else, buzz me." Watching her turn and walk back to the receptionist's desk, Kate put in a call to the Funston Fire Department.

"Fire House, this is Jake."

"Jake, this is Kate Heller over at the police department. Could you tell me if you know anything about a young Mexican girl that was taken over to Funston Memorial Hospital? It should have happened in the last twenty-four hours."

"You must be talking about the Maria Hernandez girl. Our boys picked her up at her mother 's house with an elevated blood pressure reading. The poor kid had redness on her right shoulder and was screaming that she was in pain. They had a hard time understanding either the grandmother or the kid since neither could speak good English. The paramedic riding in the back with the grandmother and girl seem to feel that whatever insect got the girl came out of some kind of jar that she was playing with. Wish we could be more helpful, but that's all we got."

"Thanks, Jake, that's a lot." Kate hung up the phone and stood before an eighteen-by-twenty-four-inch picture of the first officer shot in the line of duty in Funston. She knew that the precinct had a policy requiring that every room assigned to a command officer or detective display a picture of a fallen Funston officer who died in the line of duty. Her picture was of the first chief of police of Funston who had the unfortunate fate of having dying from a heart attack while addressing a group of high school children over forty-five years ago. The town had been actually fortunate in losing only three officers over the years as a direct result of criminal activity. Reaching for her cell phone, she placed a call to Howard, leaving him a message that she would be at the Funston Hospital. No sense in providing unnecessary information on something she had little information on, thought Kate.

Thirty minutes later she had arrived at the hospital. Until now she never gave it much consideration, but walking thought the twirling doors of Funston Hospital, it occurred to her that most hospitals are designed at their entrance much like your typical Hyatt or Marriott Hotel. An expansive atrium surrounded by patient rooms on the eight floors gave the arriving quests the feeling that the main room on the lower level was like an ancient Roman house. By those that understood, it was referred to as the lobby effect, which kept your mind away from what really existed in a hospital, the fight for life over death. "Hospitals should be places that you go to get better," but too often, thought Kate, "the opposite happened." Infections, surgical mistakes, and other medical harm she had read contributed to an astronomical amount of the deaths each year. Moving down the long passageway to the head nursing station, Kate couldn't shake the conversation that she had had months ago with her primary care doctor who in a moment of frustration had told her that there was currently an epidemic of health-care harm at all levels. "So much so that the reality of the current problem was that in the entire decade, more than 2.25 million Americans had probably died from medical harm. Think of that, Kate. Imagine if you will that's the entire population of North Dakota, Rhode Island, and Vermont. Just keep up with your regular checkups, and I'll do my best to keep you out of the hospital," her doctor had said during her recent appointment. As she now entered the nursing station, Kate was greeted by a male nurse.

"Can I help you, lady?" he asked, obviously paying more attention to the game on his cell phone than the fact that this lady was armed.

Kate, not answering, caused the tattooed nurse to look up.

"Oh, I'm sorry, Officer, I didn't realize you were from the Funston Police Department."

"That's all right, we're all overworked and stressed these days," said Kate with a little bite in her voice. Say, Mark [noticing his name tag], is your head nurse around?"

"She's on the fifth floor holding a meeting for some new employees. Is there something that I can help you with?"

"Maybe you can. I'm trying to find out if you have a young Mexican girl here by the name of Marie Hernandez? I was told she came in yesterday, and to be frank, I need to talk to her doctor if he's here. And if there's anything that you can do to find out about her condition?" asked Kate, giving Mark her best smile.

Mark, now apparently struggling to determine just what he could say, said, If you would have a seat, Officer, I'll see if I can find someone to assist you. Could I have your name please?"

"It's Detective Kate Heller."

Still looking somewhat bewildered as to what to do, Mark left the nurse's station and walked across the hall and opened the door that said Administration.

It was clear to Kate that Mark needed to talk to someone in higher authority than he had, and that was fine she thought. The truth was, no one wanted to release authority in a society where litigation was but one wrong comment away from being sued. While waiting for Mark to return, Kate walked out of the office and pulled the paper from her purse containing the phone number of the

Windham Hotel. Reaching for her cell phone, she was about to call the number when she heard Mark's voice.

"Detective Heller, the doctor will see you now."

Walking back into the nurse's station, she was greeted by a woman in a long blue hospital jacket. "Hello, Detective Heller, I'm Dr. Roberta Blue Hawk. Mark indicated that you had some questions about a patient, Marie Hernandez?"

It was clear from the name that the doctor's ethnic background was that of an American Indian or that she was married to one since it was impossible from her appearance to tell. "Doctor, I'm from the Funston Police Department. I need to know as much about the condition of Maria Hernandez that you can share with me and what might be her ailment. Frankly I may be on a wild-goose chase, but it was not long ago that this hospital admitted an adult male patient that almost died of a spider bite. It was a most unusual spider not known to be part of the spider family that you find in this part of the country. That individual who was bitten was connected to a murder case that I'm investigating where a woman died of such a spider bite. Fortunately he survived, but it later has become clear that the cases were related."

"This happens to be a child, Detective, so I doubt it has anything to do with the other cases you were commenting about."

"What can you tell me about what you have learned so far about her condition, Dr. Blue Hawk?"

"Very little, Detective, since we are governed by the rules of HIPPA, which restricts us from commenting much about any case."

"I'm aware of the law, Doctor, but if my hunch is correct, you may have a patient with the Neurotoxin PHTX3 in her system. If my guess is correct, she may have been bitten by a dangerous spider which could kill her."

"Nonsense, Detective Heller, since I happen to be an infectious disease doctor and routinely treat diseases caused by a bacterium, virus, fungus, or animal parasite. The girl only has an inflammation that has caused the skin to show a strong redness."

"Look, Dr. Blue Hawk, I'm not here to question your credentials, but have you ever treated anyone who has been bitten by a Brazilian wandering spider?"

"I have no idea about that type of spider, Detective, but I know a spider bite when I see one, and this girl has been bitten by a simple tick, maybe a mite."

"Is her family in the hospital, Doctor?"

"She only has a mother, and she's in the intensive care family waiting room, Detective."

Mark, who had remained quiet during the conversation between the two women, spoke up. "Dr. Blue Hawk, with your permission I can show Detective Heller where the intensive care waiting room is located. It's pretty hard to find since it's on the other side of this wing. Not waiting for any confirmation of authority, Mark walked out of the office followed by Kate and moved down the hallway past several offices until they reached almost the end of the hallway when he abruptly stopped. "It's through those doors, Officer. My guess is the grandmother will be the only one in the room. And by the way, for what it's worth, Dr. Blue Hawk is an excellent Doctor. She just follows the rules like the rest of us. In her case, she probably feels the rules are applied much harder," he said, hoping that Kate could pick up on his meaning.

"Mark, please don't worry. We all have a job to do. I appreciate your help," she said, shaking his hand. As he left, Kate walked into the waiting room and noticed an older woman sitting near a wide screen television set. "*Buenas Tardes*, my name's Detective Heller Ms. Hernandez. Can you speak any English?" The woman looked at Kate and nodded her head yes, but put her thumb and finger together indicating only a little." Kate was about to give up before she actually started when a cleaning woman walked into the room and started to pick up the wastebaskets. Noticing that the woman looked Spanish, she said, "Pardon, can you speak English?"

"Yes, I've been in the country for several years, Officer."

"Good, because I need your help since this lady can't speak English that well and I need you to help to interpret for us. This is a police matter, and I'll try not to delay your work too long," said

Kate. "Please ask the lady how well her daughter is doing as far as she knows."

When the woman spoke to Hernandez, Kate could tell the answer by the look on her face. "The lady said that her daughter, Maria, has taken a turn for the worse, but the doctor said she will get through her problem."

"Ask her if she knows what caused her daughter to become ill?"

The two women spoke back and forth for what seemed like three minutes before the cleaning woman spoke to Kate. "She said she's not sure, but that her daughter had said she was bitten by a hairy bug. She said at first she thought the girl was stung by a bee or wasp because her arm swelled up and got very hot."

"Tell Ms. Hernandez that I spoke to her doctor, Blue Hawk, and that the doctor feels everything will be all right."

Again the two women seemed to have an endless conversation before the cleaning woman spoke to Kate. "She appreciates your concern and is very sorry for causing this problem."

"She hasn't caused any problem. Please advise the lady not to worry."

Kate watched the two women talk back and forth when suddenly the Hernandez woman started to cry. "She thought that you were here to arrest her, Officer."

"Arrest her for what?"

The cleaning woman put her arms around the grandmother and sat down on the hospital couch and again communicated Kate's question. "She took a jar that belonged to a hotel quest. You know, one of those jars that contain jelly or something like that. She thought the guest was throwing it away, but it turned out he wanted it back. The hotel manager got real mad at her and is threatening to fire her, so she's worried for her job and her daughter."

"Ask her if there was anything of value in the jar or was it just empty? Please also ask her where is she employed?"

Kate could see that the interpreter was having problems with parts of this question since Hernandez was shaking her head back and forth.

"She's scared to death, Officer, of losing her job, so she doesn't want to tell you where she works, although she did say the jar was empty except for a small amount of grass."

Interesting, thought Kate. "Thanks for your assistance," she said, handing the cleaning lady her card. "You've been great and more than helpful, and I intend to bring this to the attention of the hospital. Please tell Ms. Hernandez I also appreciated her time and that things are going to work out fine for her daughter. I have to leave right now, but see if you can find out a way to learn where she works. It's very important to me, and I would be very grateful," said Kate as she left the two women alone and walked back down the hallway and to the main entrance of the hospital.

Outside the building, the sun has dipped behind the stone and brick buildings that make up the large campus of Funston Hospital. A church bell was ringing somewhere in the distance, sounding its daily reminder that the Sunday service was not too far off. Getting in her car, Kate retrieved the piece of paper containing the Windham Hotel phone number and dialed the number.

"Windham Hotel, may I direct your call?"

"Would you check and see if you have a Dr. Alan Ogden staying with you?"

"Yes, we have. Would you like for me to ring his room?"

"Yes please."

"Hello, this is Betty."

"Betty, this is Detective Kate Heller from the Funston Police Department. Your husband and I have spoken professionally several times on matters of joint interest regarding a case that I'm working on. Would I be able to speak to him if he's in the room?"

"He's here, Detective, and I must say that he's spoken often of you to me, so trust me that you are not unfamiliar to this family. Alan, pick up the phone. Someone wants to say hello to you."

"Hello, Detective Heller, I could tell that Betty was talking to you. Actually we were going to give you a call before we left Funston and had hoped to visit you. This is really a surprise hearing from you first."

"Someday maybe we can forget business and just enjoy each other's company. I would like to have you meet my fiancé as he's in town for the week as we finalized our wedding plan. Regretfully that's not why I called, Doctor. It always seems like I'm asking you for something. Do you have a few minutes that we can talk?"

"Sure, for you I always have time."

"I just left Funston Hospital visiting a distraught grandmother who has a very sick grandchild who was bitten by some strange bug. Sounds familiar, right? The family is Mexican, so I needed a cleaning lady to help me through the rough spots of the language barrier. The girl seems to be taking a turn for the worse, although the attending doctor, whose name is Roberta Blue Hawk, insists that things are not bad and that given time the girl will come around. The problem, Dr. Ogden, is that the girl told her grandmother that the bug came out of a jar she was playing with. The grandmother had brought the jar home from her place of employment but is scared to tell where that is for fear of losing her job. It's obviously a hotel or motel because she a cleaning maid. It won't be difficult to trace though because she would have had to mention it during admitting. Anyway she had thought that the guest was leaving the jar to be thrown away, but obviously it didn't turn out the way she thought. Doctor, you are familiar with the Funston Hospital having treated Perry Sinclair for that Brazilian wandering spider bite. Could I ask you to make a phone call to the right people that you know over there and see what the situation is regarding that girl? I don't like the smell of this bug bite, and you probably can guess where I'm going with this. It has a ring to it that has happened before. That kid may be in serious trouble, and with regret, no one understands what actually she may have been bitten by."

"Kate, I'll do you one better. Betty and I will take a drive to the hospital as soon as we hang up. I actually have met Dr. Blue Hawk over the years due to our common interest in infectious medicine. I consider she tops in her field, so it's unlikely that this one will get away from her. I'll give you a call and let you know what I find out."

"Thank you, Doctor. Look, I've got another call coming in. It might have something to do with where the maid worked, so I'll have to pick up this conversation later," said Kate as she quickly hung up."

"Detective Heller, may I help you?"

"Detective Heller, my name is Angel Galvez. You asked me to help you locate Maria Hernandez's place of employment. She works near the Funston Riverfront, where all the hotel properties are located. It's called the Hampton Inn. You'd do me a great favor if you kept this confidential as to how you learned about it."

"Angel, you don't have to worry about a thing. Thank you again."

"You know what I always say, girl, never be in a hurry to have a problem." Putting her foot down on the accelerator, Kate turned down Cambridge Avenue into the deep shadows of the drive that would take her through the forest area leading up to hotel row as it was called by the locals. If one is looking for a place on the water to ride motorcycles, go fishing, and work for people that can pay above minimum wage, one has found it in this part of Funston. Slowing the car down, she let her mind wander for a while trying to clear her head and steel herself for what might follow. Pulling over on the side of the road, she checked her sidearm to assure that the pistol's clip was engaged in the Ed Brown Special Forces .45 cal. Pistol. Thin might not be sexy, but in her mind nothing fit her better than the maximum power delivered by a .45. Back on the road she could see the hotel coming into view. Within minutes, she had parked her squad car near the front of the hotel and walked through the two large doors and looked around. The receptionist check-in station was empty, but she could see a man sitting in an office adjacent to the front desk.

Walking up to the desk, Kate was greeted by the man who was sitting in his office. "May I help you, miss?"

Kate wondered how it was going to feel like when in two weeks it would be Mrs. "Yes, I'm with the Funston Police Department, and I would like to speak to your manager please."

"That's Mr. Abdul. He's in a meeting right now. Could I have your name, please?"

"Detective Heller, and this is important, so I would suggest that you find him right now."

"Just a minute and I'll locate him." Kate watched the young desk clerk as he dialed an extension and began to review with Abdul the situation up front. "He'll be right here, Detective. Can I get you something to drink as you wait?"

"No, thank you, I'll just have a seat near the television and watch the weather report." Of course the weather report was not the channel of choice in the Hampton Hotel, so she sat back and tried to get into *Godfather IV*, where Anthony murders his little brother. Or was that *Godfather III*? Kate was just getting interested in the part where the little brother gets blown up in the fishing boat when Abdul walked up to where she was seated.

"Detective, I'm the hotel manager. What can I do to help you?"

Getting up from the chair, she said, "Thank you for taking this time away from your meeting. I wouldn't have requested to see you except for the fact I have an ongoing emergency at Funston Hospital that may be connected to one of your employees, Mr. Abdul."

"Has one of my employees been hurt?"

"No, nothing such as that, but I need to know if a Ms. Maria Hernandez is an employee here at the Hampton Inn."

"She is, err, she was, as we are processing her termination papers. Can you tell me what this is all about and what it has to do with Hernandez?"

"I will, but what is the termination all about, Mr. Abdul?"

"We have a no tolerance rule on the removing of any item from a guest's room without their approval."

"Are you taking about a simple empty jam jar, Mr. Abdul?"

"How do you know about that, Detective Heller?"

"That matter is confidential, but I can assure you that the lady is brokenhearted over her misjudgment of taking that jar. Besides, her granddaughter is in critical condition at the hospital from the contents of that container. It's important that you tell me what you know about the occupant of the room that the item was removed from."

"The guest was most upset because the mason jar, as he referred to it, was his daughter's, and he said that it meant more to him than my offer of a complementary free night's stay that I had offered. When the maid returned the item, it was in good condition. What did you mean, Detective, when you said the girl was sick from the contents from the jar?"

Ignoring Abdul's last question, Kate asked, "Did you or your staff attempt to open and look in the jar?"

"No, why do you ask?"

"I believe that the jar contained a deadly spider. The type of spider that may well have killed one Funston resident already, almost killed a second, and if my hunch is correct, has bitten that little girl at the hospital. I need the name of the occupant of that room and his forwarding address, Mr. Abdul, and as quickly as possible."

Turning to his desk clerk, Abdul barked out his request to a frightened young girl. "Give this officer the name of the person who occupied the room that we had all the problems with over that glass jar."

"He checked out this morning, sir."

"I don't care about that. We need the name of that guy. It was something like Burden or Burton. I really don't care, just get the records for the detective and fast."

"Here it is. Room 2023. It's listed under Mr. Paul Bergman, 1515 W. Peters Drive, Fairfax, Idaho. He may still be in his room since he requested a late checkout."

Looking at Abdul, Kate said, "Get me the key and fast."

Reaching for her police phone, Kate called the Funston dispatcher.

C H A P T E R   5 8

Secret No More

Howard, sitting in the Burger King restaurant, almost spilled his drink when he heard the code for officer needs assistance coming from Kate at the Hampton Inn. He immediately responded with his location and confirmation that he would be taking the call and would be heading to the hotel since he was less than five minutes from the property. Launching himself into his squad car, he sprinted out of the Burger King parking lot onto half-mile roadway. Howard knew that in another three minutes he would connect to Cambridge Avenue, which would take him right into the hotel entrance. Tactically speaking, Howard believed in the military approach to a developing situation. You can play it safe and monitor the situation from afar or opt for the aggressive approach like Chamberlain did at Galesburg during the Civil War. No bayonets today, Howard laughed, thinking about how Chamberlain had taken his smaller group of Union soldiers and overwhelmed the far-superior group of Confederates. Howard knew enough about the Hampton Hotel, having broken up several disturbances to understand the typical escape routes that could be used by the criminal element. Those that tried to escape from the front were usually taken down within the first five minutes of their attempt to flee. On the other hand, those that left through the back entry would usually follow the existing dirt trail downhill until they reached the raging Funston River and the bridge that took them to the safety of a massive forest located within fifty feet of the end of the bridge. The additional drawback was the large number of hotel walkers that usually used the trail. He knew the odds of hitting an innocent bystander with a bullet was higher than he would have liked, but then again maybe it wouldn't come to that, he hoped. Seeing the Cambridge crossroad, he turned left and pushed the accelerator down further to the floor. All things considered, he had made his cross-country car dash in just less than ten minutes. Entering the half-mile drive that would take him up to the front of the hotel drive, Howard reached over to his holstered weapon and released the safety. Swinging wide of the main entrance, Howard slowly moved the squad car around to the back of the building and parked behind one of the two heavy steel garbage containers. Getting out of the car, he ran from the shelter of the containers to the rear end of a large mobile home and began darting in between several cars parked in the hotel lot. Every ten yards, Howard would peek above one of the cars like a squirrel checking the neighborhood for the ever-present chicken hawk, and when he did, he listened for any movement that would suggest danger. He was about to continue his movement to the rear door of the hotel when he spotted a couple with their luggage waking toward the back door of the hotel. The door suddenly opened, almost knocking them over, as a middle-aged man in a windbreaker burst through the opening. Realizing that his presence apparently startled them, he appeared to stop and offer an apology. Howard watched the exchange of conversation, which went on for nearly two minutes. At the same time, his eye caught the movement of several people in a second-floor hotel room looking out the window onto the lot below. One appeared to be Kate gesturing to a man who had joined her at the window. Howard turned his attention back to the couple, who had now started to enter the hotel.

"Where's the other guy?" Then he spotted him moving down the dirt trail to the bridge. Something about the guy's anxiety to leave the hotel parking area in such a hurry set off an alarm in Howard's head.

"Hey, you!" he yelled toward the guy. "Police. I need to talk to you." Howard watched as the guy stopped and turned and made a movement suggesting that he was going to walk back in his direction. Howard, feeling that the man was complying with his instructions, started to move in the direction of the bridge. Then suddenly the man reversed his actions and sprinted directly for the bridge while reaching into the pocket of his windbreaker. "Gun," Howard's mind told him, "the guy's got a gun." Breathing deeply, Howard began to take off after the man. This time instead of the sound of the man's quick feet moving across the bridge, he was greeted by the sound of a pistol shot. "Holy shit," he said as the bullet hit a nearby wooden post on the bridge. Howard rolled to the ground and came up about six feet from where the bullet had struck. His adrenalin in full gear, he moved to the protective cover of a discarded golf cart resting at the entrance to the bridge. Not the type of police officer who stood on the sidelines, his instincts told him that he had to take this guy down fast before someone got killed, maybe himself. But he waited and watched. His eyes turned every corner widely and slowly trying to pick up any movement that would identify the location of the gunman. Ten, twenty seconds passed. Howard, still lying flat on the ground below the golf cart, raised his head up just enough to allow him to turn his vision toward the end of the bridge and beyond it, to where the riverfront was but a short distance from a massive forest and freedom from being apprehended. Still he could not see anything. Something was wrong, very wrong. Maybe the guy was somewhere on the bridge and was waiting to take at least one more shot. That was all right with him, since he knew that combative pistol craft skills are not really complicated, regardless what some people want you to believe. The skills needed to fight efficiently with a pistol were not magic or even mysterious. What made the process difficult was trying to apply them while someone was shooting at you. The first skill was to never take a shot at someone with a handgun if the suspect was more than twenty-five yards away. Most seasoned officers knew that most gunfights occur within ten feet and that training for a long-range shot with a handgun was a waste of time. However, he had often argued with trainers that the time may come when your ability to make a shot from twenty-five yards or beyond, possibly at an assailant like today, could save one's life. He knew of only one other police officer who had mastered that ability other than himself, and she was somewhere in the hotel and had probably flushed out the guy now running across the bridge. Howard raised himself on one knee and listened for any sound. All that he could hear was the sound of speedboats coming from the river beyond the bridge. His mind now told him that the assailant who had taken a shot at him had not yet cleared the bridge and was now positioned at the end waiting for his second opportunity. Howard estimated the length of the bridge to be a good seventy-five yards well out of range for a good kill shot unless you were damn lucky. With the rays of the descending sun causing him to squint, Howard yelled, "Give it up, asshole, the Marines are on the way!" Howard counted to fifteen with no acknowledgment. The guy had to be either totally stupid wanting to shoot it out with a police officer or was confident of his ability with a handgun. How could this guy possibly be Bergman? Well, one thing was for sure, thought Howard. Shooting paper targets, whether the bull's-eye type or targets that actually depict a person, was no more than a two-dimensional image. This can lead a shooter like the one across the bridge to always assume his target will be a full frontal shot during a real-world encounter. Nothing could be further from the truth as Howard stood up and began to move slowly across the bridge. Kate had beaten Howard in the annual contest to determine the best handgun score, but even she would acknowledge that to be able to hit your target under the most stressful conditions imaginable, like today, your training regimen must prepare you to be pinpoint accurate. Understanding the importance of a shooter being accurate and actually being accurate are two different things, and you need to revisit the basics first. In other words, Howard told himself, focus on sight alignment, sight picture, and trigger control. He held his breath and took five more steps. He could see the end of the bridge now, and the beginning of the banks that led to river's edge. No bad guy in sight. Gripping his .40 cal S&W with his right hand while using his left hand to stabilize his shooting hand, Howard sighted his barrel toward the end of the bridge preparing for any sudden movement. The sudden brilliance of the white light on his heart caused Howard's lower jaw to quiver. He knew what was happening and watched too late as the red dot appeared just above it along with the flash of the gun in the distance. His last awareness prior to the pain was the humiliation of surrendering control of his bowels.

CHAPTER 59

A Gun in Hand

Kate turned to the hotel manager and told him to remain on the first floor and make sure that no guests used the elevator or the stairs until she came back down. Telling Abdul that another officer would be arriving shortly, she moved to the staircase and started up the flight of stairs. Halfway beyond the first-floor level, she heard a door shutting on the second floor, followed by the movement of feet walking toward the rear of the hotel. Her plan was simple: Arrive at the top of the second floor and find no surprises waiting. Then knock on Bergman's door, pretending to be from cleaning, and get into the room before Bergman knew what was happening. If it was Bergman in that room, there was a strong chance that he might be armed when and if he should open the door. For the fourth time in the past five minutes, she had thought about Curtis and how one misstep would end their dreams. She wanted to be his wife in the worse way. For that to happen, she had to focus on moving up the stairs and dealing with what awaited her at the top. Sometimes in life there is no turning back, and today was one of those times. As she took another step up, she listened for breathing, any movement, or the sudden appearance of the face that could end her life. Where the hell was the help that she had called for? With the gun in her hand, she finished the last step and found the hallway totally clear. Breathing deeply, Kate eyed the treacherous last few steps that she would have to take before reaching room 218. As she approached the door, she heard the voice of one if the Fox anchors talking about a missing woman.

Standing to the side of the door, Kate knocked and announced, "Cleaning lady, need to come in." She waited for any sound of a movement or voice acknowledging her request. No response. "Cleaning lady, I need to come in." Kate looked at her watch and waited another full minute for any sound. There was none. Pulling the swipe card through the entry lock, the door clicked, disengaging the security mechanism, and she pushed the door open. Moving into the room, Kate moved her weapon back and forth, covering the entire circumference of the small hotel room. The room appeared empty, with the bed unused and the dresser free from any personal items, yet she had noticed that the bathroom door was closed. Walking over to the door, she turned the knob and kicked it open. Empty, with the towels still hanging unused. Suddenly the movement behind her caused her to swing around with the gun pointed at the intruder. Abdul now found himself facing the barrel of .45-caliber handgun.

"Don't shoot."

Kate, clearly pissed off, kept the gun on Abdul. "Did I not ask you to remain downstairs, Abdul? What part of my instructions, didn't you understand?"

"You didn't come down, so I thought that I better check."

"Wrong answer," she said, "now lowering her weapon. You could have been shot either by me or the bad guy if he happened to be up here. Did my partner arrive?"

"No, at least he didn't come through the front door."

Walking over to the window, she checked the parking lot for any sign of unusual movement. From her vantage point, she had a good view of everything except the rear entry of the hotel. Nothing appeared unusual, and if Howard had arrived, his car was not in sight. Turning her attention back to the hotel manager, Kate growled. "I want you to secure this room until the Funston Police arrive. What that means is, no one, and I mean no one, enters this room period. There are no exceptions, and if there's anything about those instructions you don't understand, please let me know now." Turning, she briskly walked out of the room and headed toward the rear of the second floor and the staircase that lead to the lower level and the back of the hotel building. Moving down the steps briskly, she reached the first floor and found the back entrance. As she approached the exit door, she heard the sound of a shot coming from what she judged was some distance away. Opening the door, Kate looked in the direction of the parking lot, where she thought that she had heard the shot coming from. Not seeing anything, she looked to the area where the Hampton Bridge was located and observed Howard walking across the bridge with his gun at the ready position. "Bergman, he's got Bergman," muttered a jubilant Kate. Her excitement was cut short when she saw the flash of the gun on the other side of the bridge and Howard collapsing.

"Officer down! Officer down!" Kate screamed into her police phone. "Goddamn, get some help over here at the Hampton Hotel, along with an ambulance." Finished with her call in for assistance, her instinct was to rush and see how hurt Howard was, but she knew that's not how it's done in a gunfight. Pausing, the words of her training instructor returned.

"You are either trained or untrained, and you will fall to the level of your training," he had said. As she moved slowly to her downed partner, she knew that while the instinctual desire to focus totally on who was trying to do the harm was the natural response of most untrained individuals, it was one's skills to manage their trigger control, front sight, acquisition, and movement that kept most alive to fight another day. Looking beyond the fallen body of Howard toward the end of the bridge, Kate spotted the white light glaring at her. She had seen that light beam used on pistols and rifles before, and she knew that the owner of the weapon was preparing to use the red or green tracer to finish the kill. Falling to the ground and rolling away from the crimson tracer beam, she heard the explosion of the pistol and the bullet, finding only dead air and the ground next to her. Raising up on one knee, she fired off three rapid shots in the direction of the fired pistol while falling to the ground and rolling toward the opposite direction of where she had been. She could still see the immobile Howard while she waited for the return fire. He had not moved nor uttered a sound. Hearing the familiar warbling cry of the arriving ambulance, Kate stood upright and sprinted toward the fallen Howard. In the distance, she could hear the pounding of feet fleeing, but that mattered little with Howard flat on the ground and the whole left side of his uniform jacket soaked with blood. Turning toward the hotel, she could hear the ambulance pulling up in back followed by a black-and-white squad car. Waving her hands, the two vehicles drove through the parking lot until they were within twenty feet of the bridge and got out. The two paramedics raced up to the fallen Howard, while Kate motioned the patrolman to follow her across the bridge while yelling to him that this was the location of the assailant. As they moved together across the bridge, she said, "He got Howard with a crimson light guard. You know, the type of rear-activated laser gun system that one mounts on a typical Smith & Wesson pistol. He almost got me the same way, only I got lucky. I did get off three shots, but with the distance it would have taken a lot of luck to have hit him." With Kate taking the lead, both officers moved with caution across the bridge until they reached the end of the wooden structure. As expected, there was no one in sight.

"He's obviously gone, Detective Heller," said the patrolman. "My guess is he took off into the woods, and the chances of finding him without dogs is nil."

"You're Corporal Lance Nixon, aren't you?" asked Kate.

"Yes, you and I have met once at a staff meeting about a year ago. I'm very sorry about your partner, Detective."

"Thanks, yes, I remember you now. Well, there's little to do here, so let's go back and check on Howard's condition. Our rabbit is long gone, but I know who he is, and his freedom is measured in hours not days," said Kate.

"Maybe less time than that, Detective Heller," replied Nixon. "Unless my eyes are deceiving me, one of those three shots that you fired found its mark. Look on the grass blades over there. It looks like fresh blood to me. Not much, but my guess is it'll take more than an aspirin to clear up his headache."

Kate walked over to where Nixon was standing and knelt down. "It's fresh blood, all right. I just wish that I would have been close enough to have heard him scream after what he did to Howard. Look, Corporal Nixon, I'm going to check with my contacts over at the hospital to alert them that someone might just check in with a gunshot wound. You can help me if you will check out the local physician offices in town for the same thing. If it's just a flesh wound, he can probably take care of it himself, but if the bullet found its true mark, he'll need some real medical help. Now let's get back and see how Howard is doing."

As the two officers began to retrace their steps back over the bridge, they could see the paramedics lifting Howard into the ambulance. Reaching the end of the bridge, the two police officers walked up to the ambulance and looked in at the paramedics working on the fallen officer. Kate was about to ask his condition when the driver appeared and walked up to her.

Recognizing the driver, she asked "Terry, how's my partner doing?"

"Well, the good news is that he's still alive thanks to the fact that he was wearing his vest. Knowing Howard as we all do, it must have taken some strong arm pulling to get him to wear one since he was always so careful about his appearance and I can remember him complaining that it made him look bulky up front."

"Tell me the bad news, Terry, so that when I see his wife, I have all the current facts on her husband."

"You don't have to see his wife, Detective Heller, because Captain Wagner drove over to their house and picked her up and are now waiting at the Funston Hospital for our arrival." Walking back to the ambulance, Terry got in and was waiting for the word from the paramedics that they were good to go. Looking out the window, he said, "The bad news, Detective, is as you know, vests can't stop everything, and if the bad guy uses the right ammo, nothing can totally prevent penetration. The boys in the back think that he was probably using some flex tip expanding bullet. That type of bullet creates large wound cavities and deep penetration at all velocities. Sad as it is, the guy knows his business and used probably a Hornady Magnum load that has a rifle-like performance even though shot from, let's say, a .357 magnum. He's hurt bad, but we'll get him to the hospital. From that point, it depends on the doctors."

"Let's roll," came the voice from the back.

"Sorry, Detective, but we have to put the pedal to the metal now. Good luck finding the bad guy," said Terry as he put on the flashers and the siren and pulled away.

CHAPTER 60

Hide and Seek

Funston, being the small municipality that it is, has a population under ninety thousand, so Bergman knew that it was unlikely that the police department had any tracking dogs or enough manpower to execute a serious search. An avid student of military tactics, Bergman also knew that any escape plan was one that applied the logic of doing the unexpected while applying the rule that when you're not certain, which is right or wrong, at least do something. Moving quickly through the forest, he decided that a careful movement back to his original location was the best course of action since the last thing that most people would expect was that he would return to the parking lot at the Hampton Hotel. His best guess was that if the local police were indeed searching for him, they would concentrate their maximum efforts on waiting for him to exit the forest toward the end of the wooded area, which provided an individual direct access to the major highway and opportunities to hitchhike quickly to safety. He had other thoughts running through his mind, but to follow on this plan required getting back to the Hampton Inn parking lot undetected. Now walking near the edge of the woods, he found a small wrought-iron sign with an arrow pointing in the direction of the Marriott Hotel property. Following the pointed arrow, he soon found a trail to the outer edge of the hotel property with its large tennis courts and rose garden. Approaching the garden, he noted the asphalt running track and the Hampton Inn in the distance, which he calculated was less than half a mile. As was the case with the Hampton Hotel, it appeared that the running track was designed to access all the hotel properties in the area as a common link to one another and the upscale stores that guests could shop at.

Picking up his pace, he moved in the direction of the Hampton Inn, discovering that he was the only one using the track. Looking down at his feet, he noticed the small droplets of blood that had fallen from the wound in his right side. The bullet had caught only the outer edge of his skin but still had a burning feeling. He had used his handkerchief to minimize the blood flow, and it had seemed to have worked. Within fifteen minutes into his speed walking, he had arrived in the lot where he had parked his car. Obviously the police had not found his vehicle since he had at check-in used a fictitious plate when providing the information to the clerk. Looking around and seeing no activity, he climbed into his car, started the engine, and moved out of the lot slowly until he came to the main road that led onto the roadway connecting to the highway. He was amazed at how quiet the hotel parking lot was considering that just a short time ago he had participated in a gun battle, which had brought several police and supporting vehicles. For he knew that this would be short-lived because the policewoman would continue her pursuit once she had finished doing what she could for her partner. Bergman was uncertain if he had actually killed the police officer or that he was just wounded. It mattered little because injuring a police officer under any circumstances was certain to bring out a full court press until they apprehended him. He knew that he had to get off the main highway for the time being if he stood any chance at all of escaping. He remembered that that there was a cemetery located somewhere in the area but couldn't place the exact location. He continued to search the countryside for any avenue of escape while at the same time watching for any signs of increased police presence. He had driven another five miles when to his relief the sign for the Mt. Calvary Cemetery suddenly appeared. The cemetery was located off the side of the road hidden by large ten-foot bushes that could have concealed any modern tank. Slowing his car, he drove through the iron gates and was met by rows of white military marble gravestones placed in perfect unison for several hundred feet across the undulating green hills of this small Lutheran cemetery. The marble gravestones provided the visitor with a feeling that the soldiers resting below the markers were standing guard for those whose family had chosen this cemetery for their final resting place. He shut off his engine and looked at the many graves of these men and women, dead in the service of their country. Despite what he had done, he thought that it was a far worse act committed by many who chose not to remember the sacrifices that these dead had made in service to their county. The Lutheran cemetery was by the standards of most cemeteries in the countryside well-kept. He wondered what they would do when they ran out of land. The scenery was breathtaking. The trees and shrubs with their pink and white flowers lush and full lined the walkways around the hundreds of grave markers, giving each visitor the feeling that this was just a temporary stopping place before reaching paradise. As he sat in the car and looked out into the bright afternoon sunlight, he noticed that a light wind had come up, and through the tree lines, clouds were sailing quickly across the sky. Beyond the cemetery line, he could see the ripening cornfields. The sight of developing crops brought back memories of his youth when fields as these were sometimes affected by drought, then just as quickly constant rain, and then the wheat that the farmers had planted would be ready for harvesting. All this was eventually followed by the fall hunting season, his favorite time of the year, when pheasants and duck season would begin. He used to feel sorry for urban and suburban kids growing up without a clue as to the relationship between wheat fields and hamburger buns, between corn and cornflakes. Yet in the end, he had himself rejected this lifestyle to become a minister with the idea to help people, care for those in hospitals and nursing homes, and bask in the adulation that would come from those families that respected the life of a minister. Then came the discouragement in recent years as he had become disenchanted with the low pay and how members of congregations seemed more inclined to view a minister as an employee rather than their shepherd. Today the typical member was more concerned about his ability to keep the sermon within thirty-five minutes and that their pastor not take any more than his one day a week off than caring about their pastor's health. Today being a minister was all about politics and power-freaks playing with a pastor's life and his family. The change in his attitude started slowly. He started to smell the rain before he heard it and heard it before he saw it. A lot of memory circuitry—sight, sounds, smells— began to be deeply imprinted as he approached his early forties. He started to want more out of life, not just to be taken for granted. He was human, just like the members of his congregation, who would always remember their first sex act, which had been at the time so mind-boggling that most would remember it clearly twenty, thirty, sixty years later. His wife might have long forgotten their first time on a road called Whispering Trail as teenagers, but he hadn't. Nor had he forgotten his skill level with firearms which he had acquired at the age of ten years old. Bergman now stared at the gun on the car seat. It looked wicked, black, and hard and very lethal. He imagined Detective Heller staring at the gun as she tried to swallow her fear while looking at him, waiting for the bullet that would end her life. He knew that she would try to stay brave to the end. It was not that he hated her, just her interference with what he now wanted in his life. His daydreaming came to an end as he heard a joyous bark and a black-and-tan German shepherd came bounding across the cemetery grass toward his car. Bergman opened the car door and let the dog leap onto his lap. Like most friendly dogs, this one was excited and happy to have anyone rub its head. "Who's a good boy?" he said as he patted the dog's head. "Big tough guy, I'm now undone by a stray dog," thought Bergman, looking around to see where the dog's master was.

"Jack, come over here and leave that man alone," came the loud voice.

Glancing up, he observed two men with rifles walking the edge of the cemetery. The dog hearing the voice command suddenly scampered off, reaching the shorter of the two men, and sat down while the man put a lease around the dog's neck and tied it to a tree. The taller of the two waved to him and said something that he couldn't make out but proceeded to walk in his direction holding his rifle over his shoulder. Bergman got the strangest sense that the two men were not hunting rabbits and were on a different mission. He placed the pistol in his side holster and pulled his shirt from his pants and let it fall covering the weapon.

The big man kept coming ducking under tree branches as he approached Bergman's car. Calling out, he said, "Hey, mister, my name's Sam. You from these parts?"

Getting out of the car, Bergman lied, "Matter of fact, I'm not actually from these parts. My name's Percy. I'm just visiting some of my relatives buried in this cemetery. You know how it is. You get around to doing it once or twice a year, and this just happens to be my turn to check in on our family members that lived in these parts." Watching the man's movements, he asked, "Didn't think hunting season was still on this time of year? You guys doing some coyote hunting?"

"No," he answered, looking Bergman over. "My guess is that you probably haven't heard the news yet, but there was a shooting not too far from here. A Funston police officer took a bullet, and the guy ran into the woods about three to four miles from here, near the Hampton Hotel property. Ted and I are off-duty police officers who have joined the search for the bastard, so you better be careful, fellow. We've got every available officer involved in the manhunt, but no sightings yet. No offense, Percy, but I need to have a look at some identification. I happen to notice that you have a Michigan license plate and that you've been staying at the Hampton Inn hotel."

"My god, you guys are good. How in the heck could you tell that I stayed at the Hampton?"

"Well, I'd like to take all the credit for my investigator talent, but the fact is, all these hotels put their individual brand on each guest's tire. See the little white *H* on your front tire? They do this to discourage nonguests from using their parking lots to visit other business establishments in the area. They then check the license plate against the register, and if you're not staying at the hotel, they have your car towed."

Looking at the tire, Bergman shook his head in amazement. Reaching for his wallet, he watched the off-duty cop who still had the rifle resting on his shoulder. Removing his license from his wallet, he started to hand it to Sam when he stopped suddenly and asked the

Officer, "My god, that's not a full-bore custom .375 on a model 70 action that you're carrying, is it? I haven't run into one with that type of thin-shelled walnut stock in years. That must be your personal gun, not standard issue?"

"It sure is," answered the officer. "There's no way that the department could afford the modifications that I've made on this one. Now, I don't want to be rude to visitors, but let's take a look at that driver's license, Percy," he said while placing his rifle against the tree next to him.

Bergman's quick glance to the cemetery edge noted that the second officer was engaged in playing with the dog, so he handed his driver's license to the Funston police officer with his left hand while reaching under his shirt and placing his right hand on his pistol. He watched as the officer tried to conceal his growing uneasiness over the name on the driver's license as he was undoubtedly matching it up in his head with the description that he probably had received from his desk sergeant.

"Well, everything looks good, Percy," he said as he handed the license back to him while starting to walk back to the tree for his rifle.

Removing the pistol from its holster, Bergman pointed it at the off-duty officer and said, "Sam, turn around and don't take another step, and don't even think about that ankle holster and the gun you have hidden. That was a good try, but trying doesn't feed the bulldog, does it? I could tell that you noticed that the names didn't match up, so there's no use pretending anymore, is there?"

Sam knew that the person who first sees the threat coming well in advance has a huge advantage while the person who is ambushed will probably never catch up, regardless of the training and skill level. He had been ambushed and in the process had made a mistake in judgment, and now the man now pointing the gun at him had the advantage, and that didn't bode well for him or his partner.

Bergman understood his advantage and decided to make the first move, not based on anything, but his assumption that Sam's eye movement to his ankle was to retrieve his second weapon, as was often carried by most police officers. He had anticipated the police officer to make an attempt to recover from his mistake. "If you make a move to get that gun around your ankle, you're a dead man, Officer Sam. Now I want you to grab that rifle against that tree and hand it carefully to me. Then I want you to lie down on the ground in back of the car where your partner can't see you. Think you can remember all that, Sam?"

"What are you going to do, shoot me in the back, Bergman?"

"No, but in the next ten seconds if you don't hand over that rifle, I'm going to shoot you in the head just to show you what a fair man I am."

Sam nervously gathered his rifle and handed it to Bergman while laying down flat on the ground.

Bergman walked over to Sam, reached down, and removed the Taurus Defender from his ankle holster. "Well, look at this little piece," said Bergman while inspecting the small revolver. "So this is what you were hoping wouldn't catch my eye. A man could get really hurt, Sam, with these .410ga shotgun shells. I have one of the models myself, only I prefer using all .45 Colt ammunition instead, but every man to his choosing."

"Hey, what's going on down there?" called the second police officer.

Bergman, looking up to the top of the cemetery hill, noticed that his partner had put the rifle sling around his shoulder while pulling something small from a leather case on his belt. "The son of a bitch is carrying a spyglass," thought Bergman out loud as he ducked behind the rear of the car. Looking at Sam on the ground, he knew that the one thing that can't be argued with is that the most tactical thing that you must do in a gunfight is to shoot first to survive.

"Hey, Sam, sorry about this, but wrong place at the wrong time," he said as he aimed the Taurus and fired a round into the head of the prone officer. The explosion of the shotgun round was almost deafening as Bergman dropped the revolver and immediately picked up the rifle. He didn't know who was going to make the first move, but he was fairly certain that there weren't many moves left on the board now. Bergman sprang up on one knee, aimed over the top of a large gravestone, and fired two quick rounds at the reflection coming from the spyglass. In the two seconds it had taken him to fire, he had caught a glimpse of the first round exploding into the chest cavity of the officer, with the second round missing its target. Berman waited for a few minutes despite the howling of the dog. Looking around, it was clear that the isolation of the cemetery prevented anyone from hearing the shots, and if they did, they probably dismissed them as just a typical hunter and paid no attention to the noise. That of course didn't mean that one or both of the Funston police officers hadn't radioed in for assistance, but he had not seen that equipment on Sam. "Boys probably didn't pack all their gear and just left home for their assignments," he thought. Walking up the hill using the gravestones as cover, he approached the downed officer and the howling dog. Yelling at the animal to shut up, he was surprised that his voice carried enough authority to quiet the animal as he considered shooting it to stop the howling. Walking over to the officer, he could see that the single shot had been fatal, although he had crawled about ten feet before dying. Looking at the farmer's cornfield that was near the edge of the cemetery, Bergman decided to drag the dead body into the cover of the high corn. It would probably give him a few days before anyone found it, he thought. Walking back to where the officer had been laying, he picked up the rifle and spyglass and kicked dirt around the bloodied ground. Still not certain what he was going to do with the dog, he left it alone as he walked back down the hill to his car and the second dead officer. Looking around, he noticed that the cemetery had the typical roadways between the gravestones that allowed the visitors to drive around and park near their loved ones. Although he was a strong man, Bergman doubted that he could singlehandedly lift the dead weight of Sam into the trunk of his car to move him up the hill and into the cornfield. He knew that time was of the importance because his luck could run out and someone would come into the cemetery to visit their loved ones, or worse yet, some police officer who was part of the search party would check the location out.

But what was he to do? And then he observed the little wooden shack off to the side of a large old gravestone. Walking the short distance, he found the shed had but a simple sliding latch bolt securing its door. Opening it up, he was met with cobwebs and an inside filled with rusty shovels and two buckets. The storage place seemed to have had no visitors in months, if not years. It took him less than fifteen minutes to drag the body over to the shed and put it inside. Placing the two rifles and the handgun in the trunk, he cleaned up the ground area where he had shot the first police officer and was ready to leave when the barking of the dog reminded him that he needed to do one more thing. Walking back up the hill, he found the animal lying on the ground panting and obviously thirsty. Pulling his weapon out of his side holster, he walked over to the dog and pointed the gun at the side of the dog's head. And then suddenly changing his mind, he placed the weapon back in the small holster, reached over, and unleashed the dog. Within seconds, the animal raced into the farmer's field and disappeared into the cornfield. Maybe a bad move, he thought, watching for the dog to reappear between the corn rows, but it never did. Well, every dog has his day, and that dog just had had his.

The Journey's End

Kate pulled her car up to the emergency entrance, put her police identification on the windshield, and walked through the doors looking for Captain Wagner. "Where in the hell were all the people?" she wondered, not seeing anyone around.

"Can I help you?" asked the young doctor, appearing to be a first-year resident while holding a cylinder of powdered creamer.

"Yes, I'm Detective Heller from the Funston Police Department, and my wounded partner should have just been brought in. Can you direct me to where they may have taken him? His name is Howard Singer, and my guess is that his wife and a Captain Wagner would have been here when the ambulance had arrived with him." Kate watched the doctor stirring his coffee with a plastic swizzle walk across the linoleum emergency room floor away from her as he placed his coffee on a nearby counter. Seemly only half-interested, he stared at her and said, "They took him up to the third floor intensive care area. Your friends went with him, so take the elevator over there by the women's restroom and check in with the nurse's station when you get off the elevator."

"Hey, Doc," she said. "What time is it?"

"The resident glanced up at the industrial clock, set above the receptionist desk's station. Seven forty-five. That means I've only got another twelve hours to go."

"At least you've managed something,. You've apparently be able to at least pour yourself a cup of coffee while finishing your studies on bedside manner," she said as she walked toward the elevator. "God, I'm in a piss-poor mood," thought Kate as the rattling of wheelchairs and gurneys now started to filter throughout the hospital. As she approached the elevator door, a nurse asked her if she would press the third floor for her when the door opened. Kate looked at the stretcher containing a woman patient, clearly bloodied and pale. When the door opened, Kate let the nurse in first and followed her inside. Pushing the third-floor button, the doors closed, and she could feel the slow acceleration of the elevator as the nurse adjusted the neck collar of the injured patient. When the elevator stopped at the third floor, the nurse moved the stretcher out the door and disappeared down the hall. Exiting the elevator, Kate saw the nurse's station and walked directly to it. She could see that people were busy on this floor, attaching monitors, hanging IV lines, and trundling carts all around. "Get more blood in here!" a doctor yelled. Kate stepped up to the desk and watched as a young nurse was obviously busy talking to the hospital blood bank. "I need three units and fast. No, better, make it four units. Dr. Morris said he wants it yesterday, so you better hurry. Thanks."

"Excuse me, I'm Detective Heller from the Funston Police Department. Could one of you please assist me?"

"Hi, I'm Sandra Stone, the floor head nurse. We're not trying to ignore you, Detective, but as you can see this is a trauma area, and things are going from bad to worse. We've got three myocardial infarctions, an emergency C-section, a guy who has had hot tar spilled over him, and two gunshot victims, one a police officer. Say, you're not here because of the police officer, are you?"

"Yes, that's my partner, Howard Singer. He was shot over at the Hampton Hotel where we were trying to apprehend a very dangerous man. Would you be able to tell me how he's doing or possibly locate his wife or Captain Wagner? One of them should be with him."

"I can tell you that your captain took Singer's wife home about an hour ago. She's arranging for her family members to take the kids, and then she'll be back. He's going to make it, but he's in a lot of pain. His vest saved him, but the doctor still had to use the paddles to stabilize everything."

"Would you check with the physician to see if I can see Mr. Singer for a brief moment?"

"I'm sorry, but the doctor has a surgery patient that he's attending to now. As I said, it's quite a night, Detective, but if you give me your word to stay only a few minutes, I'll let you visit him. He's been asking for you anyway. Please follow me," said Stone.

Kate entered the room, which she could see only had the one patient. Walking over to his bed, she got a glimpse of Howard's pale white skin and a smile as he recognized her.

"Kate, it's good to see you," he said in a weak voice. "Sorry I let the boss down."

"No more talk like that, Howard. He almost got me also, but I just got lucky. If there is any good news other than finding out that you will be all right, it's that Bergman has felt the heat of my bullet. It doesn't appear that he's hurt bad, but nevertheless he knows that we're on his trail. He's almost killed a young kid with his spider hobby. She's in the hospital down two floors from you. It's complicated, so we'll talk when you feel better."

"Kate, you must be careful. We're not dealing with your average run-of-the-mill psycho."

"I know, Howard. Now Nurse Stone told me that I could have only a few minutes, so I'm going to sit outside and wait for your wife to return. It shouldn't be long," she said, bending over and kissing Howard on the cheek.

"Thanks, Kate," he said as he started to close his eyes. "And just so you know, you're the best-looking boss that any man could have."

Payback

Bergman shut off his headlights and pulled the blazer into the church parking lot behind Kate Heller's townhouse. The blacktop lot ran up the back of the old brick church, where bike racks, basketball courts, and equipment sheds stood his car safely hidden behind discarded boxes that once held storage shelves for the coming school year. He sat back and relaxed as he waited. Looking across the church grounds, he could see from his location the back bedroom window of the policewoman's house. As his heart pounded, he began to work up a sweat as he reflected on the reason why he had chosen to come here tonight rather than to escape. Certainly this was not a particular smart move since the police were already looking for him. Dismissing the momentary concern, he took a short break and looked at his watch. It was one 1:45 a.m., and the woman was still not home from the hospital or wherever she had stopped. He tried to make a reasonable guess as to whether or not that she would be escorted home by another brother officer or two since by now the entire Funston Police Department had been made aware of his desired vengeance against her. They were right, of course, as he had more than a few homicidal rages about her in the last few months and was surprised at times at how badly he wanted to kill her.

Suddenly headlight beams appeared from around the side of the school and then a vehicle came around slowly and turned toward him, catching him in its beams. The car came to a stop, and getting out of the vehicle was a private security guard. Bergman couldn't make out if it was a man or woman because of the glare of the car's lights, but since the figure was walking toward him, he would soon know.

"Say, buddy, what are you doing in the schoolyard this time of night?" came the male voice.

Now he was able to make out the tall young security guard as he approached him. "I'm trying to gather some cardboard boxes for a church project," replied Bergman. "As you can see, they have tossed out dozens of them."

"Are you from around this area?"

"I live right around the block, that's how I found these boxes."

"You have nothing better to do than collect boxes on a Thursday night?"

"We all have something better to do this time of night, but when you belong to a church, young fellow, some of us follow Romans 8:28, which says, "Everything works out for the good of those Who are called according to his purpose." It just so happens my calling tonight is to gather those boxes for our church project, which involves sending clothes to our graduating pastors to help them and their families get started. I hope that you don't consider this as breaking the law?"

The uniformed guard, now looking embarrassed, responded, "No offense intended, just be careful out here this time of night." He walked back to his car and drove off.

"Dumbass," said Bergman to himself watching the security guard's lights disappear round the corner of the building. Satisfied that the guard wasn't coming back, Bergman once again returned to his car and leaned back in the seat observing Heller's house across the field. He thought about the woman not as a police officer but rather as the striking female inside that police uniform. He had first met her when she had responded to his phone call to the police when he had attempted to cover up his attack on his wife. At the time he couldn't help but notice how beautiful she was. Blond hair and full-breasted with the soft, milky skin of a child. He might have been a minister, but he was still a man with particular desires, he had rationalized. To this day, he had rape fantasies about her, along with paying back that snippy female attorney in the county prosecutor's office who had tried to put him in jail for the attempted murder of his wife. Then there was of course that uppity bitch Betty Ogden, whom he would eventually deal with also. He knew that to have any one of them would be like screwing the whole class of people who looked down on him. He often had thought that someday, he'd go for it. Now, having killed two policemen, maybe a third, there was little concern for consequences anymore. If he played his cards right tonight and didn't make the mistakes that his brother had made when attempting to do his bidding weeks ago, he'd get into her house and then kill her. But first he intended to have his fun with her and then dare her to make anything of it before putting a bullet in her head. Later there would be time for Betty Ogden. Maybe he could even arrange for him to watch, he thought, laughing at the possibility.

The next several minutes passed uneventfully. No police cars passed by the house. The radio had not reported any finding of dead policeman in a cemetery, and the neighborhood was free of the typical teenagers returning from their beer run at the local liquor stores. Stepping outside the car once again, he watched the house for any sign that she had arrived. Where the hell was she? he wondered. Everybody had to have some sleep. Then just when he was about to give up, he saw car lights illuminating the front of the house followed by the slamming of a car door. From his vantage point, it was impossible to see the occupant of the car, but it had to be her. Leaning back on his car, he watched as the security lights kicked on not only in the front of the house but seemed to cascade around the entire perimeter of the building. That could be a problem, he now thought. He watched as the lights inside the house now went on and seemed to move from one room to another, almost like she was inspecting the house before getting ready for bed. Getting back in his car, he started the engine and eased out of the church parking lot slowly, moving down the street facing the back of her yard until he circled the block and approached the front of her house. He eased his car under an elm tree and a distance away from the closest streetlight. The townhouse was set at an angle to the small roadway that led to the back of the yard so that Bergman could see the front of the house as well as the long north side. Light appeared to be coming from the dormered windows set into the sloping roofline and also from the side window, which he felt was probably the kitchen. He watched as a fleeting figure passed into the darkness with what appeared to be a dog. Bergman was momentarily puzzled, unless it was of course the family next door to the Heller house letting their animal out. That could be an additional problem besides the security lights unless he entered the house from the opposite side of the building. Opening up the glove compartment, he removed a makeshift map provided to him by his brother, who had failed in the assignment that was now left totally up to him. The map showed the layout of the house and indicated that the homeowner had no animals or any security lights. Either that or she had not turned them on earlier when she had arrived or, possibly like most women, just didn't understand how they worked. It didn't matter now because he had to deal with whatever measures of security were in place. Looking at the map, he noted that the kitchen seemed to connect to the master bedroom and the main bathroom. Bergman strapped on his holster with the .40 cal pistol in it and placed the Army surplus infrared night scope in its leather sheath. Reaching in the back of the car he removed from the back seat his H&K fixed blade knife. Small enough to fit in his front pocket, the 3.62 inch recurved blade opened to a full 7 inches. Satisfied that the street and neighborhood was still free of people and traffic, he let himself out of the car and moved swiftly across the street to the side of the house where the dining room was located. He walked in a low crouch down the side of the house and around the building, looking into each window with the infrared night scope. Looking up at the roofline, he was surprised that this side of the house lacked any security camera or lights. She obviously had used all her resources to cover the kitchen, master bedroom, and backyard, if she had any, he reasoned. Stopping, he looked in what appeared to be a guest bedroom and could see her movement through the open bedroom door. She was working in the kitchen doing something that he couldn't make out. As he watched and waited, she finished whatever she was doing and turned off the kitchen light and appeared to move down the hallway. Hearing a dog bark, Bergman froze, then realized the bark had come from several houses down the line from Heller's townhouse. Moving past the bedroom window, he carefully approached the back of the yard, where he could see another light had been turned on, which according to the map should be the master bedroom. Here he also knew that this area of the house would have the highest concentration of security lights, if any existed. Glancing up at the leading edge of the house beyond the bedroom, he could make out a control box that, if security lights existed, contained the trigger light. Here he would have to be careful because once any existing security lights caught his movements, a red light would appear, followed by the entire back of the yard and bedroom area being flooded with lights. Carefully he edged to the lighted window and looked up above the building and noticed a large security floodlight. He waited for the red light to come on indicating that he had crossed and broken the light beam that would trigger the lights to come on, but to his surprise, they stayed off. Typical woman, he thought. She had neglected to activate the total alarm system. "Could it really be this easy?" he wondered. Moving around the building, he found the back entrance, and to his shock, the door opened. The woman stepped outside for a brief moment and looked around then just as quickly went back in and shut the door. Puzzled he waited until he saw another light go on. "Must be the bathroom next to the master bedroom," he thought. Inching alongside the building, he reached the door and turned the knob. Jesus, she didn't even lock it.

A Bridge to Nowhere

Sitting on a bench waiting for Channing, he watched as the older couple approached him. Although complete strangers and just walking as he had been doing now brought them over to where he was with a sudden eagerness to bring to his attention the ongoing shooting that had taken place at the Hampton. He knew that being married to a police officer would have its moments, but the emptiness of learning about the possibility of your wife being involved in an ongoing emergency was overwhelming. Now shocked, Curtis found the older gentleman leaning over to him asking a question about his knowledge about a shooting that he had only now heard about from him.

"No, I'm afraid that's news to me since I was just walking my dog the past hour," said Curtis. "What exactly is going on?"

The man's wife spoke up. "It's at the Gold Coast. You know, where all the expensive hotels are located. It's the place where those with money go to have a good time. Fancy restaurants, upscale shopping, that type of thing. WJJR, the all-news station, is reporting that the Funston Police are involved in some type of gun battle and that at least one officer has been seriously wounded."

Curtis, now worried, asked, "Did they give the officer's name or gender?"

"That's not being mentioned," said the old man. "You know, the thing about having to notify the immediate family first. The only other thing that the reporter talked about was that the wounded officer had been transferred to Funston Hospital and is in serious condition."

Getting up from the park bench Curtis, thanked the couple for their information and yelled for Channing. Walking part of the way to meet the dog, he yelled for Channing to sit. While the dog remained at his side, Curtis reached inside his light jacket for his cell phone to place a call to Kate. Now looking at the phone, he swore, realizing that he had accidently shut it off. Quickly turning the phone back on, he immediately noticed that she had left a message for him. The message was short but comforting.

"Hi, honey. If you pick up anything on the radio about a shooting at the Hampton Hotel, don't worry. I'm fine, but I need to go over to the hospital regarding Howard. He was the officer that was shot, but according to everything that I've been told, he should pull through. I'll see you later tonight. Love you. Bye."

Now feeling better after listening to her message, Curtis walked to the car and opened the door and let Channing jump in. He smiled as he watched the dog sit down in the passenger side and waited for Curtis to open the side window. Getting into the car, Curtis buckled his seat belt and started the engine. "Here I sit worried like hell about Kate, and the dog just wants me to get the car moving so that the wind can blow in his face." Instead, Curtis sat quietly and ran his tongue between his teeth and his gums and thought. He contemplated about all the hours that he would be sitting at home or flying an airplane somewhere in the United States or across the ocean and wondering about things such as, "What's going on with Kate today?" In the end, she would come home, but before that she would attempt to put his mind at ease with the words, "I'll be fine." He on the other hand would at times be flying through the white magnificence of clouds at thirty or thirty-five thousand feet. He would then tell her many times before his trips not to worry, that he would be home soon.

All jobs have risks, but somehow today, Kate's risks seemed to be at the top of the chart for future worries that he would have to learn how to contend with. It's not a good feeling, and Curtis found himself pausing to consider the future. Now putting the car in drive, he pulled out of the park and headed back to Kate's home. Arriving, Curtis stared at the townhouse. There was no one on the porch to welcome him home, nor would there be tonight. Also, if he cared enough, to be honest with himself, and he might as well be, there would be many nights when Kate would not be there to meet him. In the beginning of the arriving twilight, he saw himself as a soon to be middle-aged pilot on the porch with a dog instead of with the woman that he loved and would soon marry. It was sort of a Norman Rockwell scene, except that Curtis Patterson began to want something more than a life with constant worries about a wife that might not make it home. Getting out of the car, he opened the front door and let Channing race into the house.

Curtis had been home only long enough to have put together Channing's dog food and hang up his light jacket when the telephone rang. It was twenty minutes past six o'clock, and his first thought was that someone was calling him with bad news about Kate. The only information that he had received was the message that she had left him hours ago. He loved this woman, but the lack of being updated caused him to be frightened and resentful. No matter what police polices, protocols, or judgment dictated, Kate could have found a moment to contact him, only she didn't. She was going to be his wife, and Curtis suddenly felt alone, a stranger to the woman who would be his constant companion for life. He quickly grabbed the house phone and was both surprised and uneasy when the voice of Captain Wagner came on the line. Curtis knew he wouldn't call this number unless it was important. Thinking that the news was going to be very bad, his heart started to race.

Wagner spoke first. "Is someone on the line?"

"Captain Wagner, this is Curtis Patterson, Kate's fiancé."

"Yes, I know, she had mentioned that you would be in town this week and staying at her house. Actually she asked me to give you a call because she has her hands full at the hospital with the serious wounding of her partner, Howard Singer. We're still trying to apprehend the shooter, but it's only a matter of time before we get him. We've got every available officer searching the entire city of Funston and the outer areas. It's our feeling, Curtis, that he may have a personal vendetta against Detective Heller along with others from his hometown of Silver Valley, Wisconsin. You need to be aware that I've assigned police to monitor her home until we apprehend this joker, so don't be alarmed if you see squad cars rolling past the house. In the meantime, it would be wise to stay close to the house, at least until she arrives. She asked me to assure you that she is fine and that she will be home as soon as it's possible."

"I'm glad that you called, Captain. I feel much better knowing that Kate is all right. I'm sure that she has mentioned that we are getting married in the next two weeks."

"Yes, and I wish you two the best of luck, but understand that I've thought of locking you up for stealing my best detective," Wagner said laughing. "Well, I'm getting the word that I have to take another call, Curtis, so just stay close to the house and everything will be fine."

Curtis laid the phone down and walked to the front of the house and looked out the picture front window and watched the patrol car move down the street. Looking at his watch, the time was now approaching seven o'clock. Closing the drapes, he walked back to the bedroom, where Channing was now sleeping on the bed with not a care in the world. Picking up the television remote, he turned on the bedroom television and stretched out near the dog.

It was 2:00 a.m. when Kate walked into her townhouse. What was that saying she tried to recall as she turned on the living room light. "Oh, yes," she mumbled to herself, "you can tell an awful lot about someone from how they clean their house." Curtis must have spent all day cleaning and putting things away. The fresh smell of lemon told her that Curtis had polished the dining room table. Tossing her police blazer on the couch, she walked down to the kitchen and turned the lights on. She could see that the wooden floor had been buffed and the coffee pot was ready to turn on in the morning. The blinking of the call identifier caught her curiosity, so she looked at the telephone screener and noted that Captain Wagner had called as promised. Clearing the screen, a second phone number appeared. The identity was blocked, which usually meant the caller was probably someone selling something that she didn't need. Trying to decide if she was going to take a shower, Kate walked into the bedroom and found Curtis still dressed and laying on the bed. "Poor guy was trying to wait up for me but obviously had fallen asleep." She smiled as see noted that he was still holding his cell phone. "He was probably worried to death about me." Walking over to the bed she gently removed the phone from his hand and felt him stir. His eyes blinked wide open.

"Kate," he said, sitting straight up. "How long have you been home?"

"I just got in. Some guard dog we got. Channing didn't even come to the door. Where is he?"

"He's in the guest room on the bed as I last remember. I guess he couldn't take my pacing the floor, so he needed some privacy and sleep."

"I'm so sorry to have worried you so much, Curtis. We have a little girl at the hospital that was bitten by a spider, and on top of that Howard Singer, my partner, took a bullet. He's in critical condition, and the surgeons spent three hours on him. Now we all have to wait for the results. If that's not enough, Bergman got away and may be in another state by now."

"Why don't you take a shower, Kate, and unwind," said Curtis. "Get some of the worry dirt off you and come to bed."

"You're welcome to join me, Curtis. Maybe you need to release some of that tension also," she said with a smile.

"Thanks, but maybe I'll chase Channing out one last time while you take that shower so that he doesn't get us up in the middle of the night. You go right ahead, and I'll see you later."

Kate watched as Curtis left the room to go get Channing. Something was obviously wrong that Curtis would turn down an opportunity to have made love to her, yet he had just refused the invitation. Taking off her clothes, and laying her pistol on the dresser, she walked into the bathroom, turned on the shower and eased into the flowing wet warmth. The feeling provided by the water cascading down her body immediately heightened her sensuality and expectations of finding Curtis in bed waiting for her. Kate felt intensely female and powerful like a witch. "Well, a good witch anyway." She smiled, shutting off the shower and stepping onto the bathmat. Drying off, she put on her baby doll nightgown and entered the bedroom expecting to find Howard and Channing. They were not there. Puzzled she walked over to the bedroom window and looked out in the darkness for any sign or movement. Where the heck were they? Walking down the hallway she moved past the dining room and pulled the drapes slightly open in order to look out upon the street. The car parked across the street was one she was not familiar with, but probably someone's guest overnight she reasoned. She closed the drapes and was about to head back to the bedroom when she heard the alert of her cell phone clicking in the kitchen. Picking it up off the counter, she walked into the guest room to check the locks on the window, clearing the phone message at the same time.

"Kate," came Wagner's voice, "we've found two of our retired Funston police officers bodies at the Mt. Calvary Cemetery. It looks to be the work of Paul Bergman. You and Curtis keep buttoned up tonight. We'll talk more tomorrow." Kate was absolutely shocked how the events were unraveling and Curtis and Channing still somewhere outside walking in the dark? She needed to find them and soon. It was at that moment that she sensed something was wrong. The shock of the arm gripping her around the waist was soon replaced with the terrifying fear of seeing the man's right hand holding a knife to her throat. She was about to resist when the man shouted to stop or he would cut her throat. Kate did as he asked.

"Baby, did you miss me?" He kissed the top of her head and pulled her tight against him until she felt his erection. "I asked you a question, Officer Bitch. Did you miss me?"

"Who are you?" she asked while already knowing the answer.

"Wrong answer, pretty Detective," he said, now using his free hand to reach inside her teddy pajamas. "I've come a long way to meet you tonight, Heller. Somehow I know that you have been waiting a long time for this meeting. Tonight I wanted to surprise you. Now one last time before I cut that pretty throat of yours. Did you miss me, Officer Heller?"

The thought of another man touching her put murderous thoughts into her mind, but she had more than herself to think about. She knew with absolute certainty that he would never get what he wanted if it was just her, but it wasn't. She knew that there was but one answer. "Yes, I've missed you, Paul."

"Good," he said. "What gave me away?" he asked, now stroking her.

"The car on the street," she said, feeling the knife just inches from her throat and his fingers attempting to probe her. "We've met before, remember? Once at your house, as your wife lay dying on the garage floor, and then at your church in Silver Valley." Kate knew that the key to any possibility of escape was to be nice to this man. "Do everything that he tells you to do and then just maybe the chance would come." She felt the knife coming closer to her neck as he continued to probe her body. "Look," she said, "we don't have to do it this way. I don't want to die over something so simple, so put the knife away and let's just pick one of the bedrooms and do it right. It's really what you want, and I won't fight you."

Surprised at her sudden offer, Bergman looked at the trapped policewoman and congratulated himself. Her beauty never failed to impress him, but her willingness was something that he never expected. Lowering the knife and removing his other hand from inside her pajamas, he whispered into her ear, "I think that you're playing with me, but let's give it a try. You may turn around now, Officer Heller."

Turning around, Kate was staring into the barrel of a pistol and a smiling Paul Bergman. "Now if you would be so kind please fetch your police handcuffs, and then we'll find your bedroom, Officer. It's not that I don't trust you," he said with a smirk, "but it could turn out that you might not approve of what I have in mind for you."

Outside Curtis had about enough of Channing watering every bush and tree that he could find. The dog had the biggest bladder of any canine that he had ever run into. One more block and they would be home, and with any luck, Kate wouldn't have recognized that he had been acting like a teenager experiencing for the first time that there were more important things than just him. She had a lot on her mind, and the least that a grown man should be capable of doing was to be patient regarding life's priorities. As he was approaching the townhouse, he noticed the car parked directly across the street from her house. When they had started their walk, it had not been there, that he was certain of. Calling Channing, he walked up to the car and bent down. It was not the Wisconsin license plates that created his curiosity but rather the license plate itself: Rom. 12:19. He tried to recall the passage, but it wouldn't come to him. Turning, he looked at the side of the house and saw the kitchen light go on and off. Strange, he thought, since Kate had earlier taken a shower and should already be in bed, unless his childish mood had kept her awake. Turning back to the car, he studied the license plate a second time and began to repeat from memory what he had learned in his confirmation class. Rom. 12:19. The words started to come back. "Dearly beloved, avenge not yourselves, but rather give place unto wrath, for it is written, vengeance is mine; I will repay, saith the Lord." Jesus! Curtis's stomach lurched. "Oh my god, the bastard is here," he said as he got to his feet and started to run across the street with Channing at his heels. Shaking, he raced down the side of the building, almost reaching the rear door, when he heard the scream. It was clearly Kate's voice yelling, mixed with the profanities of an angry male. Channing, reaching the door first, was already jumping against it trying to scratch his way in. Grabbing the door handle, Curtis tried to turn it open. "Locked, goddamn it," he said in frustration, pulling on the knob a second time. Turning, he raced back down the asphalt drive toward the front door with the dog following in his footsteps. Reaching the door, he could hear screaming and yelling inside and the crash of something heavy falling to the floor. Twisting the door handle and finding it locked, Curtis banged his fist in anger on the doorframe.

"The handcuffs are on the kitchen table," she said.

Now holding the pistol to her temple, Bergman walked her into the kitchen and picked the handcuffs from the table. "See, that wasn't so difficult, was it," said Bergman as he marched her down the hallway toward the master bedroom. Reaching the entrance to the room, he started to kiss Kate on her shoulder, moving his lips slowly up to her neck, while at the same time suddenly grabbing her left wrist and snapping the handcuff on. Now roughly pushing her away, he looked at her angrily and with hate. "That's a nice antique headboard, Officer Heller. We reached the point in our relationship where negotiations have ended. Now I want you to take off your clothes, get up on that bed, and snap that other handcuff to the headboard."

Kate knew that the time had come, and that once she secured that handcuff to the bed, she had lost. Staring at Bergman, she composed herself and smiled. "I told you Paul that I would cooperate and that there was no need to do this." Not waiting for his answer, she pulled the top of her teddy pajamas over her head, exposing her breasts.

As Bergman admired his captive prize, he failed to pay attention that in taking off her top she had move a step closer to him.

Sensing her advantage, Kate put her hands on the elastic of her pajama bottoms and tantalizingly pulled them down while turning to the side. She had a feeling that she knew what he would do and say.

"Turn around, Heller, and let me see if you're a real blond!" Bergman shouted. "It's too late to be modest now, isn't it?"

As she turned to provide Bergman a clear look at her body, she had carefully moved another two steps closer. Kate noticed that his gun began to move lower to his right side. Trained in the Israeli martial arts of krav maga, she long understood that the key to survival was being aggressive and decisive and that you must finish a fight as quickly as possible. Kate put her head down and bull-rushed Bergman, driving her head directly into his nose, crushing the cartilage and sending him flying against her dresser. Bergman yelled in pain as the blood began to spurt from his broken nose. His hands went up to his face to try and stop the flowing blood as his gun fell to the floor. Kicking it under the bed, Kate palm-heeled her foot directly into Bergman's groin, causing him to fall on the floor and roll over holding his testicles. As he tried to get up, she rotated the handcuff over her head bringing the remaining loose handcuff in full force across his cheek, opening up a wide gash and causing Bergman to tumble a second time. Now seeing that Bergman was down and clearly in pain, she ran from the bedroom.

Curtis, continuing to hear the ongoing turbulence taking place in the house, became agitated and boiling with anger put his shoulder full force into the door, splitting the wood that secured the frame and raced inside, along with Channing.

His head spinning, Bergman grabbed the edge of the bed and lifted himself up. He looked at the two bedroom windows, knowing that they were his only chance to escape. Staggering over, he pushed the window frame up as he heard the commotion coming from the front of the house and the voice of Kate yelling instructions. Pulling himself up, he squeezed through the open window and fell to the ground.

Curtis and Channing, running down the hallway, found a naked Kate now in possession of her handgun rushing back to the master bedroom.

"Turn on the security lights, Curtis, the bastard is getting away." She waited, looking out into the darkness for Bergman, until finally the lights illuminated her entire backyard. "Where the hell is he?" she screamed in frustration. Then she spotted the hobble of the injured Bergman. "Stop! Police!" she yelled. She watched as Bergman continued his attempt to reach the tall cornfield just beyond her yard. Raising the pistol, she fired four quick rounds, all missing her intended target as Bergman kept up his pace trying to reach the cover of the cornstalks. Falling and getting up, he continued to make his way towards safety. With Curtis watching her, Kate sighted the pistol a second time, raising the barrel one foot above the head of Bergman, and fired three more shots. Bergman continued to struggle another ten feet when suddenly he toppled over and didn't move. Kate turned from the window and called for Channing to follow her. Reaching the back door, she let the dog out. "Go get him, Channing, go get him!"

Curtis, watching from the window, called to Kate. "He's got him, but it looks like the guy's down for the count. He's not moving an inch."

Kate had slipped on a pair of jeans and Red Wings hockey shirt and ran out to the backyard and found Channing standing guard over Bergman. Curtis, walking up behind her, said, "Looks like one of your bullets caught him in the neck, Kate. He's bleeding out. I'll call it in while you get yourself dressed." As they started to walk back to the house holding hands, Kate stopped and turned around to look back in the direction of the fallen Bergman. "Well, at least he got to see a true blond."

"What does that mean?" asked Curtis, pulling her close to him.

"Oh, it's nothing really, but I'll tell you sometime," she said, giving Curtis a kiss.

The Aftermath

Four days later, Alan and Betty arrived back in Silver Valley. It was around 10:00 p.m., and twilight had just turned the corner into full darkness as they pulled up to their home. They had stopped for dinner at the Hill Top Beacon restaurant and were now tired from the events in Funston. Alan had once again found his magic in restoring health to the maid's daughter and even was even able to convince Dr. Patel to have an open mind on insect bites. Bergman had survived death, but Heller's bullet had left him partially paralyzed, with a future that suggested years behind bars. Opening the car door, Alan walked around to Betty's side, opened her door, and walked inside the house holding each other's hands.

Curtis and Kate's wedding day turned out to be a triumph. The rose garden at Lift Bridge's memorial park exploded with flowers, the sun shone brightly, and the bride and groom looked as happy and in love as two people could possibly be. The small group of family and friends who came to toast their union with nonalcoholic fruit punch and wine all agreed that the intimate, low-key ceremony was a perfect reflection of the relationship of these two people. Their honeymoon in Bermuda was like a short poem describing a simple, pleasant scene of newfound love. They did little but sleep, snorkel, and make love beneath the stars. Occasionally thoughts of other, earlier experiences of the beginning of their love would flash in their minds. Bergman was the past, and the past was gone. Only the present was real. Only the present mattered. The honeymoon hotel had no internet access, television, or phone. Curtis would tease and make fun of Kate's twitchiness. Lovingly he would tease her about her inability to go two days without an inbox full of email or checking up on Howard Singer's new promotion. "Must be that I haven't been able to ring your bell loud enough." Kate would then grab him, and off they would go to some deserted spot on the beach laughing all the time as their clothes came off. At last, long last, the nightmare was over.

ABOUT THE AUTHOR

K. L. Dempsey was born in Detroit, Michigan. After completing his formal education in Michigan, he joined the United States Army and was assigned to the Third Armored Division in Kirch-Göns, Germany.

Following completion of his military service, he worked for a commercial helicopter company before being hired by a major airline, where he spent thirty-three years in their marketing and sales division. After retirement, he worked in the MRI and sleep apnea business.

Today he makes his home in a nearby suburb of Chicago, Illinois, working on new material with the support of his family and friends.